M LAWLESS EASURES

VIGILANTE-THE FIGHT CONTINUES
BOOK TWO IN THE PALATINI SERIES

LYLE O'CONNOR
The New Master of Crime Thrillers

PO Box 221974 Anchorage, Alaska 99522-1974
books@publicationconsultants.com—www.publicationconsultants.com

ISBN 978-1-59433-493-1
eISBN 978-1-59433-494-8
Library of Congress Catalog Card Number: 2014945733

Manufactured in the United States of America.

Dedicated to all my children—
Matthew
Nicholas
Bethany
Justyn
Brett
Alexander
Ryan
Amanda
Kaitlin

Disclaimer

*L*awless Measures is a work of fiction. All names, characters, places and incidents are products of the author's imagination or are used fictitiously. Any resemblance to actual events or persons, living or deceased, is entirely coincidental.

Acknowledgements

Special thanks to Walter Allen Grant, author, and contributor who played a vital role in my development.

Chapter 1

Buffalo, New York

September 2002

I craved the arousal I felt as I lined up my shot. My trigger finger poised to unleash hell from my .223-caliber semi-auto AR-15. My weapon spoke twice, Shuup . . . Shuup, as the GemTech Halo Suppressor belched a puff of fiery smoke with each round. Struck in the back, center of mass, my target wobbled to the ground. Giuseppe "Pepe" Pelosi, aka the Pimp, laid face down in the alleyway. I watched for signs of movement, but the only observable motion was that of blood as it pooled around the body. I concluded my target was eliminated.

* * * * *

I vaguely remember my life before I became Walter Eloy Goe. It was out of necessity I became Walter—only a trusted few have learned my birth name. Years of struggling with dreams, nightmares, and ghostly apparitions prompted me to take action against the most vile of criminals. It was in 1996 I stepped over the proverbial line in a campaign of vigilantism. I'd figured myself in as a consequence when I saw predators serving little or no time for their heinous crimes. My contribution to justice caught the eye of a member of a secret society known as Palatini—I was invited into the society and knighted Scythian. Now I proudly crusade with the ancient knighthood—a society resurrected as an Order of freelance assassins. The society had picked up the gauntlet thrown down by its medieval predecessors. The original Palatini Knights were champions of the people, paragons of virtue, chivalrous, and all that heroic sounding stuff. Simply put, the new Palatini Knights didn't call 911. We took care of business vigilante style. We espoused our Palatini oath and delivered a less imperiled world through our personal judgment. Our mission is one of guardianship of the people, for the people, and by the people.

Not only was I proud to claim my allegiance to the Palatini, I was honored to be given "double tap" as my signature. I was willing, however, to add a few extra slugs for good measure when needed. In this present situation, it appeared two rounds were sufficient.

Some people might view shooting Pepe in the back as a cowardly act, but I would disagree. It was an execution. Pepe was assassinated. There are no rules for murder, even a righteous murder. I didn't care if he had no chance to defend himself. My one and only concern was that he was dead.

Pepe hadn't only been a pimp, and street hustler, but a soldier for the Abbandanza crime syndicate, nicknamed the Machine. I surmised he was of no great loss or importance as a person to Domenic Bacca, the ruthless Caporegime of the Buffalo and Niagara Falls faction. However, Pelosi did have a certain flair for the creation of finances. Pepe's premature death would be disruptive to the syndicate business, but not devastating. More of Bacca's soldiers had to die to shatter his illegal immigration stronghold. Their deaths had to resemble dominos falling in rapid succession to create the effective level of confusion I hoped to achieve. I had to move fast.

Why was Society Palatini interested in the Abbandanza syndicate's involvement in illegal immigration? They weren't the run-of-the-mill coyotes. The pictures broadcast on television of foreigners huddled in box vans being snuck across United States' southern border, was not the business the syndicate engaged in. Rather, they lured, tricked, or otherwise acquired underage girls with a belief they could obtain residency and nationality in America. Health, wealth, and happiness could be theirs for a small price. It was the answer to prayers for many third world inhabitants. But with the Machine there was no path to citizenship, only a lifetime of slavery.

Pimp was more than a nickname for Pelosi; he was one of the syndicate's facilitators. Anna Sasins, lead Palatini asset on this project, completed an extensive work-up on the crime family. As a result of her findings, Pepe was selected as a priority target to be eliminated. Why Pepe first? He made the "arrangements." He was tasked with logistics for moving underage girls across the Canadian border between New York and Ontario. Taking him out early disrupted the flow of girls in and out of the country and presented a greater calamity to the entire criminal structure.

The Abbandanza mobsters were involved at many levels of organized crime. They ran the gambit from gambling to cybercrime. However, the Palatini's interest with the syndicate's criminal venture was restricted to their underage sex rackets.

Kidnapping and human trafficking were hallmarks of their illegal immigration enterprise. It was an all too common and lucrative practice. Illegal immigration was a political hot potato. Rather than trying to enforce existing immigration laws, Federal Law Enforcement looked the other way. What they didn't see or know about didn't require their involvement.

Pepe, along with a couple of his minions, scratched out a scanty living on the streets of Buffalo's Lower West Side, seemingly on the lowest rung of the family's structure. His niche in the family business placed underage girls in "service" at whorehouses. There the young girls worked off their indebtedness to the Abbandanza's Freedom Underground program. Realistically it was the lowest of the scams. Freedom was a goal never to be achieved. These girls were doomed to a life of prostitution.

Capo Bacca was a stringent traditionalist. His rank and file structure followed the "old school" format Alfonso Abbandanza laid out decades before. Bacca's main interests were in gambling, bookmaking, loansharking, and labor racketeering. That was where the real money came from, but he wasn't opposed to making a dollar anywhere he could find it. The Machine reaped the dividends because of it.

I considered Bacca a target for his involvement in the immigration racket, but Anna disagreed. "There is not a direct connection between Bacca and the actions of his underlings," She said. She felt the real play for the immigration racket was in Toronto where she had concentrated her efforts. "I insist we remain aligned with the Society's guidelines. We will take out only those directly responsible for kidnapping, and sex trafficking of underage girls."

"That approach is naïve. All we're going to do is kill bottom feeders like Pelosi," I said.

As capo, Bacca called the shots. Nothing happened in his crew without his knowledge, and he profited from every decision, and the corresponding actions of people like Pepe. Therefore, he was guilty in my book. But, it seemed to be a waste of time to argue the point. It was Anna's project, and she was ultimately responsible for the outcome. It was her call. I would kill as many, or as few as she wanted.

I climbed down from the 4th floor perch atop Angelino's apartment building where I'd made a clean shot. This was Pepe's home turf. A place where he felt safe and secure. He started each day the same way, and walked the same alleys; he was a creature dedicated to habit. He'd been on his way, doing what Pepe did best, hustle. Fate changed his destiny. Or maybe it was Walter, who acting as a personal travel planner, sent Pepe straight to hell.

The afternoon was just getting started. If I hurried, I had time to catch up to "Shady Slim" Surdo—number two on my target list.

* * * * *

Anna worked across the border in Canada. She'd been invited by a fellow reporter and friend, Cal Alonzo, to assist him with material he'd collected on the Abbandanza crime family. His intention wasn't to fight crime with what he uncovered, but to write a book, and make some money. He tried to persuade Anna to join him in the research, but it was not to her liking until he mentioned the sex racket he'd uncovered. The racket of human trafficking of underage kids piqued her interest.

While I was taking out the trash in the Gulf of Mexico, Anna had flown to Toronto to investigate Cal's findings. I knew Anna was up to something while I was stalking Lou Cypher on the gulf side of Padre Island but at the time she hadn't made it clear to me what she was up to. I assumed she was busy writing a human interest story not scoping out a Palatini project.

According to Anna, Cal had been working an angle with the Abbandanza syndicate for more than three years. He befriended one of the Toronto soldiers and over the past year had become privy to some of the inner workings of the Mob. The data he provided was well documented, accurate, and concise. In Cal's world, it meant "bestseller." In the Palatini world, it meant body count. However, Anna had cautioned me to remember, Cal was a writer-reporter, not a Palatini. He had no knowledge of our Society's existence or what we would do with his research. He could not be involved or trusted with the knowledge we were Palatini, and our purpose was to kill the people he was investigating.

It was clear, Anna, was duly impressed with Cal's infiltration. She had at her fingertips a compilation of Cal's material on the Abbandanza crime family. Profiles on the organization's rackets and individual member's involvement were substantial. Not all the soldiers and associates were known, but a sufficient number of players were outlined to provide a good starting point. Anna continued to stay at Cal's rented apartment in Corso Italia District of Toronto. To her, the opportunities to sift through his notes and get daily reports from Cal were invaluable.

Cal had the inside track on the gang's activity. His infiltration as a trusted friend of a respected soldier was priceless. Like many reporters, he also had police sources. He was able to see both sides of the coin at the same time, thus providing him with an accurate image of the Mob's activity. I had not met Cal and probably never would, but I had a feeling of jealousy building. He had everything I wanted, Anna's time, attention, and respect.

Anna and I spoke daily on the phone, but it was a rehash of our current project, not about us. My new found loneliness was spurred on by the two days Anna and I spent together in Corsicana, Texas after the Cypher project was completed. Society Palatini Grand Master, Maximillian Karnage, had set a meeting between the three of us to discuss her new project. After the early afternoon meeting, Max departed, leaving Anna and me to occupy our time. We capitalized on the opportunity to explore our budding romance.

My world was coming together perfectly. If our two days together was an indicator of things to come, I was primed. Anna was a creature of beauty. She was charming, charismatic, and a stone-cold killer. What was there not to love?

Acting on a tip from a motel housekeeper, we dined at a steakhouse favored by the locals. The restaurant was cozy, dark wood throughout with tall paneled booths and shadowy lighting; an appropriate place for intimate relationships or planning a murder. I intended to steer clear of the latter. Since Anna and I kissed in Bellagio, I wanted to introduce her to the real me. I saw no chance of a healthy relationship between us if she didn't know what was genuinely me and what was Walter. This was a problem. Who was I? Did the essence of the person I once was still exist or had I became Walter, totally? I didn't know. Only time would tell—time with Anna.

After dinner, Anna suggested a walk in the park. How classic, I thought, I don't even have a gun with me. Maybe Anna brought her tactical folding knife she so skillfully displayed in Thailand. At least then I'd know we would be safe.

We arrived at a large well maintained park off Bunert Road. There were no gates or signage to indicate the park closed at any particular time. It was unlike any park I'd known. The sun seemed to drift slowly into sunset providing a warm and comfortable atmosphere for our stroll. Anna slipped her hand into mine as we walked. It was deliberate and sensational. I felt an electrical impulse that lingered. How beautiful and intense the feeling.

I was ecstatic, yet, confused and uncertain of myself. At the forefront of my thoughts were things I wanted to say to Anna. Although I was emotionally attracted to her, I feared it was mostly a one-way street. It wasn't anything she had said or done, it was me. I was insecure and the absence of a meaningful romance these many long years left me ignorant in the ways of love. I could not shake the feeling of helplessness when it came to expressing to Anna the way I felt about her and what she meant to me. From deep inside me, the nagging question kept asking, was I capable of love? I desperately needed an answer—I wanted it to be an unconditional, yes.

I maintained a gentle grasp on her hand as we moseyed across the verdurous ballpark matting. In the absence of sunlight, Anna's eyes continued to sparkle as she looked into mine. We slowed to a stop and stood silent for a moment to look into each other's face. Anna spoke first, "I want you in my life." I gently pulled her close in response, until we touched at the waist. I assured her; I too wanted the same as she did. Her eyes shifted attention from my eyes to my lips. Her body began to move forward, and I responded likewise. Our lips met in a slow caress. My uncertainty and awkwardness vanished. This was right.

Anna tilted her head back breaking contact with our kiss. It was too soon to end. I felt the power of desire released in my heart. No longer was it restrained by an emotional block of skepticism. My thoughts swirled, Anna quickly glanced into my face as if to see my expression to our kiss then leaned her body into mine. As our lips were about to touch, she gently brushed her tongue upon my upper lip. Following the response to that kiss, we embarked on passion itself.

The rest of the evening we spent together like a couple of giddy young teens at the park. We held hands and occasionally walked side by side with arms wrapped around each other. On impulse, we would stop to kiss. It was joyful; I was on top of the world.

We were delighted to have another day together before departing on our quest. On our last evening, Anna wanted to try an old Mexican style Cantina on the north end of town. After dinner, we talked in depth about our feelings and future. Throughout the night, we plumbed the depth of our relationship. In the morning, we expressed to each other our optimism for a speedy outcome with Abbandanza project. Her last words that day were inspiring, just you and me—I promise. I was going to hold her to it.

Anna flew back to Toronto while I made a trip to Portland. I wasted no time preparing for the road trip to Buffalo. I packed my gear in the Avenger for what might be a lengthy stay and I was off.

* * * * *

I had been in position for about a month with targets acquired and no "go" order yet. The thought of a speedy outcome became a haunting. Anna wanted to take care of business, but delays occurred. Interruptions from Cal, unintentional, but without his knowledge of what we were doing, his actions complicated matters. Two of the girls under Bacca's implied protectorate, slipped out of their accommodations at the urging of Cal, and into his lodging. This was great for Anna who rigorously grilled them. Each evening, Anna called to relate details from her conversations with the girls. It was all very exciting to get real time first hand insider information, but it created an ongoing delay.

The girls, each barely nineteen-years-old, runaways, and kidnapped from the New York area when they were underage, were put "in service" by Pepe the pimp. Shady Slim had transported them to Toronto in exchange for a couple Asian immigrants the local Canadian crew was exploiting at the time. Anna was determined to help Cal before she started knocking down Toronto targets. She said transportation for the girls back into America had been secured, but it would be a few days before it happened. How that would occur I wasn't privy to. Maybe I should have been.

Anna, however, gave the "go" order to take out two of Bacca's frontline soldiers and one "associate." These predetermined targets were the "feeders" who were directly involved in the Toronto immigration racket. Anna felt the disruption in Buffalo might focus the attention of the family on possibilities of a rival syndicate turf war, or maybe start one. In the meanwhile, she would get the girls out of Toronto and back in the United States.

With Pelosi down for the count, I was on my way to interfere with the second leg of the racket; prime candidate Shady Slim Surdo. He was next on my list. Cal had garnered from his Mob contact that Surdo was not well liked. He had a hankering that other soldiers disdained. Shady Slim wanted to be the first in line to "turn out" underage kidnapped or otherwise coerced girls. According to Cal, Surdo liked them young and the younger, the better. If they were virgins, it was a real treat. His actions were considered contemptuous and appalling in the eyes of the Family, particularly those not involved in the illegal immigration racket. Nonetheless, he was tolerated for business sake.

Surdo was a home grown product of Buffalo's Allen Street. He broke his bones in the street pharmaceutical trade. The Fed's turned up the heat on pushers making it less than profitable to run a business. He had grown tired of paying a street tax to Bacca's soldiers. He made the leap when opportunity knocked. He put the drugs aside for a less risky business. He made himself available to the Family. His value was soon rewarded with a position.

He had class, even if it was low class. His taste in vehicles, however, spoke a different story. He drove an old red '69 Hemi Cuda convertible that appeared to be his office on wheels. He gave me the impression he was either a businessman or a private taxi service. Regardless, he was clearly in serfdom. He frequently shuttled people throughout the city. He picked up riders from barbershops to coffee houses then dropped them off at another location, or in some cases, he brought them back to where he'd picked them up from originally. It made no sense unless he was conducting business on the move. On nice days, he drove with the top down as he cruised about. Today happened to be a sunny day.

Catching up to Surdo was far more difficult than Pelosi. Surdo didn't have a distinguishable pattern, but he did have a habit. Since I had begun the observation, I noted he had regularly patronized one of Pepe's bordello's just off Allen Street. This was chancy. He would likely have heard of Pelosi being gunned down by the time I got set up on him. He might lie low until the coast was clear. If that were the situation, I would have to flush him out.

I leaned the bucket seat of my Avenger back into an easy resting position as I cocked my Homburg fedora forward to reduce the sunlight beaming off the windshield. Pelosi's Cathouse was situated at the end of a multiple story rowhouse. This six terraced home had seen better days but matched the run-down neighborhood. This would be the easiest way to pick up Surdo's scent.

At some point during the early evening I began to consider the third name on my target list, perhaps should be second. Before I could make a final decision, number two rolled up in his 'Cuda, looking very dapper. Shady Slim left his car parked curbside to the rowhouse and trotted to the house, glancing back as he stepped through the door. The better part of an hour lapsed before Surdo poked his head out the front door. Moments later he hot footed it to his car. By his actions, I suspected he knew Pepe was dead.

I tailed him loosely for a few blocks down Main Street where he erratically veered off the main drag to one of the side roads. Maybe it was an attempt to shake the tail or worse yet, draw me out. As I watched his car, it zigzagged across and through an ill-lit neighborhood, and promptly came to a stop in front of a person standing at a crosswalk. I pulled back from the tail and watched.

Soon, Surdo was out of his convertible chasing the person he'd stopped near. I attached the moderator to my Glock M22 .40-caliber semi-automatic, jacked a sub-sonic round into the chamber and made haste in the direction of the chase. Shady Slim would return to his 'Cuda. I would take an opportunistic encounter to take him.

I strode the decrepit sidewalk toward the convertible keeping a sharp eye out for passersby. About twenty yards past his car in the direction of the chase I spotted a space between townhouses that was hidden from the radiance of the street lamp. I holed up there in the darkness, coiled, ready to strike.

To my surprise, Surdo returned dragging a female by the arm toward his car. The female's speech was pressured and too tangential to make out clearly what she had said. Surdo pinned the woman against his car's rear fender, slapping her about the head as she physically resisted her capture. If his intention was for the lady to ride peacefully with him, he had to convince her it was in her best interest to comply. At this juncture, he looked as if he was between a rock and a hard place, and losing ground. There was no evidence she was going with him the easy way. I saw no reason to wait. Surdo was so consumed by her recalcitrance; he didn't see my approach.

I surmised not many people in this neighborhood would intervene if violence occurred on the street. A do-gooder was the last thing he expected to see. My presence was certainly a jaw-dropper for him. His victim fell from his grip, and I assumed he was about to direct a cleaver taunting remark at me. But my Glock stole his attention as I leveled it in the direction of his chest—Thuup. He staggered two steps before he collapsed to the ground. Thuup—the second round blew through his head. It was a done deal.

The woman had sprung to her feet and ran. She didn't look back. My guess was she wanted distance between me and her, lots of distance. I continued on the sidewalk, back to my Avenger. If anyone had seen anything, I wasn't worried. Not in this neighborhood. On the street, a brazen shooting of one of Bacca's soldiers would spread like wildfire. It was unfriendly territory I'd tracked him to; I needed to get out of this area. Anna had designated my hotel room as our operational safe house, code named sanctuary. It was my next stop for the day.

I headed back to my hotel room, but I struggled to contain my excitement. The achievement of the day was remarkable. Especially, after such a long wait. Anna would be pleased to convey the report to Max on the success of her project. Undoubtedly, there would be kudos forthcoming from Max to Anna, and on to me. More importantly from my perspective, it rolled our timeline closer to the finish. Then, as promised, Anna and I would pursue our relationship.

I wasted no time calling Anna. Soon as I heard her voice I recapitulated my successes. I waited in anticipation of Anna's jubilant response. She was silent.

"What's going on, Anna. Something is wrong isn't it?"

"Cal, he's gone. He's missing. Something bad has had to have happened."

Cal Alonzo, a forty-year-old native New Yorker, devoted his writing career to commentary on criminal enterprises. From politicians to street gangs, he covered them all. He was a man with many friends and possibly as many enemies. He wrote under an assumed name; however, we have learned from experience, it does little in the way to protect a person's identity. Now he was missing.

"Anna, I think you need to get out of there. Come to sanctuary. I don't have to tell you this has become too dangerous to stay at Cal's."

"It's worse—the girls are gone too. I don't know what's happened to any of them. There are no signs of any struggle or foul play here."

"Wrap this up and get out—now!" I could feel a sense of helplessness emerge. I knew Anna would not put my mind at ease with her response.

"Cal is my friend. Until I know what has happened, I can't pull out. You understand, don't you?"

"Do you understand that you are in danger?" I felt myself beg of her to reconsider.

"I love you, Walter, but—I've got to do this."

"I love you too, Anna, that's why I want you to think about what you're doing to us right now."

"Don't put that on me. We are Palatini, and we have a mission."

I didn't know what to say, but the silence didn't feel any better.

"I'm going to check out Cal's mob friend, Joey Naccarella. If I can't get a lead there, I'll tie it off."

Anna set a check in time and assured me she would promptly call as discussed. Meanwhile, I would continue my hunt, but my heart wasn't in it. All that was on my mind was Anna's safety.

Chapter 2

"We weren't after a semblance of mundane and ordinary;
we wanted pandemonium."
—*Walter*

T he telephone ringer clattered rhythmically and reverberated off the walls of the old hotel room. The abrupt interruption of my sleep forced a lapse in memory. Where am I? I pondered the thought momentarily. That's right, I remember, I was holed up in a sleazy hostel Anna dubbed sanctuary waiting for her to call. My attempt at sleep had been a difficult and ongoing process throughout the night. Was it demonic activity that haunted me or was I beset by anxiety? By morning it hardly mattered, I hadn't been able to defeat it. Zombiefied, I reached for the phone.

"Hello," I scarcely recognized my own voice; harsh and gravelly. Dehydration had parched my vocal cords.

"Walter?" It was Anna. A burst of relief and happiness came over me. She had kept her word and called as promised. But, there was an unusual sharpness to the tone of her voice. "I've spent the night packing all Cal's research material. It contains names, addresses, and involvement with the different factions of the Family. I put it in a large piece of Cal's luggage and I'll place it in a locker at the airport. I'll let you know where the key will be kept in the event something goes awry."

I didn't like the sounds of her statement, "What do you want me to do?" I paused, before I offered the suggestion I'd hoped she would decide to take. "How about I swing over there and pick you up and help find Cal in Toronto?"

"No, there's no time. I'm going on the hunt. I believe I have a good lead on one of the girl's whereabouts. If I can find her, she'll know what happened to Cal. I need you to continue your takedown."

"Contact times are the same, right?"

"I will call your cell phone around the five p.m. mark."

I could deal with the sleep deprivation, but found it more challenging to remain focused on my target while Anna remained in a potentially compromised and dangerous scenario.

Emilio Zambrotta, a Bacca crew "associate" and target number three, had worked his way up the proverbial food chain of the Abbandanza crime syndicate. His goal of reaching the pinnacle of super villainy as a soldier in Bacca's crew was lofty, too lofty, one he would never attain. His lack of success wasn't because he had fewer opportunities than the next hood; but because he was a chump. Bacca played him like a fool. From an outsider's perspective, Bacca never intended to promote him to soldier, or he would have done so already.

Emilio was an honest to goodness family man with a wife and two small children. A fact he should have taken into consideration more seriously. He was a pimp. He didn't fall into the trade for lack of better options; he sought an alternate way of life. What was the enticement? Maybe the grandeur of riches, flamboyant lifestyle, or just fascinated with the seedier side of life, whatever his inclination, in the broader scheme of things, it would be brief. Walter would see to that.

Emilio spent an inordinate amount of time socializing with street thugs. He was a go-between for the crime family business. He travelled to various gang territories and "hung out" with them. Cal had never met Emilio. His awareness of Emillo's activities was compliments of Cal's police sources. The cops called him a "procurement officer" for Bacca. All Emilio really was, was a gopher. He had a "shopping list" for what Bacca would pay for. He set up deals with street level miscreants to kidnap underage girls that were homeless or runaways. Walter thought it was a smart move on the Mob's part. Girls with no accountability were easy to abduct and fewer questions surfaced that concerned their whereabouts.

The Russian Mafia was no different from the Sicilians or Italians when it came to business. They all worked the same way and there were plenty of crime families to go around. There were Mexican Drug Cartels, Irish Mobsters, and Chinese Triads. They were all mobsters, with an ethnic distinction, but without any differences. They have all learned to operate the "black market" and perfect the profitability of the underground economy.

Organized crime mastered the use of others to take care of their dirty work. A small investment in operational "layering" paid years of dividends to the manifold syndicates. Gangsters looking for recognition usually received the attention of the media and cops. If due to their lifestyle, they become a liability to the criminal organization, some up-and-coming associate trying to make his mark, offs them. The various mobsters crowed all day how they were different from the other gangs, but in the end they all operated the same lowlife way.

* * * * *

It was Sunday; Zambrotta had left his house early for the Black Rock District of Buffalo. He and his little family attended Holy Family Cathedral, a catholic parish, located a few miles north of his home. There were catholic churches considerably closer to his home but Capo Bacca attended the Black Rock parish. That was important to Emilio. Not only had the local Capo attended the parish, but two of the main crime family hierarchy, Rocco Colansante and Salvatore Giannetti, did as well. To a guy like Emilio, that was probably more important than God being at the church. If Walter ran this project, he would have turned mass into a mess. But for now, I had a more passive role.

I didn't need to tail Emilio at this point; I knew he would be returning to have lunch with his family. Later he would hit the street for work. Regardless of the day, connections had to be made. I felt hurried. I wanted to get this guy killed then join Anna in Toronto with or without her blessing. I didn't have time to watch the newspaper headlines and see how my last two kills had been presented to the public. However, I did like to read about the police and reporters guesswork. I liked the recognition, even if it wasn't by name. I also liked when a reporter nailed an accurate conjecture of what happened or why.

By now, all Bacca's troops had to be aware something ran afoul, and it had undoubtedly spread to the associates, as well. If I gave it a week, and nothing else transpired, the street view would most likely return to normal. But, we weren't after a semblance of mundane and ordinary; we wanted pandemonium.

Emilio drove a pearl colored Toyota Sprinter. It fit his persona as a family man to a tee and fit in the city environment so well it was difficult to tail. He didn't leave his house on a schedule, and for the short time I'd followed him there was no apparent order to his street contacts. The only choice I had was to wait him out.

At five-o'clock, Anna called. I was still on the observation. I explained my dilemma. She said she understood in a pacifying way. "I will put the key to the airport locker in my Lexus. I will place it under the rear license plate, and I'll put a key to Cal's apartment with it. You've got the address, right?"

"Got it. When do we make contact again?"

"I'll call in the morning around eight. Maybe you'll have good news to share by then. Maximillian has been briefed. He is pleased at the accomplishments thus far and has offered additional assets if needed. Until I get a lead, I don't think that's necessary."

Personally, I'd like to see her call in the Calvary or in this case the Palatini knights. Her safety was paramount to me. But I understood how Society Palatini did business. Danger was expected. All knights of the Order shared in this and accepted the risk.

While I waited for Emilio to make his move, I reviewed the Toronto notes on the Abbandanza family in preparation for the change I expected to make. It was possible, Anna had hidden somewhere in her notes, the right information that would allow us to locate and spring Cal and the girl's. I wanted to be ready to rock-n-roll.

Daylight faded into a spectral twilight just after seven-thirty. I hunkered down for what might be a long night. While I waited, the surrounding building's shadowy changes had drawn me back into the dream world of my childhood where I vanquished villainous predators. I enjoyed that world and grew fond of the memories. But, those were dreams, and nothing pleased me more than reality. Emilio was about to find out my pleasing dream world would be his worst nightmare.

An hour passed before the front door to Emilio's house opened. No one emerged, only the door stood wide open exposing an unlit front porch and entry way. It struck me as strange. A few minutes later, an early model Pontiac Tempest pulled up in front of his house. Emilio made a beeline to his car. He jumped into his Toyota and took off out of the subdivision in the direction of the main drag. The Tempest stayed close behind Zambrotta's sedan. Unbeknownst to Emilio or the driver of the other vehicle, there was a third vehicle in the convoy. It was Walter in his Avenger.

The two cars I tailed pulled over at an alleyway entrance ten blocks from Emilio's residence and exited their vehicles. Zambrotta and the other driver jacked their jaws for a minute then proceeded into the alleyway darkness. I was satisfied to wait. A few minutes later, the two men returned to view. Emilio retrieved an attaché case from his car and climbed into the passenger side of the old Tempest before driving off. I held my position. Before the night was over, he would return for his ride. I could bank on it.

I found it interesting, the alley had so many visitor's throughout the night. Although I didn't see anything I could put my finger on as corrupt or villainous, I was relatively sure had I ventured into the alley, I would have discovered its shadowy secrets and probably increased my body count. It was a temptation for sure, but it wasn't what I was here for.

Around two in the morning the Pontiac pulled up alongside the Toyota. When Emilio got out of the other car, he didn't appear to be in a hurry or overly concerned for his safety. He remained exposed from either vehicle for a few minutes while he conversed with the other driver. The Tempest finally darted off, and Emilio fired up his sedan. Moments later we were heading in the direction of his home, some ten blocks away. At that time in the morning, the streets were vacant. No pedestrians and only an occasional car passed by us. Most were oncoming traffic. I tailed a short distance off the Toyota's right side. I knew he could see the front end of my car, but he couldn't get a good look at me. My plan was simple; I would follow him to his house and shoot him there. All that changed a couple blocks from his house when a stoplight switched from green to red. We pulled to the stop, side by side in parallel lanes.

Emilio smiled in a friendly gesture, I lifted my Glock and unloaded half of my fifteen-round magazine into his body. The Toyota started to roll forward on its own. I watched as it drifted across the oncoming lane and slowly toward the opposite side of the road. Being a law abiding citizen, I waited for the light to change before driving on my merry way. The moderator coupled with sub-sonic ammunition made for a quiet assassination. I doubted if I could have killed any quieter with my lead-filled pipe or my newest addition to my tool box, an old fashioned Ka-Bar.

Back at sanctuary, I kicked off my shoes and stretched out on the couch. My thoughts were at ease. I knew the time would pass quickly if I slept. Soon, Anna would call and alleviate my greatest concern. During the winter months in the north, sunrise seemed to be sluggish. Freshly formed clouds covered the city and drug out the daybreak, and consequently put off my rise and shine time. No sense in rushing what I couldn't control.

I knew things could happen that might affect the best laid plans of mice and men, but with current circumstances, I couldn't help thinking it was taking too long for her to make contact. She knew how important the call was to me. As noontime approached, I realized the call I expected would not come, not as planned. I didn't want to over-react to the situation. I've been accused of being both reactive and volatile, but it was time to make contact, past time.

After a few persistent attempts had failed, the phone was answered. I expected it to be a malfunction and the call to disconnect, but there was someone on the line. I could hear the sound of scratchy movement against the phone. The noise told me it wasn't a glitch in the system. Whoever was on the phone had not covered the receiver and I could hear noises in the background. The sounds were distinctly human voices. Someone was listening, but they weren't talking. Then, the call disconnected.

I could call again; maybe someone would answer a second time. If I got more of the silent treatment, I could unload a profanity or two, closely followed by empty threats of bodily harm. I might have felt better when I was done, but ultimately I would not have achieved anything valuable by the tirade. It was time for a road trip to Toronto and get personal. If I couldn't find them, I could make them find me, and it would be on my terms. I called Max and brought him up to speed on the situation.

"Scythian, I would like you to stay in sanctuary until I get back to you. I have a contact in the Ontario government that has been helping with project information. I think he is Palatini material, and he has thus far been very beneficial."

"I could do that."

"Good then, I'll be back with you as soon as I can."

I hung up the phone. My tactical bag was loaded and ready to rock-n-roll within fifteen minutes. I'd left Max with the impression I wasn't pursuing the Toronto trip when I acknowledged him. It was only an impression. Max hadn't known me for very long, or all that well, so he wouldn't have known that I'd never been good at waiting around or following directions.

Crossing the Canadian border was rather painless. Our two nations see thousands of travelers cross each day in places like Niagara Falls. Anna had provided me with a falsified passport from our previous trip to Thailand. It didn't take me more than a couple times to figure out how the crossing station worked, and how to scam it. I crossed the Canadian border during rush-hour only to find myself being waved through without a physical check. This was especially true if I held up my passport unopened, they didn't bother to look.

Anna had already provided me with a Toronto map with Cal's apartment circled on it. All I needed to carry out was the road trip. Cal Alonzo was of Italian heritage. The Curso Italia District in which Cal had rented his apartment was a natural fit for him. The apartment on Saint Clair Avenue

West was mediocre at best. Cal wasn't presenting himself to the mobsters as someone with clout or money, but someone in need of both and hungry to get it. That made him usable, and maybe why Joseph "Joey" Naccarella had an interest in him.

I arrived at the address, waited and watched. Anna's car was parked in the lot. Not a good sign. I was apprehensive for what I might find inside. There was no amount of mental training which could prepare a person for coming face to face with the carnage inflicted on a loved one. When the thought entered my mind, I cringed.

Evening approached, and it was imperative to retrieve the keys from under the license plate before nightfall. Waiting until dark might bring greater scrutiny from onlookers and a call for a police cruiser to check me out. Anna had given me her car key when our relationship began to blossom. Perhaps it was a sign of trust between us; I understood it in that way. It was inconceivable that such a situation as this would be the reason I'd find the key necessary. I started the car and opened the hood as if I were working on it. I looked for anything that was out of the ordinary inside the Lexus then worked my way behind the car, loosened the rear plate and dropped the keys in my pocket. I shut off the car and secured it before I made my way to Cal's first floor lodging.

I listened for a minute outside the apartment door then knocked lightly. After a minute, I reached for the door knob and gave it a turn. The door was unlocked. In my book, it was detectable evidence that a condition existed that shouldn't be. It was a clue in itself. On the ranch in Oregon, tracks were more than prints in the dirt. Whether it was hair captured by the bark of a tree as an animal rubbed against it, when they passed by, or claw marks in a hollowed out stump, where a porcupine made a den. They were all tracks, and they all meant something. Sometimes the absence of a track meant something, as well. Regardless, tracks were meant to be followed.

Apprehensively, I opened the door slowly exposing the living room. Dead silence. If I had ever prayed to a higher power, it was at that moment. I feared a dramatic scene of carnage, hidden from view awaited my revelation. My senses were heightened as I crept further into the apartment. My Glock hoisted to a guard position—ready to belch fire. I moved through the front room toward the hallway and a closed door. I passed by a leather sectional sofa which formed a semi-circle around an older model console television. There were no visible signs that a struggle had taken place.

At the end of the hall, behind the closed door, I could hear voices, human voices. I opened the door slowly. My presence announced only by the squeaking of the door hinge. There was no one in sight, only an obtrusive broadcast resonated in the air. The human voices, now identified as a celluloid drama continued its play while I concentrated my effort on grasping an impression of what might have happened.

I focused my attention on the hallway. I crept forward cautiously. I'd been in similar scenarios in the past. The hunt felt the same. I'd been made uneasy by one thing, and one thing only, my fears. Never had I been fearful before, but the thought of discovering Anna's body, made me cringe.

Peculiarly, it was times like these I didn't feel very far removed from my earlier life on the Oregon ranch. Stalking and hunting skills were developed through natural consequences and a second sense arose, one identified as animal cunning. The man could be taken from the woods, but the woods would never leave the man. Hunting and tracking was a way of life. To the casual observer, the idea of tracks might seem strange in the environment of the city, but they were there. The difference was the appearance of the tracks. Forensic sciences came into existence to apply technology to tracking, but you have to be able to identify a track to understand its meaning.

Anna was the last known person in Cal's apartment. I knew from Anna's phone calls the sequence of events. Cal and the girls had disappeared before Anna vanished. I knew she had collected a majority of Cal's research material and stored it off site. Anna didn't mention any signs of foul play at Cal's residence had been evident, I reasoned she would have made me aware of its existence at the time Cal and the girls disappeared.

As I investigated each room of the rental, it became apparent there were no signs of violence. I felt confident that whatever happened to Cal and the girls or subsequently to Anna had not occurred inside the apartment. It wasn't a rush to judgment, it was a viable conclusion.

I further gathered through my impression of the quarters that what had occurred was unplanned. There were folded clothes on one of the beds, a television left on in a bedroom, dirty clothes in the laundry, food in the refrigerator, and the window shades were wide open. Further, I was unable to detect any unusual odors present. With the exception of the apartment door being left unlocked, nothing was out of place or disturbed from its natural setting. These were all tracks that led to my interpretation; the apartment was an unlikely crime scene. I felt I could narrow what transpired to somewhere between the front door and her car in the parking lot. Since the apartment door was unlocked, I felt inclined to believe it was the point of contact that involved Anna's missing person status. Most people wouldn't have left a door unlocked when they were inside their residence. It was doubly true if people left their homes. Nobody and I mean literally nobody in their right mind left a door unlocked in a city like Toronto. Not of their own volition.

I walked from the apartment door to the adjacent parking lot examining the route carefully for any tell-tale signs of foul play. I spotted the security cameras that overlooked each of the entrances to the building. With any luck, someone who had been paid good money to protect the complex assets with the recording devices had actually done the job they were hired for. Maybe that someone had the video recording of the night Anna disappeared and hadn't let the machine rerecord over the same footage. It was almost too much to ask for with a low-ball security firm like the ones usually contracted in America. They were mostly window dressing for insurance claims.

A bonded and licensed security outfit had placards on the building entrances, and the parking lot had additional signage indicating regular security patrols of the facilities. I suspected this might be false advertising to control urges that some opportunists might have, to commit petty crimes, but I decided it wouldn't hurt to examine the potential more closely. I waited to see how often one of these yahoo's came around.

It was a well-marked security vehicle that pulled into the parking lot at eight o'clock. The guard made a couple laps around the lot before pulling into a stall designated "Security Vehicles Only," in big, black letters. A smaller sign in red letters hung underneath that read, "All others will be towed at the owner's expense." The security officer seated behind the steering-wheel looked to be in his early to mid-twenties. He didn't appear to be in a hurry, he sat talking on a brick sized Motorola cell phone. I suspected it was a business call. No self-respecting young man of his age would own one of these phones for themselves.

I grew impatient, and decided to make contact with the guard; I got out of my Avenger and approached his vehicle. We made eye contact. He looked me over pretty good as he tried to decide if I was a threat. I'd seen the look before. Sometimes I was a threat. He politely excused himself from his call and pleasantly inquired, "How can I assist you?" I began to fabricate a story about dropping in unexpectedly on my dear sister who lived in a first floor apartment. I explained further, "I think she left either last night or early this morning. I would like to find out who she left with?"

The young officer looked at me for a minute, and followed with a sly grin, "You're sure it's your sister you're looking for?"

"Hey brother," I said, "you caught me. It's not my sister, and she doesn't live here, but I think she's been staying here with a guy. You know, it's got me in a tail-spin. I'm sorry for lying about her; it's just a bad deal all-around." I pulled a couple fifties from my wallet and folded them. "I'd sure like to see if she's been staying here?" I slid the money across the rolled-down window until he took it from my hand. "Let's take a look," he said with a smile.

When he got out of his pick-up, I could see the spelling on his last name, "Vaquero," that was engraved on the cheap metal nameplate attached to his uniform. "Vaquero," I said, "is that Italian?"

"No, I don't think so."

What would make a guy not know or care to know the origin of his name? "You look Irish," I said. He had light, sandy-colored hair, with bright blue eyes. They were not the average Italian features of the Corso Italia neighborhood. I could also tell he wasn't a recent settler to the area. He didn't have a detectable accent. I leaned toward a Mick in his family tree, somewhere, maybe in the woodpile, but somewhere. I said, "What's your first name?" He mulled over his response before he came out with, "Ryan." It was a sign to me; he'd accepted my presence on friendly terms.

Ryan cued the VHS tape to cover the time frames then switched on the monitor and let the recording play. The cameras were set on a multiplexer of six screens that recorded when the camera sensor picked up movement. The picture quality was poor and grainy, but it did capture Anna at the moment she was last seen. It also showed the two thugs who escorted her out of the building. We ran the footage back a couple times to watch the action. All I could see were two guys, one big dude and one, not much larger than Anna whisking her away. I wanted to cuss up a storm. My blood was boiling, but I forced myself to watch it a few more times. I could see it was useless. Not likely I'd be able to identify these perps in the future from what I'd watched. To my surprise, Ryan, leaned forward toward the monitor and remarked, "Sorry to see her with that guy."

"Which guy?"

Ryan pointed at the screen, "The little guy in the ball cap."

"You know him?"

"Yeah, he's a jerk. He's real confrontational. I caught him in the lot out here and other places I patrol, I always knew he was up to something. I think he was locating cars to steal or some kind of rip-off. He's just that sort of guy. He gets real verbal when you tell him he's got to go."

"Do you know his name?"

"No—other guys call him Jokester I think, something like that."

"Hey Brother, thanks. You helped me out a bunch. Now I know she's up to no good and I can get her out of my life, you know?" I slipped him another fifty and reassured him he's saving me more than what I had given him. I was soon on my way to the airport to retrieve the material. I wanted to see if Cal had squirreled away information on some dude called Jokester. On the way, I called Max and informed him of the developments.

"Walter, I thought we were in agreement, you were to exercise patience and stay at sanctuary until I had contacted my source?"

"That's not the way I remember it, but, what did your source have to say?"

"I haven't heard back as of yet. There is no need to panic though, Anna is highly skilled, resourceful, and not to be underestimated."

"My room at the hostel was designated by Anna as our safe house for this operation. In the event she needed a refuge, she would likely head to my locale."

"Well, alright then, call me when you pick up the material and again when you reach sanctuary. I want to know you've made it safely."

I arrived at the airport as Max and I finished our conversation. The numbered key identified which locker to locate. The luggage piece was retrieved, and I was en route to my hostel room where I'd review the material and formulate my plans.

I unpacked reams of documents that were sorted into files and notebooks. I kicked off my shoes, and made myself comfortable for what I perceived to be a long night ahead. Anna had worked the files a lot. I found them placed in order and covered a range of criminal behaviors on the Abbandanza crime family.

Unlike other mobsters who had made their fortune bootlegging alcohol during the Prohibition Era, the Abbandanza syndicate came to power during the 1960s. "Boss" Alfonso Abbandanza took advantage of turf wars that waged along the New York–Canadian border and built his empire on the less restrictive Canadian side. Alfonso was an 'Independent' claiming non-affiliation with the five notorious New York crime families known as the "Commission." In reality, there is no such thing as non-affiliated in New York's crime network. Everyone paid homage and a percentage of their take to the Commission. There were no exceptions. The Canadian faction soon learned there was no money in territorial battles; only cops and Feds ended up the winners when they fought amongst themselves. As a result, the "Boss" paid like all the other "Independent's" paid, and his criminal empire grew.

The Abbandanza family once spread throughout the Eastern Canadian Provinces but in the early 1990s lost their holdings in Ottawa, Montreal and

Quebec City. They held on to their power base in Toronto until Alfonso's death in 1993. Leadership shifted from Toronto to Buffalo, New York, in 1993 when the family mantle was passed to then underboss, Salvatore Giannetti. Nine years later, Sal was still the boss.

Like most modern crime families, they were comprised of non-blood relatives. In generations past family meant related, but not anymore. However, in the Abbandanza family there was an exception. The Giannetti power structure was strengthened when Sal's younger brother, Antonio, was made family "Underboss." He'd recently moved to Niagara Falls and was responsible for the day to day operations. It was interesting to note, Antonio was not of the low-key, old school mentality like his brother Sal. He was the flamboyant GQ gangster type with fast cars and faster women. He enjoyed being a public celebrity. He frequently entertained the paparazzi and shutterbugs alike. He enjoyed power, and had at his fingertips a great deal of it to exercise. Allegedly, he had been responsible for a number of murders.

Third in the hierarchy was Rocco Colansante, Consigliore. He functioned as Chief Financial Officer for the family and primarily handled the 'Skim' and finance distribution arm. He was a Canadian and resided south of Toronto. He too was a recluse like Sal and rarely seen in public.

With Anna's disappearance, I'd adopted the project as my baby. I owned it. I wasn't going to wait for closure; no such reality exists. The term was a myth perpetrated by psychobabblers. What I intended on doing was kill with bitter resolve anyone responsible for Anna's mysterious disappearance. The sex and illegal immigration rackets were the criteria for Society Palatini's engagement, but that had changed for me—my priority was elsewhere.

Chapter 3

". . . the law was made for the lawless, but powerless to prevent criminal behavior."
—*Walter*

I waited by the luggage carousel to greet Max. I remembered the days when you could meet someone as they deplaned, but those days were lost forever. Max would have to run the gauntlet of Customs and the newly formed Transportation Security Administration (TSA) to gain admission to the United States. If Max had a turban on his head and clenched a Quran close to his heart, he more than likely would have walked right through unscathed. It was the governments' new approach to security since September, 2001. The beacon of freedom for the world didn't want to be perceived as profiling, so they searched and scrutinized the young and elderly alike. However, searching Max might not have been such a bad idea. He likely had killed or was responsible for more dead people than any living Jihadi.

"Hello," Max said. He sounded cheerful but looked burdened. His broad smile was overshadowed by a frown. "Let's make haste to our safe house where we can talk in private."

I've learned to read human behaviors like footprints in the sand. They were directional. In Maximillian's case, his behavior displayed something heavy he had to unload. My guess was he either needed my help to carry the load, or I was the problem. It could go either way at this point. With Anna's disappearance foremost in my thoughts, it created a level of anxiety I didn't need.

Idle chat wasn't on the menu for the cross town trip from the airport. I opened the door to sanctuary and invited Max in. "Please have a seat," Max said. I pulled out a chair from the little dining table and motioned for Max to take the other chair. "I have Intel I've picked up through a very reliable source. He is a Crown prosecutor and has been very forthcoming with viable information."

"Okay."

"Authorities believe they have found Cal."

"Found?"

Canadian police agencies have matched Cal's fingerprints to a body. Police will release very little information to the public. They are not obligated in the same manner as in your country, but we have a friend as I said."

"What happened?"

"It appears he was bound, gagged, and executed with a small caliber weapon."

"Typical *modus operandi* for mobsters," I said.

I've noticed when people pause in conversation, they unknowingly create emphasis on the next thing they were about to say. Such was the case as Max continued.

"He was tortured. The report described multiple burns, lacerations, and signs of blunt force trauma to the head and torso. The body was discarded in a mall dumpster in Toronto. I believe it was intended to be found quickly. It appeared to be an intentional message; otherwise he would have been buried in a field."

What followed Maximillian's report could only be termed an uncomfortable silence. The air felt thick, thick enough to cut with a knife. As saddened as I found myself over what transpired with Cal, it only served to heighten my concern for Anna's safety.

"What do you know about Anna?"

"Scythian."

I was all ears. It was my Palatini name, the symbol of my authority within the Society's Order, and call-to-arms. We were going into action. And Max undoubtedly had a plan. Why else would he address me in such a formal manner?

He continued, "I think you should be prepared for the worst. With Anna's vanishing and the video you saw of her leaving, it is very likely Cal said something of Anna's involvement. It doesn't look promising."

I am a man of uncompromising character, or so I've been told. Anna told me that and at times with a degree of disdain and slightly different definition for my qualities. This day, my inability to compromise, would stick out like a sore-thumb. "Without our knowing differently we need to launch a rescue operation for Anna." It was my turn to emphasis with a pause before ratcheting up the intensity of my position. I said straightforwardly, "Max, I'm telling you, there are no other options. Raise hell if we have to, but we have the ability to ferret out anyone responsible for her disappearance and find out where they are holding her."

"I think you should contemplate the danger you are personally in, as well. Assuming for a minute they put Anna under duress, they might well have extracted a sufficient amount of information on our operation and perhaps the Society overall to put all of us in jeopardy. They are Mafioso. I believe they have a great deal more resources than we do. You see the dilemma, don't you?"

I knew he was trying to appeal to my better senses, but that in itself was a problem—I'm Walter. Taking a tuck-tail and run away from a fight was not my forte. I didn't like the general drift of the conversation; I demanded a clear and concise answer. Max was reluctant to engage me, and it was apparent. My pulse surged and I found myself short of breath; a convulsive trembling below the surface followed, until my anger burst out, "Abandon Anna? Is that what you are saying?"

"No, heavens no man, I think the right course of action would be to work our resources. We have contacts in both the Crown and New York State law enforcement. It's not necessary to engage in a war or risk anymore Palatini assets until we learn what has happened to Anna." Max paused briefly, "Scythian, we need to tie off the project and proceed with caution. Like you American's are fond of saying, 'until we get our ducks lined up in a row,' we should hold off making any plans."

"Not a chance!" I fought my emotions, trying to keep the rage within. If those responsible escaped it would be dangerous for all of us. I'd erupted in the past, but Max had never seen me that way, or he wouldn't have pushed it. I was a nice guy, but I had my limits. "That's a great idea Max." Max preferred to be called Maximillian, but when I slap somebody down, I didn't care about how I sounded. "Let's get all the ducks lined up, Mob ducks, like targets in a shooting gallery, and start plunking them. They'll talk, I guarantee it."

"I was only suggesting we become better organized, make preparations, and work out the smallest of details before we proceed."

"I know what you're saying Max. I may have been born at night, but it wasn't last night." I wanted to smash my fist down his throat and rip out his larynx. Max wanted to fold the hand we were dealt; I wanted to play it. What

Max suggested went against everything I believed in, and made me who I am—Walter. My pent up sentiments continued to surge as I repeated the phrase, "Not a chance," adding expletives between each statement.

Max attempted to placate my anger, but unknowingly added fuel to the fire. "Control yourself man, I understand—we all loved Anna." His thoughtful and comforting past-tense reference to a love for Anna rang hollow in my ears. There was, in fact, nothing he could say that would assuage my passion.

With a forceful tone my demands were set forth, "I need manpower and resources. No stone will go unturned. I want every Palatini available here and on the hunt. If need be, we'll kill every last one of these pukes, whether they're involved with Anna's disappearance or not. I won't rest until I get the answer I'm looking for."

"I don't think your listening Walter. I've taken over the project. I'm tying this operation off!" Max countered with a forceful resound as he continued, "A man with a hammer sees every problem as a nail. You have to learn to use something other than a hammer. Otherwise, you will never be anything other than a cretin."

"I'll put down my hammer alright, but when I do, I'm picking up my gun. I can kill a lot more of those ducks with it than a damned hammer!"

"You are going to get yourself killed, and for nothing."

"Die—perhaps. But, if I do, it will be to save Anna or to avenge her death—and I will die with honor."

Max exclaimed, "You cannot succeed!"

"You're a walking cliché! You make me sick. What are you going to say next, every cloud has a silver lining or some other crap? You're a doddering old fool to think I would abandon Anna."

Max attempted to interrupt, but I refused to yield the floor, "This is now my project, do you understand? I'm calling the shots, and I'm going to see it through to the end."

"And what end might that be," Max asked.

"A blood-bath if it has to be. If you ain't got the stomach for it, bail now."

"As you wish…I will not endanger Palatini assets or waste money on this dead project. There is no win-win to be had."

"I gotta tell you Max, I'm surprised you would let this end in a defeat?"

"Defeat, I do not think in such terms. Walter, you should be very proud. You've accomplished so much on this project. You have broken up their racket. Sometimes that's the best we can do is disrupt the process."

The gist of his argument was transparent, unconvincing, and above all, inconceivable. I opened the door for Max, turned my back, and walked to the window. The seemingly endless palaver had ground to a halt. I was numb to the core. I could barely think, let alone continue the dialogue without doing some head cracking.

I was aware when Max had left the suite, not from his closing of the door since he had not done so, but from the clacking noise of his cane as it drifted into the distance. How did he get back to the airport or where did he go? It wasn't my concern. He was capable of finding his own way as I was capable of doing what I believed was necessary without him.

I sifted through the materials Anna had packed until I located Cal's work on the soldier who befriended him, Joey Naccarella. The Toronto faction of the Abbandanza crime family was considerably different from that of Buffalo. Capo Santo De Luca, the renowned kingpin of Toronto, was a made-man and member of the Administration under Alfonso Abbandanza. He was one of the capos who selected Salvatore to assume the role of Boss of Bosses when Alfonso passed away. Naccarella was an "earner" and thereby an integral part of De Luca's illicit profit machine.

According to Cal's police source, narcotics and designer drugs boomed in Toronto during the early '90s, but De Luca didn't see the gains. His crew lost profitable territories in the West End to well-known street wranglers like the Bloods and Crips. In most cases, a change of leadership would have followed, but not so with De Luca. The elderly man kept his capo title and in all probability his life, due to his extreme loyalty he displayed to Salvatore.

The Toronto crew was forced to expand into new business ventures to make up for losses in drug revenues. The result: they cornered the market on prostitution, kidnapping, and human smuggling throughout Ontario. The Family as a whole closely followed the increased profits in Toronto and determined proliferation to their New York State factions would be beneficial. This was what the Feds called an illegal immigration racket. I was baffled by the term. It didn't have anything in common with immigration. It was another government misnomer that led away from the truth. Consequently, no one rode herd on the racket.

Naccarella was a fiftyish-year-old Canadian citizen with multiple felonies on his rap sheet. His previous human trafficking conviction caught him minimal time in the joint. Cal wrote, "Joey wore the felony like a badge of honor." It should have put a damper on his illegal activities or, at minimum, put him on a watch-list for authorities, but neither happened. Cal's notes indicated

Joey enjoyed border crossings at his leisure. Cal's police source confirmed the mobster's records were never properly coded to prevent entry into the United States, and they had no way to influence the decision. The "fix" was in for Joey.

The law was made for the lawless, but powerless to prevent criminal behavior. In a nutshell, the value of the law was wrapped in deterrence and penalty. With the modern movement to vacate punishment from the law, deterrence was non-existent. The law was therefore, meaningless. Naccarella crossed whenever he felt like it because the penalty had not been applied.

Anna had focused her attention on Joey Naccarella as the lead domino in the Toronto phase of the takedown. Despite his conviction, he had continued his involvement in sex rackets and was grooming Cal for a position with him. Naccarella's name topped the kill list in Anna's area. He would top my list now. He had a grievous amount of suffrage to answer for.

My attention, however, diverted to the pressing issue of finding someone by the name of "Jokester." He was my best lead. There were a few notes on an associate of the family, Nunzio "The Jokester" Lippa. The photo Cal had obtained was unreliable, given that it was an older photograph from a driver's license and severely faded. He also had compiled a small dossier that gave me the impression Lippa was an insignificant small time hoodlum bringing very little to the crime family's table. He had a reputation as an on-again-and-off-again drug addict. It made him a liability. At least that was Joey's perspective, but Jokester had ingratiated himself to other De Luca members with his supply of underage girls for their Toronto brothels. Some of them, according to Cal's investigation, were kidnapped from the United States. Cal's proof; the two girls he helped to escape.

I felt I had established enough of a rapport with Ryan, the young security officer at Cal's apartment complex, to revisit him with the aged picture of Lippa. If he could make a positive identification of "The Jokester" and the fellow he knew as "Joker" to be one and the same, I would be in business with a positive identification of at least one of the abductors. If, in fact, my target were Lippa, I would use the information from his dossier to arrange a little get-together. It wasn't likely he'd take kindly to my questions or voluntarily give up what I wanted to know. I would be prepared to extract it regardless of his level of cooperation.

Secondary issues of concern were sleuth-hounds. Feds had been sidetracked with terrorists for months, but sooner or later, they would come back to the business at hand, organized crime. Law enforcement at all levels had money thrown at them to combat potential raghead terrorist threats. The influx of finances had already translated into advancements for sophisticated spying technologies. In an effort to pacify the fears of the American public, the régime released some of their new advancements in electronic surveillance. According to news sources, these new gadgets were already being employed in fighting crime. Besides the new technologies, the government was also financing more confidential informants. Assuming this was true, it would further complicate things for me. I didn't want to accidently kill an under-cover cop. Inside syndicates like the Abbandanza family, it was impossible to know who was who. I couldn't just start blasting. I had standards.

I made the trip to Cal's apartment complex, and waited in the lot until I saw the security vehicle pull in. It was, as I'd hoped, Ryan Vaquero. He'd remembered me from our previous rendezvous. He seemed apprehensive at first to look at the photo, perhaps thinking he would be in violation of some moral or ethical code of his employment. However, money always talks, and so did my new best buddy.

"Yeah, that's him," Vaquero said.

"Any idea where I could catch up with this guy."

"I don't know where he lives or anything like that, but I saw him about an hour ago a few blocks from here at a place called Tine's auto garage."

"Thanks brother, I appreciate that." I followed up with a couple crisp double-sawbucks for his troubles. Whether Ryan knew it or not, we were essentially on the same team. We both sought the same results, a safer community through our actions. We just went about it in different and unique ways. Maybe someday, I'd show him how to take care of business, my way.

I wasted no time finding Tine's garage. He was not the usual target, or at least not yet. There would be no shoot and kill. I wanted him alive and verbal. We needed to discuss a few things. As I waited for a glimpse of Jokester, I became self-absorbed in thought. My altered mental state became quite enjoy-able as I educed the desired responses via gentle inspiration; I found myself completely lost in distraction. It was by sheer providence I saw a guy matching Lippa's description cross the street on foot a hundred feet in front of me. He walked on the sidewalk; his bebop was cool and carefree. A couple blocks later he slipped into an alehouse. From his nonchalant attitude, I gathered he was oblivious to the executions I conducted in Buffalo. If he was aware, perhaps he'd lived too long under the umbrella of the syndicate, and felt untouchable.

I decided to close in—Jokester had no idea what was in store for him, and I liked it that way. I couldn't wait to see his face when reality set in. It wouldn't be a joke, not at all. Lippa was a street hustler that lived on the lowest limb of the crime family tree. He had made money any way he could, short of an honest job for wages. My impression of him, he would be an easy mark. All I had to do was let him believe there was money to be made off me. I would make myself available to be scammed, play along, and he'd do the rest. I parked in the lot adjacent to the alehouse and entered through the back door. I could have easily accessed the pub through the main entrance on the street side but people customarily shoot a quick glance and tend to ignore your presence. In my experience, I have found a person entering through a back entrance, subconsciously demands greater attention. I wanted Lippa to take that second look and size me up.

I bellied up to the bar and asked for a cold brew on tap. There were a dozen or so patrons scattered throughout at small tables. From the corner of my eye, I could see Lippa eyeballing me. He was a business man looking for business and predictable. I was either an easy mark or an undercover constable. In Jokester's world everyone fit into one of three categories, family, marks, or cops. By the time he figured out which one I was, the joke would be on him.

He was seated at a table with two well-dressed hoods. They were loud at times, laughing and boisterous. From where I sat, it looked like Jokester was the entertainment with witty remarks and one-liners he had picked up in his travels. It was apparent by the trio's demeanor they were altogether comfortable with each other's company. After a few minutes, I concluded, these were De Luca mobsters. I, therefore, minimized their personal worth in a civilized society. Any or all would be subject to death.

While I contemplated the increased difficulty the extra men posed, good fortune smiled on me. The two men stood up and with a rollicking performance, made their way to the door. Lippa was alone at the table. I knew he wouldn't stay that way long, he had business to pursue; so did I.

I struck up a conversation with the barkeep in order to get this joker's attention. I was disturbingly loud as I engaged, "Hey Bud, you know anyone looking for a good deal on a couple cars?" The barkeep's eyes shot a glancing look in Jokester's direction. The bait was cast, now I had to wiggle it a bit. "I got a couple I need to get rid of quick. They're all legit, papers and everything."

The barkeep smiled and courteously responded, "You're, not from around here are you? You sound American?"

"Yep, I'm from Oregon my friend. My girl and I split the sheets and going our own directions. I'm selling everything I have left and heading back home."

Lippa had made his decision; he couldn't let an easy, transient mark, get away. An unknown person with no ties to the community and in a foreign country, it doesn't get much better. I remembered what Vaquero had said about Jokester hanging around in parking lots, and he thought he was trying to steal vehicles. Here, I was practically giving him an opportunity to steal from me. Wiggle the bait—it was fish on!

Lippa reminded me of a Timber Rattler. He slithered up next to me like a snake in the grass. He was close and cuddly at the bar. He took in every word as I described my Avenger. There didn't seem to be much interest generated in my car, but he kept listening. I laid out the description of Anna's Lexus and his eyes sparkled. He obviously didn't know Anna had a car the day he escorted her from the apartment house, or it would have been in his possession already. Jokester soon invited himself into the discussion. Lippa and I dickered about car values. I didn't believe for a moment he planned to pay if we struck a deal. When I felt the time was right, I set the hook. "Do you want to see the Lexus?" Now it was my turn to play along as he set his trap for me. It would provide the advantage I needed in the game.

"Maybe I could take it for a test drive?" He asked.

"Absolutely. Heck I wouldn't expect anyone to buy it sight unseen." I laughed. I sounded like a country bumpkin, naïve, and honest. I felt it sweetened the con for him. The more he enjoyed the rip-off he'd planned, the easier he fell into the trap.

Since I was willing to oblige, he thought he would push it a little further. "I'd like to run it by a friend of mine to look at; he's a mechanic and has his own garage?"

Again, it was not unreasonable, but deceptive. I surmised, his plan would be to strong-arm me to sign over the title or worse, but Walter was busy reeling in his fish.

"Well sure," I said. "Why don't I give you a lift to the Lexus? Then I'll follow you to your friend's garage."

Lippa couldn't have been happier. If I were Lippa, I would have set the trap the same way. It was the easiest way to get possession of both vehicles at the same time. His own transportation only served to add steps to his plan.

"You don't mind, do you?"

"No," I responded. "It's my pleasure." And it was.

Jokester introduced himself, "I'm Nunzio Lippa."

I replied, "Walter Eloy Goe, glad to make your acquaintance." We were in business.

It was nightfall when we walked outside to the Avenger. I'm sure the timing was to his liking, as well. I recognized darkness as my friend as did he, and for the same reasons. The things people like Lippa and I do are done best in the cover of darkness. He was inquisitive about the Avenger's mileage and such before he asked how far we would travel to see the Lexus. I assured him it was not far. Lippa climbed in the passenger side and carried on incessantly about buying the cars—I suspect to put my mind at ease.

We pulled out from the alehouse eastbound. What Lippa couldn't have known was the Lexus sat a half-mile or so to the west. We travelled about fifteen minutes when I began to feel a tugging on the wheel. It was only Walter.

"I need to check a shimmy in the front end. I think I might be getting a flat. Can you hang on a minute?" I didn't want to alarm Lippa when I pulled off the road. No sense getting his hackles up.

Lippa was all smiles when he replied, "Sure, do what you have to do."

I intended on it. I spotted a vacant lot on the outskirts of town. I pulled off the main drag onto a frontage road and doubled back around to the lot. I politely excused myself which further disarmed his concerns, if he had any. He was too busy plotting how he was going to take me for everything I had to think in terms of his own safety. I walked to the front of the car and kicked the tires a couple times while I kept a close eye on my prey. There was no way I could take him across the border—I had to do the deed on the Canadian side.

Lippa appeared occupied with making a phone call. He focused his attention on the phone with his head bent down while pushing the buttons. He should have been more observant. I expected better from a wannabe mobster. I charged the receiver on my Glock near his right temple and convinced him it was in his best interest to hang up on his call. Following my directions to the tee, he disconnected the call and handed me the phone.

"Turn and face the drivers' side window with your back toward me," I said. "Do it now!" I watched for any fancy hand movement that might telegraph a concealed weapon. The search would come later after I had better controls in place. I opened the passenger door and secured his hands behind his back using zip ties. I used handcuffs once, didn't care for them. Zip ties were fast, cheap, and easy, but best of all; they could stay on the body. I hooked his zip tied hands to the back of his belt and belt loop with an additional zip tie. I wanted him secure.

It may only have been my perception, but he seemed to be out of sync with the events as they unfolded, and unable to grasp the gravity of circumstances as they pertained to him. He threatened to do unspeakably cruel things to me unless I released him. He might have been more convincing if he hadn't waited until he was tied up and defenseless. I rapped him in the mouth with my gun to get his attention. I felt I'd impressed upon him I meant business and reminded him I controlled the situation. I strapped a piece of duct tape across his mouth and pulled him from the Avenger. He seemed reluctant to comply with that request. I assisted him with a couple nudges into the trunk. Maybe he'd caught this act in a movie or had seen a similar situation in the past. Regardless, he clearly became more frightened by the minute. I was gratified.

My actions were chancy. I didn't like to operate off the cuff. I couldn't afford to be seen by passing motorists, so I made the necessary moves when no other cars were visible. I secured his feet together with duct tape and closed the trunk lid. As I pulled from the lot, a police cruiser turned onto the frontage road and passed my Avenger as it traveled in the opposite direction. The patrolman gave me a good hard look. I flipped my hand up in a waving fashion but didn't look in his direction. I pulled out onto the frontage road and kept a watch in the rearview mirror as the officer continued his patrol. Lippa and I were off to an unknown destination.

I turned south and drove about an hour, travelled through Caledonia, and continued until I came across a hardtop road alongside a river. I turned onto the road and continued east until I found a welcomed turnout on the edge of a river basin. The remoteness of our location coupled with natural tree-lined embankments provided for an added sense of seclusion. I popped the trunk to share it with Lippa.

My eyes adjusted quickly to the moonlit night. I helped my passenger into a sitting position. That's when I noticed the expression of fear etched on his face. Lippa had been brought out in the boondocks for a reason. I didn't have to educate him as to what it meant. Punk wannabe's engaged in gangster lifestyles frequently heard the stories of these types of one way trips, and on occasion participated in them. My best guess was his memories were his haunting. In a restrained and polite manner, I explained the rules of how our conversation would ensue.

"I'll ask a question and you answer. I don't want to hear a bunch of mumbo jumbo or chit-chat. Am I clear?"

I ripped the duct tape from his lips. He let out with a wretched howl. As it turned out, this joker wasn't very loyal to the crime family. He was just another junkie trying to make a buck and get by. I asked a few preliminary questions to break the ice and insure we had a cooperative union between us. We went over Capo De Luca's structure of who's who, and then we got down to brass tacks. I had specific details I wanted the answers to, and willingly or not, he would provide them.

"Who is Cal Alonzo to you?"

"He's a dirty-stinking fink, a rat—some kinda snitch. That's what I heard."

I didn't interrupt him as he went on a rant. I was interested in everything he had to say, whether fact or fiction, real or imagined.

"That punk got nabbed for hiding some runaway hookers. Just like he was a somebody, you know. He ain't nobody—nobody, you hear me." He scowled as if the message was directed more at me than for my understanding. I could have taken exception to his forlorn conduct, but why debate his behavior, he would be put out of my misery soon enough.

Lippa continued, "One of those little crack ho's were tweaking, you know, she needed a fix. She went running back to her sugar daddy. He took care of her needs. Then she came clean. She ratted that punk Cal out to Bruno to get back into De Luca's good graces." Lippa looked me in the eye and said, "You can't trust no hooker, you know."

"What'd you have to do with Cal?"

"I did what I was told, that's all. Just like you do what you're told to do." My thoughts flashed back to my conversation with Max. Lippa speculated wrong. I don't follow orders very well at all. In fact, Lippa was in the predicament he was in precisely because I'm a rogue element, and before we're done, he'll pay for my misbehavior.

Lippa continued, "We caught that nark at Joey's place. He wasn't ready for it. He had no idea what was up. Then we took him to see Bruno. That's all I know."

"Joey who?"

With reluctance Lippa groaned out a barely audible name, "Naccarella."

"Who ordered him brought to Bruno?"

"Hey, it comes from above, I don't know."

I knew Cal had been beaten and tortured before he was killed, but I wanted to know what had made the rounds in this joker's circle about it. "What happened to Cal?

"Joey is a standup guy, you know. He took it personal, like—real bad, you know. He was a sucker and got himself played. Joey wanted to do Cal, but Bruno wouldn't let him."

"I thought Bruno didn't like Cal?"

Lippa chimed in on cue, "He hated that dude, man. He wanted to find out who this stoolie worked for, you know, but Cal wouldn't give it up."

"Cal didn't talk?"

"That's what I just said. Cal made it harder on himself than it needed to be. He tried to pass himself off as a crumb, but Bruno wasn't having it. He had to educate him, you know, and if you keep messin' round here you'll see too?"

"Were you there when Bruno talked to Cal?"

"Nah, I heard about it, that's all. I heard they iced him when I went to get the girl."

I knew Nunzio was one of the two culprits that grabbed Anna, but I continued the faux discourse, "What girl?"

"The one at Cal's place, you know. He was keeping that whore to himself."

"Were you alone or did others go with you to get her?"

There was a slight hesitation in his voice before he answered, "I went alone."

I thought to myself, we were doing so well up to that point. Why is it, some people have to lie? The fact he wasn't alone didn't amount to a hill of beans in the broader scheme of things, but now I can't trust what he's telling me to be true.

"What happened to her?"

"Cal tried to protect her, you know. She was staying at his place, they were all involved with each other or whatever, you know. This Cal dude didn't think Joey knew about her, but he did. Joey checked him out real close like, you know. Tuff Tony sent in some muscle from outside to scope Cal out."

"So what became of the girl?"

"I heard she didn't cooperate at first, but she came around after Bruno showed her what happened to Cal. She was real broken up and spilled her guts I hear. Bruno messed her up a bit and had taken some liberties with her before he whacked her. She got more than she bargained for if you know what I mean," Jokester smiled with a sheepish grin.

I was sidetracked momentarily as I envisioned Lippa's words. My thoughts presented a most disturbing scenario. I struggled to stay focused. He must have noticed my pause and decided to play a little hardball. He looked me in the eyes, grimaced and said, "I ain't talkin' no more. You better take advantage of the time you have and run. You better hope you don't get found."

Evidently, he forgot who had the gun. It took a few minutes to convince him how I thought the process worked best. The glancing blow with the polymer grips of my Glock had ruptured his skin. A stream of fresh blood ran from the corner of his left eye.

"I saw you and another guy, escort the lady from Cal's place, now tell me about it?"

"I was just doing what Joey said do, you know. That's the way it works. Santarossa and I did just what we were told to do."

"Who's Santarossa?"

Lippa realized he had erred. He had said a name he never intended to get involved. "He's just a guy, you know. He's a nobody."

"Yeah, well I think he's a somebody."

"What's the difference to you anyhow? He didn't have anything to do with anything, you know."

"Why are you protecting this guy? You're out taking care of business, family business, and you expect me to buy you carried out orders with a nobody?"

"Why are you so interested in the girl anyhow, huh? What's she to you?"

Again, with a little persuasion that resulted in a trickle of blood to run from his left ear, he provided a more appropriate response. Amato Santarossa was Lippa's ex-wife's brother-in-law or some meaningless concoction of that nature. Supposedly, if he could be believed, Amato was only helping out that night. According to Lippa, he picked up work here and there for a couple of the mobsters who had placed trust in him. He also worked a couple shifts a week a neighborhood tavern in Corso Italia District. Lippa was kind enough to provide me with the establishment's name so we could have a chat.

I'd left Jokester's cell phone in the front seat of the car. It rang a couple times, so I checked the phone messages, but no such luck. I looked at the call he made, it was Amato he had conspired with. "Why did you call Amato on the way out?"

"I didn't."

I took the opportunity to demonstrate how cell phones worked and showed him the last number he called. He responded, "Oh yeah, I was calling to see if he needed a car, that's all." It was getting to the point where there wasn't much I could believe of what he said, not that I expected better from him. I jotted down the few numbers he had in his phone and the incoming call numbers, as well. He was getting restless during the wait. The anxiety was getting to him.

It was time for this joker to come clean about Anna. We had beaten around the bush for more than thirty minutes, and I still didn't have the answers I'd come for. It wasn't likely he'd be forthcoming. If I continued to inflict pain, he'd fabricate a story. That wouldn't be helpful and probably sidetrack me and slow my efforts to find Anna. When faced with what Lippa had told me, I sensed she was still alive.

"I don't know. I wasn't there." Lippa flinched and ducked his head, shouting, "Don't hit me again." It was more of a begging than a demand. He gathered his thoughts and continued, his tone was stressed but calmer. "I left Bruno's when I was told to, you know. Man you got to understand, Carmine Bruno is the right hand of God." Lippa squirmed in the trunk of the car in an attempt to get in a more comfortable position. "He's the enforcer. He takes care of business."

Lippa wriggled and begged more dramatically, "Hey, how about loosening my wrists, it's cutting off the blood flow."

"Who's Bruno a henchman for, who's he answer to, what's his boss's name?" I threw out the questions in rapid succession as I lifted him out of the trunk and on to his feet. He sighed in relieve.

"Bruno is in charge of family security. He's the main go-between with the capos." He turned his back toward me, "Can you loosen these a little."

As I cut the zip tie that held his wrists to his belt loop I asked in a friendlier tone, "He answers to someone, who?"

"He takes his orders from above, probably Tuff Tony."

"Antonio Giannetti?"

"Yeah, that's right. You already know everything, so why you jackin' me for info when you already know. How about unhookin' me here, and give me a break, huh?"

Why not, I thought, he's been a good stoolie so far. I moved behind him to cut the zip ties that bound his wrists together, but I left his feet duct taped together.

"Where's Bruno live?"

"I don't know, I don't think anybody knows. He's always on the move. You won't find him unless you're connected." Lippa paused, "Maybe I can work for you, like free of course. I can help you find him, you know."

"I have other plans," I said.

Lippa turned back around toward me while he rubbed his wrists. My Glock was still in my hand and pointed at Lippa's gut.

"You can put that away, man. I'm here to help you."

"Like I said, I have other plans already." The weapon discharged, and the round I'd jacked into the pipe, roared out. Lippa bowled to the ground, he screamed in agony from the gut shot. Both hands were clenched tightly over the stomach wound. Blood oozed out through his fingers and ran freely. It was a miserable way to die.

I sat on the edge of the open trunk and watched Lippa wriggle in pain. It was all but over for him. I just wanted to watch his suffering a little longer. When he ceased to entertain me with his pain wrenched torso and laid face up as if looking peacefully at the stars, I wanted him dead. I quietly slipped up alongside Lippa and discharged my weapon again, this time blowing brain matter and debris into the air from the gravel-laden river bank. I really didn't have any further use for him.

I tossed the phone in the river near where I killed Lippa. Keeping a souvenir would be a mistake, and those pesky signals bounce off towers. GPS, it was new technology being installed in some phones. It was risky to have operational, but water killed the signal and destroyed any trace of DNA. It would never be found. That would be the easy fix.

There was going to be a plethora of forensic evidence associated with Lippa's crime scene. The alehouse may have had a camera system, but because of their clientele, I doubted it. Plausible deniability trumps any good reason to have cameras at a Mob pub. The apartment complex did have cameras, and there I was on the surveillance video for sure. If the police get a whiff I was there and could connect the dots, it might pan out as a good lead for them. If the security guard, Ryan Vaquero, heard of Lippa's murder, he might come forth with the video. If they could tie me in, there will be ballistics, fibers from the trunk of my car, too many things to anchor a case against me. I needed to get to Naccarella and Bruno fast. If the cops managed to pinch me before I found Anna, my opportunity to get her out alive would be lost.

The Machine wasn't known for reconciling events of this nature. There would be no negotiations; it had to be a rescue. Otherwise, if they thought the gig was up, they would silence her because she could finger them.

As I drove toward sanctuary, it occurred to me I couldn't continue along haphazardly. I needed somewhere to conduct business of my own, mobster style. It had to be isolated, private, and easily accessible. Potentially this could be a time consuming project, but I didn't have time. Much to Maximillian's chagrin, as long as I'm in place, it's a Palatini project, and it's not tied off.

I needed to exercise caution at this juncture. My base nature was getting the best of me. I was the proverbial bull in a china shop; I enjoyed the feeling, and it was my greatest weakness. The project was now two-fold. The original mission to free those ensnared in human trafficking and finding Anna. However, Anna was paramount. I needed to blaze a trail through leads and get the next link in the mystery secured before the project unraveled. I wasn't worried about those I would leave in the wake, when I finished with them, they wouldn't be talking.

Over my morning coffee, I perused the newspaper classified ads section for a suitable storage rental, out-building, or anything I could use with the privacy I needed. One of the beauties of Buffalo was its lagging economy. For thirty years or more the city's ruling political regime coupled with organized crime ran businesses out of town or into the dirt. The mismanagement of taxpayer funds left Buffalo teetering on the brink of bankruptcy. With manufacturing dried up there was an abundance of vacated buildings around the outskirts of the industrial area. Rent on a small building was inexpensive and private, and there were a lot of abandoned buildings, lying dormant and isolated from housing areas. I was in my Avenger before noon checking out real estate.

It took the better part of a day to find a place I was comfortable with. On the south end of Ohio Street, off a service road, sat a dilapidated-1940s Quonset hut, shabby and in partial ruin. It was unoccupied and available. The corrugated metal roof was dog-eared, rickety, and missing in areas from the semicircular rafters. The most conspicuous feature I found appealing was the rear overhead garage door that hung off track at an angle which rendered it useless. It gave the hut, personality. It was perfect for my aspirations.

I spent a few hours watching the hut for activities that might impede my primary intention. Confident I'd found a good place, I called the phone number for the property management, paid a couple months up front, and had power turned on. I stopped by the hardware store, picked up a couple portable heaters for the tiny office inside the hut, light bulbs, and a lock to secure the entry door.

It was a full day by the time I headed back to sanctuary. I worked late into the night. I developed the smaller details accumulated by Cal and Anna into a decipherable representation of the syndicates' operation. If there were criminal associates that had nothing to do with Anna's abduction or the project, but managed to get in my way, I'd kill them too—the end justified the means.

Investigating authorities swiftly connected the triple murders in Buffalo, and as expected, the news agencies ran with it. I didn't view this in a positive light. With the turn of events that culminated with Anna's disappearance, reporters only served to further complicate matters. The news agencies reported FBI sources had monitored mob activity closely, and hadn't picked up any chatter to conclude a turf battle was brewing. Buffalo police speculated it was an internal housekeeping matter stemming, more or less, from unresolved conflicts within the crime family. They were quick to discount the expansion of organized crime in their city or that there was any danger to ordinary citizenry.

Law enforcement erred before in their judgment of mob wars. New York had seen more than their share of territorial disputes that resulted in high body counts. The reporters made quick work of exposing the Feds track record. It served as a grim reminder that history had a habit of repeating itself. It was especially true when the future was dictated by the template of human nature, with greed being the underlying menace.

The media audience might have been awed by the lightning-fast pace of the police to connect the three dead men, but seriously, they already knew these guys from their rap sheets. They were all affiliated Abbandanza family mobsters. How much of a stretch could it have been to get that right? The police supposition was likewise accurate that there wasn't a territorial dispute going on behind the scenes. No police rocket science here, but rather a coy deception. Law Enforcement had paid out plenty of cold hard cash for eyes and ears on the streets. There was no honor in the criminal underworld, and everyone knew how the game was played. From paid informants to your average street junkies, they constantly gathered and sold information to the highest bidder. Sometimes it was the Feds who scored big on mob Intel, at other times; it was the mobsters that picked up tidbits that ultimately keep them out of the slammer. Being a snitch paid, but there was a risk. Snitches got stitches.

In the Pacific Northwest where I hailed from, two murders carried out in one day on a couple known syndicate mobsters, made the front page head-lines for days after the murders. In Buffalo, the local press quoted the cops and dismissed the story as insignificant. I figured these Bozo reporters were in cahoots with organized crime. There was no logical reason for them not to delve deep into the mysterious murders, unless they had no intention of exposing the crime family's existence. They had an agenda.

If I had to drop a dime and get my old friend Harold Horn involved, I'd make the call. As much as I disdained the liberal press, I held them account-able for not reporting the illegal activities of the criminal syndicates that oper-ated freely. They were themselves a viper's pit of organized crime.

The Machine had links to politicians. It was a well-known fact and undis-puted. However, most people chose not to believe it. They had infiltrated all levels of government; from the lowliest Buffalo city councilman to New York State officials. Any one of them might be on the bankroll or, at minimum, partisan to mobster behavior that benefitted their own causes.

* * * * *

To the judges, lawyers, politicians, and cops who abuse their power and authority for filthy lucre, there is one who relentlessly pursues. He will not overlook how you have allowed crimes against humanity to go unchallenged; for this your requital churns impatiently. Count the days, hours or minutes, for the guilty there awaits the lawless measures of Walter. He is no respecter of persons.

Chapter 4

"They were criminally corrupt people; not innocent people corrupted by criminals."
—Walter

It was my opinion, we had corrupt civil servants. Not all civil servants were bad, but some were, and they got my attention. Since I didn't know who was and who wasn't, I treated them all with the same respect, which was none. There were politicians, lawyers, cops, and judges that had been caught with their hand in the proverbial cookie jar. What followed, were the public's outcry, and a search for "why."

Why! Why even ask? It was just another version of the age old question, "Which came first, the chicken, or the egg?" I put the question in perspective and rephrased it, "Were civil servants caught in the web of organized crime, criminals first or were made criminals by the Mob?" Most people couldn't answer the question any more than they could answer the chicken or the egg dilemma. However, I wasn't most people. I knew the answer.

When politicians, police, or judiciary were caught with their fingers in the cookie jar their colleagues blamed organized crime. They cited mobsters for their overarching criminal influence on some of their own. How were gangsters to blame for the politicians, law enforcement, judiciary, and attorneys that were bad seeds? Did they threaten cops lives or put muscle on an elected official? Perhaps all they did was dangle an opportunity in front of them like bait on a hook, and they found it irresistible?

These were people in position that served the community. Many of them were elected to an office to represent the people for the good of the community. It was in their power to put the screws to organized crime, but, they didn't, not even close. They were obsessed with power and made bank for themselves by benefiting organized crime. As I saw it, there were two forms of guilt. Some of the civil servants were omitters. They were the ones that took bribes and kickbacks to overlook criminal enterprises operating freely. The guiltiest of these were the politicians. We were building a government full of them. Then there were the "committers" the ones that bought in lock, stock and barrel, to commit crimes straight up. Scams, embezzlement, and frauds were their life's work. They flaunted their Harvard education, shook hands, and kissed babies on their way to the top. Then they engaged in the bigger scams of housing markets, land grabs, and union trade agreements.

How was it the Mob's fault these louses did exactly what organized crime paid them to do? They weren't made thieves, they were thieves, and on the take for all they could get. How was that the Mob's fault? It was all opportunity, and they took it. An honest person with his head screwed on straight wouldn't have gone for the offer, but those guys did. Bottom line, it was a quality of their being. They were criminally corrupt people; not innocent people corrupted by criminals. They abused their positions of power and authority to line their own pockets. Whether they ended up under Mob influence or not didn't really matter to me. They would've found a way to make an extra buck off their servitude because they were criminally minded. I wasn't giving the Mob a pass. What organized crime did was create opportunities for civil servants to fall into, and they did. In fact, they jumped in with both feet. They couldn't get in fast enough. That's where the money was.

Anna had picked up travel brochures of Toronto. I glanced at them, but didn't see anything I couldn't live without. According to them, Toronto was a fascinating city to visit. I thought it sucked. All their jargon on the night life and the upscale parties were only places crime hung out. Toronto had a dark and sinister history. From its earliest days, and from what I could see, it hadn't changed. It wasn't built to provide an environment where decent people wanted to raise a family. It should have had an appeal to me because I wasn't a family man. Maybe it did in a roundabout way; it was target rich. Obviously though, not everyone felt the same way.

There was money to be made and businesses flourished. The migration found its way to Toronto by droves and brought the dregs of society with it. The morally corrupt and lawless stereotypes made it a hotbed of criminal activity in its earliest days. I wouldn't have given a plugged nickel for all of it.

I had my own ideas about what made Toronto a breeding ground for filth. This was an area of my life I carefully guarded. I tried to bring it up with Anna about the voices, apparitions, dreams and visions I'd had, but she'd dismissed it as something common among victims, except I'd never been a victim. I would have liked to have pressed the point with Anna, so she'd understand me, but I never found the liberty to explain my experiences. It wasn't her, it was me. I didn't want her to think of me as a nut job, so I'd kept it to myself.

The kaleidoscope of dreams and nightmares I'd experienced in the past had paved the way for my transition to a vigilante. I was different from the other Palatini knights. For what I knew, they'd all had temporal experiences that brought them to the Society. I had an apparitional experience. Destiny, my spirit guide, had enlightened me, as if I were an oracle. I wasn't chosen as a fortune-teller, tea-leaf reader, or a psychic. I was called to be an instrument of death. My passion was to right the wrongs for victims of heinous crimes. I didn't become a Palatini by chance. I was led to knighthood in the society by Destiny.

Carmine Bruno's dossier fell from a pile of folders I'd had in my hands. It had landed on the table top in front me. The file stood wide open with a picture of Bruno's face that stared back at me. Anna had spent a lot of time and compiled a large amount of information on Bruno's nomadic lifestyle. From her notes, I could tell she had questions about his movements. "What was the reason," she asked on her sidebar notes? I knew right off what the problem was. He was paranoid and rightfully so. When you took into consideration the people he worked for and how he conducted his business, it made good sense to be paranoid. In all likelihood, he figured his chances for a long life would be enhanced if he stayed on the move. It certainly improved his odds with me.

Anna laid it all out as plain as she could make it. All the information she'd turned up on Bruno came from Cal's notes. She'd drafted a targeting plan, personalized, just for him, but she never got the chance to put the finishing touches on it. I decided I would do the honors.

After going through Bruno's file carefully, the answer jumped out at me. He frequently stayed in the same place in Toronto. That translated to opportunity. He always rented a room at a small tavern nestled deep in the Corso Italia District. I figured that was the chink in his armor. He was a creature of habit. For a guy like him, it was a bad habit. He was called a wiseguy, but it didn't mean he was all that wise. It was a smart move to be transient, but smart guys make mistakes too, and his habit might well be his.

Bruno hung out at Musolino's in Corso Italia. It was billed as an osteria, a dago-style restaurant. Older osteria's were often used as meeting places and had rooms similar to an inn or bed and breakfast. Musolino's, touting a rich guesthouse heritage, was such a place. This particular dive, nestled in the heart of a predominantly Italian neighborhood, was host to some of Toronto's biggest names in organized crime. The way I saw it, all these upscale hoods in one place, was a plus. It was like I had all my ducks in one pond. All I had to do was line them up.

The osteria sounded pretty cozy on the surface, but unbeknownst to Cal, his records demonstrated a more sinister history behind the scenes. I don't blame Cal or Anna for overlooking what I spotted; they didn't understand the depth of the problem they were up against. I was more in tune with the deeper roots of Musolino's criminal landscape. My history from childhood to vigilantism had brought me experiences like no one I knew. I'd been there, in the darker recesses of spiritual influence where evil lurked. Musolino's was one of those places. It bore an irrefutable past. The kind of history nightmares were made from.

Musolino's, or at least the location in this district, had some sort of attraction for the worst of the worst. From the records, it dated back to the laying of the building's first cornerstone. Sometime around the 1890s, before the Mafioso presences appeared, the osteria hosted a lawless clientele shrouded in mysteries. A medley of vagabonds and motley riff-raff made up the heart and soul of Corso Italia. It was bad DNA. Immigrants poured in from every nation under the sun. While most arrived with nothing but the clothes they wore, the Italian's and Sicilian's brought with them their extra baggage. Laden with their Old World obligations to continue feudal warfare, they settled in Toronto's Italian district. Ambushes and mayhem abounded as they set about cutting out territories. It was here at the center of their bushwhacking activities a middle-aged couple decided to build a guesthouse.

More rumor than fact surrounded John Jr. and Kate Benders. They reportedly built, owned, and operated the Labette Inn in Corso Italia at the turn of the century. It would become Musolino's. The Benders were Dutch born immigrants, who initially made their way to the United States and took up residence in Osage Township, Kansas. The Civil War had ended by the time they arrived, and the westward expansion was well on the way. There was money to be made, so rumor has it, they opened an Inn. But, the Benders ran into trouble. Transients came up missing. Townsfolk made allegations and accusations against the Benders, and John Jr. and his family went on the lam. It must have been serious. The Benders abandoned their American dream and took flight to avoid arrest or possible lynching. Few people knew when they arrived in Toronto, but by 1895, they had resources enough to build a guesthouse—the Labette Inn.

As a rule unsavory types weren't pillars of the community for very long. This had been the case with the Benders. The rumor mill stirred when a vigilante committee from Kansas attempted to abduct the twosome and transport them back into the United States to face trial for multiple murders that allegedly occurred at their Kansas guesthouse. Evidently some of the missing people were found in a cellar of their guesthouse, heads bludgeoned and throats cut. With insufficient evidence of their guilt coupled with an uncooperative relationship with Canada to compel such action, John and Kate were allowed to forgo a forcible return to Kansas soil. The vigilante committee, despondent over their lack of success, set out to insure the Benders reputation would be destroyed. They marched and chanted, "Bloody Benders" in front of the Inn, which drew the attention of a reputed siege lord. He stepped in and arranged a personal favor for the Benders. After committee members received a few thug beat-downs, they left the neighborhood. According to the Kansas committee turned gossipers, John Jr. and Kate were not the traditional family of husband and wife, but rather they were brother and sister. References to their incestuous carnality spread like wildfire. They were further plagued by a series of local "missing person" investigations which, in some circumstances, had a connection to their Labette Inn. But rumors were just that, rumors, and they never gained traction in the highly transient city of Toronto. The Benders escaped, some believe for a second time, arrest and prosecution for multiple murders.

In my review, I wasn't saying they were devil possessed. I don't believe in that. I'm saying they were drawn to Toronto because it was conducive to their lifestyle. They were evil, and they were attracted to an evil environment. They built the Labette Inn smack dab in the middle of it.

By the early 1900s, Toronto had become the New York City of Canada. It was a melting-pot for nationalities looking for new citizenship. It was a cesspool. Crime sharply increased as urbanized living conditions became overcrowded, and what there was for law enforcement was overburdened or bought for a price. By the autumn of 1919, the new murder capital of Canada had consumed John Jr. and Kate, as well. They were found bludgeoned to death in their bedroom at the Labette Inn. The way I saw it, it was bad karma. It was the return on their life's investment in death. They left behind a slew of unsolved murders when they went to their graves. I figured somebody wanted it that way.

More murders, that was the way the story unfolded. More and more murders, blood flowed in the streets of Corso Italia. The new owner of the Labette Inn was Phillip Bono, a liege lord from Sicily. He kicked the Benders kids to the curb without a penny. I suppose it was only circumstantial that Bono had met with John Jr. and offered to buy out the Labette Inn the day before their brutal deaths.

Bono was a business man and wisely gave the old Inn a fresh new look and hid the old name under a new banner. Not much else changed. The newly named Musolino's was now headquarters for a Sicilian faction of gangland feudalism. More murders followed. The Bono network operated out of the Inn from 1920 to 1959 when it changed hands to Alfonso Abbandanza.

Under Bono, the Inn had become more notorious than under the previous owners. Evil had been compounded by evil. He directed a murderous vendetta against immigrant Sicilians that would not yield to his control. He killed his own and enslaved them under his operation. He ran the rackets, invested in real estate, and was prosperous. He was feared by most inhabitants. He was Mafioso.

Money could buy him henchmen but not loyalty. His wealth made him a target for other up-and-comers. His protection eroded, and other crime families moved in. It was the nature of the business. Snitches were hired to rat out Bono's activities. The Crown responded with indictments. With rising legal costs and business hampered, cash flow dried up. He wasn't the kind of guy to take the treatment lightly. He tried to make a deal, but he didn't put up the money to make it happen. The Crown turned a blind eye to what was going to happen. If he'd put his money where his mouth was, he wouldn't have been in the fix he was in, but he didn't do it the smart way.

In Phillip Bono's case, he was another victim in a string of unsolved cases for the Toronto police to sit on. Bono wasn't just slain; they did a piece of work on him. The hitter didn't come heavy. Bono was caught in his bedroom at Musolino's and perforated with an ice pick. In the end, his fate was no different from dozens of others who had crossed Alfonso Abbandanza's path. This was Musolino's history, rotten to the core, and an ideal place to focus my attention. The atmosphere was conducive to their ilk and maybe to me, as well.

Abbandanza took control of the criminal underground reins in Corso Italia and began to expand his business. Greed had always generated the Mafia's organization, and there was no shortage of greed. Therefore, the Mob could not be defeated by traditional methods.

I found Musolino's captivating. The police were powerless to impact the ruthless behaviors found in Corso Italia. Too many of the cops had steady paychecks for looking the other way. The Crown prosecutors were unable to put pressure on the criminal element to suppress their activity. Why? The Abbandanza Machine owned too many of the politicians. The Crown itself was politics. They counted on the unions and the positive publicity from organized crime to get elected and appointed positions. The Mob could make them or break them. It was the way they played hardball. I was clued in; I wasn't going to find an honest one in the lot of them. How could the people ever find justice in Toronto? You had to know what it looked like first, to find it.

I had my work cut out for me. If I figured it right, Musolino's would provide a lot of targeting solutions. If I played it smart, I would take advantage of what I had over the cops. What was it a cop couldn't do that I could do? I could kill. I could clip any one of them as the opportunity arose, and I knew how to make an opportunity happen. To make a dent in Toronto's criminal activity, I'd have to kill a lot of them, maybe too many to count.

I was deeply disturbed. If this Mob infested country was to survive, it needed plain old-fashioned predator control. I grew up around it, and I knew what to look for, and how to do it. Predators without controls consumed everything they normally existed on, and as food supplies dwindled, they expanded their menu. They consumed anything they could get their fangs into. The Mob was the same way. They were predators. As long as the money was in drugs, vice, unions, politicians, and other lowlife venues, they didn't bother the innocent and wholesome of the community. When the need for more arose to sustain their lifestyles, they operated more heavily in sex slavery, human trafficking, intimidation, and strong-arming legitimate businesses in the protection racket.

Toronto, Buffalo, it made no difference. All of these areas were deeply entrenched in organized crime. The cops hadn't shown me a thing up to now. I'd looked at their record on organized crime. Sure, they did pretty good writing speeding tickets, and cutting into some of the little ethnic neighborhood street gangs, but not the Mob.

The mobsters were more than money grubbers, they were outright murderers. They gathered together like pack animals to take down their prey. I was certain now; the Mob had to be wiped out of existence. Shooting a few would accomplish nothing. Fresh recruits were always on the horizon.

This was major league play. The porn distribution ring we took out fell apart with a few dead ringleaders. It was all minor league stuff in comparison. The Mob engaged in tougher play with tougher rules. Maybe it was a bigger bite than I could chew, but I figured I wouldn't let it concern me—I was a fast learner. I was supposed to shoot a few guys and be done with it, but not anymore. Now I had to hunt down half the city to settle the score.

Cal had written in his notes how he'd felt threatened by Bruno's presence. He would address him as Carmine to lessen the intensity, but it rarely worked out that way. In his words, "De Luca's enforcer has it in for me." Cal rambled through a hodge-podge of threats Bruno had conveyed to him; none of it impressed me. He was a loudmouth and a bully. He intimidated people with his demeanor and reputation, but I wasn't convinced he was a tough cookie. Besides, cookies crumble pretty easy, especially when they catch a hammer fist upside the head, and that was one punch I could throw, mean like. My interest in finding Bruno had quadrupled; I wanted to find him just to see what he was made of.

I continued to read through Cal's notes. I didn't care for Cal much, but then again, I had never met him either. Anna seemed taken with him, and that was all the more reason not to take a liking toward him. It riled me up just thinking about it. I was jealous. It was against my better judgment to admit that, and I wouldn't admit it to Anna. She might put it in my face, and razz me. I had good reason to be jealous, she was a real looker. I thought. Cal would've had to have been blind not to notice her, and here they were working together, hand in hand, day and night. Yeah, I didn't like him much, but the more I read his scribbles the more he seemed like an okay guy, as long as he kept his mitts to himself. Now that he'd gotten himself killed, I regretted my resentment of him.

According to Cal, it wasn't just his feelings about Bruno, but Joey Naccarella had been challenged for bringing Cal around. Cal scribed, "Carmine abruptly asked me ridiculous questions like, 'when did you get your police certificate' or 'how long have you been a snitch?' Then he would harangue Joey for not checking me out closely enough. He made me feel very uncomfortable whenever I was around him." Cal said Bruno seemed deranged at times. At one point, he had caught him out of the corner of his eye snarling and hissing in his direction from across a room. Cal finished his discourse about Bruno by writing, "Eventually his continuous questioning made it easier to repel the false accusations he leveled at me, but I should fear for my life."

Due to Bruno's habitual traits when he was in Toronto, I envisioned him as an easy kill if there was such a thing. I learned after my bout with Steward Pidd and subsequent chase from Oregon to California where I slit his throat, never again to be lulled into a mindset of "easy," especially when it "felt" it would be. There was no such thing as an easy kill, only an efficient and clean kill. I continued to examine photos and scrutinize dossiers on key players while I drafted a plan to set up an observation on Musolino's.

It was late in the evening. I was tired of the archeology dig through Cal's material; it was time to put my game in play. I put my Glock and two spare magazines on the coffee table, pulled my shirt off, and stretched out on the couch. I'd grown accustomed to sleeping with my holster on. That's when it really hit home. I was tired, too tired. My head no sooner crashed into the pillow when I realized I'd been going non-stop for days, and it was taking its toll on me. My reserve tank was empty. I was drained both physically and mentally. I closed my eyes and waited for sleep to entwine my thoughts. I laid there in wait a long time, at some point I dozed, and then came the clattering noise of the telephone ringer which startled me wide awake. Who would be calling me? No one knew I was alive, or I was at our safe house, except Anna and Max. I was pretty sure Max, and I weren't on speaking terms any longer. Maybe it was Anna. If she'd escaped the clutches of the mobsters, she would naturally try to contact me. I lunged for the phone in anticipation of the voice I longed to hear. I stopped in my tracks. It might also be mobsters. They had at least four good reasons, all lying dead, to find my whereabouts and even the score. Maximillian's prior warning rang in my ears, "Anna might have broken down while being tortured and given up the whereabouts of sanctuary." I suppose it applied to the phone number, as well. Anything was possible, but why would they call? It's not like they were going to schedule a gunfight. Maybe, they were testing the number to see if someone answered. It was easy to cross reference a number to a location. Why let it bother me, I thought, it would make my life easier if it were the Mob. They could come to me. I picked up the phone but said nothing. I would let them speak first, and they did.

"Walter?" The caller spoke my name with a questioning tone in his voice. I recognized the voice straight away. Max had repeated himself twice more before I acknowledged him. I wasn't trying to be inhospitable. The sound of his voice had dashed my hopes. I wanted desperately for it to be Anna on the other end of the line.

Max was someone I had lost faith in. I'd only been a Palatini a few months, but now I felt challenged to reexamine my relationship with the Society. In theory, they were everything I longed for, but in practice, I now had questions. I wasn't someone who needed a label. I knew who I was and what I was. I did what I was called to do before I'd met Max, and if need be I would go back to my roots and continue my calling. I could also do what I had to do in Toronto with or without Palatini support. I was not without resources.

Max was selected by the Order of Palatini knights to provide a specific role in the organization. As Grand Master of the Society, he was highly respected and carried a great deal of clout. When I first met him in Bellagio, Italy, I was taken by him. His role was carefully explained to me. He acted as a facilitator of manpower and finances for sanctioned Palatini projects. He was not considered or referred to as the boss. By virtue of our name, Palatini, we were freelancers. We were independent assassins. If we determined a need existed in a project then we contacted Max to facilitate the arrangements. Our operations were guided by our sworn oaths. In my opinion, Max had no right to circumvent this project when Anna came up missing. It was not what I had anticipated, and I felt he had further endangered Anna's life by cutting ties midstream. Perhaps, my understanding was skewed. I'd drawn from my time in military service the idea we left no one behind. The higher ranking officers and officials would leave troops for the sake of the mission, but those with boots on the ground would not.

"Walter, I have a very reliable Crown source that I have been in touch with."

"Yeah. What of it?"

"I'm afraid he has given me a bit of devastating news. You should take a seat."

I could hear it now. Max was going to say the Crown wanted me to stand down and end the project or let them handle things. I'd already decided that wasn't happening.

"Max, just spit it out! I've got work to do." My tone was hostile. I felt it and hoped it came across clearly. If not, I was more than willing to repeat it or say something else in the same quality of voice. I was not a happy camper, and I wanted him to know it.

"An attendant at a landfill near Holland Landing, north of Toronto, found a fifty-five-gallon steel barrel. Curiosity drove him to check if it contained hazardous materials. He unbolted the locking ring and revealed the contents. He wasn't sure of what it was he had found, so he called in the authorities."

It felt like Max was beating around the bush. I didn't like the treatment. It put my nerves on edge. I sat down and began to fiddle with my Glock for entertainment while Max was getting to the point. Finally, I asked, "What did they say it was?"

"What the attendant found was very unpleasant. Are you sitting?"

"We've been over that, get on to the point," I irritably said.

"Yes, well then, he had found severely degraded remains of a human body. It is currently under investigation."

His pause was lengthy and mystifying. Why? What did he still need to tell me? There were sounds on the other end of the line. I couldn't make out quite what they were. It sounded as if he was coming down with a bug. Wheezing and clearing his throat. "They recovered a handbag at the dump-site." Maximillian's voice began to crack under stress "In the pocketbook of the purse was a driver's license. It belonged to Anna." Max broke down from the emotional tension and wept bitterly.

I was stunned. I continued to hold the phone to my ear, but I was unable to hear Max any longer, although I was sure he was still on the line. I felt I should respond, but I had no idea what to say. We were both silent, the reality of what Max had said sunk in. My emotions began to react. I was unable to utter a sound. I wanted to, but I couldn't muster the strength to blurt out my pain. I sensed a surreal, out-of-body sensation, a buoyant disconnect from the pain. It was a natural defense mechanism which allowed me to escape the reality of the moment, but it didn't last.

In time, Max continued with the rest of what he knew. I wasn't sure how much of what he said I heard. I was in a fog bank. It covered me like an old-fashioned down comforter. I labored to breathe.

"The Crown source said forensics has been unable to identify the remains. DNA technologies might take months to determine the victim, if ever."

We might not have been in this boat, if we'd tried harder to find her when she first came up missing, but Max drug his feet. I was pretty sure Max felt the same way—now.

He struggled to speak, maybe it was guilt. If it wasn't, it should have been. "The value of the DNA analysis was greatly diminished by the sulfuric acid. The body had been immersed in the acid brine with water as an accelerant for a few days."

I was drifting deeper into a state of shock. I lost my cognizance to respond. I was afraid to. I didn't know what I might say, but it wouldn't be good if I did. I blamed Max for not taking the bull by the horns. I'd rather have died in a gunfight than experience what I now felt.

Maybe Max had sensed my dilemma. With great strides, he proceeded with his discourse slowly. "The police were unable to locate any teeth. The flesh was emulsified; the bones and cartilage disintegrated into smaller particles. There may not be a viable way to know the identity of the victim."

The grimmest reality sat in. It was an evil from old come to haunt me. Alfonso Abbandanza was "old school" and according to informants he had been notorious with acid baths in the early 70s as a method of problem solving. The Provincial Police were surprised, stating they had not seen this method of disposing of a victim in ten years. Alfonso had been dead about that long too. Capo De Luca, however, was another "old school" family member. I surmised this was some of his handy work. Cal and Anna had been in his territory and would have been deemed a threat to him. Old habits die hard. In this case, the practice pointed a finger at De Luca's crew. The Provincial Police should have made the connection and been all over it, but there was no evidence Maximillian's Crown source had taken any steps in that direction.

Max interrupted my thoughts, and the silence that had filled the air. "I wish I could tell you—." His words fell into silence. He lapsed into the throws of despair. It had overtaken and consumed him completely. It seemed like an eternity compressed into those few minutes. One of us had to end the stalemate.

"Thanks for calling Max." He didn't like me calling him Max, but it didn't make any difference what he liked. What I had to say was to the point. I was about to hang the receiver up when I heard Max struggle to speak in an audible voice, "Godspeed Scythian."

The receiver found its way to the phone cradle. I sat back and thought about his salutation. It had depth. It wasn't Walter, but Scythian. It was my Palatini operative name. What did he mean by saying it? I knew it was customary in some circles to use the term Godspeed like adieu or bon voyage, but I believe Max fully intended it for a blessing. Godspeed for what he knew I would do. I was fresh out of gods that were willing to go out on a limb and bless what I was capable of doing. Not even some clown they called Beelzebub would back my play. I would give him a bad rap if he did.

Chapter 5

"Morning came, as it did for all survivors of the night."
—Walter

I wasn't perfect. That wasn't news, however, I guess I expected higher of myself. People usually do expect better from themselves than they deliver. I was devastated by an unbearable sorrow. It was different than anything I'd ever experienced before, or ever knew existed. I turned on the radio to interrupt the isolation that surrounded me. I dialed through a dozen stations, none of which drowned out my thoughts. I landed on a station playing instrumental, and left it there. I settled deep into the cushions of the vintage Chesterfield chair, switched off the floor lamp, and tried to hide from my agony.

I thought I was a tough enough guy. I'd been around, seen a lot of ugly stuff happen, and dealt with it in my own way. I'd been made weak in an area that was new to me, an area I was not ready to experience in many ways. I took a risk, I loved, and now I hurt. I needed to get a grip on my feelings, but it's easier said than done. It wasn't love that caused me the galling pain, it was love stolen from me, and that was unforgivable. Nothing in my lifetime had been as special as Anna. My memories of her and my dreams of a future together, had vanished. Now, these thoughts were unbearably cruel.

What had I known about pain? Only the burdensome hurt from dreams and nightmares that shaped my destiny as an avenger. I had inflicted a lot of pain on predatory perverts that deserved to die a slow death in recompense for their filth. In their world, young innocent children were subjected to all manner of torture and abuse. They denied children the right to their childhood and stole their innocence. They used them and did whatever came to their perverse minds. In their world there was nothing taboo. I felt no remorse for them then, and I still didn't.

I retrieved my Glock from the end table where I'd neatly placed it for safe keeping. Holding my trusted friend by its polymer grips, I pressed it against my chest. Here I had a bond, a kinship, something tangible with deep meaning. I rubbed the cold-steel muzzle against my face; I didn't fear its savagery. It was a stalwart comrade, prompt in my time of need, always with me, through thick and thin. Such a friend could do much to alleviate my current distress, if I gently persuaded it. I brushed the corner of my temple with the muzzle while my thoughts were consumed by reality. I considered the ease that a split second could bring; suddenly it was there, the chilling coldness of the muzzle under my chin. It was the easy way out, fast and lethal. It would relieve the misery once, and for all. It was an answer, a coward's answer. Who could blame me? I was free to choose. There was no one left in my life I had to answer to, for what some would consider a selfish act.

I could see the headlines of the local newspapers, some meaningless unknown offed himself. However, if it were known who I was, a wanted man, a vigilante with a price on my head. A killer who had roamed their streets and murdered their Mob neighbors, it would be heralded as a just and fitting end to my story. Either way, no one would care about me. The only way anyone would care was if I stayed alive, on the prowl, and remained a threat. At least the gangsters would care and I'd be happy with that.

I wasn't like those folks that blame God for my predicament. Why should I? God had nothing to do with it. I'd watched the believers grovel on their knees in repentance and bare their contrite souls before the perception of thrones and judgment; all for not. The cup did not pass away so easily. Neither will mine. Why bother God with all of it?

Morning came, as it did for all survivors of the night. I found my actions the previous night perplexing. I felt unsafe in my safe house. I felt unable to mount a defense if mobsters paid me a visit. I had no sense of focus. So much disconnect, I knew I had to get out. Another night and it might not end the same way. I dressed warmly for the outdoors, strapped on my .40-caliber and buck knife, and set out to walk the city streets. I searched, for what, I didn't have a clue. It was midday, and the temperature had warmed to thirty-six degrees. The snow had turned to slush where the sun shone directly, and the ice became dangerously slick.

I was a long way from my roots in the foothills of the Cascade Mountains of Oregon. I missed the comfort of the wooded hillsides that hid me from society and society from me. Buffalo was a city like any other I suppose, an asphalt wilderness filled with chilly steel towering buildings. I leaned against one of the high-rise buildings and looked to the sky. The building was cold to the touch and mirrored the city's callous demeanor. The cloudless sky was without horizons, only buildings. The tinted brownish-gray haze from human pollutants filled the air. I watched the hustle and bustle of inhabitants as they scurried along. They were akin to an endless trail of ants. No verbal acknowledgment from another human being, not so much as friendly eye contact. They were in full guise for their eight-to-five masquerade.

I wandered aimlessly for more than a day, more than two, listening to the constant noise of the city. There was never silence. I didn't sleep at night but dozed occasionally on park benches during the daytime hours. I wanted for nothing. I didn't feel hunger, only numbness. I saw the homeless vagabonds. I had an inkling of how a person might choose their nomadic existence rather than live amongst others of their kind.

In the distance only a few blocks away, I could see the hostel which housed sanctuary. A block from our safe house entrance stood a corner liquor store, a familiar enough environment that would assist in my commiseration. Still sporting a trancelike fog, I entered my billet carrying four bottles of whiskey tucked neatly in a bag. I would drown my sorrows. In time, they would eventually give up, and go away.

I drank straight from the bottle. It didn't do what I wanted it to. What I needed it to do. There was no satisfaction to be found. In my langered state, I'd hoped to have lost consciousness, but instead I lost the numbness, and pain reemerged. It would not be mitigated by mere consumption of alcoholic beverage. The flames of condemnation lapped at my spirit as if it hungered to consume me; for I was vulnerable to such an attack. I was filled with guilt.

The sun rose, more than once. I didn't know how many times but a fifth of whiskey was never far from my side. I drank breakfast. It got the day off to a good start. I picked up my Glock and held it close to my heart. My weapon no longer held the choice of escape. I didn't feel the need to end my heartache. I would live with the suffering, and pass the pain on to those responsible for mine. I had been driven by mission, now it would be vengeance.

I continued to consume the whiskey until oblivion was within reach, but before I could succumb to its power, the last drop emptied on my tongue. Pure bad luck, I thought, no more bottles to befriend me.

I hadn't heard from Max, and it was doubtful I would. He paid our safe house bills through Palatini project funds. Now, I surmised I would have to draw on my own resources to remain in Buffalo. If I were going to make the Mob pay, I had to stay in the area. It might end up my life-long quest. From Maximillian's perspective, the project was defunct. I needed to sober up and make preparations.

I entered a dreamlike state in which I saw myself sauntering through a hilly field laden with lush green grass. This landscape was not one I recognized from any of my previous dreams. Always before, there were torrents of cloud, violent winds and voices. Here, there were none of these things. It was a celestial state. No light to follow through a dark tunnel, just tranquility.

The moment in time captured the dawning of a new day. Fresh, clean, and pure as the expectation of a sunrise. The horizon burst forth in rich red and deeply yellow sun rays. The sunlight sent vibrations across the meadow, the grass shook with excitement. I felt—delivered.

I sat on a western slope of the field and closed my eyes tightly as I basked in the rays' warmth. I felt at peace. It was the first time in many days. As I absorbed the tranquil nature of my setting, I imagined in my mind's eye, Anna in all her beauty. Anna was a leader. If she lived in this place, she would undoubtedly hold a position of high esteem among all the people in this heavenly domain.

I imagined Anna as she crossed the meadow toward me, scantily clad in a silky white garment, buoyant from the gentle breeze. Braided black leather straps wrapped around her, binding the sheer fabric to her voluptuous frame. The sensual sight pleasured my senses. She adorned herself with Celtic jewelry; a Trinity Knot necklace hung between her breasts and matching Celtic ornaments decorated her leather headband and upper armbands. Her flowing deep red hair and stunning blue eyes perfected her flawless erotic image. I wanted her. Anna approached where I sat; her arms open wide, stretched from side to side.

The very thought of Anna brought me tears of happiness. My heart was consoled. It was only a vision conjured up, an appearance fabricated for my dream, but dreams have had a prominent place in my reality. Perhaps, this was a vision of things to come, my reward for a race well run.

A cool and refreshing breeze wafted across the meadow and on to the brim of the hillside where I sat. I looked in the direction where I imagined Anna had been to behold an apparition coming my way. I was excited at the prospects. Could it be really happening the way I imagined? Is this a magical place where dreams come true?

I sat forward in anticipation. The spirit called my name in a sweet velveteen-whisper, "Walter." I knew the voice; it was my spirit guide, Destiny. She'd been a part of my life that I'd kept hidden, and unable to share. She too was as radiant as my thoughts of Anna had been; strange I had not remembered her in such a way. Her robe was bright white and glowed. Her hair was a vibrant honey-hued blonde, sleek, long, and fluent in the wind. She had been my closest friend and only confederate in the beginning of my vigilante crusade. She had assiduously guided my every step. It was Destiny that had delivered me to the doorstep of Society Palatini where I found meaningful direction to my life as a killer of evil doers. She had made me a promise never to leave me, all the days of my life. I wondered had she come to let me in on a secret? Was the day of fulfillment at hand? If so, I was ready.

I stood to greet her. In my anticipation, I asked, "Have I died? Is that why I am here?"

Her eyes illuminated a bright blue as she responded, "Your time is not yet at hand." Destiny reached out and touched my arm, "Can you feel me?" This was an odd question and gesture that I didn't understand. She was an apparition. You can't feel spirit-beings, and I never had felt her touch all the years I had known her.

"Yes."

"Throughout your lifetime your emotions have paralyzed you from being the person you were meant to be. You exposed yourself to love and the unintended consequence of loss. Your life has taken on a broader spectrum."

I suppose I'd known most of my life that I was different from others. I had learned that when I married fresh out of high school, and was soon divorced. I'd relegated the outcome to my military service. I was gone like a lot of the other guys, and they ended up the same way. It never devastated me. Maybe I'd never loved or maybe I knew why I felt as I did.

"You cannot hide or mask your humanity."

"Nothing makes sense to me. I don't understand why I was given a love like Anna's just to have it taken from me?"

"You have chosen a path. To understand you must live in truth and honesty with yourself."

"So what is the point? Anna is dead, and the Palatini was not what they said they were."

Destiny's eyes flashed a reddish glow, a sign I had seen before when she was angry, "In your self-pity you have forgotten why you were called." Destiny paused, "There are many trials that await you. The things that come to pass will not be your choosing. Yet, only your choices will make the difference as to how you survive them. Neither you, nor any of your kind, have been given a rite of passage. It must be earned."

"Destiny, you are talking in riddles. Name one thing I have to learn from a tragedy of love that I didn't already know?"

"You already know," she said. Destiny moved close to me, nose to nose, almost touching. I could feel the exhalation of her breath against my face as she spoke the word, "Victimization and revenge."

If anyone knew anything about dishing out a payback, it was me. That was the only reason I killed the miscreants of society. It was my chore. When growing up on the ranch, I had chores assigned to me, and I did them. If a sexual deviant crossed my path, I eliminated them. I didn't have a problem with it. It was assigned to me the way a chore had been. Outside other Palatini members, I don't know anyone more capable of vengeance than me. I laughed at her statement.

Destiny ignored my response. "You are an elite killer, but superficial. If it were not so, you would be about the business at hand and not wallowing in your sorrow."

I butted in, "I've never needed an excuse to kill the people I've killed, they brought it on themselves, and that was good enough for me. Besides, there was a time, and you remember as well Destiny, I had felt the agony of the victims."

"What you felt was impersonal and brief. You'd made a connection with the traumatic wounds of the innocent, and it led you to me. But now, you know the pain of victimization personally. It is endless sorrow with no hope of escape or relief. Victims do not have the power to change what has happened. Victims overcome through fulfillment of their lives. Your calling is your satisfaction."

I hadn't considered I was a victim, only Anna. Secretly, I suppose, I'd whined "why me," but had focused on my pain.

Destiny drifted away. Her voice resonated across the meadow, "Good happens to the just and the unjust alike, and bad happens in like manner. It is the way of your temporal existence. All things are not equal nor are all things always what they appear to be on the surface. Be steadfast, you will find wholeness in your being."

* * * * *

I woke in the evening time. Which day it was, I wasn't sure. I washed my face with cool water. My memory was intact. Alcohol had not erased Destiny's visit. I was forced to confront my thinking for the first time since the loss of Anna. No interpretation of the dream was necessary. It was clear; I had done a pretty bad job of accepting the path which was mine to take. It was a weak excuse to say, I was only human.

The grief stricken looked for ways out of the pain, and I wasn't any different. In some circumstances, there were ways to mitigate life's pain, but in the case of a loved one having died, there were no viable escapes. It was true; I wanted closure. The type psychotherapists have tried to sell where the point was reached; you shut the door behind you and move on with your life never to feel the loss again. That was me. I didn't want to remember. Memories brought with them pain of my loss.

I had read the "grief models" produced by the greatest minds in psychobabble to grasp an understanding of what victims felt. Whether they were psychiatrists, therapists or clergy, the results were always the same. No tidy ending to the confusion, pain, and anger could be found. I saw them as provocateurs of "new science" theories that didn't help anyone. They were more like entrepreneurs who'd found a niche, and lined their own pocketbooks. I assumed there were sincere people, at least some, who'd propagated the myth of closure, and wanted it to be true. Maybe they saw no other way, and hoped it worked the way they said it would, but in every sense of the word, they were wrong. Oftentimes it ended in passing the blame to the grieving person for not attaining the euphoric ideas they sought. For me, it was my expectations of closure that led me in a wrong direction and prolonged my agony. I likened my approach to beating a dead horse—it wasn't going to take me anywhere.

I had to be honest with my feelings first and foremost. That's what Destiny said. I wanted to rush the timetable and get past the grief. Who wouldn't? The truth was there was no appropriate time frame for mourning a loss. Moreover, it was a reality that had to be lived with. There was no magical door for me to close and move on with my life. If such a door existed, it would require all my memories of Anna to be hidden, as well. There was a connection between memories and loss that could not be severed without the complete loss of that person to me. Who would want to lose the memories of someone they loved?

My relationship with Anna was not over. It had grown into the deepest fibers of my heart. She was forever part of my world in my memories. My recollections of her were my treasures and locked in my heart. I knew my emotions would remain raw for some time. I would learn to live with it. Death could not take my love away. It did not possess the power.

Chapter 6

"Double-tap, he was dead. I let him off the hook easy."
—Walter

I felt better about where I was mentally, stable, and alive again. Joey Naccarella's dossier lay open in front of me on the small coffee table. It was past time for us to talk. I'd kill him quick and easy like if he came across with what I wanted to hear. If he played hardball, I'd make him pay for a long, long time. It was up to him how he wanted to play it. I didn't really care how it went down, as long as it happened.

The Naccarella home life was pretty well documented by Cal. He'd spent the majority of his time with Joey, and Joey's wife, Angelique. He wrote about Angelique's beauty, and how she was far too young for Joey, but they were together and that was that. It was one of the four cardinal rules for the Toronto Machine. You didn't talk to cops. You didn't steal from the Family. You didn't disrespect a wiseguy. You didn't mess around with a wiseguy's wife, girlfriend or daughter. If you broke one of the rules—you were dead. They weren't negotiable. Nobody touched Angelique. Joey had a bad temper, and he was the jealous type. I knew the feeling. It could make a sap out of a guy real quick, and nobody wants to be seen as sad and pathetic. Joey told Cal if someone messed with Angelique, he'd put a contract on them. I knew that feeling too, only I planned to fill my own contract.

Cal listed Angelique as a bookkeeper for Joey's self-employment. He was an earner for the Mob. He took illegally obtained Machine money in and invested it, in legitimate startup businesses. It was the best way they'd found to launder the loot. In return, he received a hefty kickback. Cal said Joey had cut his teeth on pimping, and his real bread and butter enterprise had been a string of whorehouses. The Machine got wind of his business venture, and he was introduced to the Toronto Mob. It was with the Mob connection, he became part of the phony immigration racket. Other mobsters and associates provided the underage girls and made a profit off them. That made him fair game as a Palatini target.

Joey and Angelique worked out of an office located on the first floor at Musolino's. Like all good gangsters of the modern era, he had middle men that took all the chances and did all the work. They went out on a limb to impress the Machine and make their mark in the underworld; with the hope someday they'd be rewarded with the family initiation rites. These were nothing but fall guys. You'd have thought they'd been valuable commodities to the Machine, but they weren't. They served as the link to the family that could be easily broken if things became too hot. Two shots behind the ear and the cops wouldn't be able to make their case. The connection to the family was gone.

Mobsters didn't get their hands dirty on the front line of the game. Cal said Joey was a made man, and never went close to the brothels. Joey directed operations and handled finances that were brought to him at Musolino's. I had the description of his Ford Mustang and plate numbers. That was a plus for a good recon.

Mob women didn't have much to do with the business end, usually. There were exceptions to the rule, and Angelique was one of those exceptions. Cal wrote he'd kept an eye on her because "she was ruthless" and "she would cut your throat at the drop of a hat." To some people, that'd be a real turn off, for me, not so much so. Anna was like that, and it was one of the traits I'd liked about her. Maybe Angelique wasn't so bad after all. She might have been misguided by Joey, but maybe she was my kind of girl.

Angelique wasn't in the inner circle of family business, but she was an integral part of Joey's operation. As far as I was concerned she, like her husband, was a target for Palatini assassination. Max and Anna would not have agreed. They would've said I was trigger happy or trying to get my jollies. It wasn't true. I was all about the business end of things. Angelique was not a target, but if she were nearby when I offed Joey, I had no problem sending her to the promised land either. Besides, it was my call.

I was faced with new issues I hadn't encountered in the past. Anna had brought me on because she needed someone to pull a trigger, and I was more than willing to lend a hand. That was then. Now, I'd stepped into a pretty messed up pair of shoes. I'd planned out kills before, I wasn't a novice at the game, but that wasn't the problem. I'd put my plan together before the game had been in play, not after it started. I had to catch-up, and there wasn't time for it. I had a set of flimsy notes, and I didn't know who was who. I had anywhere from days to mere minutes to make decisions and carry out plans. To top it off, I needed time to find a piece of real estate in the Toronto area where I could conduct business, privately.

I'd cruised by Joey's house for a couple days, and didn't turn up his car there or at the Inn. I didn't have a picture of Angelique, but on one of the days there was a dark haired woman in the driveway. My first impression was she fit Cal's description of Angelique. She pulled into the driveway of the house with her newer model Nissan 350Z, deep red in color. When she got out I could see she was a real looker. She tugged on the back of her red mini skirt and sashayed her hips to even it out. She was sweet to look at. She swept her long dark hair from the left side of her face and with a hooking motion, anchored it behind her ear. It was almost like she knew I was watching her every move. She looked to be in her late twenties or early thirties, her olive tone skin glistened in the sunlight. She was easy on the eyes, and it broke up the monotony of my day, in a good way. She had a key to the side door and let herself in. I watched awhile, and then watched awhile longer in hopes she might come back out. She didn't, and no one else showed up to meet her. She was all alone. At that point, I'd hoped it wasn't Angelique. I had a conflict of interest.

I took down the Nissan's license plate number for future reference, and then continued my observation. I moved the recon to outside Musolino's and continued for two more days. No Joey. No Angelique. No dark-haired beauty either, in the event it had not been Angelique. The recon wasn't paying off the way I needed. Something was in the mill. Maybe when I took Lippa out, word spread on the street and drove these tough guys into a rat-hole somewhere in the city. I was frustrated. I couldn't connect with the right people to get heads rolling.

While I was watching for Joey, I kept an eye out for Carmine as well. I had a personal score to settle with him. I wanted him bad, and I really didn't care which one I came across first. If Bruno didn't have the answers I wanted, he knew someone who did. Whoever it was who called the shots on Cal and Anna, that was the "who" I was most interested in. The rest of them I could get later. Carmine was also a no-show at Musolino's. It seemed the fishing hole had dried up.

I found the need to back-peddle on my target list and drag out a bottom feeder. Amato Santarossa had a clear connection to Anna's disappearance, and that was a good enough reason for me to have a conversation with him. According to Jokester, Amato helped abduct Anna from Cal's place. I didn't have a dossier on this clown. He didn't exist in the notes anywhere. He just appeared out of nowhere. I didn't like that. It was a loose end, an unknown player. It could wreak havoc with an already bad plan.

I knew Amato caught shifts at Musolino's, but I didn't know what kind of work he did. I'd seen him on the video security tape. He looked like a behemoth next to Lippa. There was a good chance I could pick him out of the work force at the Inn.

I had hung around outside Musolino's long enough; it was time to check out the joint. The Inn had been around a long time and wasn't very impressive from the outside. Alfonso Abbandanza made some major changes to the old structure when he acquired it. The facelift had not been solely for the purpose of modernization but served utilitarian purpose, as well.

Times had changed, and a building frequented by mobsters had to be built sturdy to avoid the pitfalls of modern society, like flying lead. Musolino's was a three-story 1960s mortar and gray brick exterior with windows set high enough to prevent a drive-by from spraying the clientele, yet it still provided light inside. It was rumored that Alfonso had sheets of steel four foot high placed between the exterior brick and interior wallboard.

The osteria was located smack-dab in the business center of Corso Italia. A couple blocks away, on St. Clair Avenue West, stood a police station with all the window dressings of a real cop shop, except they weren't getting collars on the Mob activity. The cops posed no concern for me because they didn't pose a problem for the Abbandanza crime family. The way I saw it, somebody had told the cops to layoff years ago, and they hadn't snooped around since. The Mob had free reign, and so would I.

I'd walked in Musolino's main entrance. I expected it to be a dimly lit dive, dreary, with dull blackout drapes separating the illegal gambling from view. Maybe I wanted it dark and dingy for the game I wanted to play, but I was mildly surprised. It was in stark contrast with the exterior. Musolino's interior was modern and sophisticated. Not so much elegant, but neat, clean and well lit. There wasn't one Capone style gangster in the place.

I took it all in. The bar played a prominent role stretching across the entire back wall with the exception of a food service area at one corner. The tables and chairs were solid wood with a deep ebony tint. The tables were topped with white table linen and aligned diagonally throughout the dining area. Each of the tables seated four people. I did the math. The place seated ninety-six people in the dining area and another twenty-four at the bar.

It was after eleven and if they had a lunch crowd they'd be meandering in the door soon. I took a chair that suited me. As usual, I took a corner seat with my back to the wall. Anna had referred to it as a gunfighter syndrome; I thought it was being smart. With the game we played, you couldn't be too careful.

From here, I could scope out the floor activity. I wanted to blend in. Nothing stuck out like a sore thumb. A guy sipping a glass of water for a couple hours was a sore thumb, especially in Mob territory where there were those that watched for the unusual. I didn't care much for pasta or dago food, but when in Rome…you did it the way they did it. I asked the waitress for a menu. She was pleasant and young enough to be interesting. Her auburn hair, colored from a box, was pulled back into a ponytail. The small crow's feet radiated out from the corners of her eyes, and were especially visible when she smiled. She smiled a lot. I noticed she wore glasses but had them in her apron. She didn't wear them when she took orders at a table or out in the dining area, but I caught a glimpse of her in the service area tallying up a customer's bill with them on. Women lived under a different standard than us Joes, and that was alright with me. I'd developed a liking to pretty women, and they were all pretty.

She came back to check on me so I thought I'd probe. I was in enemy territory. I assumed the employees were all loyal, so I had to tread lightly.

"Hey, how you doing" I asked.

Her expression hinted tired and overworked, "I've had better days." She paused; maybe she rethought her customer service etiquette and followed with a smile. It was a big, beautiful smile that lit up her whole face. Then she cheerfully responded back to the same question.

"Life is good."

I read her name tag, Joyce. I called her by her name and she seemed confused for a moment as to how I knew her name. It was written all over her face when it dawned on her how I'd figured it out, she smiled again. "What's the best thing in the house?" I baited her for a playful response but she was on to me.

"On the menu?" She didn't wait for my response. "All the pasta dishes are excellent. They are the house specialties." Go figure, an Italian restaurant that had pasta as their specialty.

I ordered up a plate of spaghetti and meatballs. She suggested a wine to accompany the dish.

"I'm off the juice, honey. I'm a better man without it."

"Good for you." For the first time, she took a close look at me. I felt we were on our way to the kind of connection I needed in this joint.

Joyce checked on me from time to time and kept the fresh ice water coming along with smiles, and garlic bread. I planned to stretch lunch out as long as possible without undue attention to myself. As the place slowed down in the dining area, Joyce took the time to chat. "You're not from around here, are you?"

"You're not either."

"No, I came here with my Canadian husband ten years ago, and I've been here ever since." She didn't come off happy about what she'd just said.

"Tough break," I said jokingly.

"I guess. Someday…"

"Since you're still here, I take it you're no longer with that Canadian husband?"

She was quick to turn the question on me, "Where did you say you were from?" I liked that. She wasn't brain-dead. She thought on her feet.

"I didn't," I answered and let mystery waft in the air before I continued, "Oregon."

"What brings you to Toronto?"

"Business."

She was starting to take an interest in me. My hope was she wasn't collecting information. There might be a reason she stayed at a place like this.

"What line of work are you in?" I sensed apprehension in her voice. I didn't know why, but I felt it was a good sign. Here was a gal that worked in downtown mobsterville. She'd seen lots of guys come through on business. More than likely most were unsavory individuals doing mob business. The kind of guy and the kind of business she didn't want to know about because she knew she'd live longer if she didn't. The type of guy she didn't want to get mixed up with because there wasn't a future in it for her.

"I'm a feature writer for a news magazine." I took one of my phony business cards I'd been carrying over the past few years and slid it to her.

She picked it up from the table and read the name aloud, "Walter Eloy Goe."

"At your service, my dear."

She flashed another broad smile in my direction, "That's a strange name."

I responded tongue and cheek, "So is Joyce." We had a laugh together.

Joyce reached the card back in my direction. I said, "Keep it. I'll be around for a few days taking care of some loose ends. That way you won't forget who I am."

"I won't forget you," she said with a smile.

I asked, "Promise?"

She tilted her head and with a coy smile this time and answered, "Promise."

Joyce left my bill and continued her waitress duties with other customers. She had a great smile that lit up the room; it complimented her body. I wasn't in a hurry to ask her questions. I didn't want to scare her off. I had a chance to look over Musolino's from the inside out and that's what I was here for. Joyce was icing on the cake. Real smooth icing. In a short time, I'd be able to ask her anything I wanted. As far as Amato went, I'd see him hanging around for myself unless he'd flown the coup too. I needed to get my mitts on him. I needed to pry out a lead.

On Musolino's website, they mentioned rooms available by reservation only. I made trips to the restroom a couple times to get a look down the first floor hallway. This was the office wing. The bedrooms were on the second and third floors. Cal said Joey's office, was the first office on the right in the hallway off the main dining area. The hall emptied out into a fenced parking area.

I adjusted my eating time the next day to catch the evening crew. I was in around the four o'clock mark. Joyce was waiting tables, it was near the end of her shift, and it wasn't busy. We had time to chat, flirt, and get personal.

"Why don't you give this up and move back to the states?"

She'd thought about it for a minute before she answered. "I have two boys, five and three. Their father isn't in the picture so that wouldn't make any difference. I can't afford to make the move."

I thought she seemed reluctant to mention the kids. Maybe she thought a guy worth his salt wouldn't be interested in her with the extra baggage. But if he were any sort of man at all, it wasn't what would make the difference in a relationship. She wasn't a hard bodied twenty-one year old college preppie, but she was a curvy full figured adult woman. Maybe she'd been around the block once or twice, but I didn't see anything wrong with that.

"You should be proud," I said, "A single mother raising two kids isn't an easy task. My hat's off to you, darling."

She nibbled on her lower lip and fidgeted with her wedding band that was prominently displayed on her ring finger of her right hand. "You must be married?"

I took it as a compliment. Maybe she figured a catch like me must have been snatched up long ago. "Once, many years back. It only lasted a couple years and it was over."

She pursed her lips, and blew her bangs from the front of her face, "So, you're not the marrying kind?" She said with a chuckle.

"I don't know. I never met the right woman I guess. My career became a mistress and stole all my time."

She nodded understandingly.

"Someday, Mr. Goe, I'll move back to Missouri. It would be best for my children…" Joyce paused, and I waited. I wanted to hear everything she had to say. She continued, "To be near family, and all."

There had been something painful she thought of, but Missouri was the bright spot in her future, so I focused on it.

"Please call me Walter. Where are you from in Missouri?" I hoped it wasn't a dirt bag crime ridden city like St. Louis.

"You probably never heard of it, Shell Knob."

"Shell Knob, Missouri. No, I can't say that I have. Sounds like a nice place."

"I was raised there. When I was a teenager, all I wanted to do was leave; now all I want to do is move back."

"I know the feeling, Joyce. It seems like all young people feel that way."

"My parents own a bed and breakfast style resort on Table Rock Lake. They are getting on in years and could really use my help."

I let her talk all she wanted. It helped to drag out my stay and learn the general flow of things. This was the best recon I'd been on in a while. My thoughts of Anna continued, but I was getting into my element, and that kept my mind busy and focused.

Talking with Joyce was therapeutic. In some mysterious sense, it helped soothe my pain. When I'd met Anna, I was emotionally cloistered. Why I was shut off from my feelings, I didn't know. What I did know was through my relationship with her I felt desire awakened, and I didn't care for the feeling at all. My romance with Anna and subsequent loss had opened me up like a can of worms. I wasn't as dysfunctional as I once had been. That wasn't all good news as far as I was concerned. It was a significant liability. My concern had grown about what I felt. How would my new found feelings affect my ability to kill? Was I going to be all soft-hearted and mushy or pull the trigger without remorse?

Over the next couple of days, I religiously dined at the Inn. I changed up my eating times which allowed me to get a good scope of the operation.

Carmine and Joey were no shows, but Amato worked a closing shift at the bar, and appeared to work with some regularity. He was a big guy in his early thirties. He didn't scare me, but he was plenty intimidating. I wasn't going to be able to slap him around to get his attention. It was going to be all business when it went down.

It was quiet around Musolino's at three in the morning when Amato got off work. The place closed at midnight except on the weekends when they stayed open until two. There were only two cars in the back lot, mine and his. Amato's car was backed in; I did likewise with the Avenger. We were now parked side by side with Amato's old beater between my car and Musolino's doorway exit. I mused on the idea that Jokester might have told the truth when he called Amato to see if he needed a car. He really did.

Amato emerged at the back doorway, his attention momentarily diverted from the lot as he jacked his jaw with someone still inside the hallway. In my world, it was a dangerous behavior not to scan for threats in the direction I'm moving. On past recons, I'd noticed the endless parade of potential victims streaming from stores and malls into a dimly lit parking lot, and never look for danger lurking. Not only do they not see the bad guys, they don't even watch for traffic. They just walk, head down, in the direction they want to go, oblivious to the dangers. Amato was going about life in the same way.

I could see Amato as he walked toward his vehicle with his head down and his attention on the cell phone he carried in his right hand. I'd squatted between the cars in wait to ambush my prey. I could see through the car windows as he rounded the front of his vehicle.

"What the…" He stopped short of finishing his statement. No doubt he would have extended to me the full range of his diatribe, if the notable presence of my .40-caliber hadn't pointed in his direction. I've grown accustomed to these abrupt halts, so I broke the ice.

"I killed your buddy Jokester." I opted for the shock effect. I wanted him stunned with reality, I meant business. Jokester was his brother-in-law, and this would hit home hard. I needed a lead to bigger fish. Amato didn't look like a guy you could buy a cup of java for, and he'd give it up. I laid it out straight to loosen his lips. Of course, if he could read between the lines then he knew he was dead already.

"Got nothin' to do with me." His eyebrows furrowed together as he screwed his face into a grimace. He was cold and indifferent. He acted like he didn't care I plugged Lippa. He puffed up his chest and stepped toward me.

"Uh-uh," I warned, with a slightly higher presentation of my Glock.

"Where's Joey?"

He mustered up a bitter snappish tone, "I don't know no Joeys!"

I was willing to give him another opportunity, but not the benefit of the doubt. As long as he wanted to play a game, I'd see how far he wanted to play. "Where's Carmine?"

Amato, noticeably more agitated by questions about crime family members, answered with a dismissive humph, "I don't know no nobody called Bruno neither! You need to get out of my face!"

Amato's reaction didn't faze me in the slightest. I've seen it happen before. Guys who got scared or angry said stupid things. I capitalized on it. "I didn't ask you about Bruno. I asked you about Carmine?"

I expected him to charge the gun. Why not use brute force to take control? He was big enough to give it a try. Then Amato displayed the main reason why the Machine hadn't elevated him to a higher status. He sprouted chicken feathers. I didn't expect him to well up with great big crocodile tears and fall to pieces on me. This was going to be a cakewalk.

"Since you don't know anything, I might as well shoot you right between the legs." I dropped the weapon to display my intentions.

In a whiny tone, he eked out, "There's no need for that." He wiped the tears from his face. "I haven't seen Bruno for better than a week now. That's the honest to god's truth."

I always like it when losers like Amato bring God and honesty into the picture. Two things he didn't know enough about.

"Open the back door of your car and have a seat." He looked puzzled. It might have seemed odd not to have him sit behind the wheel of his car, but there might be a gun stashed under the seat or within easy reach. On the other hand, I wanted to lessen the chance of someone seeing his massive frame standing by the car. He jumped in and folded his hands on his lap like a little school boy in trouble. I could relate. I'd been in the principal's office once or twice.

"What about Joey, I won't ask again?"

"I heard Joey made a run for it."

Amato sat quietly and looked out the front window. I suspect he figured it out by now; he'd gotten himself into a real pickle. He'd run his mouth. If Bruno found out he'd talked, he'd be another gangland statistic. If he didn't talk, he'd end up like Lippa. I had news for him, it didn't matter. His epitaph had already been written.

He made his choice. He took his chances with me. "Joey was bringing this cat around. I don't know what happened, but in the end Bruno whacked this dude and blamed Joey for the whole thing. Next thing you know, Joey was on the lam. As far as I know, no one has seen him since. I will tell you this, everyone's talking about it. I know one thing for sure; Bruno hadn't caught up to him yet."

"What about the girl you and Lippa took to Bruno's?"

Amato looked at me confused. It was legitimate. You could tell he was baffled by the question. "We didn't take no woman to Bruno. We took Cal's lady friend to Joey."

"Lippa said you took her to Bruno. One of you two are lying."

"Nunzio, he's family, he picked me up, and we drove to this dude's place. She came along, no problems. She was a real nice lady."

He asked if he could lite up a smoke. I was okay with it. He fumbled a cigarette from a crumpled pack he had in his jacket pocket, lit it, and drew in a deep drag. He held it, and I waited for his exhale. He plucked the butt from his lips and blew a stream of smoke out the open door. He continued, "We took her straight to Joey, just like we were told to do."

"Did you see her again or know what happened to her?"

"Nah, it was early when we picked her up, maybe seven or eight. It was some time before my shift started that day. We dropped her off with Joey. It was strange, you know, we met him down at the docks and put her in his car. He told us, "Get lost, you don't know nothin'!" He paused, "I guess everyone knows."

I leaned back against my car and dropped my weapon from the guard position where I had held it in for the past ten minutes. Amato fumbled for another smoke from the pack he's laid on the car seat next to him. I doubt he noticed the insignificant flash from the moderator mounted on my Glock. Double-tap and he was dead. I let him off the hook easy.

As I drove back to sanctuary, I went over what Amato had said about Carmine who held Joey responsible for Cal. That might be the reason Joey vanished, car and all. He was hiding out for his life. It was not unusual in mafia folklore to hear about acts of retribution when there was a perceived breach in their organization. Three mobsters could keep a secret as long as two of them were dead. If what Lippa told me was true, Cal hadn't given up who he was working for. Bruno might have felt further threatened by not knowing who was on his trail. The fact was, Cal couldn't name any names because there weren't any to name. But in Bruno's mind there had to be. My question was why would Joey make a run with Anna in tow? That didn't make sense.

Neither Cal nor Anna had picked up on Carmine's personal residence. According to Lippa they took Anna to Bruno's place. There had to be "a place." The pieces didn't fit the way I needed them to. Cal knew Bruno stayed at Musolino's when he was in Toronto. It seemed to be the sum of what they knew about him. He didn't live in Toronto. Why would he need a room at the osteria, if he did? Lippa must have known where Carmine lived. Maybe, I didn't put the squeeze on him hard enough before I offed him.

If Carmine was after Joey, it might explain why Joey vanished, and maybe why I hadn't been able to locate Carmine. He was busy hunting Joey. The three cold-blooded murders of the Buffalo crew probably put the Mob up on its ear. If so, Jokester's death would've put them over the top with concern.

Although local cops wouldn't snoop on the Machine because of a few Mob hits on other mobsters, there were law enforcement agencies that would have their interests piqued over the same events. When the news agencies reported on Lippa's killing they referred to him as a "reputed mobster." It wasn't the kind of advertising gangsters liked. With public awareness came public pressure, and a Crown crusader might launch an investigation to bring down the heat. Political motivation could be a powerful tool, and the Crown knew how to get the votes. Mob business might take a hit and be forced into precautions that could result in cash flow loss.

What did they have to worry about? They hadn't killed anybody. The victim was associated with organized crime. That made known associates of the victim "fair game" for the Crown. It gave the crusaders that weren't on the payroll carte Blanc to kick in a few doors of other suspected mobsters to see what they could turn up. If the cops didn't swoop in, it was a red flag that an undercover operation was in progress. There were possible informants or infiltrators already in place. Paranoia sets in pretty easily. Regardless how it went down, the Mob would retract, like the tentacles of an octopus when it was threatened. Their defensive position was to have everyone lie low. That was bad for business.

The Machine's biggest concern might have been "who." Someone was killing crime family members and associates, but who. They didn't have a clue. Anonymous was just my game. I felt I worked best when I was alone, and I couldn't be more alone now. They also didn't know "who" would be the next target. I was a predator. I could pick any one of them I wanted. They didn't know "what" I would do next. They couldn't plan an intervention. All they might figure on was there was a "next" coming. "Where" was a problem too? Toronto, Buffalo, Niagara Falls, some Podunk in between.

Pelosi got burned in a back alley, Zambrotta was whacked while driving his car home, and Lippa was taken for a ride. The fear of, "who would be next," was on my side. There were so many ways for a man to die; none seemed out of the ordinary. Maybe next time it would be them, and they couldn't do anything about it.

Chapter 7

"Never hesitate, if it's gonna go down, strike first and strike fast."
—Walter

I understood why government let crime families operate with few restraints. It was lucrative. They'd drafted laws that protected Abbandanza interests under the guise it protected the rights and freedoms of the average citizen. Politicians worked to do one thing, expand their own pocketbooks. If the citizen took advantage of the liberties under the law, and made themselves a better life, it was a good deal. But the main purpose of the corrupt financial laws was to benefit the few. Mobsters were part of that few. Consequently citizens were in grave danger. Mob victims couldn't call the cops to straighten it out. It didn't work that way. The police didn't have free reign to solve problems. Their hands were tied by law. Cops had taken an oath that bound them to live by the law, and most did; I was not so inclined.

In the absence of laws that worked to constrain crime, the Machine enjoyed their control of the underworld. And like most power, it went to their heads. Mobsters acted like a pack of wild animals on the prowl. They were animals that liked to inflict pain on anyone that crossed their paths for no other reason other than, "just because." The Mob ruled through intimidation and violence. It was the basis of their game. They played hardball to keep the image fresh in people's minds. Communities with the Machine's presence learned quickly it was a waste of time to call 911. Those that did ended up face down in a gutter, dead.

In my teenage years, I'd fought wildfires with a rural county fire department. To get a handle on a dangerous brushfire, we would set small fires in its path. Firefighters called them back-burn fires, but we called it fighting fire with fire. It was a good technique. The fact was rampant running fires with a lot of fuel were difficult to suppress. To get the upper hand on the blaze, we'd set the back-burn to contain it. Eventually, they'd burn themselves out when they'd used up everything there was to consume. Mob business was a lot like a wildfire. If the government wanted to stop the spread of organized crime, they had to contain it first, and there wasn't any evidence they could. I felt the proper application of back-burn, once introduced to the Mob, would demonstrate a better method of control than the current legal process. They'd chosen lawless measures to gain control. I'd use lawless measures to contain them. I'd fight fire with fire.

It was no secret; my moral compass was out of whack with society. The way I saw it, two wrongs made a right. My actions would be considered every bit as bad as the Mob's actions because violence was unacceptable. That was okay with me. I hadn't tried to live up to a different standard. Mobsters killed and enslaved people. I only killed bad guys. My behavior might appall the judiciary, but it appealed to the masses.

Back at sanctuary I reviewed dossiers on family members. I wanted my revenge, and I was motivated. I seethed for the opportunity to kill. My instincts, likely twisted and primitive, wanted to be in command. I took into consideration what Max had warned of, the likelihood of an unending escalation in my vendetta. The war had already begun when Pelosi took the first round in the back.

Calvino Gallo, my newest target, was the son of an incarcerated Abbandanza mobster from Mostarda's faction. He was in his mid-twenties and had decided to follow in his father's footsteps. He was a soldier that was more of a patsy than an "earner" or the muscle side of the family. He showed promise in the Rochester crew.

My impulse was to go after the hierarchy, but there was always another mobster to fill the dead's shoes. I wanted a decisive destruction, not a change in leadership. In the bigger scheme of things, Gallo's death might lead the Mob to suspect a territorial rivalry was under way. Maybe they would over-react and create a bigger problem than they had with me. The Machine had to find me to prove differently. They also had to find me to kill me, but that was a big problem for them. I was a needle in a haystack. I was literally one of millions of common ordinary people in the area that all looked alike. I didn't have business interests for them, to use to locate me. I, on the other hand, had Intel on them. Cal had milked the information train in preparation for his non-fiction book. In a round-about way, Cal bequeathed it all to me. He had gotten to close and knew too much, and it probably got him killed. The Mob hang-outs, where they lived, and many of their businesses were all neatly packaged by Anna, and now in my possession. All I had to do was follow up with them, one by one.

I picked up on Gallo at a lounge on the outskirts of South Rochester. Cal's police source identified him as the owner of the place. It was all above board and legit. Cal knew better. It was a money laundering front. I had to check it out.

I looked at my watch around midnight, Gallo had sat at the end of the bar earlier in the evening; I was on the other end. He'd been on the telephone a few times and talked to a couple guys that stopped on their way out the door, but I didn't pick up on anything unusual with him. With mobsters, normal meant being an ear. There was a lot you could learn if you listened.

The clientele had thinned out, and it was down to only a few folks left. Gallo motioned to the barkeeper to ring a bell that hung over the waitress station, signaling a free round for the half dozen of us diehard's that planned to be at the lounge until closing. Everyone bellied up to the bar for a free shot while Gallo quietly slipped out the exit. I watched to see who had an eyeball on us, but I didn't see any takers, so I slipped out, as well. I needed a lead. It seemed I was always in need of a new lead. My past leads kept dying.

Gallo looked in my direction when I left, but didn't pay attention long enough to notice I didn't leave the parking lot. Maybe it was the phone call that distracted him or the car that slowed down in front of the lounge that caught his eye. I was in the clear. He didn't suspect me of anything. A cab pulled up, and Gallo got in. I followed on a loose tail. We'd driven about two miles when the cab pulled over to the curb. I passed the cab and turned to the left at the end of the block, cut my head lights and completed the maneuver with a U-turn. I ditched into a maze of cars along the front of neighborhood houses.

Gallo was out of the cab by the time I'd swung into the parking spot. He lit up a smoke and walked slowly toward a house. The older two-story sat on the corner lot, surrounded by a white picket fenced yard. The house sat in the dark. I couldn't tell when he'd entered the front door until he'd flicked on an inside light. With the front door shut, he worked his way through his house as he turned on the first floor lights. No visible second floor lights came on.

I broke out my bug out bag, press-checked for a chambered round in my .40-caliber, holstered it, and put on my black leather police search gloves. They were more than a fashion statement for CSI. There was going to be a murder to solve. Fingerprints or DNA might be left at the crime scene without gloves, and there was an uncomfortable chill in the air. Keeping my hands in agile working condition was paramount.

I made my way to Gallo's house along the quiet neighborhood street. When I got to the picket gate, I opened the gate and continued on the slate walkway straight to the house. As I approached the three stair climb to the small landing, I deviated out of the light of the front window and into shrubbery next to the house. I stood motionless, watched and listened. I could hear it loud and clear—silence.

I looked in windows and worked my way around the house to the back door. There were lights on in the basement area, but the windows were opaque, only slivers of light shown through the framework at the window openings. I set my bug out bag down next to the single level concrete landing at the back door, drew my Glock, and attached the moderator. The lights were off at the back of the house but my night vision was constantly interrupted by looking through windows into the well-lit house. I inched up against the house and began to move to the back door. I could hear talking, a man's voice then the sliding glass door at the rear of the house opened.

"You can come back when you're done," a voice rang out.

I was poised to shoot. A cat dropped to the concrete looking disheveled from being ousted from his lair. The glass door slid shut while the cat walked to the edge of the landing, sat and twitched its tail. The cat continued a disgruntled look as I reached over and pulled slightly on the handle, it moved. I pulled a little more, and it continued to open. I moved the blind back slightly in time to see Gallo with his back toward me, opening a door to what appeared to be a basement entrance.

Cal had nothing in his notes to indicate Gallo was a family man, but he might not have known since he didn't have Gallo's physical address. At this point, I no longer cared. I wouldn't kill a wife or a child, I wasn't that kind of killer, but I would deprive them of his existence.

I'd learned early in life, through the school of hard knocks, how to fight. Skill had its place in fighting style, but in the end, a fight boiled down to one basic factor—attitude. I learned never hesitate. If violence was the option, strike first and strike fast. I wanted to be the one on top doing the damage. I'd rather throw the first punch than wait for the other guy to throw. That would've been plain stupid. My approach to a fight was different from a lot of the other people. They saw a fight as some form of contest and honor; I saw it as combat and survival. There was no honor to be won or lost, only life and limb.

I inched my way in through the glass door and slid it closed. With my thumb, I threw the lock to "on." I didn't need any unexpected interruptions. I didn't like being in the light, but I didn't want to make any unnecessary noise that turning off lights might bring. I had an immediate concern, depending on the integrity of the floor; Gallo might be able to hear my movement from downstairs. The door to the basement was ajar, I could see stairs, and there was no way to walk down them without being seen, legs first. I would wait. If he started up the stairs, I'd waste him then.

It wasn't long before I heard Gallo's voice again. This time, he wasn't talking to the cat. It was a female's voice I could hear, and from the sounds of it, she was in distress. Gallo came to the foot of the stairs, but before he climbed the stairs, he looked back and said, "Don't go away, I'll be right back." He laughed then continued, "We're going to party tonight." He laughed again, but he didn't get the last laugh. It wasn't more than a stair or two when his laugh got to me. He was still looking in the direction of the female, when I stepped around the doorway corner.

We'd stood momentarily silent before I barked my orders at him. "Get on the floor, Face down, Get on the floor."

He shrugged and responded, "Okay pig."

I cautiously scanned for any threats as I descended into the basement. When I was sure I was in control of the room, I bound Gallo with nylon zip ties and sat him up against the wall. "Hey, if you're a cop, where's your badge?"

There was a work bench in the basement with a few household tools and a roll of duct tape. I picked up the tape and started for Gallo.

"Wait a minute. Listen to me. I paid for protection. You've overstepped your bounds flatfoot."

I slapped a strip of tape over his mouth then turned my attention to the female that was chained to the basement wall directly under the stairs. She was a young woman, petite, and physically battered.

"What's your name?" I asked.

"Chloe."

The chain and restraint straps on her wrists were locked with a slide key. "Chloe, do you know where the key is kept?"

She was notably anxious when she said, "I think on him."

"I am not going to hurt you. I'm going to get you out, okay?"

"Hurry."

Hurry was a good idea, but Chloe complicated matters. I came for information. Now, I didn't have time to extract it unless he talked quickly, and that wasn't likely. It would be easier to shoot this guy, and start over with a new target.

"I'm going to find the key, but I need a little time with this guy first, do you understand?"

She began to cry. I felt bad I couldn't set her free right then, but I needed Gallo to talk. I ripped the tape from his mouth. He greeted me with a slew of meaningless profanities.

"Where's the key?"

He spat at me and laughed. I popped him in the mouth. I put my Glock down on the work bench and beat the hell out of him. The knuckles of my leather gloves were wet with his blood. He spat again, this time he aimed at the floor. In the background, I could hear Chloe as she reacted to the beating I'd given Gallo. She cried with a loud outburst when I put the boots to him. It became chaotic, so much so, I was distracted by Chloe's shrieks. I didn't have time for her, and Gallo—I had to make a choice.

I took the key off Gallo and unlocked Chloe. "Get yourself together, cleaned up, and gather your stuff. I'm taking you out of here." I helped her from the floor to her feet, and guided her to a bathroom in the basement. "Take your time; I'm going to clean up the mess."

"Who are you mister?"

"I'm a friend you didn't know you had."

"What about him?" She pointed to Gallo.

"He will never bother anyone again."

She nodded and closed the bathroom door. I turned my attention to Gallo. Over the course of the next few minutes, I tried to extract backfill on Mostarda's crew. He wasn't cooperative. He broke down and begged for his life, but that wasn't what I wanted to hear. I wanted him to beg for death. I craved it.

I had to admit, I worked him over because I reacted to the scene. Had I found him reading a newspaper or watching television, I doubt I would have felt the same way. I would have approached him in a sterile, surgical manner. But I was not willing to overlook Chloe. I made him pay severely for his actions.

Max had thought it was madness to continue the assault on the Abbandanza Machine. He'd been concerned the mobsters had the upper hand, and that

Palatini secrecy had been compromised. He didn't see a way to win. He didn't see it my way. I was a shooter, an assassin; I killed to make my point. Every round I fired was a win. Max saw too many gangsters to succeed, I saw so many I couldn't miss. Max was concerned the Mob knew too much about the Palatini, and rightfully so. Anna might have talked, under duress, anything was possible. I was concerned too, but my approach was opposite of Maximillian's. I felt the "all hands on deck" approach was the way to go. Max liked to declare victory when we finished a project. I had news for him—this was a war. I didn't see the end to the hostilities, yet. Maybe never. There was too much money for the Mob to give up, and there was too much hatred on my part to stop. In my book, it boiled down to the simplest of terms, kill or be killed. What happened to the original mission of damaging the Mob's illegal immigration racket? Anna happened. Now the project was annihilation.

Chloe came out of the bathroom, picked up a couple of clothing items, and stood by the steps. Her head hung down as if she were embarrassed.

"Chloe, take a look at this guy."

She lifted her head, her eyes watery, and tears streamed down her face. Gallo made no attempt to look in her direction. "Do you want to do the honors?"

"Do you mean kill him?"

"Sure, why not?"

Still looking in his direction, she said, "I just want to know he's not coming after me." I picked up my Glock from the tool bench and plugged him a couple times with Chloe watching. I had her start up the stairs while I spread an accelerant of paint thinner on the wood support beams and stair casing. At the top of the stairs, I lit the trail of fluid that spontaneously ignited the stairs.

We walked down the block to the Avenger and drove from the area. Chloe was young but looked well-seasoned, for her age. She'd seen more years on the street than she was old. I'd hoped she would relax now that she was out of the house, but that would not happen. She'd been physically abused, witnessed a murder, been rescued, and didn't know where I'd planned to take her.

"Where are we going mister?"

"I'm taking you to a clinic in Buffalo. You need to be checked out."

"Do you have a cigarette, mister?"

"Don't smoke."

"That's too bad, I could use one right now."

I stopped the Avenger at the first convenience store I spotted and bought a pack of the brand of smokes she'd asked for, and a couple bottles of water.

"So how did you get hooked up with Gallo?"

She tore open the pack of smokes while I handed her my lighter. "It's a long story. I was working the street in my neighborhood to pay rent and make enough money to get through school." She paused to lite up and handed my lighter back. She cracked the car window and inch and blew a stream of smoke toward it. She turned and looked me in the eye. I could see her study my expressions. She wanted to know if I accepted how she made money. It wasn't up to me to judge. She wasn't any less of a person because she'd chosen to be a hooker. Girls like Chloe didn't need a PHD behind their names to tell what someone was thinking. It was a skill she'd learned the hard way, and was good at it. Her money depended on it.

"Were you working for the Mob?"

"I don't work for anyone. Maybe that's what the guy had in mind. Either that or he would have killed me. You said his name was Gallo?"

"Forget about him. What's your last name and where's home?"

"I live on the Buffalo University campus, my last name is Page."

"Are you a college student?" I tried not to look surprised.

"Yes—full time."

"I'm going to drop you at the clinic. They treat walk-ins so make sure you tell them you're a rape victim."

"What do I tell the cops?"

"Marco Camerota settled a score."

Marco was a rising star for the crime family. He was ruthless and notoriously hungry for power. If I sowed a little strife, it might pay dividends. I swung the Avenger next to the curb to let Chloe out. "You have to walk a few feet to the entrance, but some of these places have cameras, and I don't need the attention."

"Thanks mister. Maybe I can do something for you sometime."

The emphasis she spun on her words made it sound like a generous offer, but I had to decline. "Find another line of work Chloe. It ain't a smart deal."

She nodded, said thanks again, and walked toward the entrance. I turned my car around and headed for sanctuary. In the quiet isolation of the Avenger, a thought came to me, random and roving. In the military when presented with a target rich environment you could be opportunistic. Why spend a lot of time on planning when there were plenty of targets to keep a guy busy. It had its drawbacks, but I was not in a position to set up a domino effect. There were too many ducks to get lined up to make a row. I wouldn't be able to take out all the top brass in unison as a single assassin. No matter how motivated I was, there were limitations.

I'd had a good start exterminating some of the low level hoods. But, I would save the Boss, Salvatore Giannetti for last. He owed me, and I wanted to collect on the debt. I wanted him to watch his crime syndicate come apart at the seams and crumble. I wanted him to feel loss, pain, and destruction of his Mob family, especially his own flesh and blood brother, Antonio. I wanted Sal to feel as helpless as I'd felt when Anna disappeared.

I wanted him to have time to think about death—his death. I'd beat him down then put the boots to him. When I was done, I'd beat him some more. Maybe then he'd understand what he did was wrong. Before he died, I wanted him to know what it was like, to be a victim.

It might seem bold to say, but, I had the upper hand on the Machine. I had an extensive dossier on the crime family. I knew every major player and some of the crews. It was a good hand to play. The bosses hadn't reacted with signs of concern, but human nature had taught me, they would when the threat was great enough. Nothing terrorized people more than being hunted to extinction for an unknown reason. Disorder in their rank and file would signal the beginning of the end.

Chapter 8

"There would be no negotiations—only judgment and death."
—Walter

I wanted my message to be clear, organized crime was no longer welcome in New York, Toronto, or anywhere else I encountered it. Anyone remotely associated with mobsters deserved the lawless measures of my resolve. For those that protected the Mob, from the corrupt lawyers to the politicians, my intentions were the same. There would be no negotiations—only judgment and death.

Before I became a member of the Palatini, I worked alone. It never bothered me. The camaraderie I'd had with the Palatini knights when I was invited to participate on a joint operation, I enjoyed immensely. It also made me realize the value of a well-executed plan on a much larger scale than what I was able to do alone. We hit three continents almost simultaneously, ripping the tentacles off a monstrous child pornography ring. Any criminal effort could be destroyed if men would take a stand and kill it.

As far as the Palatini project that Anna had envisioned, the writing was on the wall. I had no way to contact any of the other Palatini operators. Max was the go-between for the Society members, and he'd made it clear, I was on my own. Without Max, the others had no way to know the predicament I was in. Max had defunded the project and wanted it shut down with all Palatini assets out of the area. I was alone.

No matter, I managed to get along pretty well with myself. When I began to freelance, I was a one man death squad. I didn't like the limelight—I preferred the shadows. With the Abbandanza mobsters, there would be enough to keep me busy for ten lifetimes. I saw only one drawback; I would have to stay in the northeastern cities where the Machine lived.

Enforcer Frank Rizzi was an integral part of Capo Carl Mostarda's Rochester crew. He was my next target. By whacking Rizzi, I would expand my kill range to three of the four Family factions. That left one loose end, Marco Camerota.

According to Cal, Camerota ran a crew on Toronto's East-End. He was a Lieutenant who operated separately from Capo De Luca. There had been meetings held to establish Camerota as a capo and separate the Toronto faction into two crews, but it hadn't happened by the time Cal ended up face down in the dumpster.

I was building upon the rumored strife in the Toronto underworld; I would spread the dead around to all the crews, except Camerota's. Maybe Chloe told the cops what I said that Gallo was killed by Camerota. If the Mob got wind of an internal power grab, or a suspicion, Camerota would eventually be called to a sit down and asked to explain why everyone else was getting hit besides him. Suspicion, a basic human behavior, would go hog-wild. It was easy to create and easier to exploit. One mobsters trying to upset the balance of power for a greedier take of the pie. That's what business was about—the pie.

Rochester's Capo, Carl Mostarda, ran satellite operations along the smaller border towns in the area. He was the youngest and newest of the Abbandanza Capos; a tall, lanky man in his early forties, with short cropped coal black hair, wearing thick lensed eyeglasses. He was a hustler that earned his way to his position in the family. He ran a legitimate business in Rochester, the Double Decker Lounge—a two-story social club frequented by a host of New York State uppity mucky-mucks. From the pictures Cal had of Mostarda, he would be easily identified in a crowd. He had smarts, money, and connections. Evidently, that was enough when you're an "earner" for the Mob.

Mostarda's crew had a specialty when it came to making money. They had well established brothels spread up and down the border, but that was old news. It was also the old ways which he'd inherited when he ascended to the Capo throne. It was a lucrative crew, but Mostarda felt it could be improved. He'd found himself influenced by some of the up and coming criminals of a new generation. The brothels under his crews' tutelage found new ways to scam ignorant clientele with phone sextalk and internet webcam sex shows. They made a link between prostitution and cybercrimes. It was the new thing. It made them a ton of money.

I wasn't so much in the fog about the scam, but I boned up on Mostarda's slant. Cal's cop friend provided the low-down. It was a side note, but once again, rumors of paranoia surfaced. The Machine's factions had concerns about his operation being too large scale and strung out too far. The chief complaint centered on Mostarda's business bordering on other capo's territory. He was pushy and wanted more of the pie.

His prostitution business had gone unscathed by the Feds. However, it wasn't the usual case of payoffs or blackmail. It was a lack of interest. The attitude of "who was it harming" was customary in government circles. If it wasn't illegal drugs or arms smuggling, they didn't care. Besides, everyone knew it was the oldest profession in the world.

Mostarda was a businessman. He didn't like his assets waiting around in a whorehouse not making him a profit, all the time. Like any good entrepreneur, he had a solution. His girls would make money through cybersex. When they didn't have a trick to turn they would make their talents good in other ways. If they didn't go along with his idea, he had a solution for that too. It didn't take more than a couple of hookers to suffer his brutal consequences before the word got around what would happen. Obedience followed.

Cal laid out what he'd heard or knew about the cybercrime gig. Mostarda's associates and wannabes canvassed the red-light districts of border towns looking for suckers. As they say, there's one born every day. In New York, there seemed to be a disproportionate amount born every day. A lot more. An endless supply. "Peephole Sex" was the newest vice on the internet, and guys were lining up for it.

I wasn't so moral that I didn't know what made people tick. Me, moral—sounded more like a punch line to a bad joke. I was an assassin, how moral could I be? I didn't want to judge some "John" for getting his jollies. If cybersex was his thing, so be it. But my beef with the Johns was straight up. They were complicit in the Machine's criminal sex slavery and underage prostitution rackets. How? They fed the money to the Machine that kept the felonious behavior viable.

Johns had a choice, and they made it, but it was a wrong decision. Many of them got punked, and I didn't feel a bit sorry for them. They had it coming. They were the dirt bags of the market, the consumers which supported the abuse of women and children with their money. If there wasn't a market, organized crime wouldn't waste their time with it. Maybe they didn't know what the score was for the young girls, but I didn't buy it. The Johns were slimy narcissistic people that knew watching a twelve-year-old having sex was wrong.

I've heard it said, you can't save people from their own stupidity, and John's were living proof. The adult playgrounds were littered with victims of organized crime. Not just the hookers, but the Johns too. Mobsters didn't thump John's or roll them like in the good-ol'-days. No, now they scammed credit card information through fraud, intimidation, and extortion. Cybercrime carried a hefty price tag.

Johns were their own worst enemy. They jumped in feet first when they surrendered their credit card information for the hook up. At that point, they weren't Johns anymore; in the eyes of the Mob they became "Marks." Johns knew they were dealing with criminals, so why the surprise when they discovered they'd had a game run on them.

The Machine's minions worked the streets to hand out secret phone numbers or website addresses on used napkins at bars or whatever was handy. The John made the connection and they knew up front it wasn't free. The John dummied up and provided the credit card information, and the charge was processed. Johns expected the girls to keep them on the hook as long as possible for the cha-ching to mount up. What followed was an education. There were hidden fees in the hook-up and maybe a few extra minutes slapped on his card, but the John got what he wanted; the small stuff could be overlooked. His anonymous escapade protected his public image and reputation.

The Machine's nerdy new cybermobsters were cunning. They tapped his account for hundreds, maybe thousands extra, all in the matter of a few seconds. Do you think John Anonymous would run to the cops? Not a chance. If he did, he would expose his own deeds, and the picture-perfect little world he'd created for himself, and perhaps his family, would be destroyed. He'd take it in the shorts and count his lucky stars. It could've been worse.

The Mark, if he was loaded with loot, might have found himself at the mercy of Mostarda cybercriminals' real talents. Remember the credit card information that was handed over so freely; they had it all in their greedy mitts. It was the face of the Mob, nerds armed with computers. It had given weenie-armed little punks, mobster power, and they knew how to exploit vulnerabilities. The Mob was still the Mob, they hadn't changed a bit. They'd found a modern way to use the same old tricks to get what they wanted. However, if the nerds needed some muscle, they were savvy enough, to keep the wannabe mobsters around to bust a kneecap or two. I didn't care in the slightest if the Mark had gotten taken. My concern was with the sex slavery with underage girls forced into play.

Cal listed the cybercriminals' newest version of the older phone scam as webcam sex rip-off. The Marks were taken for a ride when they logged into the websites. It was pretty much the same gig as the phone sex, only they were secret websites, and difficult for the Feds to catch. The Internet gave the Machine new tools of leverage with IP addresses. Mostarda's crew mastered multiple versions of internet-based piracy. These guys were hackers and smart. Smart enough to stay away from breaking into government infrastructures. They didn't focus their attention on knocking off a bank with an internet heist. Such a move would put them on the Feds' radar; rather they concentrated their efforts on stealing from the commoner.

The Palatini mission had never been about who got fleeced. When bank accounts were stripped, credit cards maxed out, or their identities stolen, it was an education. The only victims I cared about had been kidnapped, held hostage and exploited.

The Abbandanza crew represented what I liked least about sex offenders as a whole; they pretended to be something they weren't. They called themselves businessmen. It had a nice ring to it, but the definition lacked credibility. They'd used their ill-gotten finances to buy highfalutin friends and influence, but it couldn't change what they were—the scum of the earth. Their façade could fool all the people some of the time, and some of the people all the time, but it didn't fool me. They weren't businessmen at all, they lacked the cajones to fess up to what they were; kidnappers and sex offenders that couldn't man up and make an honest living so they enslaved others. The Mob liked to mix with the upper crust of society. Somehow it validated their existence as acceptable. It made a good fit too. Society's elite had a slimy side, as well.

The Mob had plenty of legitimate business they'd invested in to launder their illegal incomes. When Capone ran the Chicago Outfit, he was taken down through his money. The government used paper and pen to write tax codes that could be enforced by a new law enforcement agency, the FBI. Of all the vile crimes Capone was rumored to have been responsible for, he was convicted and jailed on the least vicious of them all; tax evasion on his illegally gained fortune. It was the government's position, regardless of where the moolah came from; they had to pay their fair share to Uncle Sam. Legitimate businesses were the only way to account for where the money had come from, although it hadn't actually. The government could overlook that detail.

I was window shopping for a weak point to exploit. A person or situation that would allow me to cut them stem to stern. I wanted to rip their guts out for what they were. Suddenly, it occurred to me. There it was, right in front of my nose, and I hadn't seen it. It was the Machine's strength and their Achilles' heel, all wrapped up in one nice, neat package.

Money, the Mob loved it. They couldn't get enough of it. It came in from hundreds of different sources, but it was all tainted through illegal gain. With Anna, she was only interested in the money if it was directly associated with sex slavery or the illegal immigration rackets. I didn't differentiate. All their money was a target, and it amounted to a lot of cash. I trained my cross-hairs on what I felt was their real weakness.

In the Mob world, everyone paid upwards. The rule of thumb was 10-percent of the take. It was networking at its finest. Someone once said, the love for money was the root of all evil, and the Mob loved their money. If some bum, hit one of their drops; there'd be hell to pay. Nobody had stolen from the Mob and lived to tell about it. I wanted to slap them in the face with it.

Frank Rizzi was part of the collection process. Mostarda's crew, through various avenues of earnings, brought the money in and ultimately to Rizzi. According to Cal, Frank gathered up the cash daily and brought it to the Capo. From Mostarda, 10-percent went up to the CEO, Rocco Colansante. Capos Bacca and De Luca paid the same way. Camerota still paid to De Luca. There again was a weak point I kept in mind.

The CEO took his cut from each family-faction and sent the rest upward. The last in line were the Giannetti brothers, Boss and Underboss. How they did their split was unknown, and it didn't really matter to me who got what. I had something for each of them. They'd been living off borrowed time, and for too long. Killing Anna was a mistake they would not recover from. I couldn't guarantee I'd bring the entire crime family down, but I'd set my goals high, and it included the Abbandanza hierarchy.

Rizzi held the prestigious position of Rochester enforcer. Cal had made him sound like a glorified errand boy instead. He was a thug who cracked heads when he was told to and carried the drop like a ritzy butt-kissing bellhop. I thought it would be a good start on the money trail to have a little chat with Rizzi. Perhaps he could shed light on where to find Carmine or what happened to Joey. In the process, the money he had for Rocco would become mine. When they discovered the drop hadn't been made, and Rizzi's bullet-ridden body turned up, they might think someone was trying to muscle in. It would be a brazen attention getter, especially if I tied Camerota's name to it.

To pick up a visual on Rizzi, I used Cal's notes. It wasn't necessary to find his lair in Rochester; he had a money drop in Buffalo. Rizzi never travelled alone on the drops. The scene would be proverbial. Two birds for one stone.

It was like a discount market, "get one Rizzi and get a second rider free." Two for the price of one, it had a poetic sound.

What if the rider was innocent? I had already resolved the issue. There was no such thing as innocent. If I felt guilt, I'd learn to live with it—comfortably. Anyone who was associated or participated with the Machine was fair game. The focal point for the Palatini operation initially was to put an end to the syndicates kidnapping and exploitation of underage girls. I considered it my business as much as any soldier finds his purpose in defending his country against enemies both foreign and domestic. "We the People"—it was our fight! The fact that organized crime existed unabated, spoke to me. "We the People" could not depend on government intervention to save us. We had to act. We had to be willing to do something for ourselves. I am not ashamed to claim, I am justice by another name—Walter Eloy Goe. If I were a religious man, I'd pray for others to put on the mantle of protector of the people as Palatini had.

Cal and Anna died because they were willing to expose the Mob's corruptness. Both had different reasons why they sacrificed their lives. Cal to write a best-seller and Anna for the freedoms of others, but they both died to expose the truth. In my book, there was no greater display of love for fellow human beings than the willingness to lay down your life for another. It was the Palatini way. In that, I was proud.

It wasn't that most people didn't believe as we did. It was society which had been shamed into accepting the psychobabble that punishment, retribution, and vengeance, were wrong for a civilized society. It was a sham, perpetrated by lemmings of the educated elite. They may have sounded real smart, but their ideas were contrary to nature. It wasn't until a vile crime struck near home, that they believed, as I did. Once it was personal, like the tragedy that befell me with the loss of Anna, they too would want revenge. There was no closure in empty words, only in the smell of gun powder. Even then it was incomplete, but as close as I could get.

Rizzi didn't have a definable schedule. He made the milk run into Buffalo a few times a week. The only consistency seemed to be his destination, a shipyard just off the Niagara Thruway. In times past, the docks boomed with business. But, with the economic downturn in the area, much of the shipyard had closed shop along that stretch of road. My destination was a small single story cargo office positioned at the front of a large parking pad, maybe three acres in size and empty. This was Rizzi's drop point. I pulled into an abandoned lot kitty-corner of the office about the length of a football field away. I nestled my Avenger quietly between a small gathering of rusted out or otherwise immobilized forty-foot container vans and started my observation. Surrounding the parking pad was a six-foot high chain-link fence with four-foot wide rectangle placards attached. On the signs, printed in bold black letters on a red background were the words "Restricted". Foreboding as it might seem, the sign nearest me drooped to one side, almost touching the ground.

Sometimes luck was on your side; it was always appreciated when it was. This was my lucky day. My first set up on Rizzi, and he showed. The Machine had a history of getting up late and working late. I thought it was unusual when Rizzi arrived before noon. My intention was to put a tail on him. Establish whatever I could from locations and residences, and then have an uninterrupted person to person chat with him.

The office was manned by a couple goons who had arrived around nine in the morning. When the car pulled up, I didn't know it was Rizzi, but it soon became evident. The car was a mid-nineties 4-door Chevy Impala SS, silver-gray in color, that parked by a large entry gate next to the offices. The driver hopped out and went inside the cargo office while one of the goons came out and got into the vehicle. I could see a person seated on the passenger side of the car, I suspected it was Rizzi. Through my binoculars, I could see the two in the Impala making hand gestures. I assumed they were discussing business. Finally, the goon exited the car. Under his arm was a satchel. The prospects were good, it was the drop. The driver returned to the car, but they didn't leave, so we waited. The goons in the office, Rizzi and his driver, and me, all waited.

A second vehicle pulled up to the main gate which was located next to the offices, I figured it might be shipyard business since it was at the entry gate, but the gate didn't open. Right there, right in front of me, I watched Carmine Bruno step from the black SUV. Rizzi exited the Impala while his escort stayed put in the car. The pair embraced and walked together from the shipyard entrance along the access road in my direction, right at me.

I watched as they continued in my direction, closing the distance between us, one step at a time. I could feel a vibration, a tingling sensation, welling up inside me. I wasn't anxious; I was excited. I felt the rush of adrenaline that accompanied a kill.

They drew close, I could see their precautionary measures, and it amused me. They didn't look around like a bunch of amateurs to see if anyone was watching them. They assumed they had an audience. In a coy fashion, they covered their mouths when they talked. They wanted to insure no Feds were honing in on their conversation with a "Big Ear" and recording what they were saying or that they weren't using a lip reader with binoculars hoping to pick up viable Intel. Rizzi held his stubby cigar in his mouth while Bruno dug at his teeth with perhaps a toothpick. It was an old Mafiosi trick. Unlike the Feds, I didn't care what they had said. The FBI was tasked with building ironclad cases against the syndicate; all I had to do was pull a trigger. In this case it would be four times, for two rounds each. But first, I wanted Bruno and Rizzi to squeal like stuck pigs. They owed me that much.

They were getting close enough for an easy solution, if they saw me, I might have to resort to winging them, load and go. It was easier said than done. I would also have to kill the driver and the goons before I could get away.

I pulled out my M22 Glock, attached the moderator, and ran the slide. I worked the receiver to insure there was a chambered round. The inserted magazine now held only fourteen. I ejected the magazine and added another round which brought it up to full capacity. I reinserted the magazine and held the weapon by the steering wheel. I figured the extra round might come in handy if this went down. I held the trump card if it went south, surprise was the element. I was ready for war, they were not.

They stopped twenty feet short of my car. I could see their legs and feet on the opposite side of the container van that concealed my presence. I slipped my sunglasses on and cocked my head back slightly. I fully expected them to come check me out. A point blank encounter, perhaps out of view of the office crew, might work out in my favor. I'd smelled the sweet scent of death in the air, but Rizzi and Bruno turned away and ambled back toward the office. The scent would linger in my want, not to be realized at this moment in time.

Rizzi returned to his car. Moments later, he and his driver took off. My plan of random and roving was back in play. Rizzi was a good plan, but I couldn't pass up on Bruno. I could tag and bag Rizzi and his driver any day of the week. Rizzi wasn't going anyplace. Carmine, on the other hand, was elusive and more difficult to come up with. I gave him my full attention.

Rizzi pulled away while Bruno went into the cargo office. A few minutes later, Bruno emerged with a satchel under his arm. In mobsterville, this satchel was either a very popular fashion statement or it held something important. Bruno had a potbelly that hung over his belt if he had one on. He didn't look like a fashion statement kind of guy to me. My guess was it contained a pile of loot, the drop from the Mostarda crew.

I surmised Carmine had retrieved what he came for. He fired up his black SUV and backed away from the gate. I'd take Bruno for Rizzi, and still get the drop; it didn't get much better than that. If my luck continued, Bruno would take a road trip to Toronto to pick up De Luca's loot too. We drove north, the opposite direction I had hoped for. We were travelling the same route as Rizzi took. It didn't make sense. I kept my Glock close, loaded, and ready for action.

Traffic was light which forced me to lie back on the tail. It wasn't anything to worry over. If I lost the scent, I'd pick it up on another day. If I lost him and he had no idea he had been followed then he'd be at the shipyards again, and we would start the cat and mouse over. We travelled a few miles up I-190 to a ritzy condominium high-rise in the little Italy district of Niagara Falls. I parked off Pine Avenue where I could get a good look at the main entrance of the condo. By the time I parked, Bruno had gotten out of his vehicle and was nowhere in sight. My assumption was he'd already entered the building. I depended a lot on Cal's notes. The address I was parked near was linked to underboss Antonio "Tuff Tony" Giannetti. He was the known entity Bruno answered to. He might also have given the order to whack Cal. Tuff Tony conducted himself more Hollywood than gangster, although the two were merging in general appearance. It was a gangster paradox. Wannabes that looked like Tinseltown rappers wanted to live the thug life. They had the gangster look. The real hood rats hated the ghetto look and did everything they could to shed it. Gangsters didn't want to look like gangsters. The new breed of gangster wanted to look as if they'd posed for a cover shot on a GQ magazine. Upscale and upper class was their thing. Tuff Tony was the leader of the pack in the look. He took flash to a new level and too far for some of the older crime family members to appreciate. They didn't like the notoriety he had netted in the newspapers and tabloids.

Tuff Tony had a tough job. He was responsible for the Machine's day-to-day operations. His brother, Sal was a recluse who'd handled the interface with the other crime syndicates in New York, as far south as Florida and Texas. He was rarely seen by the media. Tuff Tony was the face of the Machine.

I'd followed the satchel of loot here, but I doubted it had found a home. The money had a destination, and Bruno had a responsibility to get it there. The road trip wouldn't be over until it made it to Rocco Colansante. Tuff Tony got the cut after Rocco did his thing. This was all according to Cal, and it was possible he was wrong.

I had to speculate why Bruno was here instead of Rocco's. Maybe they were pulling some shenanigans on the drop. Skimming from the take wasn't unheard of, and after all they were criminal types. More likely their meeting had to do with other business; the recent killing of mobsters might be a hot topic, I hoped so. Bruno was responsible for the security of the business, and it was threatened. I'd given them plenty to talk about, mostly in the way of dead bodies strewn about, and I wasn't done giving the family hierarchy a motive for secret meetings.

I waited. What choice did I have at this point? I wanted Bruno in the bag, and the drop in my pocket before the day was up. He was a primary player in the Mob, more important than Rizzi by far, but he was still an errand boy. If I pulled it off right, Marco Camerota would be the fall guy. If it didn't go smooth, it would still crank up their paranoia a notch. If the local crews thought someone put the muscle on them, they might lash out and start a gangland war. There was always plenty of tension on the street over territorial ownership. The ethnic drug cartels were struggling for dominance and didn't like the "street tax" structure where they had to pay the Mob for protection to conduct business.

As I sat on the observation, a police cruiser pulled in close to where I parked, then a second car, then more unmarked cars with an unmarked van. It looked like a meeting of the minds. I sat low in my Avenger. The marked cars pulled into the condo parking lot and sealed off the entrances. Moments later the unmarked police vehicles pulled up to the condo entrance while officers in commando styled vests from the van took up positions at the condo exits. Officers walked quietly from their unmarked cars and entered the building.

Time stood still. Bruno's SUV was parked at street level in clear view. I hadn't seen hide-nor-hair of him. Officers exited in three small groups a couple minutes apart. Each group had a man in custody. The prisoners were placed into the back seats of the unmarked cars. Bruno was in the first group.

The show went on; gawkers crowded the street while news reporters were held at bay by the police. As night closed in, I decided to head back to sanctuary. I was disappointed, I'd hoped to end the day with a higher body count, but I wasn't without a way forward. There was tomorrow, and there was Rizzi.

Chapter 9

"I know other criminals will fill the void the dead will leave."
—Walter

I awoke in a panic. I didn't know what had triggered the alarm that I sensed, but it caused me to leap from the couch. I knew it was early in the morning, but not much else had registered. I heard music playing in my head that reminded me of the old black and white television series Twilight Zone. It was another nightmare of sorts, the kind I'd had over the past couple weeks. I'd had nightmares before and found ways to enjoy them, but these were different. They were about Anna as this one had been, and increasingly unpleasant. The strangest part of the dream that had awakened me was the harsh sound of knocking. It didn't connect in any meaningful way.

Before I could return to a prone position on the couch, I had to check the house. I didn't think it was any different from what most people would do; if they'd been startled awake. I knew I wouldn't find a rational reason why something went bump in the night while I slept, but I had to make sure the house was safe before I closed my eyes again.

Then I heard it again; a thumping on the safe house entry door. I quickly retrieved my .40-caliber from its resting place on the end table next to the couch. I ran the slide, and it snapped back charging a round into the chamber, loud enough a person with an ear to the door might have heard. While I waited, I picked up two fifteen round magazines, and slid them into my back pants pocket.

I thought to myself, the knocking noise might have had another origin, a sound from something else in the complex, but it sounded like knocking. Who was the question? There was no maid or room service, and no one knew I was here besides Max. Management had no reason to knock on my door unless the rent was due. Max said he wasn't funding the project any further, maybe he'd stopped the money flow, and I was on the hook for the stay. For a fleeting moment, I hoped to hear Anna's voice from the other side of the door. If she were still alive she would come to my safe house, but in my heart I knew it wasn't her. We had protocol. She wouldn't have made that mistake.

The knocking had not repeated again since I'd picked up my weapon. Whoever it was might have left. Still, I couldn't think of a good reason to open the door to see. They might be waiting me out. Whatever the circumstance, there was a slew of reasons why someone might stop knocking, not the least of which would be to avoid drawing attention.

It could be cops, but again, no reason to answer the door. I wasn't in the mood to talk voluntarily with detectives. If they wanted in bad enough, they knew how to get in, but knocking was hardly their style. A police raid would swarm the place with S.W.A.T. or snag a pass key from the desk attendants. Whatever the purpose of the knockers on the other side of the door, I wasn't buying in.

Thump, thump, thump. The "Whoever" I'd been concerned about, was still there. I could hear my heartbeat hammering away in my ears. Thoughts of the previous night came rushing at me. The Machine might be wise to me? Three were in custody, and I assume they were all family members since Bruno was the first one hauled out in cuffs. But, I still didn't know what their meeting was about. It might have been about me. Maybe they'd issued some orders to take me out. The worst case scenario played in my mind. Anna, under extreme duress, had given up sanctuary to the Mob. Did I believe that was possible? It would be understandable. Most people rapidly broke down under torturous conditions. At my door, there was silence. Anticipation had become worse than the knocking.

If they wanted a war, they'd come to the right place. They might get me in a rush, but it was going to cost them. Thugs would have to breach the door to get me. I intended to make it difficult. I moved back into the bedroom. The hostel was from an era when they built buildings thick and heavy. The doors were solid core, and the door jamb where I took up position was sturdy, and thick enough to protect from smaller caliber weapons. The type of guns most mobsters carried, cheap, Saturday-night specials, the famous throw-away guns.

I didn't live prepared for a standoff; I quietly made a suitable barrier in the doorway with a light-weight metal book shelf. I kneeled to conceal myself and waited with my weapon poised and ready. I didn't have time to think about the endless possibilities at my door, not anymore. I had the necessary response for whatever tried to come through.

Bang. Bang. Bang. The thuds became more pronounced. It was reminiscent of a hammer pounding on the door instead of the knuckles of a balled-up hand. "Mate, are you there?"

No way! How could it be? I was dumbfounded at the likelihood of Seymour Bludd at my door. I stood and inched my way to the door, still unsure of the right course of action. Bang. Bang. Bang, "Open up mate, I know you are in there?"

Standing to one side of the door as I cracked it open slowly, I asked, "Bludd?"

I was met with a resounding, "Giddaymate!"

I opened the door further. Standing before me was a barrel-chested fellow, sporting a ball cap and smiling ear to ear. "Sorry for the intrusion this way, mate. Can I come in?" Seymour gently pressed his way through the door opening and into my living quarters.

I was relieved to see it was Bludd at my door, to a point. I was still hyped with a lot of adrenaline; it would take a few minutes to work through my system. Until then, I wouldn't be able to talk much. Bludd seemed aware of my condition and didn't press the conversation. I peeked down the hall then closed the door. Bludd clamored about in the little kitchenette apparently looking for something. As I stood with my Glock still in hand, he pulled out a teapot, filled it with water, and placed it on the stove. I looked out the security viewer peephole, I wasn't sure why, an instinct I suppose. The million dollar question sat poised on the tip of my tongue. Why was he here?

Still digging through cupboards, Bludd asked, "Where's your tea, Mate."

"In America we drink coffee." It was a mindset. Everyone knew Americans drank tea, too, but where I was reared, we drank coffee year round and iced tea in the summer when it was hotter than blazes. The only time I recalled having hot tea was when we ate at a Chinese restaurant.

"So it is." Bludd laughed, and continued to scrounge around in the cabinets until he came upon a cache of tea in a plastic container. Anna had stocked sanctuary with items she thought we might need. I'd bet my bottom dollar she didn't have Bludd in mind when she bought the tea.

It was a nerve-wracking way to start the morning. Bludd was still rummaging through the pantry when I put my gun back on the end table. I placed the two extra magazines from my pants pockets next to the Glock and aligned them in such a way they could be retrieved quickly should the need arise. It was a habit, a good habit.

Captain Seymour Bludd was how he was introduced to me in Houston, Texas. He was a skilled and dedicated Palatini operative with years of service—I was a rookie. He sported a solid reputation amongst the knights of the Order and was responsible for the Brazilian project, my first joint operation. The more I thought about it, the more I realized, I really didn't know jack-squat about the guy or why he showed up here. I chide the Mob for their paranoia, but I guess any of us with a stake in the game, would be a little distrustful considering the same circumstances. He had questions to answer before I relaxed my guard.

I watched Bludd as he lollygagged behind the kitchenette-counter while he presumably waited for the water to boil. I had to ask myself, what if Max sent him to tie off all the loose ends on this project. I was probably the only real loose end Max would have been concerned with. Nothing else of the project remained. Had Max directed Bludd to dispose of me and thereby safeguard the Society? With my comfort level challenged and deteriorating, I slipped my Kydex paddle holster on my belt and placed my Glock securely into it.

Bludd eyeballed the bedroom barrier and said, "Were you expecting guests?" He laughed and continued, "I don't want to interrupt anything if you are."

"No, it's the way I keep house."

He removed his cap and hung it on a protruding cabinet handle. His receding hairline exposed, he wiped his hands over the tuffs of hair covering his temples. I caught his eyes as he carefully followed my every move. I tightened my belt.

"Do you always put your gun on before your shirt?"

"Always."

Bludd nodded, I don't know what it was, a posture or a particular gesture, but something non-verbal was communicated that brought emphasis to our uneasy scenario. A moment later, Bludd turned his attention to the boiling water. He remained at the counter while he poured a small cup full of steaming water. Nonchalantly he dipped his tea bag; more notable was the avoidance of eye contact. His decision not to engage in a stare down, precisely at that moment, was the right choice. Any face to face encounter would have transmitted a distinctive threat. I'd seen it before with animals on the farm. Stare them in the eyes and they would react to the anxiety that was created.

People were the same way, although they don't like to admit it. It was as if the reaction was a bad thing and meant to be denied rather than utilized for survival. It was an instinct. There was nothing wrong with having them. It helped to recognize a threat when it was present. I felt the tension subside. We had managed to get through a mutually uncomfortable situation.

"I suppose you're curious as to why I'm here?"

That was the understatement of the day, and he knew it. I'd come to understand communication worked like a game. For equal players, there were rules to be followed. I walked around behind the kitchen where Bludd stood, filled the coffee pot with water, added enough coffee, from a can I kept on a shelf, to insure it would produce a strong brew and then switched it on. Bludd smiled with a big toothy grin and said, "Touché." He wasn't drinking coffee, I wasn't drinking tea.

Bludd took a seat at the little two-person dining table with his back to the wall. I would have done similar and wouldn't have expected anything less from him. He sipped his tea slowly and repeatedly rubbed his hands over a seriously balding head. A subconscious behavior I'd seen before. Bludd had something on his mind. I waited for the idea to pop out like a Genie from a bottle. The coffee aroma filled the air.

I poured a cup of the cheap drip-grind java and topped it with skim milk. As I stirred the blend together, Bludd interrupted my thoughts, "Have a seat mate." I slipped into the chair opposite of my visitor and stirred my coffee. A peaceful quiet sat in. Only the spoon clinking against the sides of my cup and the sound of Bludd sipping his tea broke the stillness.

"So, to what do I owe this pleasure my friend?" My tone was lighthearted and noticeably insincere. Although I was relieved to see Bludd at my door, I was filled with contempt and mistrust for anything Palatini. I trusted no one.

Bludd stood to his feet; my hand left the spoon and moved toward my holstered weapon. He turned his back to me as he reached across the counter to retrieve the teapot. "You are not one to trust very much, are you," he said.

"A guy might live longer if he didn't." I waited for him to respond with a different opinion. I didn't care if he did. He could have his opinion, and could have argued the point until he was blue in the face; it wouldn't have changed my mind one iota.

Bludd sat down in his chair and with a fresh tea bag began the ritualistic dunking into his cup of water. I intently watched the dip, dip, and squeeze of the bag. He replied, "Good, I like that in a person."

"So why are you here?"

Bludd peered over the top of his cup as he took a sip. "You can't keep all the fun to yourself, mate. You have to share."

I felt better. His words were sincere. He was the kind of guy that lived the Palatini lifestyle to the hilt; he lived to kill. I wanted to hear more.

"How did you know where I was?"

"Maximillian, of course." Bludd held his cup level with his lips and continued, "He rang me up and asked if I was interested in lending a hand." He smirked as he continued, "He said it was apt to be sporting. What say you mate."

"It might be too late to do much about the project." The way I saw it, the original project had died with Anna. The only remnant left of the plan, was the killing, and I'd expanded on the idea.

"I doubt that mate. I've heard reports. That's why I'm here; to finish it."

His sincere response and warm smile lifted my spirits. I had a sense of rejuvenation. I was not alone. That would make a difference on how the end game played out. If he was in it for the long haul, two Palatini could wreak havoc ten-fold over what one could do.

Bludd leaned forward, lowered his cup and whispered, "Frankly, Maximillian was surprised you stayed the course. He feared you'd give it up. Kudos mate."

I presented the project scorecard, "Before Anna disappeared I'd taken out three targets on her list. It undoubtedly put a damper on the sex slavery trade in Buffalo, but I doubt it'd be a long standing deterrent. Since Anna disappeared, I've taken out a few low-level players. Honestly, I've had a hard time with leads. I was used to having had my homework done ahead of time, not playing catch up in the middle of the game."

Bludd erupted in laughter, "I'd bet Maximillian you'd have downed a hundred of them by now." He wiped his forehead, and said, "Glad you left some for the rest of us mate!"

"Rest of us? What rest of us?"

"You have the lead on this project. Maximillian has made that clear. He has also fully funded the project regardless of how long it takes."

"I count you and me. What rest of us were you talking about?"

"Maximillian put out a call to all knights of the Order. There will be other lads show, I know it."

I had my reservations. Why hadn't Max called me and let me in on the bigger picture? He knew Bludd had committed to show up, how many more Palatini operators were en route? Manpower was a game changer. Management of assets would be new to me; I wasn't sure I wanted the responsibility. I didn't have a plan that included others. It would take time to construct, time I didn't want to waste; it was time that wouldn't involve killing. It would be a slow process to get a new asset on board with the information to be efficient. I gathered up the exposé and laid it on the table.

"This won't be the extensive briefing you're used to on a project. It's an ongoing process with new developments every day. I intend to dismantle the Machine. It's rather plain and simple. I'm going to inflict as much damage as I can on their resources and kill as many of them as I can. I know other criminals will fill the void the dead will leave. I can't do anything about that. Anna is dead. She's not coming back, but they will pay. If you don't want any of this, we can part ways now, I won't think any less of you for keeping to your oaths and bond of righteousness." Bludd said nothing. He opened up Cal's writings and began to read. I let him have a few minutes to grasp the scope of the operation.

"What are you driving?" I asked.

"I bought a '97 Chevy Tahoe in Corpus Christie where I moored *The Haphazard* until I return."

"While I'm gone, store your gear, and park your rig in stall number two-zero-five."

"Will do, mate."

I'd prepared for a recon while Bludd studied up on the who's who of the Abbandanza crime family. I loaded the Avenger with my bug-out bag and set out for Toronto. Progress, however slow, had to be made. Manpower would not be allowed to hinder me. When Palatini operators drifted in, I'd double them up based on skill sets, and send them out on a target. What I needed at the moment were more leads.

I cruised by Joey's place to see if there was any action. I hoped to see his Mustang parked in the double car garage behind his house, but the garage door was closed. The cool temperatures had set in a couple months earlier, and the garages were used more and more as the weather deteriorated.

I'd spotted the change at Joey's place right away when I pulled into my observation point. The newspapers that had accumulated on his front porch over the past few days were gone. Maybe Joey was back in town.

I was hungry. Sometimes, when I'd get busy, I'd forget to eat. I could kill two birds with one stone this time. I could eat and check out the mobster's lair at Musolino's. I'd arrived after the lunch crowd had left. Joyce was busy working the floor but took the time to say hello. I ordered up their specialty, an endless bowl of cheesy ravioli with garlic bread. Joyce came back by after I'd finished my plate, and sat next to me. It was small talk at first, but she soon warmed up to me. I noticed something different about her, something I needed to comment on.

"Joyce honey, you're not smiling today, what's wrong?"

"Nothing."

I wasn't convinced. People frequently answered that way, but I've learned if you prod enough, they'll share their woes. Most people with troubles needed someone, they could trust, to listen to their problems—Joyce was a troubled lady. She had practically begged me to inquire further about her concerns. So I did. I reached across the table, placed my hand on the top of hers, and with a gentle, caring squeeze, asked again, "What took your beautiful smile away?"

She flashed a smile in my direction, but it wasn't real. "I have to get out of here."

I didn't know the problem or what she needed to escape from, but nervousness in her voice validated her concerns.

"You need out of Musolino's?"

"No, Toronto! I need to pack my boys and go."

"Why? And where would you go?"

"I'm sick and tired of this awful place. We had a murder right here in our parking lot."

I felt responsible for Joyce's fears in the wake of the tragedy.

"Well, maybe Amato hung out with the wrong crowd?"

Joyce quietly studied my eyes. "How did you know about Amato? I don't think it was on the news yet?"

I realized I'd made a slip. Never hem and haw or stutter your way through a lie. I did the right thing and took a moment before I responded. "I work the journalism business, remember. We get a lot of information before it's released to the public."

Joyce nodded. She'd bought my song and dance routine, but she didn't know the backstory. Amato had been a co-worker, and he was an okay guy with the people he worked with, but he wasn't okay with everyone. She didn't see the side of him I did. She didn't know, for a few measly bucks he abducted a woman and transported her to be killed. That was the Amato I knew. She had no way of knowing him for what he was, any more than she knew me.

"You're a journalist, you should write articles to help stop this craziness. Any violence is useless, and they should outlaw guns too." She looked at me in earnest as if she had a good idea. Sweet naïve Joyce, she believed people could be persuaded by a silly tabloid story against violence, and people would cease their human ways. It made about as much sense as confiscating all the guns from the law abiding gun owners, and somehow that would disarm the criminals. The root of the problem was human behavior, not a gun. I chose to avoid the debate, it wouldn't change a thing.

"How about Missouri, that little place you told me about?" I hoped I'd impressed her by remembering she'd spoken of a move before.

"Shell Knob is a safe place. My boys would love it. My parents have never seen either of them."

"Joyce, I think you're on to something. It sounds like a good decision."

"I'm going to find a way soon." In the corner of her eye, a tear formed. I felt my own emotion for her. Something that was foreign to me a year ago. I'd given way to change. Not that I tried to, I was happy the way I was.

"Perhaps I could help?"

Joyce's smile returned. Her eyes sparkled as her smile radiated her beauty. "That's so sweet of you," she said. Our eyes fastened together. It was our moment, a connection, deeper than physical attraction. There was an unexplainable chemistry going on that brought a measure of enjoyment.

Seconds later, a young, shapely woman, tightly squeezed into a baby pink mini dress, entered Musolino's, and stole my attention. She was a vision of beauty, with olive skin and long glossy black hair that flowed as she sunk her five-inch spike heels into the oak wood floor. She crossed the dining area and to the hallway. She was the woman from Joey's place.

Joyce patted my hand as she stood. "I've got to get back to work." Her words sounded reasonable, but the body language was all wrong. I'd offended her. I apologized for the distraction, then I apologized again, and once more for good measure. Joyce had been cool about it.

"You don't want any of that." We both knew who she had referred to. I felt an explanation was in order. It wouldn't be the truth, but it would be an explanation. Joyce wasn't stupid, she'd been around, and she made any lie, tougher to spin.

"The woman reminded me of a friend's daughter."

"Sure." Joyce smirked.

I could tell I had to go the extra mile with this line to get her to buy in. "His daughter disappeared about three years ago. She was from Oregon but wanted to go to one of those specialty colleges in Buffalo. It was sad. She disappeared without a trace." I put on a lost puppy dog face. "I just thought, maybe." Joyce sat back down next to me to listen. I'd turned the corner on the conversation and was heading the other way.

"I don't know if it is his daughter or not, but if it is, your friend is better off not finding her."

I looked at her quizzically. Her cheeky comment had taken me off guard. "Do you know her?" I asked.

"I know who she is." Joyce's smile had once again disappeared. She watched the hall as she continued, "best not to talk about her."

"Why's that?"

"You ask too many questions, even for a journalist. I've got to go." Joyce stood to leave. I took her by the hand; a soft smooth hand—unexpected. She was a waitress, mother, and single parent. Her hands had every right to be harsh, callous, and dry, but they were tender and pleasing to touch.

"Joyce, you haven't given me your last name?"

"It's Farmer. It was my maiden name." Then with a smile and a slight embrace she was off waiting tables.

It was four-thirty, and the osteria would be jumping soon. With a casual ambling, I made my way toward the restroom, located in the hallway. I wanted to get a glimpse in the first office that Cal had identified as belonging to Joey and Angelique. If Angelique and the dark haired beauty were one and the same, there was definitely something of interest to be seen.

As I walked by, suddenly the olive skinned woman came out of the first office. We nearly collided. It would have been okay if we had. Luckily, I'd caught her as she fell from her spiked heels. I held her for a moment in my hands, until I was sure she was stable on her platforms. This was a great opportunity to strike up a conversation, I thought. A good deed never goes unrewarded. I'd kept her from a potentially nasty fall, at a minimum there would be the traditional "thank you," and open the door for dialogue.

She smoothed her dress against her hips as she gained her balance. She flicked her head to one side and with her hand tossed her hair away from her face, and gazed into my eyes. Her eyes were dark like rich chocolate and commanded my attention as she rewarded me.

She began with a tirade of foul four letter words followed by a few nasty innuendos. Her voice filled with intensity, and her language became filthier as she made personal reference to my body parts which were hidden from view. I'd worked in a factory for years, and I couldn't recall a time when I'd heard so many cuss words strung together in such a fashion. There was no thank you to be had. Evidently it was my fault she'd walked into me and fell off those lousy stilts she'd worn. But still, I apologized, it was an accident. I continued toward the restroom thinking it was over, but she followed. Her lingo changed, I supposed it was Italian, but I didn't understand a word of it. Regardless, I suspect it was nasty too.

116

I'd stayed in the restroom for a few minutes before I peeked out into the hallway. The devil incarnate was nowhere in sight. With the coast clear, I slipped out the back exit to circle around the building where my Avenger was parked curbside. There it was, right there in front of me, I stopped dead in my tracks. In the parking lot, the very spot where I iced Amato was her Nissan 350Z. I high-tailed it to the Avenger, I wanted to be ready to rock-n-roll on a tail when the little princess took off. Maybe Joey was holed up, and she would lead me to his burrow. It made sense; I doubted he would let his gal out without a leash. There was nothing wrong with her on the outside, not that I could see. Nothing duct tape couldn't fix. She was the type of woman that knew what type of woman she was. She could make a man's mouth water. I had duct tape.

I waited, and thought about how our encounter might work out, then I waited some more. It was nearly ten when her car pulled out onto the street. I didn't know if she was alone or where she was going. All I could do was tail. We were headed in the general direction of the house where I first laid eyes on her. If that was our destination, I wouldn't have a long drive.

She'd arrived at Joey's house alone. I hadn't been parked very long, but midnight was just around the corner, and I was getting antsy to score a good lead. She had led our brief chat at Musolino's. It was my turn this time. The interior lights dimmed, and it was time for me to get a closer look. The Flood lights on the garage illuminated the driveway sufficiently; I could see how they might prove their worth as a deterrent to prowlers. Lights also created greater darkness to the sides of where the lights shined. It provided a cloak of obscurity for the advanced predator, like a Palatini assassin. I holstered my primary weapon and grabbed my bug-out bag. I pulled on a simple knit face mask, black leather police gloves, and slipped extra latex gloves in my pocket. The mask and gloves went fashionably well with my dark jacket. I made my way to her backyard.

I stealthily moved in position behind the house. I knew it was risky, but some risk had to be pursued. I wasn't concerned with a dog. There was none. The value of the recon earlier paid off in some ways. If they'd had one, the yard would likely have been fenced, and I would have seen the animal. I wasn't concerned with an alarm system. Cal said none of the mobsters wanted anything to do with alarms that would trigger a cop response or camera systems. Joey had told Cal, "Let those suckers try to get in, I got a surprise waiting for them."

I located the bedroom at the back corner of the ranch style home. It was the only room visible from the outside that remained dimly lit. I wasn't able to see in the room through the window blinds, but I could hear. I placed my acoustic listening device on the window glass and listened in. Within a couple minutes, two things were notable, no voices, only noise. I could hear music and the spray of water. I went to the back door, slipped a bump key into the door lock and cracked it with a small rubber mallet. The dead bolt hadn't been thrown, so I walked in. It took less than thirty seconds from start to finish.

I dropped my bug out bag inside the house at the back door. When I left, I wanted to make sure I had it. I passed through the anteroom, which was separated by an unlocked interior door. I unsheathed my M22 and attached the moderator. From there, I went in search of the target room. The house was dotted with plug-in nightlights which provided some advantage in navigating the hallway. I saw a light emitting from an open door in the right corner of the hall. I'd closed the distance to the room; the sound of music was now noticeable. I peeked around the corner into what appeared to be the master-bedroom. A single bedside lamp lit the room. The shower could be faintly heard. There was a large walk-in-closet just to the left at the room entrance. It was fitted with double bi-fold doors which stood partially open. The lamp from the opposite side of the room held the closet in cavernous darkness. It was a good place to hide.

The shower stopped, and a few moments later the bathroom door cracked open which hurled a plume of moist hot air toward the bedroom ceiling. I could see the entry to the master-bath through a vanity mirror on a dresser located on the opposite side of the bedroom. The woman was drying her hair, at first with a towel followed by a hair dryer. Moisture from the shower had formed on the bathroom mirror, which obscured her nakedness from my point of view. This conversation I expected to have wasn't going to be easy, there were a lot of distractions. Too many. She moved out of view and then back in view, the moisture had cleared making for a clear view. She was less naked. Minutes later, she came from the bathroom, hung her towel on the bed post, and with her back to me, shimmied into a silky looking piece of lingerie that barely hung down past the bottom of her panties—had she been wearing panties. She looked more like a Victoria Secrets model than a notorious mobster's wife. She was the type of girl that could've made a ragged tee-shirt look like designer sleepwear. She had it all, sexy and elegant. Why had she chosen to be with a stinking Mafia bum like Joey?

She turned the music volume up then sat on the edge of the bed and brushed her hair. She stood, picked up a purple satin robe, and slipped it on. She looked good in purple; she looked good out of purple too. She walked toward the closet, but was interrupted as she opened the bi-fold doors. The moderator on my .40-caliber automatic often had that effect on people. It was time for a formal introduction.

She was startled by my presence, but not unnerved. I wanted her away from anything that might conceal a weapon. I remembered Cal's warning that she was ruthless. "Sit on the floor at the end of the bed. I think you'll find it comfortable."

She sat without saying a word; I was surprised at her behavior. I expected fear, but she showed none. I figured at any moment she'd read me the riot act with lots of added nastiness. "I have questions, I want answers, Capiche?"

Her lips pursed, and a snotty defiant attitude was written all over her face. "What are you, some kind-a-joke, eh?" She spoke pretty good English for an Italian-Canadian. It didn't sound much like English that I was used to, but I could follow her drift.

A joke, I thought, maybe she was right, maybe I'd taken this all too lightly. I pulled off my mask, "Remember me?" At that moment, I saw the fear in her eyes. She remembered our meeting, but that wasn't the reason for her concern. Masked people wore masks for a reason; if the mask came off, it marked a change in plans, a more dangerous change for her.

She knew how to make a man forget she'd flipped out in a cussing tirade. She could've made me forget about a lot of things. But then, she opened her mouth again. "You are a clumsy fool. You almost knocked me down. You are a stupid oaf."

Why is it, beautiful women so often end up such a disappointment when they open their traps? "My name is Walter, and you're smart enough to know I'm not here because of your foul mouth. I have questions."

"Okay, Walter with questions, just so you know, I do not tell you nothing, capiche?"

Her sarcasm stunk and she could stop repeating my name; she made it sound—ugly. I put my .40-caliber to her temple, "I'm not here to hear your sassy mouth. Do you understand?"

She gently nodded as she said, "Do you know who I am?"

"No, you tell me, so I don't get it wrong."

"My husband is Joey Naccarella. Have you heard of him?" Before I could reply, she was off and running at the mouth again. Usually when I conduct an interview, I like people to talk, that's why I ask them questions, but this girl was getting on my last nerve.

"You still didn't tell me who you are."

She donned a sly look. "Do you know who the Abbandanza Family is? No, you don't know. My husband Joey is a made-man. Do you know what that means? No, you don't know because you are a stupid man, stupid, stupid, stupid, man. You don't know nothing."

"What is your name?"

In a sharp tone of voice, she said, "Joey is connected. Do you know what that means? If you were a smart man, you'd leave right now and maybe you'd live another day or two."

Thuup. I grazed her thigh with my .40-caliber. She screamed, rolled to the floor, and careened in pain. I placed my gloved hand over her mouth and held it there until she was quiet. I whispered in her ear, "All I asked for was your name." I uncovered her mouth to speak.

"Angelique Naccarella."

"That wasn't so hard, was it? I know who Joey is, what I want to know is where he is? We need to talk."

"I don't know. I haven't seen him."

I sat her up on the floor and handed her the wet towel from the bed post to hold against her flesh wound. "You don't know where your husband is?"

She winched in pain as she answered, "He was called to a sit down. Before he goes he told me to move money to new accounts, take out cash, and go see my family. He would get back to me. He knew it don't look good."

"Who called him to this sit down meeting?"

"If I tell you what do I get out of it?"

"Are you religious?"

"I'm Catholic."

"What you get is your sins absolved sister. That's all any of us can hope for."

"Carmine told Joey that De Luca had called a sit down."

"What happened at the meeting?"

"I don't know." She paused before asking, "Can I get a cigarette?"

"Yeah, why not?" I picked up her pack of smokes, and a lighter that was on the bed stand next to the lamp, and handed them to her. She'd become remarkably pleasant, now that she had a wound to nurse. But then again, I wasn't fooled; she was a schemer, a gorgeous, sensual schemer. She lit her cigarette, the smoke drifted upward gently from her lips. She sighed. Her face conveyed a brief glimmer of relief.

"Keep talking."

"Bruno came to Musolino's to see me the next day. I thought I was in trouble for transferring the money, but Bruno never said nothing about it. He said Joey never showed for the meeting and asked the same questions you are asking."

"What do you know about this Cal guy?"

"Joey told me Bruno whacked Cal. He said he wasn't happy about it, he let Bruno know it. Bruno tried to convince him that Cal was an agency plant. But Joey said there was something wrong with the story, Cal was no cop. That made Joey dangerous. When Bruno left me at the Inn, he said he was going to look for Joey because he might have flipped, but I knew better. Joey was no rat. He wouldn't enter the Feds' program without me."

Angelique's lips were alluring, thick and flush. I sat down on the edge of the bed as I listened to her talk; she sat on the floor at the foot of the bed. "Well you're not a cop," she said as she adjusted the towel on her upper thigh.

"Guess not," I said. "In a roundabout way, I'm a friend of Cal's."

"So you are trying to get to the people that killed him?"

"I will avenge his murder. Where's the cash you pulled out?" I hadn't noticed the luggage stacked neatly in the corner of the bedroom before she motioned to it. "In there," she said. I walked over to a leather zippered handbag that sat on top of larger luggage piece, unzipped it, revealing stacks of bills, hundreds, fifties, and twenties.

"So, what's your game, big man?" Her voice took on a sultry tone. "You a hitter?" Her movement caught my eye. She had leaned forward; her purple robe had fallen open, exposing another form of distraction. She knew it too. Her plan was in motion to lure me into her captivity and secure her freedom, and maybe my demise.

"I take care of business."

"I don't see what that has to do with Joey and me?"

"Maybe nothing," I said. "Tell me about your job at Musolino's?"

"I'm a bookkeeper. I collect money, make deposits, and handle pay-outs."

"What about the kidnapping?"

"What kidnapping?" Her rich chocolate-brown eyes and long eyelashes gave the perception of truth and honesty. Her hand slipped up on my leg as I stood before her. I had to give it to her; she was one hell of an actress. She could have made it in Hollywood.

"The sex slavery, the lying illegal immigration, the kidnapping underage girls, and the rackets you and Joey are running?"

"We saved those girls from the street. You don't know what it's like on the street for them. We gave them shelter, food, and clothing. We were the ones that protected them. If they were drug users, we gave them a fix. We bought them Christmas and birthday gifts."

Was this blind justification? I doubted it. The criminal mind was too predictable. It made a good story, though. I just hoped she hadn't brainwashed herself with that saving and helping bit. They'd bought kidnapped girls off the street from hustlers, and lied to other girls to enslave them.

"You buy and sell girls like farm animals, and that's why you took care of them. They're nothing but a money crop to you. You can justify it all you want. At the end of the day, it's all smoke and mirrors. You are guilty of the worst kind of inhumanity known to mankind. You are a human trafficker."

She didn't have an answer this time. A shrug of her shoulder told the rest of the story. Now I understood why she was with a Mafia bum like Joey because she wasn't the picture of perfection she appeared to be. She was a cheap imitation of a lady and was rotten to the core. I paced slowly back and forth across the room while she watched. She pulled out another smoke, but it fell to the floor, so did she. A .40-caliber round left a gaping hole in her forehead where it emerged. Large caliber exit wounds usually did. After a well placed second shot at the base of the neck, she wasn't as pretty as she had been. She was also very dead.

I didn't waste time looking through the house for clues about Cal and Anna. What mobster would be dense enough to have left evidence around in the house? I grabbed the leather handbag with the money along with my bug out bag and slipped out the back door. The Machine would take extreme offense to a wiseguy's wife being clipped. In the traditional Mafia world, it was a sin and punishable accordingly. They would be out to kill me for what I'd done. I wasn't worried; I'd already crossed that bridge. Who were they to tell me what's acceptable and what wasn't. The Mob didn't exactly have a moral compass. She was as guilty as the men for committing the same crimes. If not, I wouldn't have killed her. It may be their world, but they're in my book and sex slavery carried a death sentence.

The drive to sanctuary was quiet. I had plenty of time to think about the execution of Angelique. I was haunted. I didn't want to shoot her, and I knew why. Anna had awakened in me a new appreciation. I was happier without the confliction I felt.

Chapter 10

"Anonymity was a killer's best friend."
—Walter

The next day Bludd and I had awakened early. With him, it was intentional—for me, not so much. He'd slept in the bedroom while I took the couch. I hadn't tried to be hospitable about the arrangement; I preferred the central location of the couch. In the event a need arose to act or react, I felt less trapped. Besides, I didn't really sleep anymore; it was more a series of catnaps, interrupted by dreams. Still, it would have been nice to have slept later. Bludd's continuous clattering in the kitchenette, followed by his personal apologies to me for all the noise, prompted me to rise and shine—well, maybe not shine. There was no need to dress. I'd slept in the clothes I'd been wearing the day before.

We sat at the kitchen table and drank our morning beverages, silently at first until the early morning cobwebs had washed out of my throat. I did a quick recap on Angelique, down and dirty, not the type of Palatini briefing he was used to. What he had to understand was I wasn't the typical Palatini kind of guy. If he hung with me, he'd have to adapt. The standard Palatini way of doing things was out the window. He'd have to get used to the idea of operating off-the-cuff.

"What is the scope of the project?" Bludd asked.

I boiled it down to the simplest terms possible. "We're going to beat 'em to a pulp, and when we're done beating 'em, we're going to beat 'em some more, just for good measures." Bludd nodded. I was satisfied our mission had been made—clear.

"What about the money, mate? We've never been a pack of thieves."

We counted it out together on the table, twenty-grand in all, nice neat stacks of spendable unmarked bills. But, that was only the tip of the iceberg.

"Why should we leave the money for the cops or the Mob to find? Why not put it to good use?" I asked.

Bludd had thought for a few moments before he answered, "As long as we're not pocketing it for ourselves, I can live with the decision mate."

"It's settled then."

I introduced Bludd to my cockeyed idea of random and roving assassination. It was the catch-all phrase I used for a concept that required clarification. "Whatever we do on any given day will depend on manpower about as much as it does on what time of the day it is. Random and roving, get it."

"Where is the cutoff point that we say we've finished?"

"It'll never be finished. I reckon as long as there is an endless supply of mobsters, it'll never end."

Bludd said, "So there are no plans, and there is no end."

I scoffed at him, "Sure there are, we just haven't made them yet, and it'll be over when we get done."

Bludd laughed, probably at the absurdity of the non-plan, plan. "You came up with this all on your own, did you?"

"It's a natural talent."

"What about today?"

"I don't have a clue. All I can promise is fun will be had by all."

Bludd looked puzzled, and responded, "Fun?"

"Those were your words, mate." I couldn't resist the sarcasm. "You're the one that said I can't have all the fun, remember?"

"I do, mate, I surely do. So where to from here?"

"Next on my agenda is the target, Frank Rizzi."

Cooling my heels and jacking my jaw wasn't part of my non-existent plan, but with the added manpower of one person, it had become the bulk of my day already. I had places to go, things to do, and people to kill.

The phone rang. The phone, that ingenious electronic modern leash on humanity, which kept us all connected, all the time. Some would say it was a marvelous invention, and they'd be right, but it had its drawbacks. It was a constant interruption to life, and in Rizzi's case, it was interrupting his appointment with death. It rang again.

"Say mate, are you going to get that?" Bludd asked as he watched the phone as if he expected it to spring off the cradle on its own.

"I suppose," I told him, but it continued to ring. I looked at it, and then looked at Bludd. He continued to watch it like a hawk, and it rang some more. Phones have a knack for ringing until someone on either end finally gave up. I reached over slowly and picked up the receiver. Bludd was noticeably relieved.

"Yeah."

"Hello, how are you today Scythian?"

"I'm hard at it Max, What can I do you for?" I didn't know what to think toward Max. He'd put the call out to other Palatini for assistance, and I should be thankful, but he had acted without my knowledge. He'd made me feel as if I was alone when it hadn't been true. Was he trying to make up for his stupid blunder of not supporting the project? I didn't know, and that made me suspicious. For now, my feelings would have to stay in check; I had bigger fish to fry.

"It has proven valuable to our projects if updates are provided daily and when something out of the ordinary has happened in the field. Communication is the key element to a successful mission," Max said.

I mumbled under my breath, "You got to be kidding."

"What's that?" He said.

"Okay, I'll make contact daily."

"Good show."

Here was a guy in a control position who had the audacity to tell me how important communication was to a project, and he hadn't done jack squat to let me in on what he had done. I felt a bad attitude coming on.

Max, however, was pleasant and cordial. I gave him that much. It appeared to me it was as if nothing had gone down badly between us. I figured what he really wanted, was back in control over the project. It had to look bad on him to abandon operators still in the field. It might cause other knights to question future projects. No one wanted to be left behind. I suspect piling on Palatini operating procedures might make him feel in control, but it would slow me down. I didn't have the time or place for it.

"Cal harbored two of the girls that had escaped the Mob. He should have gotten them out. I think it was the mistake that unraveled the whole project," Max said.

"Maybe, we'll probably never know."

"It is highly probable, with your talents, you will free more hostages. How do you plan to handle it?"

"I don't have a plan."

"We have a contact in the area that has helped kids off the street. She is not Palatini and has no knowledge of our existence, but she is a good soul. She can be contacted to assist without any questions asked."

This was a nice option to have. The fact I'd inherited the project in midstream, I lacked the customary assistance I would've had on a controlled Palatini operation. Something was better than nothing. "Hit me with it Max."

"Gladys Louise Mitchell, she's a known entity in the Buffalo area and runs a legitimate business for wayward children. I think you will find her to have a heart of gold. She has helped many young ladies to a stable life." Max followed with her phone number and seemed pleased with my acceptance of his labor.

In the process of eliminating mobsters, I hoped not to get hamstrung with rescues, but if I did, I had a go to gal, to get me out of the bind. I wished I'd had her name a couple days back for Chloe. I dropped her at a clinic door. Without help, I doubt she'd ever get out of prostitution alive. Soon as I could catch a break, I'd give Gladys a call and pass Chloe's name to her. Maybe with a little luck, it wouldn't be too late to salvage her from self-destruction.

"By the way, has Kuhl arrived yet?"

"Who is that?"

"Thomas Orlando Kuhl, he is a top-notch Palatini operative."

"I haven't seen him. I'll have him call if he shows."

"He will be there soon, I'm sure of it. Until then, Seymour can fill you in on Thomas. Godspeed and remember to call daily, will you?"

"Sure."

I placed the phone in the cradle and took a minute to think about the call, a long minute—there was a lot to think about. Perhaps I was being paranoid. Events had unfolded so fast they had taken control over me. It should have been the other way around. Cal, Anna, the project mission, arguments with Max, unknown manpower, and a few guys I'd knocked off, all played in my mind. In order to see the complete picture I needed to unscramble the chaotic images in this project. Bottom line—I was in charge.

I poured a drink. That was a good start to any fresh undertaking. It was early in the day, and I was tired of the java I'd been pumping into my blood stream all morning. I wanted to slug down something with a little more kick in it. The bottle said distilled spirits, eighty-six-proof. It went over ice, cracked the cubes, and I tossed it down. It was smooth. I poured another. I had little appreciation for an audience, and I noticed Bludd watched intently.

"Want to join me?"

"Thought you'd never ask, mate."

"Who is Thomas Orlando Kuhl." I had nothing against the guy. I was skeptical of his value as an operator, having been dropped into a project, without a plan in place. "Max said he'll be joining us."

"I've never met him, but he is reputable."

"Max said you could fill me in on him."

"Kuhl has had experience with the Mob. He led a project in South Africa against Italian Mafiosa when they expanded their criminal enterprise. He did a lot of damage to them."

I listened to what Bludd had to say. Kuhl had taken on some grease-balls and had a measure of success. That was a plus. There were differences within the Mob, even within one of the same flavor. There many variations existed around the world. You'd almost think being involved in organized criminal behavior was normal human behavior. And for some, maybe it was.

Every ethnic variant had a form of mobster. Criminal families weren't families at all. They were organized criminal enterprises. From the Irish Mob to the taco-bender cartels, they all represented their ethnic origins. Some of the crime families worked with different ethnicities, but rarely were the outsiders allowed into the inner circles of a crime family. Other mobsters killed their ethnic competition. In the end, none showed to be more successful, or ruthless, than the Mafioso.

Westerners were under the delusion the Mafia had been stamped out in the 1970s because a couple big names in New York and Philly had been locked up. It didn't mean a thing. What happened in the '70s happened in the '30s, and again in the '50s. The reality that had to be faced was criminal empires continued to expand, and were stronger now than ever, in both numbers and wealth.

The Mob, like all corporate businesses, had gone global. They lived in places like New York and Toronto, but they conducted business ventures in struggling third world countries. Westerners didn't believe it because they didn't want to.

Bludd interrupted my thoughts, "This will be right up his alley, mate. Kuhl was a military man of some sort, a Black Ops fellow, and one of your own."

"He's American?"

"He is."

It sounded as if Thomas Orlando Kuhl was a man of many useful talents. The kind of guy I could work with.

"Why would a guy with his skill set go vigilante?"

"Your President, I forget his name now, shut down the program in the early 90s. With expanding social programs, military cutbacks, and all that political rubbish, Kuhl was cut in the process. That's when Max picked him up."

Bludd loaded a black canvas bag which had one word, Foster's, embroidered on one of its sides. He stuffed it with the supplies he hoped he would use before the day was over. I could see the hope in what he packed; a change of clothes, tools, poly rope, adhesive tape, weapons, and ammunition. I grabbed my bug-out bag and refreshed my supplies, which included reloading my 15-round magazine. I'd only spent a couple rounds the night before on Angelique, but maximum capacity was always the correct amount of rounds to have in any given situation. Ending up one round short in a firefight would not be my epitaph.

I had told Bludd before we headed out I was going to call Gladys Mitchell and get my options lined out with her. I wasn't sure what I was going to say, but after I had heard her voice, a kind, gentle voice, I found myself at ease with her. I made it simple, "I've got money, and I want to give it to you for the rescue of kids living on the street."

"All right, you can send a check to my…" I cut her off mid-sentence, "No checks, cash on the barrelhead, anonymous, and I have two conditions."

"Sir, before I could agree, I'd have to know the conditions."

"I have ten-thousand dollars to donate, but I need you to contact a young lady, a prostitute, and see if you can help her get off the street. I can't tell you much about her; let's say she was an acquaintance. Her name is Chloe Page; she reportedly lived at Buffalo University campus. I dropped her off at a Buffalo clinic. She needs help to get out of the business."

"I am more than happy to help her. What is the second condition?"

"There is a lady in Toronto, Joyce Farmer, she has a couple young kids and needs help to move to Missouri. I have ten-thousand bucks to pay for her move. I need you to get the money to her and help her get out of Canada."

"Okay. I'll do what I can. It sounds as if you meet quite a few unfortunate people."

"Yeah, more than my fair share, I guess. Why don't we meet up somewhere? I can give you Joyce's work address and the money."

"Will tomorrow work? I have to be downtown in the afternoon."

"You call it?"

"About three-ish at Pearl Street Grill, do you know where it is?"

"I'll find it."

"What's your name or how will I find you?"

"If I don't see you come in, ask for Walter."

While I was finishing my conversation with Gladys, Bludd had come to an abrupt halt in front of the television. A newscast had broadcast a report that covered the police raid from two days ago, the one I witnessed at Tuff Tony's place. The reporter said, "Thirty-two-year-old Antonio Giannetti, reputed Mafia Underboss for the Toronto based Abbandanza crime family had been arrested at his condominium in Niagara Falls, New York, on charges of firearms trafficking and participating in a criminal organization. Five other members were also in custody all stemming from the same criminal charges."

The reporter covered a slice from an afternoon press conference held in front of Buffalo FBI Headquarters that featured an array of law enforcement agencies from local police to Alcohol, Tobacco, and Firearms (ATF) officers. The FBI spokesman took his turn at the cluster of microphones to report, "Five search warrants were executed in the Buffalo, Niagara Falls and Rochester areas resulting in six suspects arrested. All were members of the Abbandanza crime syndicate."

Next to speak was an ATF spokesperson, "The investigation started more than a year ago with the goal of cracking down on firearms trafficking along the border." The reporter was quick to seize on the lack of specific details on the investigation, however, a small cache of unregistered firearms, a yacht, and two exotic cars, were seized. IRS Agents were looking into bank accounts, as well.

The local Police Chief followed suit with his statement, "We will do everything in our power to remove illegal gun trafficking from our streets and dismantle the organizations that are responsible for bringing those guns into our community." The reporter finished with a list of alleged key members of the crime family arrested with Tuff Tony including, Carmine Bruno, Rudy Cantu, Paul Favassa, Fred Millar, and Lucan "Spooky Luke" Russo.

Why is it I find myself suspicious of the raid? Why did law enforcement, after a ten year moratorium on crackdowns, choose now to exercise their power? For a yearlong investigation, they barely scratched the surface of what these guys were guilty of. It had the smell of a political agenda all over it. Somebody needed a score. Maybe it was the State prosecutor who was up for re-election that needed to show the populace he was effective at controlling crime, or perhaps it was as simple as, law enforcement needing a morale boost from the collar? Whatever was really going on was all behind the scenes. They moved fast and got nothing in return.

"Did you notice no one from Toronto was indicted?" I said.

Bludd added, "Police didn't nab the head guy either."

"It's a flimflam, you can bet on it."

The phone rang.

"Criminy!" I yelled. "What am I, PBX central?"

Frustration had gotten the best of me. I wanted to kill a mobster and everybody and their dog wanted to talk to me. I snatched up the receiver. My "Yeah" was curt and tense.

"Hello, this is Maximillian again, sorry about the intrusion, but I have terrific news. My Crown contact, who is a very prominent fellow in the Provincial task force of Ontario, wants to assist our project. He is in the know concerning the Abbandanza crime family. We have spoken daily since Anna disappeared. He wants these gangsters out of Toronto. I have kept him apprised of our progress and he has likewise kept me informed on happenings."

"Somebody else knows what we are doing?"

"He is aware. He knows our interests are in what happened to Anna and Cal, and for justice to be served, our way, for those responsible. He is supportive of our direction on this."

"Did he tell you about the police raid?"

"No, there was no mention of it."

"Mob arrests were made in Buffalo, Rochester, and Niagara Falls. Maybe he doesn't know as much as he says he does."

"Are you sure?"

"I was setting on a target when the raid went down. It's already been covered in the news. It's out there in the open, Max. I'm surprised this guy hadn't mentioned it."

"I will check with him and see what happened. Sit tight until I get back with you."

I hung up the phone. I had a bad feeling about someone other than Palatini knowing we had an operation in progress to kill members of the Machine. It made me uneasy. I turned to Bludd, "Lets rock-n-roll." We jumped in the Avenger and lit out to find Frank Rizzi.

We were too late in the day to go by the shipyard where the drops had taken place previously, besides, the police raids would have forced some change to what I saw go down last time. The collar on Bruno might have set us back to square one with Rizzi.

Bludd and I swung into Rochester and stopped at the Double Decker Lounge, Mostarda's social club. I wanted to see who's who in their neck-of-the-woods. I entered, followed by Bludd a few minutes later. As far as anyone was concerned, we were just a couple regular guys that had met up for a beer; unofficially, we cased the joint.

As much as I'd like to think I'm not easily noticed, when I stepped through the front door, I felt every eye in the place on me, and there were plenty of eyes. The lounge was dimly lit, and shadows filled the booths that were against the wall. The bar was short holding about a dozen people if all the barstools were filled, but they weren't. One man sat at the end farthest from the entrance door. Of the forty or so people in the place, not one had their backs to the door. People sat semicircular around the tables in groups of two or three.

Bludd joined me as planned. We tossed down a couple cold ones and watched the clientele. We hadn't been there long, when I saw a young woman descending the spiral staircase from the second level, her hand gliding confidently on the railing. She held my interest, Bludd's too. As she reached the bottom stair, she paused and scanned the barroom from side to side. I didn't send her a green light gesture, but I had a chair open on either side of me at the table. With eye contact made, she began her approach. Bludd was big, bald, and barrel-chested. I hoped his presence at the table wouldn't scare her away. She was a classy looking gal with sex appeal. Her dress wrapped tightly around the package she advertised. She was a platinum blonde with long-legs, even without the heels she wore.

"Is this chair taken?" She asked.

Before I could answer she pulled the chair and planted herself, next to Bludd. I didn't figure on that. I was considerably more athletically built than Bludd and better looking too. The only thing I could come up with was he had "sucker" written all over his face."

"Buy a gal a drink?" She said to Bludd. How could he resist the temptation of her thick wet lips?

"Reckon so Sheila." She didn't have a nametag on, and I was sure he didn't know her by name; it had to be an Australian slang of some sort. He motioned to the waitress for service.

"I'll have my regular," the gal said. When the waitress walked away, the Sheila started in with questions.

Bludd chose to introduce us; I couldn't have cared less, now. "I'm Seymour, and this is my mate, Walter."

"Mate," she said. "Are you guys—together?"

"It's not like that," Bludd said. "I'm Australian."

Well, that explained to her a lot about his weirdness right off, I thought. She politely told us her name was Candy and casually asked us another dozen questions. I couldn't put my finger on what she was trying to find out if we were cops, running some kind of game, or run-of-the-mill citizens, but she was pumping us for information and wouldn't stop until she was satisfied.

"Are you fellas interested in some action?"

"What kind of action?"

"I have my own live webcam show I star in; I'd love to have you watch. That is if you'd like to watch me perform." She leaned close to Bludd, and in a whisper said, "I'm really amazing." Candy had given Bludd the browser address and a kiss on top his bald head before she made her rounds of the barroom. While Bludd was busy paying full price for Candy's watered down drinks, I'd broke off and wandered around the lounge. I had plans to visit here again and wanted to see the security features and layout of the building. I slipped upstairs to the second level. It had the customary bar station for social clubs and a young man taking care of a couple tables. Huddled in the corner was Carmine Bruno. He was a guy that gave the term, potbellied slob, a bad rap. Bruno wasn't alone. Capo Carl Mostarda sat with him. If you counted the four hired guns he had nearby, he was far from being alone. If I didn't know better, I'd say he was scared of something or someone. Gunslingers come in different sizes, but some of the most notorious of the mobster's gunmen weren't big muscly guys, but average to small in size. The gun made everyone the same size. The exception was in the behavior. The smaller guys had fewer options and had a tendency to use extreme violence to make their point. I wasn't going to be able to get to Bruno here, not under the current conditions. On a positive note, he'd bailed out of jail, exposed himself, and was vulnerable.

I went downstairs, passed by Bludd, and said, "Come-on, Camerota wants us." I said it loud enough for Candy and the barkeep to hear.

We jumped in the Avenger, Bludd asked, "What's this all about?"

"I didn't want you to end up with a disease penicillin couldn't cure, and besides she's one of Mostarda's girls peddling the webcam scam, maybe she'll hightail it upstairs and rat us out as part of Camerota's crew. That should put a burr under their saddle. By the way, Bruno's not in jail any longer."

"Wow, do you know that for sure?"

"He was sitting next to Mostarda upstairs."

Chapter 11

"Suspicion and doubt had given way to chance."
—Walter

Wwe had slept late into the morning since Max wanted us to stand-down
our operation until he'd heard from his Crown source. Of course,
we didn't, and were out to all hours of the night casing the Double Decker
Lounge in Rochester. Capo Mostarda and Carmine Bruno had crawled into a
gloss-black Hummer and left together with a convoy of vehicles in tow.

We'd barely started our morning routine when the phone rang, it was déjà
vu. Bludd and I stopped in our tracks. A small voice spoke to me and said,
"To hell with that," but a subconscious prompt, one I'd rather have kicked
to the curb, took over, and against my better judgment, I answered the leash.

"Yeah."

"Hidey-ho," Max said. He sounded chipper, more than I felt for sure. Max
dished out the usual cordiality followed by a few formalities, and then we got
down to brass tacks.

"I spoke with the Crown source about the police raids. He said he was
unable to transmit the information to me; it was a total black-out on their
end. He was apologetic but recommended a solution to the glitch."

"Go ahead, shoot."

"If you are agreeable, the Crown contact would like to meet with you and
Seymour face to face in an effort to work more efficiently together."

"I don't know, Max. It seems risky."

"The attorney I'm speaking of has been very helpful. He is not aware of our Society as such; however, he has been made aware of the Machine's culpability in Cal's and Anna's death. His hands are tied. He has no choice but to follow the law. He has told me he understands that my interest is purely a case of revenge, and he fully supports us. But, he has an ulterior motive for helping us work outside the confines of the law to get things done. I would caution you, he is not aware we initiated the project. That is very hush, hush. He might feel differently if he discovered information he provided was used for assassinations without his knowledge. It is best not to divulge too much.

"What did he think the information was for?"

"What we had discussed previously was routine mob information. He believed we were engaged in data research."

This set me to rethinking the proposed meeting, and the more I thought about it, the less I liked it. Palatini assets did not share contacts. To my knowledge, it was a cardinal rule. Anna shared Nontawat in Thailand, but he was a pawn, not a contact. He took an active role, with or without Palatini involvement. Contacts were treated as confidential informants, CI's, and their identities were closely guarded.

Palatini members were always after Intel for missions. If they sought information in an area, they'd let Max know, and he would put the word out. If operatives had viable sources, they would collect the information then pass it back through Max. In this scenario, Anna had not mentioned a CI. I assume she had not met with him.

"Why is he in such a hurry to have contact with us?"

"He said arrest warrants had been prepared and were ready to be served on the Canadian side. This would likely trigger additional arrests in the United States. He said he would have fluid information that would need to be passed rapidly."

"Give me a couple of seconds, Max." I held my hand over the receiver while I ran it by Bludd.

"If the bloke feels it's necessary, we should go with it."

I related his opinion back to Max. "Good, his name is Talbot Pembroke of the Crown Attorney Offices. I know you don't hold lawyers in high regard, but there are good attorneys who are good people. He is a key player with the Provincial task force on organized crime. Talbot and I have been friends many years, we are fortunate to have him in our corner. I will give you his private cell phone number to contact."

"Okay, we'll do what we need to do on this end."

It was early winter in the eastern states. Bludd and I had been blessed with good weather up until now, but we were forced to fight off the blistery cold wind of a nor'easter that was centered further south. Nonetheless, we were catching some of the snow and winds. The converging air masses rapidly brought blizzard warning conditions to the area. A city like Buffalo would be paralyzed in a matter of hours if power outages occurred.

We made it to the Avenger and dove inside. We thought we'd warm the car up before we braved the cold once again to scrape the ice and snow off the windows. Once we succeeded in that task, we took off. As expected, it was a slow-go around town, but we made it to Pearl Street to meet with Gladys Louise Mitchell. Bludd sat this one out and remained in the car to keep it warm while I made the deal with Gladys. I arrived earlier than expected at Pearl Street Grill, thanks to the storm putting the skids on traffic. Gladys hadn't mentioned anything out of the ordinary about our meeting place, or for that matter, how we would meet up. I assumed the grill would be a dinky little place, and all I had to do was watch for a single lady looking around for someone, and it would probably be her. I was surprised to see the grill was located in a brewery, a large, four-story corner lot brewery, with multiple terraces for dining and leisurely drinking when the weather improved.

I stuck to the ground floor and went exotic with an order of burger and fries. I topped it off with a draught beer. I was about half way through with the meal when Gladys arrived. She looked cold, and she had good reason to. Her double breasted Peacoat might be classically chic for winter wear, but not for blizzard wear. We gestured a "Hi" by a wave of the hands, and she pulled off her coat and hung it on the back of the chair, to drip dry.

"Hello," she said as she formally extended her hand, "I'm Gladys Mitchell."

"I'm Walter, nice to meet you."

She shivered a bit and asked the barkeep for a light brew. After brushing her hair with her hands a couple times to get the wet snow out of it, she smiled a warm and caring smile in my direction, and then asked, "How do you know who I am?"

"Everyone knows about your work. You're a legend."

"I don't think I'd go that far, Walter, but thank you. I do suppose we're fairly well-known around the area."

"You're, not from around here, are you?" I asked.

"Yes and no. I've lived all over from North Carolina to California, and Arkansas to Alaska."

"So how did you get into this line of work?"

"I saw a need mostly, and I acted on it."

I finished off my beer and lifted Angelique's leather handbag to a chair that was between us. I pulled the zipper across the top as it opened, stacks of money were revealed.

"Twenty-grand, just like I said. You'll find what information I had on Chloe and Joyce in the side pocket."

She said, "That's it. No receipts or tax credit, nothing? I'm just going to walk out of here, and you'll never know what happened to the money?"

"I'll know inside because I believe you are an honest woman."

"We're done then," she said.

I nodded and said, "That's it." I sat back and folded my fingers together. I could see she didn't trust the deal; I could see it in her eyes, they were questioning me, without saying a word. I didn't blame her; I might have been an IRS agent trying to set her up on tax evasion. Maybe, since she was a down to earth type, she was mulling over the old adage, "If it's too good to be true, then it probably is."

Gladys got up, slipped the straps of the handbag over her head so that the handbag was secure under her left arm while the straps rested on her right shoulder. She shook the water from the fiber mesh of her Peacoat, donned and buttoned it. The bulge underneath her arm was obvious, but a mugger would most likely pass her by, snatching the handbag would be difficult.

"Thank you." With a simple nod, she turned and left. Suspicion and doubt had given way to chance.

Bludd and I lit out for the shipyard cargo office where I'd picked up on Frank Rizzi, maybe we would get lucky again. I wanted to show Bludd the money drop location. When we had more manpower on board, he might have to carry out part of the operation in the area without me. I didn't know the frequency of the pattern for money drops, but I was sure the Mob had a plan in action. All creatures of habit set patterns; it was one of the common denominators of human behavior. Humans, held the highest position in the food chain amongst the animal kingdom, but we were still animals. Some humans were more animal than others, but animals nonetheless, and the laziest creatures, as well. With a fantastically cunning mind and deceptive ways, the criminal might try to mislead their trackers, but in so doing, develop a characteristic pattern that once again could be followed. If it was every day, or every other day, or they rotated between morning and night drops, or locations, it was insignificant. The Mob designed it; therefore, there was a pattern to be found like tracks on a muddy trail. The pattern would emerge, and we would ambush our prey as planned.

We squeezed the Avenger back in between the ramshackle trailer vans where I'd parked previously. We watched and waited. Bludd and I discussed the turmoil we'd cause when we took Rizzi out and ripped off the drop. The crime family would not overlook such an offense. More than an hour had passed; in some sense it was a waste of time. The snow had drifted in around the car, and the winds made it impossible to see the cargo office through the blowing snow.

Bludd and I talked until six in the evening. It took me back to my earlier days in the military and the camaraderie I'd had with Sergeant Gary D. Stone, my friend. If Gary was alive today, we'd have been partners on this mission. "Bludd, let's check out the bar scene. Rizzi lives in Rochester and Bruno was at the Double Decker yesterday, I don't think we'll find a more target rich environment."

"Let's do it, mate."

We cut a brodie in the road, the snow aided my Avenger's quick turn, and we were headed to the lounge. We struggled with road conditions as the nor'easter breathed down our neck. It wasn't so much the amount of snow, but the blowing sideways and drifting snow that hampered our way. A trip that normally took less than two-hours to drive ended up nearly four-hours long. Bludd and I had plenty of time to address our sanity, which came into question, as we fought our way through the blizzard to South Rochester.

Once parked in the Double Decker lot, Bludd stayed in the vehicle while I ran a recon inside. The first floor bar area was nearly vacant. It would appear the gangsters were smarter than we were.

"What's your poison?" The barkeep asked.

"Looking for a friend is all."

"You were here last night, weren't you?"

"Yeah, another guy and I stopped in. I really liked the place."

"Candy's gone for the night."

I grinned like the Cheshire cat, "It shows, huh?"

"I know your kind," he said in a sardonic tone.

I turned to leave, and thought, "I'd kill that grease ball just for sport." I hated urges I couldn't act on. It's like an itch you couldn't get to and scratch.

I tromped through the snow to the Avenger, jumped in, and warmed my hands over the heater vents. I had found an unexpected value in working with a partner. They could stay in my car and keep the vehicle warm while I go about doing my business.

"Well?" Bludd asked.

"Candy's gone for the evening."

"If she was there, it would be livelier than sitting here with you."

Eleven rolled around, then twelve and into a new day with nothing to show for it. My random and roving killing spree had become milk toast. We could start indiscriminately killing Mob peons at Musolino's and the Double Decker, but I had a carnivorous taste for red meat, not minnows. I had to kill something big.

"Let's bag it mate?"

It was going to take us a long while to get back to sanctuary. I suggested we crash at a cheap motel and get a fresh start tomorrow morning. We didn't talk much, but found the nearest acceptable lodging, and turned in for what remained of the night. I wanted to sleep, but did a lot of thinking instead. It was nine in the morning when I woke Bludd, and hurried him out the door.

"We'll grab some breakfast on the road."

"Okay, mate."

I swung the Avenger into a Food Mart gas station and filled the tank. I picked out some burritos, microwaved them, and got in the car. I gave Bludd his pick, but the idea of fast food didn't seem to set well with him. It might not have been so bad, but I added insult to injury when I handed him the coffee.

"You'll have to tough it out without the tea buddy."

It was time he learned what I was really about. I'd sacrifice comfort and security to make a kill. He'd have to do the same.

The wind had settled down, and streaks of blue had appeared in the sky. An odd patchwork of gloomy storm laden clouds continued to roll through, while white bulbous clouds formed like cotton above the horizon. It was a good sign we would catch a break from the nor'easter. The radio reports on traffic conditions were positive with most main thoroughfares plowed. The usual snarls had been elevated only slightly by government offices and school closures. It was past noon when we backed into our hiding spot to watch the shipyard cargo office.

"Let's call this Pembroke guy and see what he's got for us."

Bludd nodded.

"This is Talbot."

"Max gave me your number to call."

"Uh-huh. Do you have another person with you?"

"Yeah."

"Can we meet tomorrow?" He asked.

"Where?"

"On your side, it's too dangerous to meet here. I'll call you tomorrow with the details. I've captured your phone number in my phone."

Bludd and I talked about the meeting with Pembroke, it helped to pass the time, but then a break we hadn't counted on, drove right up to the shipyard gate, and parked. A tall lanky guy got out of the gloss-black Hummer. This time Mostarda didn't have a convoy of thugs with him. He pulled his jacket collar up as he looked around, a look I'd seen before, the look you see when someone was watching for others that might be watching them.

Carl Mostarda, legitimate business owner of the Double Decker Lounge, Rochester crime family Capo, and all around bad guy, strode into the cargo office. Mostarda to me was better than a dozen Frank Rizzis, but didn't equal one Carmine Bruno.

We watched to see who else might show, but a half-hour later, Mostarda came out and climbed into his Hummer, backed out, and headed in the direction of Buffalo.

"Let's tail him."

Bludd nodded, and we were back on the road. We drove into North Buffalo and veered off into the suburbs of Black Rock. I showed Bludd I was in the know when I called our destination in advance. Minutes later, Mostarda swung his rig in behind Holy Family Cathedral. I'd been there before. Emilio Zambrotta had brought me here as I prepared to kill him. We took up a position curbside on the street. His Hummer was neatly hidden between three towering concrete walls, which gave the church a mediaeval appearance.

"I don't know who the priest is, but he must be in cahoots with the Machine."

"Are we going to kill a priest?" Bludd's face bore the signs of shock at the prospect.

"If I knew he was involved with the Mob, I'd kill him in a heartbeat." I didn't mince my words. I felt that way and I would act accordingly. If I did decide the priest owed a debt, I might as well load the sacrament plate Sunday morning with plastic explosives instead of bread. When it exploded in the congregation, about half of the Machine would be eliminated in one foul swoop. There'd be more than the blood and body of Christ splattered in mass; it'd be a mess. But, foul for sure. Indiscriminate killing violated the most basic rule I lived by. If the parishioners weren't involved with the Mob's hustle or muscle, I didn't want them in my crosshairs. At the end of the day, I had to be at peace with whatever I'd done. A moral failure of that magnitude would be my haunting. Innocent people could not be killed. I was a better person than low-life mobsters, and I intended to keep it that way.

"What do you think he's doing in the church, mate?"

"Confessing—I hope. I'd like to have all that crap out of the way before I facilitate his final absolution of sins."

Bludd reached over and pulled up the cuffs of my gloves, "There are no nail marks in your palms."

"That's their belief not mine. Here, put these on," I handed him a set of leather gloves. He squeezed his big mitts into the size extra-large gloves, and clinched his fist a couple times to stretch them to a more comfortable size. "Keep 'em," I said.

"What do I need these for?"

"So you don't leave prints and DNA all over the place. Geez Bludd, it's like working with a novice."

He laughed, a deep bellied laugh, and he had the belly to back it up.

"Can you drive a Hummer?"

"I'm a tugboat captain, I can drive anything."

I shook my head jokingly in dismay, "We'll see soon enough."

"Get ready, we're about to do a capo." I paused, took out my six-inch fixed blade buck knife, and said, "I told you I wanted an attention getter; Mostarda will make it happen."

Bludd pulled his knife, a combat relic of World War II fighting knives, an Applegate-Fairbain with an equally long blade. Great minds evidently thought alike.

I wasn't surprised to see Mostarda in this area. He ran satellite operations up and down the border. Of all the capos in the Abbandanza family, he controlled the largest physical territory. He was also the most culpable in the human trafficking racket. He needed to die almost as badly as Bruno.

It was five-fifteen. It hadn't snowed during the day, but the cloudiness had aided in the arrival of an early dusk. The side door of the church opened and Mostarda appeared, shutting the door behind him.

"Let's go Bludd."

Mostarda fired up the Hummer and sat in the vehicle. It's a good idea to warm a vehicle in the wintertime. It was risky driving with windows fogged up, and that's what would happen if the defrost wasn't blowing warm air. In Mostarda's case, it was risky to sit in a vehicle as it warmed up. He didn't know that evidently. It didn't take long to fog up the windows, his body heat and exhalation put warmth and moisture into the air, which condensed, and hung like a shade on the windows. He wasn't able to see someone if they approached his vehicle, not even someone the size of Bludd.

I pulled the Avenger into the back lot of the church and alongside the cathedral wall out of sight of my target's vision. It was a fast tactic. Bludd and I got out; walked around the corner of the wall where the Hummer was parked. I reached the passenger door first; Bludd was a close second at the driver's side. I opened the passenger door quickly with my weapon pointed point blank at my victim's head, the diversion allowed Bludd to open the driver's side, and place his .44-caliber against Mostarda's head.

He stumbled for words, finally spitting out expletives and a question, "What do you want? Do you know who I am?"

"Shut up," I said. "We're going for a ride."

"Over my dead body."

"It can be arranged."

We might have carried on a longer conversation, but Bludd had wrapped Mostarda's wrists with Duct Tape followed by liberal amounts of tape over our target's mouth. It was an ugly tape job and I told Bludd so, but he stuck to business, and had Mostarda immobilized. Bludd shook him down, found no weapons, and then pushed him into the back seat of the Hummer.

"Where to mate?"

"Follow me; we're going to ditch this tin can."

We took it nice and easy. No need to draw anyone's attention, especially not the cops. We ran south on Niagara Street a few miles, swung into La Salle Park, and dumped the Hummer. Bludd and I tossed Mostarda in the trunk of my Avenger and cruised another mile to the southern end of Ohio Street where the rented Quonset hut was located.

The service road to the hut had become squirrelly, brought on by weather conditions. The build-up of snow and the lack of travel in the area made it a challenge. We yanked Mostarda out of the trunk and pulled him along through the snow to the entrance of the hut. I didn't have much for furnishings in the place. A couple metal folding chairs I'd picked up at a Salvation Army store comprised the seating arrangements. I fired up the heaters in the office and went back to get our bags from the Avenger. When I got back, Bludd had Mostarda strapped to one of the chairs.

"Geez, Bludd did you have to use the whole roll of Duct Tape?"

"He tossed me what was left of a roll, and said, "It's not all of it mate, besides we have plenty more."

Mostarda couldn't move. Bludd ripped the tape from around his mouth. His eyebrows pinched together as he let out a moan, and his face twisted into an agonizing grimace.

"I'm not going to mince words with you; I want to know about your operation?"

"I'm an honest businessman. Who are you?"

"I'm going to ask the questions, you are going to answer, understand?"

"I'm not answering to nobody, you understand? Who are you yokels working for?"

Bludd slapped a piece of tape over Mostarda's mouth, reached down and pulled his shoes and socks off. Mostarda wrenched his body back and forth as much as the tape would allow him to move, but it wasn't much, and in the end, not enough to avoid getting what was coming to him. Even if he'd gotten loose from the chair, what was he going to do? Bludd grabbed an old busted piece of two-by-four lumber, weathered dingy-grey by the years, and smacked Mostarda's bare feet. Mostarda howled under the tape until one side gave way to the screams and shrieks. When he was done reacting to the pain, he screeched and hollered bloody murder. Finally, Bludd placed a new piece of tape over his lips.

"He needed an attitude adjustment," Bludd said. He took a couple more swings with the piece of wood then checked Mostarda's cooperation level. Bludd ripped the tape off. We waited while Mostarda gained his composure.

"Here's the deal, I want the names and addresses of anyone involved with the immigration racket?"

Mostarda seemed out of breath as he mustered up his strength. "Why, why do you want to know?"

"I also want to know about Cal?"

"Who's Cal?"

"And before we're done, I want to know about the lady kidnapped from Cal's place in Toronto. Tuff Tony and Carmine Bruno had something to do with it. I want to know what you know."

Mostarda lifted his sagging head to reply, "Why don't you call Canada if you want answers, you filthy jamook?" His lip had curled up like a smile, but it wasn't a smile at all, it was a condescending sneer, and I didn't take kindly to it. Bludd wrapped his mouth with tape and beat him some more. Not just his bare feet, but he moved up the body striking the two-by-four flat across his shins and knees. Behind Mostarda's chair, I laid four-ply plastic sheeting on the floor and doubled the layer for maximum benefit. I had a feeling it would come in handy before we were through.

Bludd stopped the beating and threw the chunk of wood onto the plastic. I covered Mostarda's head with a Muslin cloth bag and pulled the drawstrings tightly around his neck. I'd bought a dozen of these bags, and this was the first time I'd had the opportunity to use one, in this manner. The box the sacks came packaged in had advertised they were ideal for a variety of uses. I considered writing a review for the company on how handy I'd found them.

Bludd appeared solemn. "Are you going to kill him with the drawstrings?"

"No, let's move him to the plastic."

Bludd pulled out his combat knife and began to cut Mostarda loose from the chair. I picked up a few pieces of scrap steel inside the hut. The pieces were a foot to eighteen-inches in length and resembled pieces of railroad track. I guessed them each at twenty or more pounds.

Mostarda was alive and barely conscious as he waited for us to dispatch him. He was wrapped up tight with Bludd's tape job and the Muslin bag secured on his head. I didn't want to drag this out all night; it would only cut into my sleep time. I didn't see the need, he wasn't talking, and I didn't need him to. I was killing him because he needed to be killed, and it might create the splash I wanted it to in the local underworld.

"Let's wrap him," I said.

Bludd joined me on the hut floor, holding Mostarda in place as I put the rail between his legs and taped his legs around the piece of track. When we were done, we'd made a plastic burrito of the guy. The Muslin bag kept the plastic from resting against his face and probably alive for a spell before suffocating.

"Are you comfortable with this?" Bludd asked.

"They owe for pain; they'll pay with pain. All of them."

"Where are we going to dump him?"

"In Lake Erie, but we're not going to dump from one of the bridges. Too many of them have camera systems set up. It'll be a road trip."

"Which way?"

"South, out of the populated areas."

"Sounds good to me mate, is there any place to eat out that way?"

"C'mon, I'll buy you a happy meal."

We loaded our cargo in the trunk and closed up shop. We found a dumping spot on Old Lake Shore Road. Last we saw of Mostarda was as he sunk from sight into Lake Erie. This time of the year with cold weather and snowstorms, the beach area, didn't get much traffic. I felt his disappearance would remain shrouded in mystery until someone found the body. On the way back, we'd swung past where we'd abandoned his Hummer with the keys in the ignition.

It was already jacked. The link to potential foul play might rest on a chop shop or street punks caught cruising in it. When his vanishing was made known, I planned to capitalize on the paranoia. The psychobabblers were wrong—revenge had a sweet taste.

Chapter 12

"I checked for signs of life, but there wasn't any left in him."
—*Walter*

My cell phone rang. I looked at the clock, it was eleven-thirty. It seemed late in the morning to still be sprawled on the couch, but in fairness, Bludd and I hadn't made it back to sanctuary until the wee hours of the morning. Nevertheless, it was time to roll out or at least answer the phone.

"Yeah."

"I have information for you."

"Who's this?"

"Talbot."

"Hang on a minute; I was up late last night taking out the trash."

It was no secret; I hated being awakened from any level of sleep by a phone call. I liked it even less when it was a lawyer on the other end of the line. Max said Talbot was one of the good guys, but how could that be? He was a lawyer. Marvels never cease, or so they say. I've never met a lawyer worth a hill of beans; maybe Talbot would be the exception to my rule.

"Okay, what do you have for me?"

"Names and pictures of police officers that we believe are on the crime family payroll."

That was viable Intel. A guy armed with this information could cut the legs out from under the entire Machine.

"Where do you want to meet?"

"I have family property in the Village of Gowanda, New York. Drive west from the Village toward Highway 90. There'll be a sharp right hand corner at Stafford Road. Keep an eye out for the sign, Gnarly Oaks. There will be a road to the left just after the sign. Follow it to the end; you'll see a one-story farm house. You can't miss it; it's the only house on that road. Seven o'clock sharp this evening."

"What do we need to bring?"

"I don't want to see any guns. You have no use for them here. Keep them in your car when you arrive."

His directions sounded simple enough. I placed a call to Max with the update. I gave him the meeting location and what his source stated he had. Max felt the Intel would be very beneficial to disrupt the Mob's illegal immigration racket. I was glad he had reminded me. I had momentarily lost sight of our goal, the Palatini goal. Annihilation had become mine.

Bludd and I hadn't discussed our expectations for the meeting, but I had a niggling perception of how it was going down, and it was beginning to get the best of me. I kept pondering the logical question. Why would a confidential informant put himself under a spotlight the way Pembroke had done? Did he see fame and fortune in this move? Were we his tools to get something done he otherwise was unable to get done. His stated motive for cooperating with, as far as he knew, a couple of ragtag killers taking revenge on the mob, was stuck in my craw and difficult to swallow. Finally I blurted out: "I don't like the set-up, Brother. He's not an anonymous CI anymore, he's made himself the center of the stage and directly involved in calling the shots on this operation. Supposedly he doesn't know we have a project. At least that's the word I got. I smell bogus."

"You're letting your imagination get the best of you, mate."

"Maybe so. This out-of-the-way meeting and no-guns bit have given me a bad feeling, and I can't shake it."

Bludd shook his head side to side but held his tongue.

"Listen to me, and think about it, I feel as if we've been baited." I let that sink in for a minute. "Look, it's exactly the way I would bait prey. Pembroke has offered us information that we didn't ask for and that we don't need. Why would he give up cops' names to a pair of guys he doesn't know? Supposedly, he thinks we're here for revenge on a couple mobsters over a dead friend or two? It's bait."

Bludd looked puzzled, but agreed, something didn't feel right. "You think it's a set up then do you mate?"

"Pembroke's a lawyer, I think we'll have to slap him around for a while then he'll fess up to what he's really up to."

"You might as well get that idea out of your mind. You can't slap a CI around. It's no wonder you haven't developed any CIs of your own with that sort of attitude." Bludd jokingly continued, "I may not want to be your friend anymore either if you act like that."

"Remember, he's not a CI anymore."

From Buffalo, it was about forty miles to the farmhouse outside the village. With the snowy road conditions, I assumed it would make travel slow. Even so, by my calculations, we'd still arrive before the meeting time. Bludd and I loaded our bug-out bags and strapped on our weapons and backups. Pembroke hadn't convinced us he was calling the shots. I holstered my .40-caliber and tucked my 9mm Sig Sauer into my ankle holster. I didn't worry about a silencer for the Nine if a situation escalated to the point where I had to pull my backup, I wouldn't need a silencer. I would need to survive. Bludd's backup handgun was the same type as his primary weapon, a .44-caliber Smith and Wesson revolver. He had a pair of shoulder holsters he'd strapped on to allow each revolver to be concealed on either side. I nicknamed him, Doc Holiday, after the infamous western gunslinger that was known to strap on four or five pistols for a gun fight. If Bludd had known who Holiday was, it would have been funnier. Western folklore evidently wasn't taught in Australia.

I cranked up the Avenger, and when it had warmed up, we headed south toward the township of Gowanda.

"Gowanda," Bludd laughed, "Sounds like Africa."

The drive seemed longer than expected, but it wasn't. It was one of those psychological experiences that threw a guy's perception of reality off. The distance to a place and return were the same distances, and took the same amount of time, but sometimes it seemed longer to get there than the trip back felt. That was all it was, but it could fool the wisest. Consequently, I almost missed the sign to Gnarly Oaks. I thought I'd travelled too far by the time we reached it. I noticed someone had taken the time to brush the snow off and make it more visible. The turn off appeared almost out of thin air, and I reacted. I slammed on my brakes, fishtailed the Avenger onto the side road as if I were "Big Daddy" Don Garlits. Bludd didn't know who "Big Daddy" was either. I concluded Bludd didn't know who many people were, at least not in America.

The dirt road was blanketed with snow. I stopped the car and got out. Bludd watched as I got down on my knees and looked at the tire imprints.

More than a single vehicle had traversed this fresh snow. Why or how many, I couldn't be sure, but notably two or more different vehicles had driven the road. The area was remote with plenty of trees along both sides of the road. It looked like a good place for an ambush. I drove slowly.

"Bludd put a gun in your hand, just in case." He didn't ask me why. He drew his .44-caliber five-shot belly gun from under his jacket with his right hand and held it low against his right leg.

We pulled up toward the house and stopped fifty yards out. A man appeared on the rickety looking front porch and motioned for us to come closer. We inched forward and kept an eye out for anything out of the ordinary.

"He's only one man," Bludd said.

"You mean one man is all you can see."

As we pulled closer, our host neither smiled nor waved or made any friendly gesture. He only motioned us forward. I surmised he was all business. We stopped behind a silvery two-door coupe with a round BMW emblem and a Canadian license plate. It didn't take an Einstein to figure the Beemer was Pembroke's ride; it looked like something a lawyer would drive.

"Don't let him see our guns and be careful of hidden recording devices, something's rotten in Denmark."

"You mean in Gowanda don't you mate?"

"Let's go with that."

Bludd stayed by the car, acting as if he had something to get out while I made the approach. "Pembroke?" I asked.

"Attorney Talbot Pembroke."

Well that was matter-of-factly to the point, and without a handshake. Not only did I not like the set-up, I didn't like Pembroke. In all fairness, I didn't like him before I met him. He'd made a bad first impression, but then again, he was a lawyer. What could I have expected differently?

"I have prepared a cursory review of materials. The packets are on the kitchen table."

Pembroke led the way through the front room which had an old paisley-print couch with two matching easy-chairs, the type of décor that had to have been bought as a set, and probably a long time ago. I can't imagine they sold many of these sets, but it was New York.

Pembroke and I walked past a large wooden coffee table that sat center of the couch, with the chairs on either end. Bludd purposely lagged behind. We continued through the kitchen area to a breakfast bar nestled against the back corner of the house. A small bay window in front of the breakfast nook overlooked a pole-barn behind the house. I've seen farm houses like this before; the bay window was useful to a farmer but had little value for our needs. My hackles rose. I tried not to show my reaction. The front room with the couch and chairs looked to be more comfortable and well-lit to facilitate the meeting. Bludd's eyebrows pinched together, and one side of his lip clenched tightly. I could tell he wasn't happy with the arrangements either.

Assembled on the table were two small piles of papers. Pembroke invited us to have a seat and take our time reviewing the paperwork. Our host was nervous, and he had good reason to be. If he had the goods on bad cops, he was in danger. I continued to be bugged by whys. Why the meeting and why in the back of the house. If we met out front our backs would be against a solid wall, and we'd have a terrific view of the road. Too many whys didn't add up? There was a reason for every detail and purpose. I'd bet my lucky stars on it. I picked up a stack of paper and walked out of the breakfast nook and into the kitchen area where I had partial visual of the front room and my Avenger through the window.

Pembroke, an athletic looking fellow of six-foot plus, seemed rattled by my actions, and came unglued.

"We can start as soon as you are seated," he snapped.

"Go ahead and start," I said passively.

"You are disrupting this meeting. Now have a seat so we can start," he demanded.

Bludd caught the drift. "Mr. Pembroke, why don't we move into the front room where the light is better?"

Furious, Pembroke's anger burst forth, "I'm wasting my time with people like you. I was given the impression you men were serious. You wanted revenge for two of your friends. I agreed to help. If you're not interested in cooperating, I have better things to do with my time than babysit." He opened his briefcase and picked up one set of the files that lay on the breakfast nook.

"Put the papers down mate; put the papers down on the table," Bludd ordered.

Pembroke spun around as if he was a real tough guy, and discovered he wasn't tough at all. Maybe he thought he'd put Bludd in his place, but he ran into a problem, a .44-caliber problem. Bludd snatched the attorney by the collar, pulled him nice and close, and dusted both sides of his face with the back and palm of his hand. Holding him close, Bludd stuck the barrel of his Smith & Wesson against his cheek and flashed a cheesy smile in my direction.

"What happened to not slapping him around?

Bludd shrugged his shoulders, "It just happened." Bludd turned his attention back to Pembroke, "What's going on here?"

"You were told no guns at this meeting," Pembroke barked.

Bludd drug our host to the front room and tossed him on the floor. I looked over the packets briefly.

"Who are these people?"

"I told you, cops."

"You're a liar, Pembroke. You have rap sheets on criminals; none of these felons are cops."

Bludd put pressure on Talbot's face with his gun.

"So why'd you bring us out here, Pembroke," I asked.

Pembroke was a punk, a scared punk. His plan had backfired, and the meeting had spiraled out of his control.

"I've never seen a lawyer that didn't sing like a canary," Bludd said.

I opened the files again and read to him. "Here are the names, mug shots, and rap sheets that all go together. It looks as if they're all criminals that are affiliated with street gangs in Ontario, not the mobsters we're after, and not a single Toronto cop in the group. Before we leave here today, you're going to explain this real clearly."

"Should we call Maximillian and let him know about Pembroke?" Bludd asked.

"We have plenty of time to make phone calls later when we are finished here."

Pembroke laughed, "You think you're leaving here alive? You better make me a deal, and I mean real soon. You are in over your head. You're involved with something that's bigger than the two of you."

"Why don't you tell us what we've gotten into?" I said.

"You don't understand, I'm giving you a chance to get out alive, and you better take it."

"Sounds like a plea deal to me. Is that your offer, a plea deal? I've never known a plea deal to work out for anyone other than the criminals and their lawyers, and since you're both, I'll have to decline, disrespectfully," I said.

Bludd snatched our host by the collar, and made an indention into Pembroke's cheek with the muzzle of his gun. "I'd talk if I were you, mate, you're time is running out."

I went to the window to watch for movement. Pembroke had made a threat. The only way he could carry it out was with help. Bludd smacked Pembroke on the head with his pistol, which dropped him onto the floor. Bludd quickly ran a sweep of the house. We didn't need a surprise waiting for us in one of the rooms.

"Clear," Bludd yelled from a back bedroom.

I stayed at the corner of the front window while Bludd continued his unorthodox interview techniques. I overheard Pembroke invoke the Fifth. To Bludd, being an Australian, a Fifth was a bottle of hooch, not a Constitutional courtroom plea. I explained to Bludd that our host had no intention of incriminating himself by saying anything. Bludd laughed as he continued his interrogation. "I'm reasonably sure mate, the Fifth doesn't apply to a Canuck in the USA," he said. I had to agree; besides it sounded like Pembroke was giving us attitude when he'd spoken.

My partner, a brawny barrel-chested man of considerable girth, made Pembroke look tiny. Bludd wasn't the shy type either; he had no problem with addressing business issues in a straightforward manner. He smacked Pembroke around some more until he coughed up a statement. Between gasping for air and spitting blood, he said one word, Omerta. Maybe he thought we were a couple country bumpkins, but I had news for him, I understood what he said, and I was going to stuff his code of silence where the sun didn't shine.

"Hey pal, you ever heard of a capo named Mostarda?" I asked.

"Never heard of him."

"He's dead," I said, "I killed him last night, but that wouldn't make any difference to you. It was slow and painful. Probably coincidentally, but at some point during our chat, he, too, uttered Omerta."

"You killed Carl?"

"Is that what you called him…Carl? The guy you don't know."

Pembroke's lips loosened up, "I will not let you destroy what we have built to revenge your insignificant friends' death. If they hadn't meddled in other people's business, they would still be alive."

"They got iced in your neighborhood; did you have anything to do with it?" I asked.

Pembroke laughed, "You'll never know."

"Who killed them?" I demanded. "You're a big shot in the Mob. Why don't you man up and tell me right to my face?" My voice quivered with anger, and a thirst for blood stirred. "You're nothing but a clown, Pembroke. You're just another pawn in the game."

"You don't know me, and you don't know who I am. Let me tell you, I'm the one who decides who gets what. I'm on the top rung, not the bottom rung. You're the pawn, and you better wise up. You better wise up while you can."

It didn't take me long to size up Pembroke. His narcissism stunk. He had the same problem politicians had, a delusion of royalty. They were elected to be servants, but servitude was never their true goal. They wanted to be worshipped.

"Do the names, Lippa, Santarossa, Pelosi, Surdo, Gallo, and Zambrotta mean anything to you?

"Sure, I've heard the names, and I know some of them are dead, so what… do you think reciting names scares me?"

"If it doesn't, it should. When I met them, they were all alive. Now, none of them are alive."

Bludd chimed in, "We have a lot more to kill, mate, before we go anywhere."

"It was never about vengeance for your friends, was it? Pembroke asked. "That was only an excuse to get my help to destroy the family. It's some kind of takeover of our area. You're all in this together, Maximillian too. Why, what's in it for you? What are you after?"

"You're going to die here tonight, right here, and I'm going to kill you slow and easy. Then I'm going to take down every one of your mobster pals and shut down your sex slavery racket."

Although Pembroke had my attention, I wasn't distracted enough to miss the headlights that crept slowly toward the house. Novices, I thought. What fools would use lights. They were too lazy to hoof it in the snow, and now it was too late. They had sacrificed their biggest advantage, the element of surprise.

"Bludd, we have company!"

I saw Pembroke smile, "I told you, didn't I?"

I scanned for the best place to facilitate the expected intrusion. There wasn't one to be found. We could improvise and make do, but there was no 'best' place in the house. Bludd released his grip on Pembroke, who fell backwards to the floor in a pool of his blood. We left him on the floor whimpering. He was a sad excuse for a man. He'd been a hired gun for the Crown and for the Mob, and now he wasn't any good to either of them. He had used his ability to prosecute and inflict pain on the Mob's competition. He'd no doubt beat a lot of people down with paper and pen, then walked away laughing. That's the way I saw him, but the shoe was on the other foot now.

The vehicle had stopped in the tree line along the roads edge, we doused the lights inside to get a better view outside. This, of course, tipped off our visitors to the fact we were on to them. The porch light illuminated the area outside the front room window and the snow added to our advantage. The brightness of the snow had made dark silhouettes more visible and the depth of the snow more difficult to move through. It was uncomfortably cold. I kept a keen eye out as my night vision improved. Soon, I saw shadows moving that weren't shadows at all.

"Where do you think they'll try to enter," Bludd asked.

"I don't think it makes any difference. Let's set up at a narrow point and have a fallback position. Once we've drawn contact, we'll improvise."

"Is that part of your random and roving plan too, mate?" Bludd quipped.

I answered him with confidence, "Absolutely!"

The ranch style house had three bedrooms and a single bathroom located off the main hallway. Bludd took up the forward position in the hall, and I at the opposite end. Too much light illuminated Bludd's position at the front of the hall, but to make a shot they'd have to be in the house. That shot for them wouldn't come without paying a price.

Pembroke broke for the backdoor, running on all fours like a wild animal. We didn't want to shoot and give our positions away; we did, however, want to shoot Pembroke. The door, centered between the kitchen and breakfast nook, now stood wide open from Pembroke's exit. If nothing else, it made a convenient entry point for our intruders.

"Don't shoot, don't shoot," I heard Pembroke yelling outside. He'd caught a lucky break and escaped, for now. You win a few, and you lose a few, but he'd be the big loser at the end of the day. Maybe not today, but his last day was coming soon.

A man like Pembroke played a dangerous game of two sides against the middle. Maybe it was a lawyer trick he'd learned in the school of higher lying. Where I went to the school of hard knocks, double-crossing tricks didn't play forever. Sooner or later you got caught in the squeeze, with pants down around you ankles, and Bludd and I would be there, waiting to serve up a plate of fresh justice. He was deep in the Mob's grasp, either willingly or unwillingly. I didn't know and I didn't care. He had set us up to be taken out. Pembroke was a louse and deserved to be hunted down and squashed like a bug. First, Bludd and I had to get out of our predicament. The party was thrown in our honor and was about to kick off.

Again, there was yelling outside. It was clear they weren't concerned that we knew they were all around us, and they must have banked on us not being cop callers. And they were right. Why screw up a good thing with cops. It wasn't every day we were given such opportunity. By the sounds of the voices outside, they were all around us; there was no way they could escape us now.

The shouting of what sounded like orders tapered off. What had Pembroke told the late arrivers? We could assume it was everything he knew from weapons we carried to the killing of Mostarda and the others. Then it was quiet, deathly quiet. It was the type of stillness you get when you walk across a cemetery; cold, and eerie. Death permeated the air.

Bludd maintained vigilance while I opened the bedrooms and bathroom doors to see if entry could be gained through the windows. All rooms had a single sliding window that opened about ten inches. It was too small to crawl through. Access would be by one of the two doors. In the middle of a fire-fight, I imagined a thug or two might try the front door, but only after a diversion, unless they were really novices. The back door would be the most likely point of contact. Bludd fell back to the first bedroom and used the door frame for cover. I followed the same line of reasoning with the last bedroom.

The stillness was broken by a single gunshot through the front room window and struck in the hallway lath and plaster. I suspected it was a diversion tactic, but neither Bludd nor I moved. Then, the party crashers unleashed a barrage of bullets into the house; I listened for automatic weapons fire, but I didn't hear the cadence. The popping noise of the weapons fired sounded like small caliber handguns, but there were five or six shooters unloading on us at once, and that might have been all there were.

It was adding up amateurs wasting ammo on nothing besides breaking glass and punching holes in the plaster walls. They might have been good at putting the muscle on someone, but they were out of their league in an assault on a fortified position. Bludd and I would hand them an education they'd never forget.

It was quiet again. I suspected they were maneuvering into position to try something more stupid than shooting up the house. If they thought we were cowering in a corner or shaking in our boots, they'd been watching too many old Hollywood black-n-white gangster flicks. There was only killing or dying going to happen next. I wasn't afraid to die, and I didn't think Bludd had thought about it, one way or the other. I crouched and duck-walked forward on the smooth Oakwood tongue and groove flooring to where Bludd was positioned.

"They're getting their courage up to come at us," I said.

Bludd responded with a sharp sanguine nod.

"Okay, let's set the wheel in motion. It may catch them off guard before they can spring their plan on us. Let a few rounds fly toward the kitchen, and I'll do the same toward the front room. Then we'll drop back to the end of the hall. Let's draw them into this long hallway."

Bludd nodded again, but before we could kick it off, gunfire erupted through the living room window. Bullets zinged into the walls and penetrated the bedroom where Bludd took cover. I returned fire, sending a couple rounds down range in the direction of the front room window as I slipped down the hall to the back bedroom. Bludd dropped a couple rounds into the kitchen then pulled back to my position at the back bedroom. While we were setting the trap, a voice called out from the breakfast-bar area which was veiled by walls from our view.

"Come out here, we won't shoot. We want to talk to you. That's all, just talk."

We played it smart. We didn't engage in small talk. I figured they'd weaseled their way into the kitchen and were prepared to launch an assault. Pembroke had questions he needed answers to, and I knew his crew would be relentless to get what he wanted, there was never another consideration.

They probably counted manpower by counting heads, and they had the numbers on their side; but the way we'd counted, the odds were still in our favor. We would play a costly game of hide and seek, winner take all. Anyone militarily trained knew that it took an overwhelming force to rout an enemy that was dug in. They didn't have it, and what they did have were unskilled street punks. What it boiled down to was strategy. Ours were simple; our aggressors had to expose themselves to the greatest risk to advance on us, and we knew they didn't have a choice in the matter. They couldn't leave it like it was.

Body count would tell the story. If we got the upper hand on the first assault and took out a few shooters, they'd likely tuck-tail and run. They weren't fighting for God, country, and mom's apple pie; they were fighting for money, but it was only peanuts. The inherent problem with paying peanuts was all you got were monkeys. We were fighting for our camaraderie and survival. It was a better motivator than peanuts.

We sat patiently and waited the way boxers lay in wait to throw a counterpunch. Let the other guy take the chance and open up first. When he committed to the punch and had closed the distance, he was most vulnerable to the counter strike.

We heard voices and shuffling around by the kitchen. They were amassing their force to bum rush us.

"One of their mates was hit," Bludd said.

I asked, "How do you know?"

"I heard one of them say it"

I could hear the panicky sound in the voices. If we'd hit one of them with a lucky shot, it didn't change a thing. I remained suspicious it was part of a ploy to draw us out. If they were being tricky, they were really good actors. The panic in their voices sounded genuine.

Again, a man called from the kitchen area, "Give up your guns. If you don't, we're going to shoot you up."

The stage was set; they'd drawn a line in the sand. We continued to play it safe and not say a word. I could hear voices in the kitchen area. They were in disarray. Confusion had set in, and arguments were discernible. Suddenly silence. I could see a trickle of light that streamed to the end of the hallway. The passageway by which they would come was now illuminated. They were afraid of the dark; I embraced it as a friend. Maybe they needed light to aim their guns because they lacked the skill to shoot directionally in the dark. Regardless, we were in the dark recess, and they would be silhouetted. They were foolish.

"Slide your guns down the hall to us, buddy."

They had to act soon; I was bored with the stand-off. I wanted to have action, so I threw a monkey-wrench in their works.

"Why don't we liven up the party?" Then I let fly a volley of lead, down the hall, in their direction. I'd no sooner stopped firing when the mobsters made their presence known at the end of the hall entrance by a slew of bullets spewed toward us. At this rate, the winner would be determined by who had ammo left when the other side ran out.

"I'm hit, I'm hit," Bludd screamed.

He wasn't a bad actor either. The fix was in. If they believed Bludd took a bullet, they might become overconfident, and walk straight into the ambush. I told Bludd, "Nice touch," and we dropped back from the doorway of the last bedroom, to a fortified position we'd haphazardly thrown together. Something was better than nothing. Bludd used a metal desk he'd tipped on its side; I took a chest of drawers, pulled them away from the wall, and squatted down. Bludd was in the left corner of the bedroom and I in the right. The grease-balls had to make their way the length of the hallway, exposed, with no place to hide. They would be a nervous wreck by the time they made it to us. We counted on it.

Slight sounds of movement in the hall broke the silence, and shadows moved against the wall.

I whispered to Bludd, "Rock-n-roll."

"Aye, aye, mate."

Chaos and confusion soon followed. One of their crew busted out the sliding glass bedroom window from the outside the house. Glass shattered and flew throughout the room. I believe it was intended as a signal to overrun our positions, but it was launched prematurely. The men inside were not ready. It was a mistake they couldn't correct.

Keyed up and ready for anything, I was set to kill. Through the broken window, a flash-bang grenade was tossed. It struck the floor and rolled toward the front wall before it exploded. Bludd and I ducked low behind our barriers. The Mob shooters made their advance.

Men with guns blazing entered the room through the plume of smoke given off by the grenade. They didn't blaze long. My hearing was toast in the matter of a millisecond, but my vision was intact, unaffected by the flash. The men, who'd rushed into the room, were stopped by the flash-bang smoke, but silhouetted in the doorway by the light they'd used to traverse the passageway. The flash-bang had not worked in their favor. We opened fire with deadly accuracy.

The smoke drifted into the hall and away from the bedroom, aided by the slight breeze through the broken window. Bludd advanced on the downed men to determine the status of their wounds while I secured the hallway from the bedroom doorway. Bludd searched the men for weapons and threw their guns into a pile. He took their wallets, looked in them, pulled out their identification, and dropped their wallets to the floor.

"All Canadians," Bludd said.

I was just about to laugh, when one of the downed men beat me to it. I motioned to Bludd to cover the hall while I pulled the grease ball to a sitting position against the wall.

"Who put you up to this?"

"I don't have anything to say."

They all say that, at first, but I've found ways to persuade people to talk. "Kid, that stuff works with the cops and maybe in court, but not out here." I followed up with a couple swift raps on the beak then stepped on his leg wound and squished it around. He screamed in pain. If there were others still outside, they would get an earful of what I had for them as well.

"What's your name, pal? Your license is right here on the floor with the others, but I'm giving you a chance to be up front with me."

"Dino, Dino Bianchi."

"How many people are with you here?"

"I don't know, the three of us came in one car, the others came in another. I don't know them."

"You're just a snot-nosed kid; you're sure as hell not the brains of this outfit. What are you twenty years old?" He didn't look that old, but I was giving him the benefit of the doubt.

"Twenty-two."

"Twenty-two, and almost dead; it's not a good start. Did Pembroke put you up to this? Did he fork out the dough?"

Dino scoffed at my statement. Maybe he didn't know the role the attorney played. The muscle end of the business wasn't able to be trusted with too much info. They don't earn enough money to keep their mouths shut when the chips are down. In Dino's case, I wanted to make sure we had an understanding. I pointed my Glock at one of his comrades that lie bleeding from a sucking chest wound, and blasted him. This time the shot was to the head.

"Who do you work for?"

He struggled with his words, "The guy you just shot."

"Who was he to you, your boss?"

"He's my uncle, Valente; I help him out sometimes, that's all."

"Well, he's been a real bad role model, kid." I pointed my pistol at the other survivor of their trio. He too appeared mortally wounded from multiple bullet holes in his torso. "Who's this guy?"

"Just a guy, he worked as a bouncer at a strip joint. Uncle Valente gave him some side work, that's all."

"Sounds like your uncle was the boss?"

"I guess he's a boss, I don't know about that."

"I'm sorry for you kid; sorry he got you into this mess. Do you know who De Luca is?"

"Everybody in Toronto knows who he is."

"You give him a message for me. He doesn't run Toronto anymore. I do."

Bludd looked uneasy. "He's seen us mate. We can't let him go."

"Don't worry about it; he'll make a good errand boy. He doesn't know anything, "Do you kid?"

Dino shook his head. I snatched him up by the collar, "Don't ever come looking for us, boy. If you do, you'll die a slow and miserable death. That's a promise. We're not mobsters, and we're not in it for the money, we're assassins. That's all we do, kill."

Bludd said, "I duuno mate, that's awfully chancy."

I looked at Dino, and said, "I don't think so. He doesn't want to die that badly. Do you, kid?"

Amidst Dino's muffled sobbing he said, "No."

It was our turn now. Bludd and I started to inch down the hallway when an explosion ripped through the silence of the night. We crouched low to the floor and waited to see what followed.

Bludd said, "I think they blew up your car, mate."

If Bludd's speculation were true, I'd not be able to contain my anger. It also meant there were still other targets nearby. Now in the absence of noise, our adrenaline ridden breathing became audible. At the entrance to the hall, Bludd turned his attention toward the kitchen and back door while I ducked down and quickly made a beeline for the front room. With a flick of the switch inside the kitchen, Bludd extinguished the light. The shadows once again hid us.

We remained quiet and motionless until our night vision improved. The outside porch area was still lit, and a skunk light on a telephone pole had kicked on, probably automatically at dusk. I could see something burning, maybe a car, but considerably farther away from the house than where my car was parked.

It had taken a couple hours to learn the truth. Pembroke, Maximillian's secret weapon in our crusade against crime, was himself involved with the seedier criminal elements of the underworld. We'd successfully held off the first wave, but there were more mobsters lying in wait somewhere outside the doors of the old farm house.

We were all in the same boat when it came to time. None of us could hang around here long. After the explosion, and with the fire burning, cops or emergency vehicles were likely to show up. With one or more dead bodies in the house, a witness, and plenty of Mob affiliation to go around, Bludd and I decided it would be riskier to stay than leave.

We gathered up the files Pembroke had brought, but left behind when he scampered out the back door. Bludd covered me as I went to my left out the back door toward the corner of the house with the broken window. I expected whoever was outside might be still be in the area. I'd planned to secure that corner first. I stayed close to the building, my Glock poised at the ready.

Bludd headed to the opposite rear corner and secured it. Once at my corner, I squatted down and pivoted around the edge. I'd raised my gun to fire, but the body didn't move. In the foreground lay a man, face down. I kept my eyes riveted on him as I drew close. I checked for signs of life, but he had none left in him. Blood had pooled under his body. There was enough blood loss I knew he hadn't died from natural causes; unless you considered being shot a natural cause for a mobster. My best guess was he'd caught a stray bullet by accident. Bludd said he'd overheard one of the mobsters claim to have been shot earlier. Maybe this was as far as he'd made it. Let sleeping dogs lie, as the old saying goes, it applied to dead dogs, too.

The body count had climbed. I was happy about finding dead mobsters instead of live ones. I came to the front corner, but my attention was drawn down the road, to where a small fire burned. What was it? It wasn't my car. It was visible and parked where I'd left it. Maybe the explosion and fire down the road was Pembroke's ride, it was nowhere in sight.

I assumed Bludd had made it to the other corner by this time, but the porch light made it impossible to see him. I moved out into the yard. The skunk light illuminated the snow, which made it easier to see movement. I squatted down and stayed put until I spotted Bludd moving up on the Avenger. He checked it inside and out, and then signaled for me to join him.

"There's a body in the backyard," I said. "It looked as if he caught a bullet."

"Think Pembroke killed him and ran?"

"No, I doubt it. Didn't you say one of their guys was shot earlier?"

"That's what I heard; maybe the bloke did eat one."

"Let's check out what's burning."

Bludd and I crossed the field until we reached the smoldering remnants of the fire. Two twisted masses of debris, unrecognizable, sat motionless on the edge of the roadway. If Dino could be believed, these had been the cars our welcoming committee had brought to the party. Bludd and I took a closer look.

"What do you think went wrong on their end?" I asked.

"I dunno mate, but take a look over here. It's one of them," he said as he pointed to the charred remains on the ground.

Satisfied, neither vehicle was Pembroke's BMW, we backtracked to my car. We could only see so much in the dark, and we weren't hanging out until daylight to figure out what had happened outside while we shot it out inside. We loaded into the Avenger, and for a brief moment, I had second thoughts about cranking the engine. What if the Avenger had been bobby-trapped to blow? Sometimes you have to take a chance. The engine came alive at the turn of the ignition switch, and I whipped it around, and high-tailed it for sanctuary.

As we passed by the cars, Bludd asked, "Where do you think our attorney ran off to?"

"He's on the run to the only place he knows to go for help, Capo De Luca. With some luck, this'll get dropped in the Boss of Bosses, Salvatore Giannetti's lap."

I could tell from the smile on Bludd's mug, this was his cup of tea.

Chapter 13

"He didn't become a rat, he'd always been a rat;
what he became was a confidential informant,
So he would be a better rat."
—*Walter*

I didn't see the need to hurry; however, Bludd disagreed. Max wasn't going to like my phone call whether I called as soon as we got back or waited until morning. When all was said and done, the call wasn't going to change a thing. Attorney Talbot Pembroke, Maximillian's buddy, project resource, and Crown jewel of Toronto's attorney's office, would be a hard pill for Max swallow. It would be for anyone. Max had put a lot of stock in Pembroke, and unfortunately, had provided him with too much information. It spelled danger for the Palatini. He should have known better, and did, but it didn't stop him from making a bad decision to involve Pembroke. The wool had been pulled over his eyes. Pembroke was a connected man, a crime family member, a mobster in his own right. It was an error in judgment Max would not make again. It was a hard lesson learned.

I understood how it happened. Max trusted Pembroke. People seemingly had a need to trust other people, but if the trust was placed in the wrong person, it could get you killed. Max had brought Pembroke in on the project; on the surface, considering his credentials, he would have been a good fit—but only one side of him fit. Pembroke was supposed to have provided us with input on the Abbandanza Mob. Instead, he got his hands on inside Palatini information and ratted us out to the Mob. Maybe Max figured he had to trust people like a prosecutor. However, it was a mistake I wouldn't have made. I didn't have a need to trust. In Maximillian's situation, the adage, "loose lips sink ships" had come back to bite his butt along with the butts of the Palatini. If Max had given the idea more thought, he would have realized he had no way of knowing who would hear the things he told Pembroke, or how the attorney would use the information. Pembroke had sold Max a false bill of goods, and then betrayed him. The price tag was a heavy burden to accept, but Max owned it.

Mobsters had eyes and ears everywhere; it was a fact, and everyone knew it. It was a misconception, of a false belief that they were all on the street. The truth was the Mob owned a boat load of politicians, cops, and evidently prosecutors. Everything Max had told Pembroke had made its way to the Toronto Machine. In my book, his double-cross made him the primary culprit behind Cal and Anna's disappearance. He had a lot to answer for, and I wanted to ask the questions.

I aimed the Avenger in the direction of Buffalo and put the hammer down. Pembroke was on the lam, and my guess was he hadn't made it a half-mile away from the farm house before he was on his cell phone jacking his jaw to the grease balls. Without question, my name would top the Machine's hit list. Bludd's name would be a close second. No more random and roving targets. We would concentrate our efforts on Palatini enemy number one—Talbot Pembroke. He needed to die, and I needed to kill him. That was my version of a win-win solution. We arrived back at sanctuary, unloaded our gear, and turned in for the remainder of the night.

The morning greeted me with the aroma of freshly brewed coffee. Bludd was already sipping his tea when I joined him at the table. Over tea and java, Bludd and I rehashed what we knew, what we thought we knew, what we didn't know, and what might be on the horizon. No matter how Max received my phone call, Bludd and I were going to forge ahead, locate Pembroke, and kill him.

In Buffalo, it was one in the afternoon when I placed the call across the pond. For Max, the time frame would be perfect. The call more than likely would catch him during his evening meal. I'd hoped what I had for him would kill his appetite. I counted on it. I was prepared for an uphill battle with Max. He had to be convinced, beyond doubt, of Pembroke's involvement with the Mob.

Maximillian's phone rang. Some people get worked up over the littlest things. Not me. I relaxed and waited for him to answer. My dad told me many years ago, "If you don't want a bad reaction; don't make a bad first action." My reaction would wait until we had our conversation.

Max answered with a cheerful, "Hello."

"Hey, this is Scythian." The news would be ugly, no sense setting the tone before the conversation got underway.

"Yes…good," he said, "do we have progress?"

I started with the good news first. I could have started with Pembroke, but we would have dwelled on it and not focused on what we'd accomplished. We had done some good, and the project was still in motion. He needed to see the positive side. "I met with Gladys Mitchell as you suggested. She's a first-class act. I gave her some names and a couple bucks to help her cause."

"Delighted. Have you met with the source?"

"I have, I hate to say it, but it didn't go as well as we'd hoped." The cat was out of the bag.

Max cut to the chase, "Are there new developments?"

"I'd say that's an understatement." I ran through the scenario with my allegations of Pembroke's loyalty to the Mob. It was met with silence, the kind of silence that strangles the life out of the air around you, and made it hard to choke out another word. I could cut the tension with a knife.

"Is he terminated?"

"On the loose."

We would have been considerably safer had he died at the farmhouse. Now he posed an extreme threat.

"We suspected a mole inside our operation had been providing the Mob with Intel. Our fears were confirmed when Cal Alonzo came up missing. Anna and I discussed it in depth. She was not willing to shut down the project and get out as I requested." Max said.

"She told me the same thing Max. I couldn't get through to her. She knew it was no longer safe, but I couldn't persuade her to pack it in."

"I told Talbot about the girls who had escaped the clutches of the Abbandanza crime family. He was aware Cal was hiding them out. He suggested they stay there, and he would coordinate efforts with police. We looked to him for help with their placement, but something went awry. And now we know what. We had not suspected Pembroke to be the mole."

"It's all twenty-twenty hindsight."

"How could someone like Talbot become an informant to the Mob?" Max asked, but I suspected it was rhetorical.

"I think you have it all wrong, Max. "He didn't become a rat, he'd always been a rat; what he became was a confidential informant, so he would be a better rat."

Max was silent. It was an uncomfortable stillness. Finally, he asked, "What could Talbot have hoped to gain? He had money, power, prestige, and honor."

"My guess is greed. He wanted more money, more power, and more prestige. He never had honor; it was a self-serving façade he'd created in his mind, and displayed to the world."

I could hear the sound of disappointment in Maximillian's voice as he sighed. The knife that had cut through the tension had choked the life out of the air and was now squarely planted in his back. With every memory of Anna it twisted and with every word, it stabbed at his heart. Max had become a victim too.

"This is my fault," Max said.

"It doesn't make any difference. All mistakes become history. It's over. The only thing that makes a difference now is where we go from here." Casting further blame and criticism on Max might have made me feel better, but I didn't have time for that. Killing the mole, the man that made the events unfold the way they did, was the only thing that would give me satisfaction—even then it wouldn't be enough.

"What is your plan, Scythian?"

"I don't have one at the moment. What you can do for me is to trust no one from here on out. We have boots on the ground. Let us run the operation the way we see fit. We'll thin the herd."

"Agreed," Max said.

Bludd and I sat down together and made a shopping list of targets. We couldn't complete everything on our list and continue to work as a team on every project. I wanted Pembroke as a trophy; he was a two-faced rat that would look good mounted on my wall. Carmine Bruno, the guy that ordered Cal and Anna's torturous death, deserved the same treatment, and I had the stomach for it. There were capos, and enforcers like Frank Rizzi who was culpable in the immigration racket—the reason for Palatini's involvement—and they needed to die. For the rest of the mobsters, if they got in my way there would be no mercy. It wasn't just tough talk. I would kill any and all comers.

Bludd was concerned that sanctuary might have been compromised. Staying put was no longer an option. We decided on a must-vacate timeline and started the countdown. There was no way of knowing what information had passed back and forth between Max and Pembroke. He may have unintentionally let slip our location. Since he trusted Pembroke, he'd given it to him having thought it would be in our best interest. We intended to make it as difficult as possible for anyone to find us. We surmised our best bet was to motel hop, one cheap room after another, along the outskirts of the cities in our area of operation. We would stay in one place only as long as we considered it safe and convenient. We would discard our throwaway cell phones for new ones, and do so more frequently. We would become ghosts.

The phone rang. I figured Max was going to be a pest. He wanted a piece of the killing action. However, with the wind in my sails, and an overabundance of energy, I was quick to answer. I wanted to get the show on the road.

"Yo!"

"This is Kuhl, I'm coming in."

The line went dead. I racked a round into the chamber of my Glock and holstered the weapon. Bludd grabbed his holsters, tossed them on over his shoulders, one .44-caliber draped on either side of his torso. I ejected the magazine from my .40-calber and added another round, bringing it up to sixteen opportunities, then reinserted the magazine.

"What do you think, mate, gangsters?" He suspected a sequel from the previous night. His eyes were bulging wide open from the prospect of such an encounter.

"Kuhl says he's here and coming in."

We waited for the knock. It was a single rap on the door. Bludd responded. With one .44 in hand, he opened the door with the safety chain in place. It wouldn't take much to bust the chain, but the slightest edge in a gunfight could make the difference between who lives and who dies. When Bludd was satisfied, he looked toward me, winked, and opened the door.

In walked Thomas Orlando Kuhl. I wasn't impressed. He didn't look tough, and he wasn't a big guy. Less than six-foot tall, fortyish, and in the one-hundred seventy pound vicinity didn't bring me excitement. I could see his eyes shift quickly from side to side while partially hidden behind the military style black-framed glasses. It was a scan to size up the situation he'd stepped into. I respected him for his behavior, but I still didn't have anything for him. He introduced himself and put his right hand forth. I had a problem with that. I didn't want to tie up my shooting hand, not yet.

"Good," Kuhl said. He walked to the little dining table and took a seat, "Bring me up to speed on the project." Bludd went to the kitchenette and started another teapot of water while I sat at the table across from Kuhl.

"Do you have something to drink?" Kuhl asked.

Bludd offered him a cup of tea which he readily accepted. I thought to myself, just great—two tea drinkers. Was this an omen? Whether it was for good fortune or bad luck, was yet to be seen. Kuhl removed his Blackwater ball cap, and revealed another commonality he had with Bludd; a shiny bald head. His most prominent feature was on his face where he sported a bristly horseshoe mustache. If he'd had a cowboy hat, he would have taken on the appearance of a western outlaw from yesteryear.

"How did you find us?" I asked. "How did you know where we were?"

Without batting an eye Kuhl said, "Maximillian."

"Okay," I said. I realized Kuhl was here to stay. It was time to get down to brass tacks. I gave him the low down straight and in a nutshell. I started with how the project was trashed and continued with a brief synopsis on the crime family, their structure, and their rackets. I ran down the loss of Anna, the people we'd killed, and the fact we were being hunted by the Mob while we hunted them. I included Pembroke's escape and his priority status on the target list. I sprinkled a little of my philosophy in along the way. The project now was to kill as many mobsters as humanly possible. All of them. Every last one.

As far as I was concerned, there were no innocent mobsters. If they were members of the crime family, they were guilty of a get rich scheme where kids were being used as sex slaves. I was aware there were mobsters that looked down their noses at the human trafficking racket. They should have put a stop to it, but they accepted it. They were likewise guilty.

"We could have used you last night, mate," Bludd said. "We had a god-awful shootout."

"At the farm—I was there," Kuhl said.

"If you were there, why didn't you come forward," I asked.

"One of you cowboys might have shot me," Kuhl said jokingly, "besides; I left my calling card for you to find."

Bludd piped up, "What calling card was that?"

"You found dead guys that you didn't shoot, didn't you?"

His question was rhetorical, or at least I assumed it was. "You killed a couple thugs and set the cars on fire?" I asked.

"No, I didn't set the cars on fire," Kuhl said with a deadpan look. "I rocked their world!" As Kuhl recalled the event, he became noticeably excited. "I detonated plastic explosives. The same type as y'all use," he said.

Bludd and I shrugged as if we didn't know what he was talking about. I didn't know what Bludd's background in explosives was, but I'd never used plastics.

"Well, I have plenty more where that came from. I've found it to be handy when dealing with the Mob. There's a large market overseas for plastics. I have Semtex with me, it's a commercial grade explosive used in the construction trade for demolition. It's used all over Europe, very stable, and an easy product to work with."

I was interrogating our newest volunteer; why not, I felt uneasy. More so now that I had found out Max, and Anna suspected a mole inside, and hadn't told me. I felt Max didn't trust me; usually it was the other way around. Now, I had a hard time trusting anyone else. It felt strange to have had the shoe on the other foot. "How did you know where we were last night?" I asked.

"You'd given Maximillian your coordinates for the powwow. I'd called to let him know I'd arrived in Buffalo, and he gave me the info. It wasn't rocket science. I essentially followed the same route you had taken to the turnoff, turned my lights off and crept down the road until I saw a couple cars parked together. I pulled off the road into the tree line…"

"Wait, wait, wait," I interrupted Kuhl, "You pulled off the road into the woods, how could you have done that, there must have been a foot of snow out there?" That part of the story sounded too farfetched for me to believe.

"I have a four-wheel drive van, and the snow was more like six to eight inches," Kuhl responded matter-of-factly then picked up where he'd left off. "I used a parabolic sound amplifier, probably similar to the ones you have; only mine is military grade." Kuhl stopped short of finishing his statement. For a moment, he looked back and forth between Bludd and me before he asked, "You don't have a listening device, do you?"

"I've never found much need for one," Bludd said.

"I have a smaller version, an acoustic listening device, used for hearing through walls, but nothing for long range listening." I said.

Kuhl, again jokingly said, "Y'all sure are a bunch of underprivileged killers," but it wasn't that much of a joke. Maybe we were. I had become impressed. Kuhl had skills and capabilities that would expand the Palatini abilities to bring death and destruction on a wider scale. Kuhl continued, "I listened to the group of men talk when they were by the two cars at the edge of the field. It was hard to dial in on them; one of the car's radios was playing, which created interference with the clarity. The group split up and headed down the road to the house. One guy stayed with the cars."

"We saw him," Bludd said, "or what was left of him."

"I'm never sure how a set up like this will turn out. I grabbed my gear, and brushed it until I was close enough to plant some insurance in the wheel wells of the two sedans. Between the music and one guy's attention directed at the house, it was a cinch to plant the charges. If I had to light'em up, I could; otherwise, I'd shoot them one by one."

"How did you know they were bad guys?" I asked.

"I don't know how you wouldn't know. There was no way they could have been mistaken for cops. I could hear them talk, I could see their mannerisms, and how they handled their weapons. They were low-life, and up to no good."

"Then you blew up their cars," Bludd asked.

"No, I came up to see how y'all were doing first. The larger group of guys had moved behind the house. They left one guy at the front corner. I shot him, but he managed to get around back of the house. I stayed hidden behind a fancy sports car for a couple minutes then moved around to the barn behind the house. All hell broke loose; I couldn't make heads or tails out of the mess they had going on. One guy came out of the house in a panic. He left in the sports car."

"That would have been Pembroke," I said.

"The guy I shot was yelling. The group sent him to the cars. It struck me funny, but the guy in the sports car wouldn't give the injured guy a ride. He had a bad limp, and had to stop every couple steps to rest. He wouldn't have lasted long; he was leaking too much blood. The group entered the back door. One guy went around the corner of the house. He's the guy that broke the window and tossed the flash-bang in. He started for the front of the house. I shot him a couple times and dropped him. When the gun battle ended inside the house, I came up to the broken window, and heard y'all talking. I decided to go get the wounded guy. He'd almost reached the cars when I ran up on him. He might have thought I was one of his crew, or he didn't care anymore; he didn't sound an alarm. The guy at the car must have seen my Uzi's muzzle flash. He cranked the engine, and I detonated the charges."

"Wow," Bludd said, "Too bad you didn't get Pembroke, he had the sports car."

"He was the damned double-crossing lawyer Max had as a source." I said.

Kuhl was himself a contrast. He had a warm smile and icy-blue slit-like eyes. His appearance was one of evil concealed beneath a thin veneer of human flesh. I liked him more by the minute. Kuhl said, "Are you familiar with vehicle tracking systems?"

Bludd beat him to the punch line, "I don't have one of those either."

"Are you talking about a Lojack?" I asked. I also didn't have one.

Kuhl nodded and said, "I put a GPS tracker unit under the BMW's front bumper."

Bludd asked, "When did you do that, mate?"

"Remember me telling y'all I stayed by the cars for a few minutes. Now y'all know why. These tracking units have become common with fleet services. I planted a unit made in Europe. The newest version manufactured this year, and it has had very good results in the New York region. We should be able to locate your man without much difficulty. I'll set up my laptop and start monitoring for the car's activity. We'll be able to get a fix on places he goes before we take him. We'll get the best bang for the buck that way." Kuhl's emotions were once again on the rise. I surmised it had something to do with the bang he referred to, and his hidden cache of pyrotechnics. I figured I'd let him have his fun, and enjoy the work. Will Rogers once said, "If you find the right job you'll never have to work a day in your life." Kuhl had found such a job.

"I've got a Quonset hut, with a little heated office that would work well for you." I said.

"Sounds good. I'll stay there with the equipment, if that's okay?" Kuhl asked.

"That works; Bludd and I will be mobile. We're moving out of here today. We don't know if it's safe anymore. We'll check in daily. Let's get you moved in over at the hut." I said.

Over the course of the next couple hours, we loaded our gear and moved Kuhl into the hut. Bludd drove his Tahoe over to the hut, and I parked the Avenger out of the way. Pembroke had seen my car. It would be risky to drive. Kuhl called Max to provide an update while Bludd and I found a motel to work from. Bludd suggested we camp out at Musolino's in Toronto or the Double Decker in South Rochester. Musolino's was not a good choice. That was Pembroke's territory. We didn't want an accidental encounter to foul things up. We'd be better off to concentrate our efforts on the United States side of the border.

A block from the Double Decker lounge was a cluster of inexpensive motels. Big neon signs lit up the skies, each with a different name, but other than the color scheme, they looked about the same, and the price for a room was cheap and competitive. We had a wide choice of rooms, so we selected a second floor end unit which overlooked a portion of the Double Decker parking lot, ideal for our purposes.

Carl Mostarda was dead, but organized crime was big business, and the cash flow didn't stop because of a small police raid, or a capo getting killed. Rizzi would continue his errand boy duties of moving money through Mostarda's top lieutenant, Lucan "Spooky Luke" Russo. The Machine wouldn't miss a beat when it came to the money.

The Mob had to be aware that assassins were hot on their trail to kill them. Pembroke knew, they all knew, but they still didn't know why. I wanted to keep them in the dark. It was enough that they knew they were hunted prey. In fact, I liked it that way. Max had a different take on the situation. He believed we should send a message to Russo, and let him know the mortality rate for his crew would continue to climb unless they got out of the illegal immigration rackets. I only had one mandate, run or die. I hoped they didn't run. They might lay low for a while, but they felt superior—they wouldn't run.

Mob business was about dominance, and the crime family dominated through violence. It was the only language they spoke. If they cowered down to threats of violence, they might as well have packed their bags and moved out—they would do neither. To get the upper hand, and squash their sex slave business, we had to take their control away. That meant we had to over-power their hierarchy; and the only way they understood was with violence.

Mostarda was the first real step. The soldiers and associates I killed had knocked a few holes in the Mob's muscle, but they were replaced overnight. The streets had an endless supply of wannabe mobsters. I thought we ought to send a message to the Bosses, in the language of vendetta and spoken in blood—their native tongue.

Two days passed. Two long days that I'd listened to tea pots whistle and ate fast food until I was blue in the face. I needed to kill. According to Kuhl, Pembroke's car was at his personal residence. The police and news agencies had discovered the farmhouse crime scene and were exploiting the story for all they could get out of it. Dino Bianchi, the boy gangster, was in custody, in a hospital, in serious condition, and the only survivor. The gangland shootout had been attributed to organized crime. I assumed they made the determina-tion from the players they found at the scene. It was cut and dried in the eyes of the police agencies because they didn't know any different, not yet. Big crime scenes take time to process. I hoped it kept them busy for a long time.

I left Bludd at the front room window overlooking the lounge while I made a road trip to the shipyards. There was no reason to believe the drop had been compromised. I pulled into my previous spot between the old freight vans and waited. The day wore on, and I was antsy to check out Musolino's. Maybe Joyce was there. It would be sort of nice to visit with her again. Before I pulled out on the road, though, Bludd called. "Mate, I think you might want to head this way. Cars are lining up alongside the lounge; it looks like a meeting. They have guards on the vehicles."

"I'll head that way."

I cruised through the lounge parking lot and scoped out the vehicles. There appeared to be a security detachment keeping a watch on the area. Bludd was right; it must be a big wig meeting.

I called Bludd, "Come on down, let's get a beer."

Bludd and I walked to the Double Decker lounge. We chose a corner table near the rear of the main floor. That allowed our backs to be against the wall. Once the gunfighter syndrome took over, it was impossible for me to expose my back in a public place again. We had a good view over the entrance and bar, but we couldn't see up the stairs. Two thugs had positioned themselves at the bottom of the staircase. Traffic flow upstairs was by invitation only. A couple bar patrons wanted to shoot pool upstairs, but the thugs convinced them in no uncertain terms, they were not invited.

The bartender was new to us, which was a relief. The last guy had the customer service skills of a turnip. The waitress was polite and fetched us our libations. We were on our second round when Candy entered the lounge with her flawless, fluid stride. She didn't miss a beat as she crossed the dance floor. Her hips rolled pleasingly from side to side. Heads turned, and men smiled. She stood near the curved end of the bar. She glanced sideways over her raised shoulder which highlighted her curves for all to see. She tilted her hip to one side as she leaned slightly forward under the bar lights; her platinum blonde hair shimmered from the neon accent. Candy was dressed to kill. Her one-piece, form-fitting, black mini dress drew attention; her long, lean tanned legs snuggly fitting into her black knee high leather boots.

She stopped and talked to a couple of guys along the way but clearly had our table as her destination.

"How you fellas doing tonight?"

Bludd was quick to answer, "Marvelously, sweetheart, and you're looking fine as well."

"Do you remember us from the other night?" I asked.

"I do," She touched the top of Bludd's forearm in a stroking manner, "Seymour, right?" Bludd smiled but kept his teeth to himself. Candy looked toward me, "I'm sorry," she said, "I don't remember your name."

Bludd piped up, "That's Walter."

"Yes, that's right, Walter." She gave me a visual once over and asked. "So, what are you boys up to tonight?"

"It looked as if the bar was rocking, lots of cars outside, so we thought we'd stop in and check it out. Everyone must be upstairs. It must be a private party or something because I don't think those guys there are letting anyone upstairs." I gestured in the direction of the men at the foot of the stairs.

"Leave it alone," Candy said as she took control of my gesturing hand and pulled it down to the table. She turned her attention to Bludd, "I feel like partying tonight," her voice changed to a sultry tone as she spoke. Bludd bought her a glass of wine.

Bludd and I were stuck entertaining our table guest. We were there to see who came down from the second floor, and weren't leaving until they did. Candy ran her hand up and down the stem of her wine glass in a cylindrical fashion. When she wasn't fondling the glass, which wasn't often, she talked about the success of her webcam business. I excused myself for the men's room and left Bludd and Candy alone. I needed a break. She had a classy look, but she was damaged goods. She came off like a two-bit hooker. I didn't care for being judgmental, it wasn't my style. In general, I believed to each his own. However, if I found out these grease balls poisoned her mind and forced her into the sex business, I'd make sure they paid. When I came back to the table, Candy excused herself and slipped over to another table.

Bludd whispered, "Candy told me she was cheap tonight."

"I'll bet she's cheap every night."

"Two-hundred dollars mate, two-zero-zero."

I was wrong about her; she was not a cheap two-bit whore, she carried a hefty price tag on her collar. She must have been the cream of Mostarda's crop and trusted.

"C'mon, I'll buy you another brew. By the way, what did you tell her?"

"None of your business, mate."

Maybe it wasn't, but I couldn't pass up goading him a little with it, "I just wanted to know if you needed a loan?"

We had knocked off another beer before people started meandering down from the second level. The meeting was over. Thugs at the bottom of the stairs whisked a portly old man away as if they were secret service. They slipped behind the bar and out through a door. Where it led to, we didn't know. A few minutes later one of the thugs escorted Candy through the same door. Maybe her business was picking up.

A couple mobsters came down and mixed with the few people still at the bar. We got eyeballed pretty hard, but they shrugged us off as a couple nobodies. I didn't recognize most of the thugs only one or two looked familiar. While I watched the Machine mingle, I saw Frank Rizzi pull up a stool at the end of the bar. I nudged my partner and let him know it was Rizzi. We finished our drinks and checked out. I kept a watch from the edge of the parking lot while Bludd trotted over to the motel for his Tahoe. Without knowing how much time he'd have before Rizzi left the club, he quickly gathered up as much of our gear as he could handle, tossed it in the Tahoe, and swung by to pick me up.

We sat for the better part of an hour behind the lounge before Rizzi came out and climbed behind the wheel of a red Audi. That made news. As far as the Intel went on Rizzi, he was known never to travel alone. Evidently, that was not the case. He exited the lot; Bludd and I were on his heels. We hit Highway 390, ran north until we came up on the Latona Road exit, and followed him another block where he turned off to the right into a private driveway. At the end of the driveway sat a large two story home. We decided to catch a view from a distance and see what happened.

Early the next morning, cars started to arrive. We counted the vehicles, jotted down license numbers and descriptions of the cars. It was routine until the fifth car showed up around eleven. This visitor stayed longer than the others, and signaled a change in behavior. The older model white Ford four-door sedan we had waited on to leave finally drove past us; only now the car carried a passenger. I assumed it was Rizzi and had a hunch the drop was in play.

We tailed the sedan and followed it to a diner, where the driver and Rizzi exited the car and had lunch. We stayed in the Tahoe. Mobsters didn't hide. They were exposed to conduct their business. We could have killed them any day of the week and wherever we wanted to hit'em. But for the risk we faced, we wanted maximum carnage and to take the drop. There was always that chance Carmine Bruno would show for the wad of dough these gangsters carried.

It was one-forty-five before Rizzi was back on the road. I felt good about the tail; we were heading in the direction of the shipyard. The white Ford sedan pulled up next to the cargo office gate while we tucked the Tahoe back between the cargo vans. As before, Rizzi stayed in the vehicle while his driver went into the office. Soon, an office goon appeared, walked to the sedan, and climbed in behind the driver's wheel, but they weren't going anywhere.

"Get ready," I said. "If Bruno shows up it'll be a perfect day." I couldn't tell from the set up what their plans were for the drop pick up, but it didn't matter. I had a plan. I'd rob the Mob and turn out the lights on the cargo office Machine. Bludd prepped my Remington 870 for close quarter action, and I had strapped my .40-caliber on after we'd left the lounge. Time ticked away slowly as we waited.

Ten long minutes passed. The office goon opened the driver's door, got out, and headed for the office carrying a canvas type bag with handles. We rolled out slowly. Bludd pulled the Tahoe in and blocked the Ford from backing out, although there was no one in the driver's seat. I had bailed out before Bludd brought the vehicle to a stop. I started toward the office. Bludd jumped out with the shotgun in hand, stepped up to the Ford driver's side window and blasted Rizzi once.

I heard the shotgun slide jack another round into the chamber, but Bludd didn't take another shot. One Double-aught round was sufficient. The driver, a man I didn't know, had cleared the office steps on his way back to his car when Bludd had opened up on Rizzi. The driver was slow to react to what unfolded in front of him. He reached under his jacket, but if he had a weapon, I never saw it. I peppered him, center of mass, with three shots in rapid succession with my Glock. His bloody bullet-ridden body plunged face down on the walkway as I quickly made my way to the cargo office door.

I stood behind the cinder block wall, and pushed the office door open slowly to reveal the foyer with no one in sight. There wasn't a chance they hadn't heard the gunfire, and little chance they weren't on a cell phone calling for reinforcements or arming themselves with weaponry they had stashed at the place. Bludd went to the rear corner and kept an eye on the back door.

I hollered, "Throw the money out and I'll let you live," but no one listened. Maybe it was because they thought they'd get the best of me. I didn't know, and I'd likely never know. Their response told me everything I needed to comprehend. They unloaded their weapons aimed in my direction.

The office foyer had an eight-foot long clerk counter on the back wall to the left side in the room. There was a see-through docking station for a laptop that offered zero cover and concealment. To the right was an open area waiting room with high-back armchairs, coffee pot and a magazine rack. A four-drawer metal filing cabinet stood next to the entrance of a short hallway off the back of the foyer. There was a coffee mug and laptop on one desk, and a plastic water bottle on the clerk's counter.

The office wasn't the ideal place for a gunfight. I hadn't thought this part through. If I hid behind the counter, which was the best cover and concealment, I wouldn't be able to dislodge these cockroaches from the back office. They had to come out. If they did bum rush me, they'd expect to find me hidden behind the clerks counter. There would be no element of surprise.

I moved up to the left side of the hallway entrance near the counter. I was about fifteen feet from the doorway in the hall where the goons were held up. I fired off a rapid succession of rounds, they returned fire. These guys had the advantage; they knew the lay-out of their office. I had to make it into a disadvantage.

From the shots I'd fired, they would be able to tell I was on their right side if they entered the office from the hall. I fired two suppression rounds then quickly moved to the other side of the office, where I'd use the cover of the filing cabinet. My plan was to bring them to me.

Silently I ejected the magazine from my Glock and stripped the remaining two rounds out, then slipped it empty into my front pants pocket. I reloaded my weapon with another fifteen-rounds of opportunity. Ready to continue the action, I reached over the file cabinet, let two quick rounds fly toward the end of the hallway. They returned fire. I pulled the empty magazine from my pocket and dropped it on the tile floor. A tinny-twang echoed in the absence of gunfire. To further get their attention, I followed up with a couple cuss words. Maybe they thought I was in the middle of reloading when the magazine hit the floor. I'll never know. Whatever they thought they acted on it and sealed their fate. Both thugs ran down the short hallway and into the office with weapons blazing. They turned toward the counter where they expected me to be hiding. It was a truly brave and bold move on their part. It was also very stupid. They were dead wrong. From behind the metal filing cabinet I shot them in the back. Some might consider my ambush to be a cowardly act. I'm an assassin. I was there to kill mobsters. Anyway I could.

I crept down the hall and listened for noise. I had cleared the bathroom and back office before I went to find the money. I didn't know when the Mob planned to pick up the drop at the cargo office, but my wait time was limited. With cell phone capabilities, the pickup could be called off, or an army of mobsters might be on their way. I had no qualms with more notches added to my .40-caliber, but it wasn't a smart move to wait.

I grabbed the canvas bag full of loot and headed out the front door. I called to Bludd, and we jumped in the Tahoe and headed to our motel room.

"This was a major slap in the face" I said.

Bludd smiled a big toothy grin.

Chapter 14

"The criminal justice system is a misnomer. It should be called the victim justice system, maybe then they'd have their priorities right"
—Walter

We arrived at the hut where Kuhl had set up operations. He had a few items of interest spread out in the tiny office space, but when I asked, he said, "We'll get to them shortly." Bludd and I were excited to fill Kuhl in on what transpired at the cargo office.

"We killed Rizzi and took the Drop," Bludd said, still sporting the wide toothy grin. I noticed there wasn't much that didn't make him smile.

"Cool." Kuhl said.

I chimed in, "Besides Rizzi, you can up the body count by three more."

"Wow, you guys did have a good day," said Kuhl.

We started the count on the canvas bag, and it turned out better that we had imagined.

"Eighty-grand, give or take a few thousand," Bludd said.

"Hey, that's great news," I told Bludd. "It won't cripple them for long, but it'll stir up a hornet's nest. We'll have to take it further." No one disagreed. The problem, as I saw it, was police pulled off raids, confiscated their property and drug money, but then they'd go soft on them. They should have brought the hammer down over and over, year after year—but they didn't. The cops constantly chased their own tails. It was as if they had to balance their attacks between the different gangland elements to be fair. Rival gangs did likewise; they'd pull off some caper, take some territory, then laid back and tried to work their profits. The Mob would retaliate, tit for tat. The Palatini strategy had no such equivalent measures. With the Mob it was always about the money. We needed to hit the Machine, as fast and often as possible.

"We need to hurt them in the pocket book," I said, "where they are going to feel it." No one thought differently.

"I'm amazed at how much y'all are able to accomplish without using technology from this century," Kuhl said.

"Funny," I said. "Not everyone is trained in black ops or has these electronic toys to help them. Some of us operate with our guts and a sense of right and wrong." I paused briefly, "So, you'll just have to be amazed at our success."

"Y'all do good. I give you credit for that. Maybe I can show you a couple pieces of equipment that y'all can find a use for in the future," Kuhl said.

"That works for me," I said. "What about Pembroke?"

"His car has been parked at his residence. That doesn't mean he hasn't gone any place. Only his car hasn't. I called his office; he's not expected at work this week. Let's assume he's put the word out about the farmhouse incident to his Mob family, but he's not using his car. He might think it's too risky to drive it around. I wouldn't put it past Pembroke to use his influence to misdirect the police away from De Luca. They were his boys and the police likely know who's affiliated with whom." Kuhl said.

"When you think about it, Pembroke had his hands in a lot of the mess. He's made the cops ineffective. I think that little raid I saw the other day was staged. It meant nothing. It might have been to protect a few of these mobsters. Pembroke didn't know who or where we were. He only knew through Max we were here," I said.

"It's a good bet, mate, if it hadn't been for the likes of Pembroke, the Machine would have been eaten' alive by other gangs. They're like bleeding piranha in the underworld," Bludd said.

"I don't have anything against cops," I said, "but I do with the whole idea of justice. The criminal justice system is a misnomer. It should be called the victim justice system, maybe then they'd have their priorities right." To me, the criminal justice system didn't represent justice at all. The system was self-evident and apparent; the laws were about criminals' rights, not victim's rights.

I knew I was preaching to the choir. The whole legal system was too impersonal; victims were nothing more than nameless statistics on a piece of paper that ended up logged into a computer. The law was itself too imperfect; the concept of punishment was non-existent, and had been replaced by reform. It was now entrenched as a bureaucratic fallacy and propagated by every two-bit

Harry that came along with a psychobabble degree. They knew damn good-and-well there were types of criminal behavior that could not be reformed or ever trusted in society again, but that's where the money was. These political pimps were as much about greed as was the Mob. The system needed an overhaul of common sense to combat the growing onslaught of liberal mind-sets. One-by-one, citizens learned the hard way. Never trust the lawmakers and liberal judges to lead the fight for justice. They were as much of the problem as they were the solution. It was up to ordinary citizens, like Walter, to provide the people's response, the proper response; one and the same.

"Check this out." Kuhl said. He laid on the table several handheld radios with wireless headsets. "When you work with others, it's nice to be able to coordinate a strike." Then he held up two vests and said, "These are ballistic vests. Some people call them concealable body armour. They can be handy in a shootout. Walter you'd take an extra-large, Bludd you'd need two of the biggest ones I have." Kuhl threw one to each of us and said, "Try 'em on." I'd fit into the one he pitched to me. Bludd shimmied to get into his triple-extra-large vest. Kuhl picked up a weapon and said, "Have you seen one of these before?"

"Yeah, I carried one for a while, I said. "It's an M79 Grenade Launcher."

"That's right. It's lightweight, extremely quiet, and easy to deploy the weapon for when you want the value of an explosive round at a distance of more than thirty-meters," Kuhl said while he dug through a green military ammo canister with his right hand and retrieved a couple grenade rounds. He held up a pair of 40mm HE (High Explosive) rounds which I'd had some experience with in the military. "It's yours," Kuhl said, "I picked up a case of them. They were leftovers from 'Nam when they replaced them with the M203."

"Modernizing is a good thing," Bludd said as he continued to struggle with the fit of his body armour.

"What about Pembroke?" I asked.

"We have communications, and I can run the vehicle tracking from my van. We should relocate to the Canadian side," Kuhl said.

"Let's go for a visual op," I said. "Kuhl, your van won't cut it. Those four short antennas make it look like a spy rig." Pembroke had seen my Avenger at the farm; it would be a dead give-away if we were seen in it. We had one viable option left short of another rental. "Bludd," I called out. "It'll have to be your rattle-trap."

We loaded up the Tahoe and were ready to roll-out before dawn the next morning. That night we made pallets on the office floor, relaxed, and mulled over people, names, and places we'd hoped and intended to encounter. As we chattered back and forth, I got nostalgic with memories of my Thailand trip. Anna and I had lain on the beach and drank spiked fruit drinks with little umbrellas in them. We flew from there to Italy and walked the Romanesque streets of Bellagio and dined in the richest atmosphere imaginable. The life of an assassin; it seemed promising, but it was nothing like that. When the window dressing had been peeled away, what was left wasn't exotic or glamorous at all. The life was in reality a cold, isolated existence that required an assassin to wallow in the filth of humanity to extract a necessary vengeance. Tomorrow would be another day, a new dawn, and nothing to look forward to, except death. Mine or theirs; it was no matter.

It was sunny and cold at seven in the morning. We cranked the Tahoe. It moaned and groaned as it came alive. Kuhl had plugged in his block heater on his van. When he started it, it responded more lively. I said good-bye to the Avenger; as much as I hated to leave it, it had to sit this round out.

Kuhl had gotten the jump on us. By seven-fifteen, he was en route to Vaughan in North Toronto. Pembroke's Beemer had been parked at a residence just off Keele Street. Bludd and I planned to take his Tahoe and check out Musolino's. Bludd favoured the plan the way I'd outlined it. I would monitor the outside area and keep a watch over the parking lot while Bludd grabbed some grub inside.

Capo De Luca had a Davenport Road address in Corso Italia near Musolino's. The other big cheese in the area were Marco Camerota, the would-be capo of Toronto's east end, he lived on East Danforth. Pembroke's car hadn't gone to either of those residences. Where he had gone and what he had done, remained a mystery. What I did know was he was in the same boat I was in. His car was easily recognized by us. It wasn't safe for him to drive it around. He probably had the same thought.

The phone rang. "The Beemer's on the move," Kuhl said, "it's heading south into Toronto. Let's get eyes on."

Bludd was in the diner, when I called. I'd never been one to talk much on a phone, and Bludd knew that, so his attention was immediately aroused.

"Rock and roll time," I said.

A minute later, Bludd leapt into the Tahoe with his raviolis in a to-go box and said. "What are you waiting for, mate?"

I brought my partner up to speed as I drove. He nodded, as I talked, and gobbled down his leftovers. I tossed him the phone and said, "Make use of it."

"I asked about your Joyce."

"She's not mine. She's a good gal, and she needs a break in life to show the world she has the grit to make it."

"Well, she's gone already."

"Good," I said as I glanced at Bludd. A lopsided smile drifted across his face.

"I'm glad she's made it out of Musolino's," I said in a sharp tone as if I'd planned to argue the point.

Bludd's smile widened and appeared permanently planted on his face, like a rat that got away from a trap with the cheese. "I'm sure you are, mate." The phone interrupted our discourse about Joyce. Bludd gave a couple of uh-huh's and a nod the caller had not been able to see. "Got it," Bludd said and disconnected the call. We continued north while I repeatedly glanced at my partner, who wasn't very forthcoming. We had the tool for communication; we needed to learn to use them more efficiently.

"Well." I waited for a response.

"The Beemer stopped at a grid coordinate on Kingston Road, in Pickering. Take Saint Clair Avenue East, get on Highway 401, and take the Brock Road exit. Kuhl will be there before us. He'll give us a heads up when we get to the area."

It was six in the evening and traffic was snarled at its worst with commuters. I hated traffic at this time of the day; unless I'd planned to knock someone off, then traffic was good. I could stay hidden until I struck and then blend back into traffic and disappear from sight. We had more than twenty miles to travel to get to Pickering. Another hour dragged by as we jockeyed our way to our rendezvous. As we drew near, this time Bludd placed the call and turned on the speaker, so I could get the goods first hand, and not filter through him.

"It's a swank nightclub," Kuhl said. "The name on the place is Reservations. There are a few street-side stores with a long continuous parking area across from the nightclub. I'm in front of Wyman Hardware."

"We'll be there soon." I said.

We spotted the van and pulled in next to it. Kuhl came up to the driver's window and said, "I'll go in and check out the scene. Don't mess with the Beemer; I've rigged it to blow. It's parked on the side of the nightclub."

We ran through a description of Pembroke with Kuhl. We included the tidbit that he might show signs of being recently pulverized, and the possibility he might cover it up. Kuhl made his way across the street while Bludd and I hunkered down—for how long was anybody's guess. Fifteen minutes later we got a call.

"He's here and has a couple ladies at his table. I think it's noticeable he's taken a beating. It's dark in the club, and this chump has on sunglasses and a ball cap," Kuhl said. "He ain't foolin' anybody with that get-up."

"Okay, I want him alive." I said. It was in all our best interests not to get trigger happy, especially with the plastic explosives. I wanted this guy to talk, and if he wouldn't, I'd make him pay for his silence. Extra.

Kuhl called a couple more times to keep us in the loop. It was appreciated. I kept telling Bludd, "See, that's the way communications work." But he ignored me. Kuhl related his observations. Pembroke had sucked down eight stiff drinks over the past couple hours, and he was hammered, according to Kuhl. He'd walked with a drunken stagger to the restroom the last couple times he was up. In the past thirty minutes, he had two guys join him at his table. They had run the ladies off. There were some eye shots around the room and some quiet, whispering type conversation amongst them.

I'd known criminals like Pembroke. I didn't know them long, but I did know them well. I might have known them longer, but because I knew them well—they were dead. Criminal behavior didn't bother Pembroke in the least. Even when it was his own. He could go to his home, mingle with family, go out to a movie, and continue his social life like nothing vile had ever happened in his world. Yet, he aided and abetted every racket the Mob ran and every crime the Mob committed. Whether it was murder or human trafficking of children, he supported it by his actions. I'd planned to interrupt his routine criminal life.

Pembroke was a coward like all other mobsters. Sure, I knew some of them were tough physically, but that didn't mean they weren't cowards. The brave were the kids that were prisoners in the Mob's makeshift brothels. Children were subjected to a life that was no choice of their own. Their only apparent means of escape was death, but they refused. Instilled in them through nature was the instinct to survive. And it made them brave. It was up to me and others like me, to free them. Since politicians and lawyers protected the Mob's rights to enslave people in human trafficking, I took the right to kill every last one of them. I held each and every member of the crime family responsible, the whole cowardly bunch.

As I thought about my second meeting with Pembroke, Bludd asked, "Why didn't he run?"

"He knows."

Bludd asked, "He knows what, mate?"

"He sees us as criminal just as he is, and he's right. We won't call 9-1-1. So—why not surround yourself with muscle and hope for the best outcome." Bludd nodded in silence.

It was another call and another update. "They're coming out. Pembroke is with them, and the ladies too," Kuhl said. They emerged and stood in a group for a few minutes in front of the club. They then moved in separate directions. One female walked with Pembroke to his Beemer. I was concerned, if he got behind the wheel, he might kill himself—and that was too cheap. His female companion loaded him into the passenger's seat and then climbed in behind the Beemer's steering wheel.

She wasn't a bad looking gal, but she wasn't a head-turner either. She had a remarkably pretty build for being hidden inside an oversized dark-grey, hooded, full length coat. She stood around five-foot five without her two-inch heels and wore dark slacks. She looked business like, kind of classy, with her coal-black hair pulled back in a ponytail. She sat behind the wheel and warmed the car before she slipped it into reverse, backed out and headed south.

Bludd and I trailed the Beemer while Kuhl held a good distance back. His van might be well equipped, but it was easily spotted. We travelled for twenty minutes south on Highway 401, hung a left and were back on Kingston Road. The Beemer turned into a motel parking lot and pulled into space twenty-nine. It was a sure bet she'd been there before. The space corresponded with the same number on a ground floor door, which they entered. Pembroke's escort was tucked neatly under one of his wings as she assisted him over the threshold. We cruised through the lot and parked in the area marked over-flow. Kuhl parked by the main road.

The motel lobby and office area was a two-story structure with two single level wings that jetted out in opposite directions. Twenty-nine was an end unit on the west side. It was likely the escort's place of business. I might have been mistaken. She might have been his girlfriend, a friend, a Good Samaritan, or maybe plain neighbourly. However, my gut instinct was she was a hooker.

Kuhl joined up with us on the west end of the parking area. We prepped to enter by force. At door twenty-nine, I took centre stage, Kuhl and Bludd on either side. Each of us with our weapons hidden under our jackets, moderators and silencers attached, and bug-out bags in hand. The door was not equipment with a spy-hole-security viewer. Not uncommon in 1940s construction.

At midnight, I rang the doorbell. Two more short rings and I heard the sound of the metal safety chain being removed. We pulled ski masks over our faces. The door opened a sliver, and a woman's voice said, "Yes?" We breached the opening.

My hand went over the woman's mouth as I spun her behind the entry door and against the wall. "Sssssshhh." I whispered in her ear while my partners bum rushed the target. I slid the door shut with my left foot as I pressed the woman against the wall. She'd had only a sheet wrapped around when she answered the door. In the scuffle, it had dropped to the floor. With my hand over her mouth and tightly squeezing her body against the wall, her eyes filled with tears as fear gripped her.

Bludd and Kuhl were faced with a different problem. Pembroke was passed-out. I saw the pie-eyed expression of the woman when our target was drug from the bed without as much as a whisper. Pembroke was yanked up by his hair and seated on a wood-framed desk chair; Kuhl used electrical zip ties to secure his ankles, wrists and arms, just above the elbows, to the chair frame. Bludd used less than a half roll of Duct Tape this time. He made me proud.

Bludd scoured the room for anything we preferred not to be there, like covert cameras. Kuhl reached into his bag-of-tricks, pulled out one of his gadgets that looked like a voltmeter that he used for counter surveillance. He swept for bugs around the room; I continued to hold the naked woman. We all had our jobs to do. Some jobs were better than other jobs, but nobody complained, I certainly didn't. We all carried our load.

Kuhl gave the thumbs up and put his bug detector back in his bag. He started to zip the bag closed, snapped his fingers, apparently he'd remembered something he needed to do. We all watched as he reached back into his bag to see what he would come out with next. He looked up at his audience, smiled, and pulled out a can of potted meat.

Although neither Bludd nor I had commented on what Kuhl had done, he responded, "What can I say, I'm hungry." I turned my attention back to the woman, "I want to talk to you. Do you understand?" I asked.

She nodded.

"I can't do that if you're screaming, and I can't do that with a wad of tape around your mouth, okay?"

Again, she acknowledged with a nod. I slowly dropped my hand. I reached down and picked up the sheet for her to cover herself.

"Thank you," she said.

"It's okay. Just stay chilled, okay?"

"Yeah," she responded.

I didn't figure a tough guy approach was necessary to gain her compliance. Not at all.

"I'm not going to hurt you—I'm not here for that."

She adjusted the sheet around her as she said, "I didn't think you had planned to. You could have done it already. A man like you could do anything he wanted to, and I couldn't stop him." She had paused before she added, "Even if I wanted to."

She was intuitive, smart as if she'd had an education from something other than a book. The type of education only a hard life could teach her. She knew how to survive.

"Smart girl," I said. "What's your name?"

"Samantha, but my friends call me Sam."

"Okay friend, have a seat on the bed." She looked for a spot away from the action. She sat with her back against the makeshift headboard that was attached to the wall then adjusted the sheet around her.

"You shouldn't have done that mister. He's a Crown prosecutor. It could spell big trouble for you." What a nice gal. She was looking out for me already, and we'd only been friends for a couple minutes.

"I'm going to take my chances," I said.

Bludd used a little cold water, and a couple slaps to make sure Pembroke was coherent while Kuhl dug the potted meat out of the can with a plastic Spork. I positioned myself in front of Pembroke. I wanted to make sure he could see and recognize me. "You don't look happy to see me, counsellor." It was rhetorical. "You didn't want to talk the last time we met. Well, you're about to have a change of heart. As an attorney, you're accustomed to asking the questions. That's about to change. Before I leave, you're going to tell me everything I want to know, and then some. You can make it easy on yourself or.... Well, you know the rest"

Kuhl finished his can of cold potted meat and fished around in his bag for something else. "If you've finished with the Alpo, could we to get back to business?" I asked.

"Count me in," Kuhl said, "I've had some experience in this sort of thing when I worked for Uncle Sam."

I watched Samantha as she took it all in. We didn't have much time, but I didn't want Pembroke to know that. What he needed to know was we had the entire week to devote to him. Kuhl evidently spotted a plastic bottle of rubbing alcohol in an open bathroom cabinet. He must have known what it could do. He uncapped the bottle and poured it on Pembroke's head. The alcohol ran down his forehead and cascaded over his eyelids that he had squeezed shut. The muffled screams through Bludd's tape job were barely noticeable; the dance he did while tied in the chair was more memorable.

I engaged Sam in small talk as Kuhl set the pace, but it was impossible to divert our attention from the torturous scene that unfolded in the room. I'm not proud of the measures we'd been forced to undertake to get the job done. If it were up to me, I'd simply double tap behind the ear and let the carcass rot, but in Pembroke's case, he was a way to a means and a means to an end. If he wanted to cooperate, and talk as I'd asked, I'd kill him outright. If not, we could drag it out for a week, and I would have without any remorse.

After Pembroke had bounced around in the chair for a few minutes, Kuhl picked up a small under-counter plastic storage drawer from the bathroom, filled it with water and flushed his eyes then pat dried his face. Sam had collapsed her face into a pillow and tried to hide from the nightmare she was in. She was a victim of circumstance, but it couldn't be helped. This wouldn't scar her any worse than she already had been, by her choices in life. I assured her none of this involved her in any way. When we were done, we'd leave, and she'd never see us again.

Bludd stood behind Pembroke and removed the tape from his mouth. Bludd was ready to slap another piece of tape over his mouth if he started screaming or yelling. "Okay, let's talk," I said, "Who do you work for? And I don't want to hear your jargon of being a prosecutor. You know what I mean?"

I had to give it to Pembroke; he had a way with words. A bad way. The rubbing alcohol hadn't dampened his spirits any or maybe it was the booze talking, but he continued his tough attorney act, "You and your criminal league of friends are those sucker fish at the bottom of a tank. You eat all the crap at the bottom, like a scavenger. I told you before, you need to wise up and realize you're on the wrong side," he said.

He was probably right. The odds were against us. We were few in numbers, and we didn't have the bankroll the Mob had, to get things done. Bludd applied a liberal amount of fresh Duct Tape to Pembroke's mouth. Kuhl unwound the razor sharp metal ribbon from the potted meat key he'd opened his can with and let the peeled strip fall to the floor. I had no way of knowing what Kuhl had in mind, but he was highly trained while in service to our country. There was no way any of us could have fathomed such an interrogation technique. I just wanted answers, but sometimes drastic measures were forced upon us to get the job done. Such was the case of Pembroke. The faster he cooperated the better it was for everyone involved.

Pembroke, however, was not so easily swayed. Kuhl removed a small Spyderco pocket knife from his front pants pocket and with its razor sharp blade, carved a strip of flesh less than a quarter-inch in width on Pembroke's upper arm at the shoulder. The little piece of skin hung out like a hangnail. Bludd held Pembroke in place while Kuhl took the meat can key he'd used to open the potted meat, slipped the slotted end over the piece of skin and twisted the key.

Kuhl continued to twist the key and wrap the skin around the key while Bludd helped control Pembroke's dance. "Mate, where did you learn to do something like this?"

"You don't want to know," Kuhl said, "but it's not my first rodeo."

Thomas Orlando Kuhl, aka, T.O. Kuhl, had a past, and he didn't want to share it. I didn't blame him. It was probably better left in the past. I wasn't a novice when it came to extracting information. None of us were. Some techniques were efficient and gruesome; the two went hand-in-hand. Prolonged pain equalled information. In more modern times, information sought after, focused on painless and bloodless extraction. It was a nice thought, but it had one major drawback. It didn't work. With the facts known, society continued its humane approach to fruitless interrogation. Boring a prisoner to death should be inhumane, as well.

Pain could be overdone, and shock would render torture utterly useless. That wasn't our goal. That's why it was necessary to apply it in small amounts over a period of time; time we didn't have. Otherwise, I would have subjected Pembroke to hours of Tiny Tim's version of "Tiptoe through the Tulips." Humane, but cruel and unusual punishment, that would undoubtedly lead to revealing everything he knew; or insanity, whichever came first.

I wasn't after his confession. I already knew he was a Mob associate. I had bigger questions for Pembroke to answer. A good interviewer like Kuhl could extract everything he asked for, and then some. A moral hazard for the truth. With Kuhl's methods and expertise he would have Pembroke admitting to being the second shooter on the grassy knoll. That was not the goal. People would tell you whatever they thought you wanted to hear, if they thought it would end the torture. I wanted truth. If he wouldn't talk, he would beg for death before we were finished.

Kuhl had hooked the outer layer of the epidermis and rolled it off the dermis where the pain sensors abound. The small strips of skin peeled easily. When Kuhl had finished a couple short strips, Bludd once again removed the tape. Pembroke's actions and attitude still needed adjustment, proven when he spat in Kuhl's face. Lawyers were known to be a nasty and infectious bunch, evidenced by the foulmouthed rant he flew into after he spat.

Bludd covered Pembroke's mouth with another piece of tape, and Kuhl poured a little dab of rubbing alcohol on the fresh wounds of Pembroke's arm. He danced some more. Sam kept her face buried in the pillow, but she could hear everything being said. Bludd pulled Pembroke's head forward, and Kuhl began to strip layers from his upper back. He passed out at one point, which was common enough behavior when an adequate amount of pain had been delivered. Kuhl used smelling salts to bring him back around. As Kuhl continued, I thought to myself, what was my greatest advantage with Pembroke? He was a lawyer, and lawyers were always ready to play let's make a deal. What I had to do was show him how to put the deal I had for him in his win category, and it would be a done deal.

Pembroke looked more and more like a Striped Bass as the better part of two hours took their toll. Sam hadn't lifted her head since we had begun the interrogation. Bludd ripped the tape from Pembroke's mouth, and I asked the questions, again. "What's your business with the Mob?

"They're Family," he said. "Omerta."

"A blood oath," I said, "Well my friend, you will have paid your oath before today is over. How long have you been a made-man?"

"Twelve years."

"Why are we here?"

"Some writer friend of Maximillian's got his nose in our business. He gained a foothold with one of the made-members and wanted to uncover dirt to sell a book. When your boss told me about those two runaway girls, I knew we had to put a lid on things. I clued Bruno in on where they were. I put the word out to Maximillian and family that one of the girls defected back for a fix, but it wasn't true. She was still on the run when she was caught. We needed to make it go away for good before we got pressure from the cops or media. Bruno took Cal's cell phone and sent a text message to the girls to meet him. They didn't know it wasn't him they were meeting. We had to get rid of Joey to make sure we didn't have a rat in the family."

I thought it odd that we would meet like this. The crime family and Palatini were both working our way to the common ground. The mobsters tried to smoke out a rat, and the Palatini tried to ferret out a mole. There was no rat to be had, and I had my mole in hand. "What happened to the writer?"

"Cal?

"Yeah, Cal."

"Bruno killed him."

I didn't have to ask why. I knew why. What I wanted was a confirmation. "Where are the runaway girls?"

"Dead—Bruno took care of them."

"How do you know he killed them?"

"He told me himself. Bruno doesn't need to lie about anything."

"The girls, how did Bruno know their cell phone number?"

"Cal broke and told Bruno he had their number in his phone."

"You said Bruno took care of Joey?"

"That was the idea. Maybe he did, maybe he didn't."

"There was another woman helping the writer, what happened to her?"

"I don't know. Bruno learned about her too late."

Pembroke had avoided eye contact since he started to roll over on the family. He now stared into my eyes and measured me. "Who was she, one of Maximillian's killers?"

I could have ignored the behavior, but for the sake of saving time I thought the best course of action was to cuff him one on the side of his chops and put him back on the right path.

"I ask the questions, I said. "Where's Bruno?"

Pembroke had talked; he knew he was already a dead man. If we didn't kill him, the Mob would. The only thing he could hope to achieve at this point was a swift death to end the game. He opted for the deal.

I had more questions. Questions he couldn't answer. If Bruno had not killed Anna, who did, and what had become of Joey Naccarella? Maybe Bruno didn't tell Pembroke everything, especially if they were concerned with a rat. Pembroke was a lawyer after all. How much could he be trusted?

Pembroke was slow to respond. Kuhl held the potted meat key next to his face, and said, "Answer the question or I'll peel your face."

"He's under De Luca's protection; you'll never get to him. I told De Luca the whole thing with your insignificant little group. Bruno had thought it was about revenge, but we know the truth now. We know it's about business...our business. You are in trouble. De Luca ran with it up to the Commission. They will take action. Maximillian stuck his nose in a place it didn't belong," he paused, "but I will tell you this, you are known, and they will hunt you and kill you. You are out-gunned and out-matched. Maximillian told me all about your little band of killers. Yeah...sure, Maximillian sold you out for nothing."

"If De Luca has Bruno then he's in Toronto?"

Pembroke didn't answer. Kuhl closed in on Pembroke's face with his knife. "Okay, okay…he's in Toronto. You'll find him at the Galaxy Icahn."

I was satisfied that we'd gotten what we were going to get; Pembroke was of no further service to the project alive or for the revenge I was after. Bludd taped his mouth one last time, and I pulled a Muslin sack from my bug-out bag and slipped it over his head. Sam lifted her head. The curtain was on the way down for Pembroke. She didn't want to watch, but she couldn't help being drawn to the final performance. Bludd went into the bathroom and returned with a hair curling iron, tied the cord loosely around Pembroke's neck and slipped one end of the curling iron inside the loop, twisting it into a tourniquet. Bludd cranked it tight and held it. He squeezed down on the cord a minute more than necessary before releasing the tourniquet and cutting the body loose from the chair. I checked his vitals. Pembroke was dead.

It was zero dark-thirty and just before daybreak when I turned my attention to Sam. The car was parked around the corner, and she hadn't seen it, nor would she. Bludd and Kuhl gathered up our belongings and sat them by the entrance door. She had not seen our faces under the masks, any identification she could make was nil.

She wasn't the cream of the crop as far as a witness went; she wouldn't be especially credible. I figured her past was tainted with a rap sheet of miscellaneous petty crimes. I didn't know if her profession were a chosen path, or she was forced into the game. In the end, it didn't matter; I wasn't there to rehabilitate her. She had value and I wanted to exploit it. When the cops arrived on the scene, they'd comb through the crime scene for evidence. Her story would be an integral part of what they collected. Everything she heard Pembroke confess to, she'd tell. Her input would be collaborated at the highest levels of the Crown. If they failed to investigate, there would be a public outcry. Cops would love to catch the killers of a high profile murder, such as in the death of Pembroke. They would glory in the positive news reviews, for a job well-done. A rare event for the media. But the real story would be Pembroke's association with the Mob. The cops would really get their jollies if their investigation turned up more dirt at the Crown attorney's office.

I saw it differently. Any further Mob connection in the political arena, especially at the Crown Attorney's office, would be swept under a rug. They couldn't lose the trust of citizens with more scandals. I was already there. I didn't trust government to do the right thing. Not Canada's. Not ours.

"What are we going to do with her?" Kuhl asked.

"Bind and gag her." I said. Sam was resistive to the idea, but I explained she would only be that way for a few minutes while we made our getaway. Although she objected to the gag, she did favor one aspect of the plan—us gone. I told her I would call the front desk and have an employee do a welfare check on her room. She seemed satisfied. We had her put on clothes before securing her hands and feet. Bludd was about to tape her mouth shut, but Kuhl had seen his tape job earlier and said, "I'll take care of that." He placed one piece of tape gently over her mouth and sat her on the bed.

"Tell the cops everything." I said.

We departed with our bags in hand. Kuhl walked to the Beemer, reached under the front fender of the wheel well and removed his ordinance and the lojack before he took off in his van. Bludd and I went for breakfast. It was more than an hour after we'd left when I made a call to the motel desk for the welfare check in room twenty-nine. There were no sounds of panic in the clerk's voice; my guess was Sam had not yet been discovered. After breakfast, we blended into the heavy morning traffic crossing the border. We'd decided to lay low for a day, get some rest, and meet the following day at the hut. "Let's find a cheap place in Buffalo to crash for a day and tomorrow we'll tackle the Bruno thing," I said.

"When do you intend to call Maximillian with the updates?" Bludd asked.

"It'll wait." The call was not all that important to me. It was Maximillian's trust in Pembroke as an ally that had cost Anna her life. I didn't say it, but Bludd got the message.

Bludd nodded, "Okay mate, you have the lead."

Chapter 15

"I wanted to know how anyone could judge the outcome before the end."
—Walter

On the lower east side of Toronto, the Galaxy Icahn hotel stood as a landmark, or so their advertisement said. I called Kuhl at the hut the next day. He had barely taken the time to rest his eyes before he was back on the mission. His plan was to get inside the hotel and put some monitoring bugs around. Foremost would be near the front counter where many conversations took place. With a little luck his surveillance would locate Bruno.

For some reason, Bludd was antsy to call Maximillian. I wasn't. I didn't see the need. I didn't buy into Pembroke's claim that Max had sold us out. What I saw was an error in judgment, not malicious intent on Maximillian's part. I supposed it might cheer Max up a little to hear the details of Pembroke's interrogation. It certainly made me feel better. I reluctantly made the call.

"Hello," Max said.

"This is Scythian."

"I was hoping to hear from you."

"The hunting guide you suggested turned out to be useless." I found myself guarded more than usual. I didn't like the idea of an unsecure phone line as a means of communication, not with what we'd done. I didn't care if Max knew what had transpired, but the fewer that had access to the information, the better. I spoke as coded as possible that Max could understand. "I fired him."

"Where do we go from here?" Max asked.

"Hunting was good at lower elevations. Shot a nice mess of game birds, but the bigger game has moved further up the mountain. We're going to move to a higher elevation for our next hunt." I would have preferred to have told him that I'd planned to kill all the Abbandanza hierarchy, and shutdown the entire crime syndicate, but I couldn't. Apparently he picked up on the fact I was on an unsecured phone and went along with me.

"When do you think you'll end your vacation and return home?" Max asked. He was fishing for something without bait. I could hear it in his voice. If he was after operational specifics of when and where the next target would be taken out, he was barking up the wrong tree. He didn't have a need to know. As with most plans, if you wanted to keep them secret, you didn't tell anyone. Once the cat was out of the bag, it was hell to get it back in. "Just as soon as we're done," I said.

"We need to talk soon. I have someone I want you to meet. They will help wrap the project up." Right then, I wanted to say, which one of your friends did you want me to meet and kill this time? I'd become distracted by Bludd jumping up and down in excitement as he pointed to the television. "Okay, I said to Max, "I gotta go."

The local news broadcast brought its viewers a breaking news story, but it wasn't news at all. Not to us. Bludd watched to see what, if anything, surfaced about Pembroke. After I had hung up with Max, Bludd laid out the particulars, "The report was pretty sketchy, mate. They didn't give any graphic details—yet."

"What about Sam, did they mention her?"

"Well I suppose they did, mate. The reporter said there was a witness to the brutal murder. She was placed into protective custody. It had to be her," Bludd replied. "What did Maximillian have to say?"

"Not much," I said. "He was fishing for the lowdown on our plans." I grinned and continued, "He said he had someone else for me to meet." I shrugged, "I don't understand Max; I think he's a slow learner, sometimes." Bludd ripped a deep-bellied laugh.

I placed a call to Gladys Mitchell. I wanted to unload the hefty bundle of cash we'd taken from Rizzi. What better place to put it to good use, than with someone who wanted to get kids off the streets. When Gladys answered, I told her I had another donation to deposit. She agreed to meet at the Pearl Street Grill again and shoot for an afternoon rendezvous around three-thirty. I was mindful Kuhl might call and I'd have to forgo the meeting with Gladys.

"Don't take it personally if I'm a no show," I said. "My job might call me out. If so I will reschedule with you." She seemed satisfied with the arrangement.

I was able to make our scheduled meeting at Pearl Street without interruption, although I'd hoped for the call from Kuhl instead. The idea he had Bruno in his crosshairs aroused me. Since I had nothing else on my docket, Gladys and I chatted for a spell. She had something I rarely found in people, a genuine heart. It was refreshing, and a real treat to listen to her talk about her concern for the lost kids of the city. While she spoke, my thoughts took me back to what I'd felt when Walter was conceived in his original state. Gladys had virtue and character and was a positive influence in a negative world. She'd brought a touch of heaven to the process of deliverance. Society didn't recognize the virtue because the concept was too difficult to comprehend. They had been ruled by the philosophy of every dog for himself. My part in the process was a notably darker and more sinister role in the rescue of kids. I looked at it this way; people like Gladys and I were both necessary for the process to work. We made a cycle of life; both positive and negative were comprised in the complete circuit. It was an honor to meet a counterpart in the cycle.

I'd placed the money in a leather and nylon rucksack before I met with Gladys. The last time we'd met, she'd ridden the bus. If it was her only means of transportation, then the rucksack would be easier than a canvas bag to pack. The eighty-grand was a mixed bag, from sawbucks to C-notes, and altogether weighed around twenty pounds. When I told her how much the wad contained, give or take a couple Gs, she got all teary-eyed. I gave her a hug, and said, "I gotta go." She nodded and said, "God Bless you." I was humbled by her prayer for me. God knows I needed help, but I doubted any God would bless what I did.

It was rush hour and traffic was snarled all across the city. After firing up Bludd's Tahoe, I waited until the temperature gauge started to climb before shifting the transmission into drive. I flipped on the radio and listened for traffic reports, by the off chance I might miss a pile up somewhere along the route. It was a survival mechanism I'd learned since I'd been stuck in urban sprawls. Even expecting Kuhl would call momentarily; when the phone rang it took me by surprise. I flipped the phone cover up and fumbled it to my ear, "Yeah."

"Scythian." It was Max. It was a disappointment.

"I don't have time to meet with anyone right now, Max, I'm busy." It was a snappy response, more rude than abrupt. I'm sure I put icing on the cake when I called him Max. More than once, in the past, he'd made clear his disdain for the abbreviated version of his name. I'd also been clear in the very recent past, I didn't care.

"Yes…well, I have someone here who wants to talk with you," he said. "Just a moment, please." I didn't know what part of, "I don't have the time," he didn't catch, but I had higher priorities than a phone call, from Max or any of his buddies.

"Hello Walter." I was floored. Time stood still as I reeled from the confusion that overwhelmed me. I pulled the Tahoe to a stop alongside the road, I felt disconnected from reality. I waited for the voice on the other end of the line, a female voice, to speak again. It had been a simple, "Hello," but it was an unmistakable voice; a voice from the grave. She spoke again, "Walter."

I uttered her name in disbelief, "Anna?"

"Hi, Walter." She waited for my response, but how could I? It wasn't that I was speechless, because I wasn't. But I froze up inside. I didn't know what to say. It didn't make any sense. What is going on? I wondered. Maybe I was speechless. As realization set in, I was flooded with emotion.

"Are you hurt…are you okay?" I whispered.

"Don't worry, I'm fine, but I need to talk with you as soon as we can?"

"Get together," I said. "Where are you?"

"Here," she said, "I've been here. In the best interest of the project, I remained out of the picture until the mole was caught."

I didn't know where here was. Not exactly. If she was here, it was clear, Max was here too. They were both here, wherever here might be. A bad feeling came over me. I had been used and perhaps setup to be used again. Why wasn't I told what they were up too? I had taken control of the project, but Max clearly wanted to shut it down. At least that was what I was led to believe. If I'd gone along with Max and shutdown the project, how would it have caused Pembroke to come out of his rat-hole and show himself for what he was? I had questions, too many of them for a phone call, and the wrong type questions to ask over open airways. A meeting was necessary.

"When and where?"

"Maximillian and I will come to you, what is your location now?"

Tact was not my forte and I needed time to get a handle on what I felt. "Not now, not today," I said. Questions ran rampant through my thoughts as if it was a playground. Anna's being alive wasn't a game changer. We'd set the wheel in motion to eradicate child sex slavery hidden within the crime family's immigration racket. It escalated because of what had happened to Anna and from a determination to extract blood for blood. It wasn't a smart move to interrupt the game while it was in play. We had pressure on the players; it didn't seem smart to back off now. Secondly, it didn't seem smart to let someone know our whereabouts until we understood what had happened.

"I'll call you," I said. "We'll set a time and place then."

"Okay honey, I want you to know how much I care about you," Anna said. "I saw how much you cared for me through your actions. Walter…it's been hard for me too."

We left it there, for now. It was a dream come true or should have been. I was thankful Anna was alive and relieved to hear she hadn't been hurt. But my emotions were all over the place. It was a mixed bag which made it difficult to focus my attention on Bruno. I didn't like the confusion I felt. It fostered a greater distrust for the Palatini ways. It was a further reason to distance myself from the organization and embrace individual vigilantism.

It was ten minutes before seven when I made it back to the motel room on Buffalo's north side. I'd had time to mull over what I would say to the team concerning Anna and the project as a whole. I felt we'd all been misled into thinking we were on a vendetta for Anna. It wasn't true. On the same token, I didn't want to call the project to a halt. There were kids to save. In my book, we could hash out the news later, after we took care of the business at hand. If we didn't live through it, there would be nothing to resolve.

I had no sooner walked into the motel room when Bludd snagged my attention with an abrupt demand. "Call Kuhl." His tone of urgency was out of character. It was enough to stand my hackles on end. I didn't hesitate.

Kuhl blurted, "He's here, room two-zero-niner."

Project on, I thought. The main thing was to keep the main thing, the main thing. And the main thing was to kill Abbandanza mobsters. As many as possible and as long as possible. There was no other level of win conceivable. I would not let a peripheral issue like a meeting come between me and my prey.

"Can we wrap up business on the spot?" I asked.

"Let's hook up here and take care of it," Kuhl said.

That was great news. "En route," I said, and turned to tell Bludd to clear out everything and mount up, we were moving to a new location, but he was a step ahead of me. His coat was on, and his bags were in hand. "Stop blathering, mate. Hurry and pack your things and let's go."

Kuhl hadn't mentioned there was any need to hurry, but I felt an internal prompt just the same. I'd never been an adrenaline junkie, but I had an unexplainable urgency that could only be controlled by action. I didn't live for the rush, but I could live *with* it just fine.

It was less than a two-hour drive to meet up with Kuhl at his surveillance van. He'd strategically parked in a lot adjacent to a large grocery store that operated twenty-four hours a day. The busy store acted as cover and concealment. On the road trip, I wanted to tell Bludd about Anna, but resisted the urge. I felt the timing wasn't right. By not telling my comrades up front, I ran the risk of being as guilty as Max was for withholding the truth. Once Bludd and I joined Kuhl, maybe I'd find the opportunity to tell them what I'd found out from Max. However, at this point, my priority was Bruno's imminent death.

When we arrived at Kuhl's van, he had us enter through the back doors and take a seat. He had a pretty fancy get-up. A five-foot long piece of two-by-twelve rested on top of two five-gallon paint buckets meant for visitors. Although, I imagined he hadn't had many that lived to tell about it. Kuhl sat in a beat-up rusty looking metal folding chair that retained a hint of its beige enamel factory paint. It was comfortable though, in comparison to the bench Bludd and I were on. Kuhl was perched at a custom designed workstation that was neither futuristic nor ergonomic. Nonetheless it contained the essentials of his high-tech electronics.

He adjusted his headset over his ears and sat motionless with his eyes shut like he was a participant at a séance summoning a spirit from the afterlife. I had news for him; I had spoken to one raised from the dead just before I'd answered his call.

Bludd and I made ourselves as comfortable as we could in the tight quarters while he continued to monitor the spy bugs for "voices." I took it all in. From the electronic gadgets to the poorly constructed plywood counter. It was a curious mixture, much like Kuhl himself.

I wanted to bring up the subject of Anna, but when I started, Kuhl put his index finger over his mouth and uttered, "Ssssshh." As I waited for an opportune moment, I noticed his lojack system was operational. He scribbled a cryptic note to himself on a yellow sticky Post-it pad and removed one side of the headphones. "He'll be heading for his vehicle in a few minutes. I'd suggest you get a bead on him."

"Where's his rig parked?"

"In the hotel parking lot," Kuhl said. He raised his hand and pointed, "Right over there." The black SUV was in plain sight and backed up to the outer edge of the lot.

"We need to get a lojack transmitter on it."

"Yeah buddy," Kuhl said, "I've already done that."

"Outstanding," I said, but then I saw a twinkle in his eye that made me question, was there more to the story? Kuhl had something up his sleeve. "What else?" I asked. There had to be something else. He came off too smug.

"I rigged it to blow," he said. As fun as that sounded, the reality was we were in a waiting game, and it was Bruno's move. I caught a glimpse of Bludd's big toothy grin out of the corner of my eye, he liked the idea of fireworks too.

Kuhl had picked up a transmission at the hotel desk that Bruno was checking out. When he left the hotel we'd tail and take advantage of the first opportunity. I wanted a piece of this guy, but because he was a high priority target, I wanted to interrogate him first. What could I achieve? Maybe nothing, but he might hold the key to the annihilation of the crime family, a thought that appealed to me. Anna wasn't dead or hurt, and Cal got mixed up with mobsters he knew were dangerous. He didn't deserve what happened, but he jumped out of the frying pan and into the fire. It was no surprise when he got burned. Outside of the whereabouts of Joey Naccarella, I didn't see where Bruno could shed much light on anything. I conceded to Bludd and Kuhl, either way worked on Bruno, but I made it clear, "He's not the end to the vendetta. The Machine has to be destroyed completely, and forever."

"I don't think we can make a significant enough impact to run them out of town," Bludd said.

Kuhl nodded in agreement. "We've hit 'em hard already; I'd say we've slowed them up, but we need to be realistic. I don't see a way to affect any permanent damage. The money drop you took probably upset them more than the loss of a couple street hustlers, but the more earners we take out, the greater impact it would have on their money."

"Did you forget about Pembroke?" I asked.

"He was a patsy. Money can buy another one that looks just like him and does the same thing," Kuhl said.

Kuhl was right. The Abbandanza crime family was resilient and numbered over three hundred known officers, soldiers, and associates. How could a small band of assassins make a long-term change? Kuhl's response continued to resonate with me.

"How do you know what we can do?" I asked. I wanted to know how anyone could judge the outcome before the end.

"The problem is how do we know when we've reached the end?" Bludd said.

"There is no end," Kuhl said, "the government has tried for a hundred years and they can't shut down the Mob, not even with all their manpower and money."

"Maybe I'm wrong, but I don't think we're spinning our wheels," I said. "The Machine can be brought down. They are at the disadvantage, not us; they have never met the likes of a Palatini vendetta." I let my comrades think about a solution, how we win or how we end it, but no one spoke up. I knew the Abbandanza history. There were times in their past when they'd engaged in territorial wars, and came out more powerful. They'd survived the onslaught of government agencies who had corralled a portion of their activity, but the Mob was never deterred. They have continued to expand their influence and wealth.

"I know this. We won't know until we try," I said. "We can't compare what we do to the cops or judiciary; they are constrained by the laws they've made." Kuhl and Bludd acknowledged the truism in my words with a sideways nod and a shrug. "As Palatini, we have no such restraint," I said. "We are the law."

"Mob wars have gone on for centuries," Bludd said, "and they are rarely able to shut one another down. How do you suppose we can do it with force and violence?"

"That's a fact; mobsters are always in competition with each other for a bigger piece of the pie." I let it sink in for a minute. "We aren't mobsters, and we aren't interested in the pie. We want to destroy the market. We have to bring their reign of terror against young girls to an end."

"Even if we take down the Machine, another brand will move in, and we're right back in the same boat," Bludd said.

"You're probably right," I said, "but it's no different than the child porno ring you busted up less than a year ago in Brazil. We disrupt the business and slow their progress, and maybe in the end, we'll weaken their structure enough for the cops to further damage their organization, the lawful way. It's a crapshoot, but if we don't try, more kids will end up in misery at the hands of organized crime."

I didn't know if I'd convinced them we had a chance, or not, and maybe I didn't need to do either one. We were Palatini; we had chosen to engage in the battle. These knights weren't afraid; they just weren't used to a non-specific goal. I thought, "Kill them all wrapped it up just fine."

While I had their attention, I thought I'd drop a bombshell in their lap, "Everything is fluid in this project. I found out today, Anna is alive." Kuhl leaned back and blew out a sigh which unmistakably contained nasty fragmented words. Bludd reacted in a similar fashion. His words were coupled with a deep bellied laugh. Anna had been the reason, the only reason, both men came to Toronto.

Kuhl was quick to compose himself and asked, "What's the story?"

"I don't know," I said. "We haven't talked about it yet. I wanted all of us to get together and hash out the mess. I can tell you this. It had something to do with Pembroke being ferreted out, but I don't have the full story yet. We're in this together. Anna can address us together."

I knew they respected my decision to include them when we met with Anna and Max. We sat quietly. Glances were tossed around from person to person like a hot potato, but no one maintained eye contact for long. Kuhl waved his hand back and forth in a motion for silence to an already silent audience. I watched as he adjusted his headset, leaned forward, and picked up his pencil. He reached for a sticky Post-it notepad, pulled it close, and prepared to write.

Suddenly Kuhl said, "He's checking out." His voice had notably gained in pitch; excitement replaced silence as if it had never existed. Bludd and I watched the SUV through the back window of the van. Bruno was cautious. He used his remote auto start from the corner of the Galaxy Icahn to crank up his vehicle. In the Mob world, vehicles had been known to explode. A safe distance was a smart move. He approached his SUV and continued with a complete circle around his vehicle, stopping to inspect each wheel well. He opened the driver's door, slipped inside, and closed the door. He warmed his vehicle for the next fifteen minutes.

I made an abrupt decision. Bludd and I would run a loose tail while Kuhl monitored the SUV's movement through the tracking system.

"You're at the wheel," I told Bludd. Why not? It was his vehicle.

We climbed through the van and out the driver's side door. It would have been easier to unload through the back door, but that would have exposed us to Bruno's view. Watching a couple guys crawl out of a van might tip him off to our presence. He might think we're cops. However, more than likely, his first thoughts would be that we were the killers he'd been warned about. As I stepped from the van, I said to Kuhl, "Don't blow up the SUV—not yet."

Kuhl chuckled, "I'll try not to, but I can't guarantee anything."

Bludd climbed behind the wheel of his Tahoe, and I rode shotgun. I kept the cell phone close by. Modern society had made the old fashioned "tail" obsolete. "Let Bruno get out of eyesight, and we'll rely on directions from Kuhl. The lojack will track him," I said. I then placed a call to Kuhl.

We travelled northwest, and soon entered the familiar neighborhood of Corso Italia where Musolino's osteria was located. I told Kuhl over the phone the restaurant would likely be our destination. Minutes later my hunch proved correct.

He pulled into the parking area of Musolino's and sat in his fancy, pimped-out ride for a couple more minutes before two thugs appeared from inside the restaurant, and walked to Bruno's vehicle. He got out of the SUV, hugged both men, and then accompanied them back into Musolino's. We sat on the observation for more than two hours. You could learn a lot by watching behaviors, and it was evident, security had become an issue. One of the two thugs, who had greeted Bruno in the parking lot, pulled security checks in the lot. He walked to the SUV, checked the surrounding areas, and then returned to the restaurant.

Bruno went through his routine again when he was ready to leave. The lights flashed when he hit the remote start and announced his impending departure. He and his two mobster buddies walked to his SUV, scanned the parking lot, and did a 360 degree check of his vehicle, inside the wheel wells, the whole bit. There was a brief exchange of affection between the three men before Bruno climbed behind the wheel and drove off. I called Kuhl and gave him heads up. We waited for Bruno's pals to go back into Musolino's before we pulled out.

The tail was mobile in the direction of the border. It was thirty minutes past midnight. I felt we had plenty of time left before daybreak to do what needed to be done. All it required was opportunity. We proceeded to Burlington, hung a course to the left, and traveled to the border crossing. At the massive six-lane entry point at the Lewiston-Queenston Bridge, we picked up the visual on Bruno's SUV. I called Kuhl, "We've got an eyeball on the target and are tightening the noose."

"I'll close up shop and head in," he said.

"Anything changes, we'll touch base."

Once upon Niagara Thruway southbound, I figured we'd cruise for a while, but Bruno had a different idea, and took the exit toward Lockport. We followed. I surmised his destination would be Rochester, but couldn't take that chance. We needed to take him before he reached his destination. Traffic would become heavier if he passed through Lockport. Morning commuters started early.

It had been my experience; people who committed criminal acts were guarded and overreacted to anything that caught their attention. On the other hand, people who lived a criminal lifestyle didn't. They conducted themselves in a normal manner, as any other law-abiding citizen, on any given day. It was their habit. We rode close to Bruno, but he didn't appear to notice. We hadn't travelled far on this stretch of the road when the SUV brake lights came on.

We were on the outskirts of Sanborn, New York. As we entered the hamlet we passed a couple gas stations alongside the road. He swung a U-turn and headed back to the nearest one.

You had to love old habits because they really did die hard. You could count on it, and Bruno was living proof. He swung his rig in by the west side of the building, near the rear of the station, and parked where the lot was poorly lit. Bruno and criminals of his ilk avoided light like it was the plague. Whether it was daylight, limelight, or spotlights, they hated them all. Light exposed their presence, and they loathed being known because of what they were—criminals. Bruno was called the muscle of the family. He was notorious for extortion, intimidation, and murder. When I looked at him, all I saw was another slimy, belly crawler, who needed a gang to impose his will on others.

We pulled past the front of the station and went down the east side of the building. We circled around the back and parked.

"Drop him or take him?" Bludd asked.

"Take him alive."

"Okay, mate," Bludd said. "I've got ether in my bag. I'll get a rag out, and soak it."

"What…in the car?" Ether was not to be used in a confined space. We'd likely succumb to the vapor before we got it on Bruno's mug, and then we'd probably end up dead.

"Nothing to fear, mate, I'd planned to do it outside the vehicle."

I felt better about the ether with Bludd one step ahead of me with the working knowledge of the product. I've led an isolated life and was pretty much a shooter type assassin, but I dug the idea of new tricks to the trade. "Where do you pick up stuff like that," I asked.

"Well, I tell you, ether is inexpensive and super available in overseas countries. I picked this bottle up in Brazil when I finished that last project."

"Okay, what's my part? What do you need me to do?" I knew enough to ask the right questions. I knew with ether the induction was slow. It varied so much between individuals; there was no way to know how long we'd have to hold him. There was also a chance he'd die by accident when we applied the rag. A risk I could live with.

"When Bruno comes around the back of his vehicle and before he gets to the driver's door, we'll go for a grab. You pin the arms, and I'll put the rag on him," Bludd said. "When he's out, place cuffs on him, and we'll push him in his SUV then I'll drive him out of here. We can meet down the road."

We didn't have to wait long. Bruno started his vehicle with the remote start. It was a signal to us he was near his car. Bludd hurried to soak the rag with ether while I went to the corner to watch Bruno approach his car. I scanned the area and there wasn't a soul in sight. At two in the morning, this stretch of the old highway wasn't busy at all. I heard the automatic door locks, unlock. I was about to meet Carmine Bruno in person.

I heard the slam of Bruno's portly body; face first, into his SUV. He'd gotten the door partially open when I tackled him into it. He'd managed one pudgy arm, inside before I was able to get to him. He tried to reach the horn, he swatted and missed. His bulging frame made him extra hard to handle, he was as wide as a door. My arms could reach only part way around him. Gentle wasn't on the agenda for the day, so I pressed his body against the car. I wrapped up his arms any way I could hold onto them. Bludd had his problems, too. Bruno lacked a neck. His head sat flat on his shoulders. Bludd had gotten Bruno's mouth covered, but struggled to get the rag over his nose to make a good seal. However, the more he struggled, the more he inhaled the vapors, and the weaker he became. I pulled his hands behind his back and slapped on the cuffs.

I opened the back door to his vehicle, and we pushed him in face down. Bludd climbed in behind the wheel while I jumped in the driver's side of the Tahoe. Bludd followed. We traveled State Highway Thirty-One, backtracking about ten-miles until we got to a frontage road along the east side of a reservoir. We took it. With no houses in sight we dumped the vehicle.

We pulled Bruno from the vehicle and stuffed him into the back of the Tahoe. We'd locked up Bruno's rig, and drove off. As soon as we reached the Interstate, we crossed under the road and up the access ramp. Every fifteen minutes, I gave Bruno a few sniffs from the ether-doused rag I'd placed in a plastic zip-lock bag. I was careful to roll down the window for ventilation. The cold night temperatures wouldn't kill us. We were headed for Buffalo. I called Kuhl.

"We have the package wrapped up and en route to the hut."

"I'll meet you there," Kuhl said.

"I need a favor. Punch the button and touch off that pimpmobile?"

"Stand-by," Kuhl said. A couple minutes later he said, "Done deal."

I was semi-relieved. It was another piece to an enormous puzzle that spelled trouble for the various task forces and government agencies engaged in the fight with organized crime. Every new piece of evidence we'd provided created coordination and jurisdiction issues, and we gave it to them as often as possible. We wanted them knee deep in puzzle pieces. When Pembroke was alive, he had the inside track, and led the task force members astray or notified the Mob when something was brewing. They'd lost that barrier and were free to interpret the puzzle pieces for themselves.

Any vehicle, abandoned in the boonies and blown up with explosives, brought higher levels of concern to the law enforcement community. When it was a well-known mobster's vehicle, it involved more agencies and greater concerns. On top of that, Bruno would be a missing person, and it was to our benefit to keep him that way. Pembroke, then Bruno, would have government agencies hopping with excitement. News agencies would consume much of their time.

At the hut, we strapped Bruno in the chair and waited. Kuhl called, "I'm twenty-minutes out." The timing was right. Bruno was coming around and was about to discover the truth to the age old question; was there a hell? "Hey, Bludd," I said, "I don't want to do what we did to Pembroke." I was loud when I said it, intentionally loud; I wanted Bruno to hear me. I wanted him to remember. Psychobabblers called it side talk. I didn't care for most of the crap they regurgitated on a regular basis, but this was human behavior. Bludd shook his head, "It was a bloody mess, a big bloody mess for sure. I've never seen anything like that." The Machine had people on their payroll. Cops, judges, and politicians would tell everything they knew to the Mob. Not only were they aware of Pembroke's death, the mobsters had probably seen pictures of the Crown attorney already. It's the way it was.

I planned to exploit Bruno's knowledge. He would have to be stupid to think we wouldn't do the same to him. I glanced in Bruno's direction, and said to Bludd, "I want him to talk. If I have to, I'll take every inch of skin off him." His reaction told me he heard and understood what I had said. I could see it in his eyes.

I hovered over Bruno, face to face. "You're a little bit stupid, aren't you?" I asked. He gave me the cold shoulder and turned his head away from me in disrespect. Who'd he think he was talking to, a choir boy? He knew the shoe was on the other foot. He'd doled out similar harm and torment to others in his past, or ordered it done; now it was his turn. He knew exactly where he was at—his end.

I shot a brief look at Bludd, "My bet is riding on stupid," I said, "but I'm gonna educate him." Bludd pulled Bruno's chair near the old military style metal desk. He looked as if he'd be a hard nut to crack. The biggest nut-cracker I had was a one-pound single-jack sledge hammer. It was a great hammer that

I used for breaking through anything the bump keys wouldn't open. Its value would take on a new dimension with Bruno—a not so gentle persuasion.

Kuhl arrived, "Where are we at with this clown?"

"Have a seat, kick back and relax. Carmine Bruno thinks he's a tough guy. We're going to soften him up a bit, then see how tough he is." I told Kuhl.

"Hold grease balls' hand out there," I told Bludd. He cut one hand loose from the chair and after a brief tug-o-war with Bruno's arm, Bludd flattened it against the metal table. Bruno was a dangerous man—in a round-about way. He was a killer. Ruthless and cold-blooded. He'd been known to work guys over as long as the guy was held by a couple of Bruno's goons, and he'd ordered the murders of others, but he wasn't physically capable to take care of business by himself. He was obese. He lacked muscle tone and endurance. His resistance didn't last long. With his arm stretched out and held flat against the old military type desk, I asked my first question, "Why'd you kill Cal, what threat was he to you?"

"Go to hell."

My single-jack slammed down on his left index finger. He shrieked and bellowed; his payment had begun. "I want the answer, and you're going to give it to me. We can do it the hard way or the easy way, it's up to you. Why'd you kill Cal?"

I could see Bruno made a quick study of my face, flashed an impudent grin, and responded with a tirade of foul language that included references to my mother, dogs, and disgusting sex acts. I might have been offended by his words, but I took the high road and slammed the single jack down on his little finger. He let out a loud ear-piercing scream. I grabbed a greasy gob of hair, pulled his head toward me, and callously said, "I can work my hammer all the way up to your collar bones, and break every bone along the way, unless you talk." Bruno cried in response, but he wasn't ready to talk. I lifted the single-jack again, took aim on his thumb, to which he cringed and cried out, "Wait…I'll talk, I'll talk." Bruno wasn't too stupid, after all.

It made sense to most people if you're going to die, why endure hours of torture, then get whacked. Make it easy on yourself. Bruno knew his fate. All he could avoid was the additional pain. It was up to him, but it was only the mental ascent to the idea of cooperation. I could go either way on the deal. Bludd wrapped a couple paper towels around his mashed fingers while Kuhl cut Bruno's other arm loose from the chair. He wasn't free to move around, his feet remained secured by zip ties and his legs and chest remained taped to the chair.

Bruno's mouth was hanging open and his tongue protruding slightly, "Could I get something to drink?" I nodded to Bludd, who unscrewed the top from a plastic water bottle and handed it to him. He took a long, slow drink, put the bottle down on the table, wiped his lips with his shirt sleeve, and kept his end of the bargain.

"Cal was Joey's boy. I never liked the guy; I didn't make any bones about it. I didn't want this cat around." He took another sip of his water and continued, "He snooped around, asked too many questions, and got his nose in business that wasn't his. I had him figured for a Fed at first, you know like FBI or ATF, something like that. I couldn't figure out his angle until I talked with him one-to-one."

"You figured him out, did yah?"

"Yeah, I found out he was no big deal. He was just a writer that wanted to make a big splash with a book." Bruno polished off the bottle of water and asked for another. "Why not," I said and signaled to Kuhl to grab one since he was standing nearest the case of water. He put it down in front of Bruno. "This guy Cal got all wrapped up emotionally over a couple hookers who were looking for a Sugar Daddy. You know, they just wanted off the street, and didn't want to work for their keep anymore. Cal was the sucker that fell for it. He should have stuck to writing books." Bludd reached over and popped the top on the fresh bottle of water for Bruno. He took a quick swig and continued, "He was a do-gooder and was going to save the world or something. He told me about it. He thought these girls were being held captive or forced to be hookers."

"I'd heard they were kidnapped as underage girls," I said.

"Maybe that was Joey's gig, not mine. I had to clean up his mess, that's all. The whole thing was Joey's fault; he brought this guy around and shouldn't have. He knew too much for his own good." Wow, I thought. Bruno had a Joey that trusted someone outside their crew with too much info. Max trusted Pembroke with too much of our family business. What a parallel.

"Why'd you kill him, if he was no big deal?"

"He had it coming. I had to make an example out of him and those hookers too."

"What happened to Joey?"

"You know Joey, huh? His eyes darkened, and his bushy foxtail eyebrows pushed out. "Joey was a punk. When he got the word De Luca wanted a sit down with him, he ran. I told him to get that broad at his boy's house and bring her to me. I wanted to know what she knew, but Joey hustled her away. Maybe he thought she'd be a bargaining chip or something."

"So you don't know where this gal or Joey's at?" I asked. Of course, I knew Anna was safe, but I didn't know the details.

"I've got eyes and ears out; he won't be able to stay underground for long."

His answer was good news. No emphasis on finding Anna. She evidently hadn't meant that much to him. He wanted Joey for some unfinished business. Maybe Joey heard that Cal told her everything he knew, and he couldn't afford another set of loose lips. Joey needed Cal's woman out of the picture, and on ice. So he took care of it, and sent those yahoos I killed to pick her up for him.

"Who gave the order to kill Cal?"

"Nobody has to give me orders. I did what needed done."

"Come on, who's your boss?" I asked.

He struggled momentarily with the answer. It wasn't that he didn't know; he didn't want to say. I picked up the single jack, and with a gesture in Bruno's direction, he was able to articulate an answer, "The guy's name is Tony."

"Tough Tony—is he the one that gave the order?" I asked.

He nodded and said, "It was more like I told Tony what the solution to the problem was and he agreed." He took another drink of water and said, "Pembroke told us all about you guys. You're going to be discussed at the meeting."

"What meeting?"

"It don't matter none. The meeting is going to happen, and you and your crew are the topic. The Boss will call for a stragismo on your whole organization." Smugness returned to his face. I didn't care for the look.

"What's a stragismo?" I said. "If you're gonna threaten me with something, it's not very scary if I don't know what it means."

"They will make you their life's work. It'll be a campaign of terror," he said. "You will pay dearly. You will pay for everything."

I didn't like his attitude. "Where's this little pow-wow taking place? He got cocky with me and called me some choice names. Bludd and Kuhl strapped Bruno back into the chair, Duct Taped his mouth, tethered one hand and pulled it across the metal desk. That's where I started. His fingers were first to receive the punishing blows from the single-jack, then to the back of his hand and finally the wrist. Bruno was delirious with pain. Kuhl doused him with water and used his smelling salts. When Bruno gained his awareness, I checked his level of cooperation with a question. He could have responded with a nod or made some gesture, and the punishment would have stopped, but he wasn't a "wise guy" after all.

Bludd and Kuhl cut the other hand loose and tethered it. Bruno entered a state of shock from pain, and I doubted he would recover with the ability to communicate. If we beat him continuously, it only sped up the process of death. I thought how easy it used to be when I stalked a perp and shot him to death. I missed those days. As I prepared to crack down on Bruno's other hand, Bludd removed the tape, and I halted my assault.

It took Bruno a minute to gather his thoughts then said, "The Double Decker." Why he told us now, I didn't know. It might not have been the truth, and there was no way to prove it. Bruno hung his head. Tired from the ordeal or in shame for not holding his tongue, I couldn't tell. What I believed was he had lost all hope for his life. He knew he would endure hours and maybe days of torture before he died, and he would not die until we got what we came for. He made the decision to end it. I didn't fault him. It was the only way out.

"When, what time?" I asked.

"Wednesday…late."

I glanced at Bludd and Kuhl. It didn't appear we had any further use for Bruno. Kuhl standing behind Bruno, took the initiative. He pulled out his piece, strapped on the silencer, and fired two rounds into the back of his head. We wanted to ensure he stayed a missing person for at least a few days. Mornings weren't the best times for dumping a body, so we wrapped him up and stuffed him into the Avenger's trunk where he'd freeze; then, with the return of darkness, we could offload him with little chance of being seen.

We decided to finish the cleanup, and catch a nap. Then we'd follow up with a call to Anna. It was time for the scoop.

Chapter 16

"This war won't be about who's right; it'll be about who is left"
—Walter

The Quonset hut had been useful. Quiet and remote was to our advantage. Saturday we caught up on rest and jawed about the possible upcoming meeting. There wasn't much time to prepare for a Wednesday night gathering at the Double Decker. Tentative plans were scratched on a yellow legal notepad and put on the desk for review and input. Bludd talked fluidly about the meeting while I paced the Quonset hut floor and made additional notes on the legal pad. Kuhl busied himself with gadgetry, and distorted the Semtex as if it were Play-doh.

"When are you going to call Max and Anna?" Bludd asked.

"I don't see the urgency," I said. "I think the Mob meeting is our highest priority."

Bludd shook his head, "I think we need to let Maximillian know we are no longer a secret society, mate."

Kuhl, who hadn't shown any signs of interest in our conversation, chimed in, "It's the responsible thing to do. Their lives are in jeopardy just like ours will be if they order a stragismo. We can't wait until after the meeting to tell them. You never know how the meeting might turn out. We might not survive." Kuhl's smile expressed a glint of malice.

I didn't want to agree, but it made sense, in a practical way. "If it'll make you feel better, I'll make the call today," I said.

It was just after two when I placed the call to Max. He answered, and the usual exchange of cordial greetings followed. "We'd like to meet tomorrow morning at ten thirty. There's a greasy spoon in Cheektowaga at the Walden Galleria. You and Anna will find the diner without any difficulty. They have a decent breakfast."

Max agreed.

We waited for nightfall. Under the cover of darkness, we would pay our final disrespects to Bruno's corpse. From my earlier studies on crime, I'd learned serial killers set patterns. If and when they were caught, it was usually due to one of two things. They either returned to the scene of the crime, or returned to where they'd dumped the body. I wasn't going to let it be that easy. I'd travel out of my way, a long way, to make sure Bruno was deposited appropriately. A mile or two extra on the Avenger wasn't going to hurt a thing. Besides, Bludd wanted to get some fresh air. Kuhl, on the other hand, was busy soldering parts together. Every now and then we'd catch him talking to himself while he handled the various instruments of death he had strewn about. Like a little kid with toy soldiers, he'd speak to the pieces, "Die suck'r," or "Ka-boooooom." This was frequently followed by eerie laughter.

It was seven fifteen on a Saturday night. Most of my old friends at the aluminum factory would have been ready to party the night away. That wasn't a bad idea, but before I could get into the revelry mode, I had to take out the garbage. A layer of dark clouds had filled the sky and carried a fresh threat of snow. That wasn't a negative scenario, but rather a good thing for our plans. The ground had already been covered in a blanket of white; more snow would not make a dramatic change to the landscape. It might, however, conceal a body. Regardless if it snowed or not, we needed to find the right site. We hit the road.

We headed south. The population was spread out amongst a number of small hamlets along the route. Rather than run the Interstate we decided to use the more remote and isolated State Highway system. An hour into the road trip, we'd explored a couple side roads, but nothing had panned out. However, crossing the railroad tracks gave me an idea. We stayed near the tracks and kept an eye out for a remote area that would allow us to drop off Mr. Bruno.

On the northeast side of Irving, New York, where a set of railroad tracks crossed Highway 5, Milestrip Road angled off to the south. According to our map, the road would dead end near Cattaraugus Creek and a railroad bridge. We ventured in that direction. As we approached the end of Milestrip Road, the bridge exoskeleton loomed before us in the darkness.

We stopped short of the end of the road, and dragged Bruno's body from the trunk. The frozen tub-o-lard hadn't lost much weight. Maybe three liters worth of blood, and that wasn't much weight at all. I'd wrapped the corpse in a white linen sheet when I'd dropped him in the Avenger's trunk that I'd lined with plastic four-ply sheeting. It all had to go, and it would come in handy now as a makeshift litter. We drug him up the slight incline that led to the railroad tracks. Neither Bludd nor I wanted to pack Bruno alone, or together, and not far for sure. With the snow cover of six or more inches in depth, and the light dusting that had begun to fall, it made the job easier to slide his body.

It was more than twenty yards we had to pull Bruno to get him up on the railroad ties, but that wasn't far enough. We pulled him another twenty-five yards to the north end of the bridge trestle. On the metal bridge grating, the snow had fallen through, and we lost footing on the ice that had formed on the grate. We left the body laying flat and parallel to the tracks. If the train hit the body as planned, it would likely tumble and drag it for a long distance.

We left the sheet over the body, as well. With the fresh snow on the white sheet wrapped body, there was a good chance the engineer wouldn't see the body at all, or tap on the brakes after impact. If, by chance, he did see the body, the cops would have a chore on their hands with a mangled corpse. Identification and cause of death might take the coroner a long time to establish or be forever obscured. If it bought us time, we wanted to do it.

We said goodbye to Bruno, jumped into the Avenger, spun her around in a 180—an easy maneuver in the snow—fishtailed back onto the main road, and headed north toward Buffalo.

"Mate, all the exercise made me hungry. How about we pick up one of those American cheeseburgers?" We pulled into the first fast food joint I found and ordered up at the drive through window. Bludd called Kuhl to see what he wanted to eat, but he'd already downed a couple cans of cold spam. We cruised back to the hut and spent the remainder of the evening in casual conversation while knocking down shots of Jamison's.

Sunday morning greeted us with fresh snow. It wasn't a blizzard, and we didn't have to dig ourselves out, but it was as much of a hindrance as it was a help. The media had declared an "above average" snow fall, and there was no end in sight to the weather pattern. We needed to get this project done and over. I recalled how miserable I was in Texas when I took out the child porn distributor with the Brazilian link. The shoe was on the other foot now. Next time I'd schedule Texas in the winter and New York in the summer.

Max and Anna were first on our agenda for the day. There were questions I needed answers to, and I needed them quick. We had mobsters that wouldn't wait. Kuhl had more of a one-track mind than Bludd, and me. Gadgetry had consumed his life, and he had a hard time breaking away from his toys, except to deploy them.

The three of us rode together in Bludd's Tahoe for the half-hour drive to the restaurant. It was a quiet half hour; I felt we were talked out. There were no longer any "what if" scenarios to discuss or be had. All we wanted were answers and to move on with the project. It was ten-fifteen, we were early, and I wouldn't have had it any other way. We walked inside the diner, and more or less, all chose the same six-foot round table which was nestled into an L-shaped corner. We played musical chairs for a few minutes and jockeyed our positions around until we'd ended the game with all three of us back into the corner. It couldn't have ended any other way.

Max and Anna entered the diner right at ten-thirty. I considered them late for our ten-thirty meeting. Max was bundled in a heavy down parka and walked with the support of his cane. Anna followed behind Max. She was lovely as usual. Her long red hair had taken on a deeper tone than I'd remembered. Anna chose a seat nearest me while Max had taken a centralized position facing all of us. I'm sure he felt safe.

A young waitress in our area brought menus, water, and a cheerful smile to our table.

"Can we have a few minutes before we order? It's been a long time since we've seen each other, and we'd like a few minutes to catch up on things." I asked.

"Not a problem, honey. Give me a signal when you're ready."

When the waitress had moved away from our table, Max started off the talk with a round of congratulations for smoking out Pembroke. "It was a marvelous job. I must say, each of you performed like an A-team." It didn't lead to handshakes or slaps on the back amongst the rest of us. It was the reason we'd come to Buffalo—it was business.

"I owe all of you an apology," Max said. "Anna, this includes you. I felt a kinship with Talbot Pembroke. I'm sorry I overstepped my boundaries and violated our code. I did so honestly. I wanted to bring him in as a Palatini. It was an error that placed all of you in jeopardy…Especially Anna. For this I am truly sorry."

"I feel I have an apology to make too," Anna said. "It might have been a wrong decision to have remained hidden after I escaped my…" Anna began to cry softly. After a moment, she'd regained her composure and collected her thoughts enough to continue. "Cal was a really good man. His heart was in the right place, and I think he was a rare find in journalism circles. We will miss him."

Max again spoke, "It was obvious we had an inside leak when the kidnapped girls and Cal vanished. Anna had stayed on against my wishes and suffered traumatic consequences. We were very fortunate she was able to get away alive."

"I knew we had a mole." Anna said. "What I didn't know was how much information Maximillian had provided Talbot or I would have suspected him, but…"

Max interrupted, "We've covered that Anna." Then he laid out the story from his perspective. "Anna called me after she had escaped her capture. Once I knew she was safe, I made the decision to have her remain "missing" for her safety. At that point we focused on where exactly the project had been compromised."

"When was that? At what point did you know Anna was alive and had escaped?" I asked.

"Excellent question," Max said, "I believe it was late in the evening after we had that nasty confrontation on whether to proceed with the project. Since you were determined to push forward, I thought you might succeed in flushing out the mole. As it turned out, it was a capital idea that panned out rather nicely. Since I feel defensive right now, I might add, I had called for other Palatini to assist you before I knew Anna was alright. I was certain you would find them valuable."

"Well your decisions and actions cost me more than a little heartache." I grimaced and flashed a glance at Anna. Our eyes made contact, only briefly before she slowly looked down toward her hands that were folded in front of her on the table. "I was shocked when I heard about Anna. Then I find out weeks later there was no reason to have felt the way I did. You let me needlessly suffer when you were aware she was alive and safe."

Max tried to cut it, "Yes, well I've explained…"

I lifted my hand toward Max with a gesture to stop, "Understand, I'm not crying and whining about anything. It is what it is, but I want you to know this; I've lost trust in our Society. When you wanted to shut down the project, I figured you for a coward. I felt betrayed and I questioned my loyalty to the Palatini. I was paranoid when Bludd showed up at my door. I wasn't sure if I would have to waste him to survive. You didn't tell me you had put out a call to assist the project."

Anna piped in again, "Sometimes it is impossible to predict what circumstances will develop or the outcome of the circumstances."

"Truth would have been inspiring," I said.

"I did what I felt I had to do to keep Anna protected. It was your decision to continue the project. I might add, against my wishes. All of that was before I had heard from Anna," Max said.

"My decision was based on your cowardice Max."

"I made a decision to let the project play out and see where you took us. Anna told me you would display a harsh reaction. I think she said, 'like a bull in a china shop,' if my recollection is correct."

"Here's the deal, Max. I didn't sign on to be used like a guinea pig."

Max rapidly tapped his cane twice on the tile floor which echoed a hollow clacking noise that drew the momentary attention of others seated nearby then leaned into the table and said, "I believe we have here, a case that the philosopher Nietzsche addressed when he said, "That which does not kill us makes us stronger."

Anecdotal, I thought. Not much of a summation. I felt my tolerance level being challenged. It was likewise mirrored by Bludd's reaction. He fidgeted with his napkin, and dug at his fingernails. Kuhl seemed to be in la-la-land, but in all fairness, he wasn't much on talk. He was a man of action. If I had to wager a bet on what Kuhl had his focus on, my money was on his passion for bomb building and making an impressive pyrotechnic surprise for the Mob.

Out of the blue, Bludd motioned to our waitress. "Could I get a cup of coffee? Black."

I was stunned. Bludd was a dyed-in-the-wool tea drinker. I looked at him and said, "Coffee?"

He shrugged and smiled. No one else seemed to notice.

"What happened to Joey?" I asked.

"I had to win his trust before I escaped," Anna said. "Maximillian told me you knew a couple of Joey's men had taken me from Cal's place and brought me to Joey. That's true."

"Joey was concerned; he told me De Luca would put a contract on him. He needed me to be a cop or a government agent so he could broker a deal for protection. I guess he didn't know about Pembroke. If he had made a deal, Pembroke would have handled it, and would have set up the hit. Joey erred when he thought the Canadian government would have protected him from the Mob."

"So how did you get away?" Bludd asked.

"He wasn't the gentleman he should have been. He had needs, and I was able to gain his trust. I will leave it at that. He saw me as a defenseless woman he could overpower at will. He took me to a cabin in a remote area about seventy miles southwest of Toronto. He said no one knew about his cabin and it would be the perfect hideaway until he worked out his plan. He didn't live long enough to see the plan through. He wasn't as tough as he thought he was and I wasn't as defenseless as he supposed. He had me make dinner. He wanted a large Porterhouse steak with oven steak fries. I'd served the steak in front of him and stepped back to the stove to get the fries. At that point, he didn't watch me very closely. I shoved the two-pronged carving fork into his neck and grabbed the steak knife still on the table in front of him. I bled him out."

That's my Anna. I'd seen her in action in Thailand. There was no doubt in my mind Joey had underestimated her.

She continued, "I gathered my things, helped myself to his cash, and drove his car to Toronto. I dropped it curbside, walked a block from there to a convenience store, and called a cab. I had the driver take me to Niagara Falls where I rented a motel room, and a car. The next morning I did some shopping. I picked up a disposable cell phone, and later in the evening I gave Maximillian a call."

"So y'all decided to be hush-hush about the change in circumstances then?" Kuhl asked. He'd been listening after all.

"That's right," Max said. "I flew to Toronto to be with Anna. I felt she needed the support. I was also able to monitor the project's progress, although sadly, much of that was done through liaison with Pembroke. I want to express once again, the remarkable job each of you has done. It must have been very difficult for you in light of what was believed to have happened to Anna."

"I think the most important aspect of the project was accomplished when you took Talbot out. He was a key factor in their power base. He had the ability to negotiate around law enforcement," Anna said. "We can close out the project. The Machine has been severely crippled."

"Sure, soon as we're done," Kuhl said. His icy cold blue eyes squinted almost to a close.

"It's pointless," Max said. "This is a war we can't win."

"Bruno told us the Mob already planned a war for us. He called it a 'Stragismo,' I would call it a vendetta on their part. Thanks to you, Max, they know something about us. They know there is a league of assassins that are working against their interests. You, Max, are a primary target. Therefore, what we do, we do for the greater good of all," I said. Bludd and Kuhl nodded while Max vigorously shook his head. His disagreement was noted as was his desire to cut ties and run. "I know the way you've always done things. Sneak in, kill, and sneak back out, but it's different this time. This war won't be about who's right or who's wrong; it'll be about who is left."

"What can we do to help?" Anna asked. She understood we would not cease our actions against the Mob.

"Stay out of the way," I replied. It sounded harsh, even to me, but necessary. We didn't need any interruptions. We had a thing to do.

Anna had listened and understood the score. The Palatini didn't have a choice. We needed to severely cripple them or the hunters would become the hunted. Besides, we hadn't put the kibosh on the Mob's involvement in human trafficking. Not yet. She knew as Palatini operatives, we wouldn't stop until we succeeded.

"We'll finish the project. With Pembroke out of the way, we can weaken their structure. Maybe then the cops can put the screws to them," Kuhl said.

Max sat back in his chair. I read him like a book. He was unhappy with our decision. The Palatini team assembled for this fight had rejected the notion that we were washed up and had to pull out. It wasn't going to happen that way.

"If we're clear, there's work to do," I said. My mood had shifted to a less defensive posture with my coworkers, now I felt their support.

"Let's go," Kuhl said. He was anxious to get back to the task at hand. He was in his element as a bomb builder, not jabbering about the "what if" scenarios of the operation. I thought it was time to go as well. The longer we sat at the table the more I noticed Anna's prettiness. Intimate snippets from a time past forced their way to the forefront of my thoughts. I didn't want to entertain them. Not at all.

By six in the evening, the three of us had relocated into two motels near the Double Decker Lounge. Bludd and I shared the room we'd used previously at the motel that bordered the lounge parking lot. It would take around the clock observation. We decided upon four-hour shifts to make it happen. Kuhl had asked to work independently, and resided in a motel about a block west of our position. We parked vehicles strategically according to need. We didn't schedule any daily meetings; we'd get together whenever a need arose.

Ten-thirty Sunday night, the three of us met in my room. Bludd continued his watch over the Double Decker Lounge while Kuhl and I pulled chairs up near him.

"I don't think we should mike the place," Kuhl said. "When they have their meeting they'll check for transmitters." Kuhl had first-hand experience with the Mob. He was in the know, and we went with his call.

"The one thing we can't do is allow their meeting to take place. Whatever measures we have to take or whatever we have to do, we can't let the meeting end naturally. If they pull off the meeting, they will come out unified and aggressive in their vendetta against us," Bludd said.

Mob meetings had gone through many changes over the years. Every ten to twenty years, a new generation of mobster came along with ideas to reform their established revenue systems. What they wanted were ways to make more money. But, after they reinvented the wheel, it looked the same. Racketeering, drug-dealing, loansharking, and prostitution, the list went on and on. It was the same urban-based criminal enterprise it had always been. The only change was the changes in technology. Otherwise it was the same old song and dance.

However, some changes had been destructive to the Mob. John Gotti, Jr., took the helm of the Gambino crime family in 1985. His crew had pulled down hundreds of millions in loot every year, but he broke with many of the old line traditions. His love affair with the cameras and media made him dangerous to the Mob's way of life. He was flashy and enjoyed the attention, but it brought the heat with it. The consequences were felt not only by the Gambino mobster's, but by the other New York City crime families as well. And they didn't like it. One time Lucchese crime family boss Anthony "Gaspipe" Casso said, "What John Gotti did was the beginning of the end of Cosa Nostra." But it wasn't the end. It created change. Not an end.

The Five New York crime families and the Chicago Outfit comprised the governing Mafioso body referred to as The Commission. The "Bosses" of the crime families were the ones that called all the shots for organized crime. The Abbandanza family had been subject to their decisions and directives, as were another twenty or so Mob factions. But, in 1985 the bosses stopped meeting. Rather, mini meetings took place with representatives of the Five Families. Quiet meetings in diners and social clubs became the typical way to conduct business. Gotti held his meetings at the Ravenite Social Club in Manhattan's Little Italy, right under Federal agent's noses. They couldn't get a thing to stick to the "Teflon Don." It took a snitch, Sammy "the Bull" Gravano, to put him away. The Feds could have shot Gotti any day of the week if they worked as we did, but they didn't.

What the Machine faced was considered a local problem, but they still had to report their decision to The Commission. "I think it'll be a low-key meeting. We run the risk of civilians and Mob representatives from other crime families being present," I said.

"More likely it'll be the local hierarchy and some soldiers in this initial meeting," Kuhl said.

At three in the afternoon the following day, Kuhl stopped by to check in. We'd watched him enter the lounge twice. We were curious as to what he was up to. When Bludd asked, Kuhl said, "I'm getting the lay of the land. They've posted signage on the Double Decker front door for an early closing this Wednesday."

"It's a good sign, blokes. We'll be on for it," Bludd said.

The Abbandanza mobsters hadn't had a good challenge to their authority in thirty years. If they'd been hoods, who had fought for territory on a regular basis, they'd have been better prepared for what they were up against. But these guys were fat, dumb and happy. They'd relied on trump cards like Pembroke, who'd kept them out of hot water, and an emphasis on any rivals in their area. They had further clout by their connection to the other New York crime families. They also used payroll to own police protection in Toronto and pimped out politicians on both sides of the border. We didn't know who was who. If we did, they would have been dead "who's". It seemed as if there wasn't anyone money couldn't buy.

I wanted to make their meeting memorable. Something they would never forget, but wanted to. I had a philosophy about violence. It might not have been the best option, but it was always an option. When I chose to use it, I didn't take the tuck head about it. There was nothing shy or bashful about my approach. Cops were allowed the use of force, but only the amount of force necessary to control a situation. I had no such restraint. I used violence as brutal and severe as I could make it, and maybe then I wouldn't have to come back and do it a second time.

Once we started our assault, I assumed herd mentality would kick in. It was an impulse to gather together for protection; a natural survival instinct. Psychobabblers called the response, fight or flight. I called it recreational shooting, like ducks on a pond.

The lounge was headquarters for Lucan Russo, otherwise known as, "Spooky Luke." He was a well-known crime figure in the Rochester area, and newly appointed crime boss for the Mostarda operation, since the capo's disappearance. Russo had been a police officer in the early '90s. His career ended when it was discovered he had Mob ties with the notorious Abbandanza clan. He was a guy who leaned heavily on the old school tactics of extortion and strong arm rackets. What I saw was a thug, who professed in the 'old ways' because he liked being a thug, not because it was more lucrative. Tough mobsters weren't always rough, but Russo had a reputation for violence. He also had close connections with Marco Camerota, his cousin, and would-be capo of Toronto's East-End.

"Spooky Luke" would be the meeting's host. I'd dealt with tough guys like him before. Since he was newly appointed capo he had to come off hard, and what was harder than being perceived as fearless. Mobsters like Russo had an image to uphold. It would never cross his mind that anyone would attack his crew when they were all together. They were too strong. It would be an act of suicide. To us it was the chink in the armor we watched for. How would it manifest? It already had. Russo strutted around the lounge all hours of the day and night. We watched him come and go without so much as an escort to his car. I considered his judgment and actions brazenly disrespectful to us.

* * * * *

Wednesday morning around eight I moved all unnecessary personal items to the Tahoe. We kept our weapons, ballistic vests, and warm clothing. I drove the vehicle a block away to Kuhl's motel and parked it. Kuhl arrived at our motel room at eleven for a prearranged meeting. I was on the back of the sofa-couch with my binoculars, working point. The observation hadn't paid any great dividends, but we did gather general knowledge of Russo's operation. Kuhl had brought a flyer back from the Double Decker which read, "We will be closing tonight at nine o'clock for maintenance. We apologize for the inconvenience. We will reopen Thursday morning at our regular time."

"A neatly packaged bit of deception," I said. "It's going down tonight."

Kuhl had taken advantage of his two days free reign to get inside the lounge. He was a new face in the joint and could get in unnoticed where Bludd or I could not. The bartender had it in for me, or at least that's the way I felt. I certainly didn't like him. It would have been trouble if I'd tried to hang out there. We'd watched Kuhl make multiple trips into the lounge, with his pool cue in its case and a small rucksack over one shoulder. He was a *poseur* who made good his cover as a pool hustler. Sometimes he spent an hour there. At other times; he was in the place for more than two hours. By the end of the third day, he had the wherewithal to know who was who of the regulars that hung out at the lounge.

Just after two in the afternoon, Kuhl came back by our motel room carrying a large Buffalo Sabre hockey bag. "I think we need to line out a few things for tonight," he said. "I have a plan I've been working on." He pulled from the hockey bag two M79 grenade launchers and a dozen high explosive rounds. After he neatly lined them up on the coffee table, he removed a gun case and laid it on the kitchen counter. "I'll be using this one," he said.

"What is it," Bludd asked.

Kuhl opened the case and removed a bolt action rifle. "She's a Winchester Model 70." He assembled the bi-pod and attached one of the two scopes that were in the case, and then a silencer. "She's a .308-caliber—a real beaut. Don't you think?"

"Nice," Bludd said. "What kind of scope is that?"

"She's equipped with a thermal night vision scope and a silencer—she's all part of the plan."

"We can do a plan, mate, and a backup plan. But thirty seconds into the firefight we'll need a different plan. Nothing ever goes as planned," Bludd said.

Kuhl rubbed his cheek along the forearm grip and barrel of his rifle as he held it against his body in an embrace. I understood what I saw; it was sensual. Kuhl eyed Bludd and with an air of confidence about him said, "Well my Aussie friend, at least we'll own the first thirty seconds of the fight, and I plan to do a lot of damage in that amount of time."

Once again with Kuhl, I could see action behind the curtain. I'd learned, with him there was more to the play than what was shown on the stage. "What's up your sleeve?" I asked.

"I've rigged the lounge to blow."

"How?" Bludd and I asked in unison.

"With ten pounds of Semtex."

"Explain it to me," I said.

"I went in the lounge the first night looking for a way to make a prop, something I could use they would not likely notice. Next to one of the pool tables on the first floor is the men's bathroom. There was nothing out of the ordinary in the bathroom. It's a standard design all the way with three urinals, two toilet stalls, and a double sink vanity with a five-foot long mirror. I packed two-inch PVC pipe full of Semtex, nearly nine-foot in all. It's more than enough to bring down the entire building."

"How did you get it in the lounge?" I asked.

"Eighteen-inch pieces of ABS, one at a time and a coupler to hook them together. Wasn't hard at all, they fit nicely in the cue case."

"Won't they see it when they give the place a thorough going over before the meeting?"

"I don't think so. It's up under the front of the sink counter top and blends into the existing pipe nicely."

"How do you plan to set it off?"

"I put a cutout in the ABS and put the detonator, a throwaway cell phone, in it. I put a blasting cap in the Semtex and wired the whole thing to a relay and a nine-volt battery for a power source. When I call the phone number, the vibrator on the phone will send a charge down the line, and there will be a hellish boom."

"What if they find it when they're poking around? They'll be on to us."

"No worries. If one of those guys tried to disable or remove the trigger, it'll set off the fail-deadly switch I put on the phone. It's a dead man switch in reverse."

We spent the next few hours in discussion about offensive positions and how we would initiate the event. We continued the observation, tested our radio communications, and completed a second weapons check. What never came up was the "what if" questions that dawg every operation. There would be no "what if" this time. "Anyone at the meeting when the bomb goes off will die. We are the topic. If they're there, they're a target." I said. It wasn't a family gathering with women and children, it was a business meeting with the hard core of the family. It was in a nightclub late at night. I expected the chances were slim we'd have other than mobsters and associates show up.

By eight-thirty, darkness had set in, and the temperatures plummeted. What did that mean for us? Two things we could figure on, less activity outside the Double Decker, and the thermal display on Kuhl's scope to be crisp and clear. We could also figure on being cold.

The lounge closed its doors to the public at nine as expected, and we readied ourselves to deploy to our stations. Bludd spotted two cars with occupants that were positioned at either end of the lot; plumes of exhaust rolled from behind their vehicles. The frigid air swiftly dispersed the exhaust. Nearly an hour passed without any further sign of the meeting taking place. Cars had pulled into the lounge parking lot, only to be contacted by the men from what we called the sentry vehicles, east and west, and sent on their way. At ten fifteen, the first vehicle arrived that was allowed to line up along the south side of the building. Parking on the south side shielded them from view of the main drag which was to our left. It also put them in a direct line of sight for our observation. Car by car the traffic continued to arrive. By midnight, there hadn't been a new arrival for a half-hour. We felt it was safe to assume the meeting was in progress.

Kuhl loaded his hockey bag with his assembled .308-caliber rifle, wrapped himself warmly, and said, "Let's do it." I accompanied him to the north end fire exit of our motel, walked up one staircase to the landing that led to the flat roof. I prepared to bump the lock open on the roof access door when I noticed it was not secured. "One less thing to do," I said as I opened the roof access.

"Tell Bludd I'll see him in thirty-seconds," Kuhl said. I acknowledged with a nod, and I was on my way back down to the motel room. We put our ears on and made radio contact with Kuhl.

The first radio traffic we picked up was, "I have two bogeys on the roof top, east and west." Kuhl's thermal scope was doing the job it was intended to do. We had turned off the lights in our motel room and watched the rooftop of the lounge. The exterior lights of the Double Decker were arrayed in a manner that limited us from seeing Kuhl's bogeys from our room or from the ground view.

"Prepare to launch 40 Mike-Mikes at the line." Kuhl said. We loaded HE rounds in the M79s. It was now up to Bludd and me to coordinate our efforts for maximum damage. The M79s report was barely a whisper when launched. More than likely, the mobsters wouldn't have a clue what hit them. When the grenades exploded, the mobsters might think it was a car bomb under one of the vehicles. If it confused them even slightly, I was all for it. We counted on the thugs of the sentry cars to be drawn into the action. The hierarchy inside would be pushed to the opposite side of the building from the explosions, and more or less over the top of where the Semtex explosives were located.

Bludd and I had our headsets and awaited the 'Go' order. We opened the two-foot wide windows on either side of the large front room window, and poised, ready to fire. I would lead the countdown to synchronize our shots, Bludd would shoot for the west end which was seventy-five yards away, and I would shoot about twenty yards further in an attempt to hit midway on the line of cars. What I didn't want to do was overshoot.

"West end bogey is down," Kuhl reported in a whisper. We had heard nothing and there were no visible reactions to his shot. Almost immediately Kuhl reported again, "East end bogey is down. Hit'em! I repeat hit' em."

I counted down, "Three, Two, One," and we fired the grenades. The explosions were simultaneous, or close enough, and incredibly loud. The sound of the explosions echoed off the rectangular mass of structures which encompassed the parking lot. Bludd and I loaded for a second volley. The front door to the lounge swung open, and two of the henchmen ran out in the direction of the line of vehicles. They no sooner had stopped by the corner of the building when the Double Decker ripped apart at the seams. Kuhl had detonated the plastic explosives. It didn't flatten the building completely, but not much of the structure was left. My immediate guess was no one made it out of the meeting alive. The thugs and the sentry guards outside were down. One or two of them were rolling or moving slightly. They were low level players or they wouldn't have been outside. If they lived through the attack, they should count themselves lucky. If they'd been part of the inner circle of trusted family members—they'd been slaughtered.

Kuhl radioed he was inbound. Bludd stayed at the window on point.

"The building is on fire!" Bludd called out.

I waited by the door for the knock. I was anxious. A second felt like a minute, and a minute like an hour. I cracked the door and watched. A moment later he appeared at the end of the hall moving rapidly in my direction. Once in the room with the door closed Kuhl pulled his .308-caliber from the hockey bag and began to break it down and into the gun case.

"I hear sirens in the distance," Bludd said. "There are people out there helping the downed blokes in the lot."

"That's okay, stick to the plan," I said.

"If you're not wearing it, load it in the hockey bag. Everything!" Kuhl said.

The M79s were light, and we only had cold weather gear which we wore. Once the gun case was put into the bag, we were ready to withdraw to the motel a block away.

We went to the fire exit, straight down to the ground level which exited into the back parking area. We saw a young couple walking from the lot into a back door of the motel. We waited until they were out of sight. We were able to slip down an alleyway to Kuhl's ground floor motel room.

* * * * *

We hunkered down for the next few days. We'd stocked up on food and water for the event. We watched the news coverage; it was a big deal. Nationwide coverage, and it continued as information leaked out. If we could get through the first forty-eight hours of the police investigation, our further withdrawal would be made easier.

226

Chapter 17

"There are no happy endings, not in this life"
—Walter

I placed a call to Max to let him know we'd kicked some tail. He wanted to get together for a full run down, but I nixed the idea. It wasn't time to toast our wine glasses and slap each other on the back. It was time to be very small and quiet. News reports broke on the destruction of the Double Decker. Bludd stayed glued to the television watching for coverage while I found myself mildly disinterested in the reports. Who and how many was all I cared to know. Kuhl might have had the best idea and ignored the news. His interest was in activity on police radio bands.

The Mob had people in journalism; a lot of them. We knew that. We also knew you couldn't trust the accuracy of what was released to the public. Not even what the cops put out to the news agencies. Everything had a spin to it. You had to be naïve to have believed differently. Initial reports were confusing. Mobster names were mixed in with heroic actions of first responders. Two firefighters had been injured battling the blaze. One report focused on a recently discharged United States Army medic who had been instrumental in saving the life of an injured man in the parking lot. The injured man was later identified as an associate of the Abbandanza crime family. All interesting stuff, I suppose, but it was all smoke and mirrors as far as I was concerned. Whether it was intentional or unintentional, it led people from the knowledge of the truth about the Mob. Government agencies confirmed the blast was from an explosive device, but quick to dispel the rumor of terrorism. A conclusion jumped to by many since the September 11, 2001 terrorist attacks in NYC and Washington DC.

The morning of the third day we began to shuttle our equipment to the Quonset hut. By mid-afternoon, our transfer was complete. I called Max. I wanted a meeting. We had ground to lay for our next target. I intended to further cripple their money flow. We felt it was their Achilles heel. Max insisted Anna had to be included in the meeting. I told him I didn't care, and left it at that.

Sunday, before we met with Max and Anna, Kuhl wanted to go to church. Not just any church, but Holy Family Cathedral in the northeast end of Black Rock. It wasn't so much a religious thing with Kuhl, but more of an opportunity to visit the spiritual watering hole of some of the recently departed members of the crime family, and see if any of the familiar faces in our profile photos showed up at the service. I figured if they were still alive, they were hiding under a rock, and rightfully so because it wasn't safe for them.

This was capo Domenic Bacca's jurisdiction. He held the strongest arm of the family and we'd hidden under his nose. Pembroke would have passed that along before he died, especially since he was affiliated with the Toronto faction. Bacca wouldn't be too happy with us over that piece of trivia, and I intended for it to be leaked widely amongst his kind. If we couldn't get to him, maybe some of his own people would. More importantly to Kuhl was Rocco Colansante, Consigliore and crime family CFO. Kuhl had his eye out to make Rocco the next target. You could never go wrong if you followed the money trail. One more boss was known to attend services at Black Rock. Salvatore Giannetti, the crime family's "Capo dei capi." I wanted him, but he was proving to be a tough target to catch up to. He was rarely seen, and we suspected well protected. I might have to become a devout church-goer after all, just to get a shot at the head mobster.

Bludd had parked curbside a hundred yards away from the church and let Kuhl walk. I was shotgun for this leg of the trip, and tried to keep an eye out for bad guys. But both eyes closed, and I dozed off. I'd gotten used to power naps; it was almost my only form of sleep anymore, and I could do them anywhere. I startled awake at one point. I sat up and in a panic.

"You're okay, mate. I have you covered," Bludd said.

Church let out, and there was a stream of people exiting the cathedral. After a few minutes what remained of the congregation lingered on or around the big double doors at the top of a wide set of steps. We watched Kuhl as he shook hands with people, and seemed to carry on a conversation with a couple of parishioners.

When Kuhl got back to the Tahoe, we were eager for the report.

"Let's go," Kuhl said with an urgent tone.

I interpreted the seriousness by which Kuhl spoke to mean there was trouble afoot. I pulled my .40-caliber, press-checked the slide to insure I had a round in the chamber, and held it on my lap. We headed west from the church.

Kuhl leaned forward and asked, "What did you see?"

"You tell me." I said as I turned to look into his face. "Why did you say let's go like the house was on fire."

"Sorry, didn't mean to alarm you. I'm hungry for some grub," he said.

I shared a few filthy expletives with the occupants of the Tahoe. It helped me to get back on track.

Bludd asked Kuhl, "Who'd you see in the church?"

"Nobody. They offered prayers for the families who lost loved ones in the bombing, and world peace. That sort of stuff."

"Nobody?" I said. "What about the people you were talking to outside and shaking hands with. Who were they?" I hoped he'd made contact with a crime family member or blood relationship to those who died. We might get the skinny on what's going on behind the scenes.

"Just some nice people, they didn't say anything about the bombing."

It was twelve-forty-five when we pulled into the Village Restaurant; the pre-arranged destination for our meeting. We weren't first to arrive for a change, Max and Anna were seated to the right from the main entrance. We had the corner booth. With its tuck and roll padded bench and matching semi-circle back, it was all very cozy. The kind of coziness a sardine felt in a can. I didn't like it at all.

Our waitress was quick, and hooked us up with drinks. Then took our food order. Max had a look about him that made me immediately question what was wrong. His expression of painfulness increased as he explained. "I received a call today from a gentleman who would like to meet with us and discuss an end to hostilities along the New York border."

"Who is it this time? A governor or a mayor?" It wasn't sarcasm. I was dead serious.

Max understood my concern. "I suppose you could say it is the residual effect of Talbot on the project. The man's name is Vincent Telese. He referred to himself as a spokesperson at one point, and a representative at another. He informed me he had been selected to make contact and attempt an arrangement of sorts to end the issue."

"A representative? "We don't know what we're dealing with, do we? Pembroke had both cops and mobsters in his pocket," I said.

"I suspect he is a Mob affiliate," Max said.

"How did he know to contact you? I asked. Something sparked my suspicious nature. "How did he get your phone number?"

"Well, frankly, he was given my name and number by Talbot. He gave me the impression he had not talked to Talbot directly, but the information was filtered to him through someone else."

"Why are we talking with these grease balls? What can he offer us? Maybe he'll give us a free get out of town card? What are we talking about here? Are we considering making a deal with the devil?" I asked.

Max squirmed in his chair, "At some point we have to consider alternatives to killing and blowing everything up."

I didn't like the sounds of that at all, but I knew it was coming.

Max continued, "There are other issues to consider here. We might not have won everything, but the tide was sufficiently turned on their illegal immigration racket."

I looked for support to take a stand, but quickly realized there was none to be had. I could see it in their eyes; they were in agreement with Max. End this thing and move on.

"What's the down and dirty on where we're going with the project?" I asked.

"We have arranged for two representatives from either side to meet. Walter, why don't you and Anna meet with them?" Max suggested.

"I'll meet with them," I said, "but if he tries to bully us, I'm going to kill 'em on the spot."

Anna smiled. She knew I meant business. She also knew she should plan on going down that way.

"Okay, set it up with Anna as spokesperson." By their silence Kuhl and Bludd elected me their representative in this powwow. Max and Anna decided on a Christmas Day meeting. The call was made to Telese, and the tentative arrangement made. It was a go.

Since no one had asked about the Rochester bombing, I figured they waited on me to bring it up. "You have undoubtedly followed the headlines on this event." Anna and Max nodded. I continued, "We now have confirmation of the dead, Toronto's kingpin Capo Santo De Luca, Capo Domenic Bacca of Buffalo, Toronto East End Lieutenant Marco Camerota, and the Rochester host, Capo Lucan "Spooky Luke" Russo." Palatini smiled and exchanged glances with each other.

"Another twelve soldiers inside, two soldiers outside and three associates in the parking lot have died," Bludd added.

"I will make it more if the deal goes south." I didn't want to leave anyone in doubt of where I stood. If Society Palatini was satisfied with how this project was ending, they'd set their sights too low. Absent was Rocco Colansante, CFO and third in the Abbandanza hierarchy. Why was he a no-show for such an important meeting? We didn't know the answer. After the Double Decker Lounge went up in flames, we'd found out underboss, "Tough Tony" Giannetti, had landed back in jail on another drug charge. Salvatore Giannetti hadn't been seen or heard from since I'd taken control of the project. The most likely scenario had been voiced by Kuhl, "The capos were there to make a plan to present to the hierarchy. We intervened in the process before it ever got that far."

* * * * *

Christmas Day in Buffalo, I speculated on the headlines for the following day. Chicago had its St. Valentine's Day massacre. What would Buffalo's be? Christmas Day Annihilation had a nice ring to it. Anna picked me up in her jet-black Crown Vic before I could come to a conclusion as to what I thought would ring best in the newspaper.

"Where are we going?" I asked.

"A luxury hotel in Niagara Falls. I've rented a room for the meeting."

"What's the plan?"

"No agenda for the meeting. We'll see what they have to offer."

"Go with the flow—got it."

"I'm not willing to make any agreements without the other's input. We all have a stake in the outcome."

"I can," I smiled as I drew my Glock and checked my magazine capacity to insure it was full. "If I have to, I can make a decision for you too."

Two-thirty on the dot, we rolled into the parking lot. The meeting was scheduled for two-thirty, and I was upset. I would never arrive late, but I kept my opinion to myself.

We entered the lobby. I kept an eye out while Anna went through the process of checking in at the front desk. Vincent Telese was nowhere in sight.

I didn't know what he looked like, but you could tell from the behavior of those around us, there was no concern for who we were.

Anna motioned to me to follow her to an elevator nestled near a back door exit. We rode to the seventh floor, and walked halfway down the hall to room seven-twenty. Anna ran the cardkey. The green light flashed, and Anna turned the handle. I pulled my .40-caliber up to the ready position. Anna looked both ways in the hallway, and said, "Put that away."

Once inside, I did a quick scan of the rooms while Anna placed a call to Telese. She gave him the hotel and room number.

"Okay, what's up Anna?"

"The arrangement I made with Telese was to wait by a diner two blocks from here, and I'd call him and provide directions at that point."

Anna placed another call where she repeated the name and address of the hotel and our room number.

"That was Kuhl and Bludd. I had them watch from outside the same diner. I told them Telese and another man should be waiting inside…Walter, try not to be so suspicious. I have the matter in hand."

Anna's cell phone rang. "Do you have them?" She asked. "Okay, great, see you soon."

As she disconnected her call, she said, "Seymour is tailing a vehicle that pulled out of the diner, carrying two men, heading in our direction."

"Where's Kuhl? I asked.

"He'll be close by, watching the street for any developments."

"Do you really think these guys are coming alone?"

"If they don't, I have you to make the final decision." Anna gave me a teddy bear hug and said, "Let's get ready."

I figured I could talk from any angle. I moved around the room until I found the best feel for a gunfight. Two chairs sat diagonally opposite a small coffee table in front a large window which overlooked the city to the west. I asked Anna to unlock the door and have a seat. "Why don't we wait for the knock and I'll answer the door?" Anna said.

"Not a good idea. If either of us answers the door, they might grab us, and they'd have an immediate hostage to bargain with. How about I yell 'come in' and see where the chips fall? If you sat in the far left chair, you'd be out of their view from the doorway." Anna took the seat I'd suggested. I sat at the end of the breakfast counter. Its slight curve and four-foot high counter would provide a small degree of protection. I walked to the door and unlocked it, returned to my seat and waited.

The knock was light and rabbit like. I waited for it to stop before I yelled, "Come in." The door opened slowly to reveal the silhouette of a tall and broad-shouldered man. With his deep voice, he called out for Anna.

"Come in. Have a seat," I said.

The large man walked directly toward me. He was all of six-four and carried near three-hundred pounds on his frame. A second man and smaller by far trailed behind the big guy. It was a smart move. I didn't like it at all.

The big guy moved to the opposite end of the breakfast bar. At that point, I could see he held the same advantage as I did from the curved design. I didn't like that either. He slowly unzipped his coat while he maintained hard eye contact with me. I eased off my stool and readied for action. For a brief moment, it was possible I'd experienced what old-fashioned gunslingers might have felt before they threw down. It was the rush of adrenaline. I felt an intense surge of power. My senses heightened to the point where I anticipated his movement, if he were so inclined. I read his face as he sized me up—his eyes were cold as ice. From the corner of his mouth, I saw a twitch, followed by a lopsided grin that accented a distinctive Capone like scar on his left cheek. He was cautious. He knew the score.

The second man stepped from behind the big guy, extended his hand, and introduced himself, "I'm Vincent Telese." I nodded my head to the left, where Anna had been seated until our visitors arrived.

"She's the one you want to talk to," I said, but that was as cordial as I got. I didn't shake his hand. Not as long as the big guy stood too close for comfort. I refused to be distracted or let my shooting hand get tied up in a handshake.

Telese smiled, turned, and addressed Anna. They shook hands, and before they sat in their respective chairs, Telese introduced his associate, John Salcucci. I could see some similarities between the thug and me. He didn't acknowledge the introduction. Nor did he extend the same cordiality as his counterpart with a handshake gesture. He never took his eyes off me. He only stared.

Anna introduced herself as a spokesperson for an organized community of individuals, drawn together by a common goal. It sounded nebulous to me. It probably sounded the same to Telese. She casually pointed with an open hand in my direction, "This is Walter. He's a friend of mine." The informal introduction didn't bother me. Although, I would have liked her to have mentioned how I'd killed a bunch of his loser friends. That didn't come up. "One of our goals is to end child slavery in all forms," Anna said.

"I represent men of business," Telese said. "Men who stand to make a great deal of money in their ventures when they expand along the New York-

Canadian border. They intend to remove some of their competition. To do so, they need things to be quiet."

"Who is going to expand?" Anna asked.

"I think the most important thing would be to find common ground and work to resolve the issues," Telese said.

"What would that common ground be?" Anna asked.

"There are occasionally unfounded allegations against the people I represent, but rarely do they end up in a court of law. We do not want trouble… trouble hurts business and interrupts profits. Trouble brings cops around, and they get tied up in business matters. That takes them out of our communities where they fight crime and keep our families safe."

I could see by the time he was done with his spiel, I'd wished I'd worn a pair of stovepipe cowboy boots.

"What is it exactly you are offering?" Anna asked.

Telese looked around the room, his eyes searching for something that wasn't there. He leaned forward and said in a quiet tone, "My people have made an arrangement to reorganize business operations in the areas of Toronto and along the border." He was careful not to say too much, but enough we could figure out what he meant. "Your group wants kids off the street, out of the sex trade, whatever. We do to. We are family men. We don't like this sort of thing going on in our neighborhoods. It's bad for business."

"How do you know what we want?" I piped in. All eyes were on me. It wasn't customary for the escorts to talk.

"A former associate related the problem as he understood it. If it's not the case, perhaps you could help us understand."

Pembroke must have said something either to these grease balls or the Machine's hierarchy. Regardless, Telese was smart enough not to speak names, or relate anything that would incriminate him.

"Let's say I have a trust issue when it comes to the Mob," I said.

Telese frowned at my mention of the Mob. "Détente is good for everyone involved. You may find the people I represent to be despicable, but I can assure you there are worse choices that will fill the void you have created."

Telese was right. After the street punks fought for the territory, the replacements would be worse. They'd be hungry to exert power and reap profits.

"How will we know or what assurance can you provide us the problem will be corrected? Anna asked.

"Listen to what I'm saying to you," he said. "I'm not here to give assurances or compromise. We don't have to compromise anything with anybody, understand. Now that we're talking, New York families don't like the kind of thing you've alleged has gone on. Our people are coming in. They intend on a change because it's in the best interest of our business."

The room fell silent, but the silence didn't last. "When we expand our business, we will take care of the issue. In return, we expect life to be quiet and peaceful," Telese said.

"I'm not buying it," I blurted out. "The mob is going to police the mob?"

"No one is talking about the Mob!" Salcucci retorted.

Telese looked me up and down a couple times then with a touch of shrewdness, he said, "Why is that hard to believe? We rely on our government to take care of internal problems in the government. We are no different."

Telese was correct when he drew the parallel between mobsters and politicians. However, the correlation failed to prove his point as valid. Everyone knew politicians couldn't be trusted to clean their own house. How could the Mob be relied upon to maintain a housekeeping regiment better than government?

"Things are not going to be quiet around here for a long time. Haven't you read the newspapers? I asked.

Telese turned his attention to Anna. "We have some influence in this area. We intend to assemble the right people to make the necessary changes as we reorganize. If by chance, we were to discover a known juvenile engaged in prostitution or other illicit affairs, we will assist them out of the business. As far as your interests go, we will arrange the Rochester bombing to be covered up. We will sanitize the past and look toward a brighter future. You will be in the clear."

"It sounds too good to be true," I said.

"I think it's opportunistic." Telese smiled broadly as he responded.

"I'll take the offer to the others and get back to you," Anna said.

"Good," Telese said, "We will proceed as planned. It is imperative there be no events that draw attention to your group while we make the necessary adjustments."

Telese and Salcucci left quietly. I figured I'd see them again, when we came back to clean up the mess, and finish the job we'd started.

We waited to leave until we were contacted by our security detail outside. Anna looked upset. "What's the problem; you got what you came for, didn't you?" I asked.

With a sharp intonation, Anna said, "You tried to bait them into a fight, didn't you?"

"I only tried to save on gas. They represent organized crime. We'll be back. You can mark my words."

Anna called for a meeting that night. The Palatini discussed the offer, and they liked it. However, the decision to end the project wasn't unanimous. One vote abstained.

* * * * *

Two days after our meeting with the "representatives," confirmations of change showed in the news. A local gang, fresh from the hood, was popped by ATF agents for the Double Decker Lounge incident. Agents supported by police had rounded up a baker's dozen of the South End Deuces. Media reported on the sweep as the culmination of a yearlong investigation on arms trafficking by the Deuces. Multiple charges were filed against gang members for conspiracy, possession of explosives, illegal weapons, drug charges, and a half-dozen more. According to the news reporters, the Machine and the Deuces had a long-standing territorial feud.

I didn't know what I felt about the police raid on the Deuces. They weren't responsible for the demolition job; on the other hand, they weren't exactly good guys either. They were slimy punks that made a living off stealing from others in their neighborhoods. Maybe the bigger issue with me was credit; I didn't like to share, and I probably didn't play well with others either. It had a bright side though. The cops looked good with the quick nab on the Deuces. If the community was satisfied, the cops would be willing to take the credit and leave it alone.

A second confirmation came the next day when underboss, Antonio "Tuff Tony" Giannetti, missed his court date and his sleazebag lawyer was unable to come up with his whereabouts. A mystery that I suspected would remain a secret.

There were changes, but I didn't believe for a minute it was because some New York City mobsters cared about our interests. They cared about their interests—profits. They had moved in on the Abbandanza crew's territory swiftly and were supported by the Commission, or at least that was the rumor. Whoever they were, they were big enough to make it happen, and that's all that counted. Given a little more time, I would have made some of the same changes. Only there wouldn't have been any replacements.

I guess I'm not as optimistic as my counterparts in the Society. Palatini exuberance was based upon the changes they saw. Me, I had a problem with what we couldn't see. How would we know if the kids that had been trafficked by the former regime had gotten out of the racket successfully? It was a question that would go unanswered. Max said we'd have to take Telese at his word and have faith in what he'd promised. Evidently, I was lacking in the faith department when it came to trusting gangsters.

We'd spent a week cooling our heels in Buffalo. If we were done, it was time to go. We'd stepped back and were no longer on the hunt. Max received a call from Vincent Telese with an assurance the people he represented had the situation well in hand. "These things take time to unravel. We have, however, made progress in the area and will soon have it cleaned up." I gave Telese credit; he could have been a politician. He said a mouthful and never said a thing.

If I stuck around Buffalo to keep an eye on things, I knew I'd get myself in hot water, and roll out the project again. Anna invited Seymour, Thomas and me to the sleaziest bar in Buffalo. We knocked down a couple shots of rotgut and told a few meaningless stories before we said our good-byes. We'd barely turned the corner into the New Year, and already each of us had a destination that awaited our arrivals.

Kuhl headed out first, followed shortly afterwards by Bludd. Where to? I didn't know. Anna recovered her Lexus from Cal's parking area, drove it from Toronto to Buffalo, and parked it. She felt safest driving the rental until she left. She planned to spend another couple of days with Max to recap the project, and then she'd drive back to Oregon. I supposed Max would fly back to somewhere in the United Kingdom. Anna invited me along for the trip back to Oregon, but I had more important things to do.

With Kuhl and Bludd having bailed, I got the itch to roll. Anna stood next to my Avenger as I climbed in behind the steering wheel. She looked frustrated as she followed me with her eyes. "Are you in a big hurry?" She asked. Truth was—I was. It was mid-afternoon, and I wanted to get on the road. That was reason enough.

I'd charted a route to Oregon that avoided the larger cities along the way. To me, big cities were just to drive through. There was nothing of interest to see. As I fumbled with the maps, Anna said, "I was hoping we still had plans to get away on a vacation together?"

It was a nice gesture. Maybe she had hoped to repair the damage that was done to our budding relationship. But sometimes, when you've ripped something up from the root, it dies.

"I'll have to get back to you on that," I said. "It'll take me a few days to drive back to Oregon. Right now, I need the time and space," I said.

She leaned forward, and with a hug through the window, she whispered in my ear, "I'm sorry." At the end of her embrace, she caressed the back of my neck and slowly moved her lips from my neck to the bottom of my ear lobe, and whispered again, "I'll be waiting to hear from you."

I was deeply saddened by the turn of events. It wasn't what I'd wanted for either of us. I was further saddened that I didn't feel anything when her lips touched my neck. I thought I should have. I remembered back to when I did. I didn't know if she still felt something for me or if she'd hoped to breathe life back into our relationship. I fired up the Avenger and said, "Gotta go." I felt like I had more to say, or should have more, but it eluded me. Anna nodded and took a couple small steps back from the car. She waved and forced a tight-lipped smile. I did the same.

The fastest way from Buffalo seemed good to me, but south and westerly felt especially right. I spent night one of the journey at Mentor, Ohio. It wasn't far from New York, but still, I'd felt the weight of the project lift from off my shoulders when I crossed the border into Ohio. I logged five-hundred miles the next day, but I wasn't much closer to Oregon. I'd drifted farther south, just driving where the wheel took me. The cool night air at Bowling Green, Kentucky, reminded me of the Pacific Northwest. The next day I was up early and continued westerly to Springfield, Missouri and spent a leisurely evening. I thought I'd be plagued with thoughts and emotions about Anna, the project, or both, but surprisingly I was void of stress.

On the fourth day I rolled out and drove a little more than an hour south on Highway thirty-nine toward the Mark Twain National Forest. It wasn't by accident. I arrived in the small community of Shell Knob, Missouri, turned into the Bridgeway Plaza and had an early lunch at Carole's Restaurant. From there, I crossed the bridge over Table Rock Lake where Shell Knob continued its sprawl.

A few miles further, I located the address I had committed to memory. A small sign hung from a tree limb, which announced the tiny resort. I pulled up in front of the large two-story home that resembled a bed and breakfast that was nestled in the tree line. On the lake's edge sat four rental cabins. Many people would have commented on the scenic view, I saw peace and tranquility. Something I didn't have much of.

I put the Avenger in park, left the motor running, climbed out, and stretched. I knocked on the front door. An elderly woman answered the door. "Hello, how can I help you?"

"I'd like a room"

"Did you make reservations?"

"No, not yet." I grinned an unexplainable smile. The product of a subconscious thought that had slipped through the maze into my realization.

"Why don't you step right in here and I'll have you fill out an occupancy card? How long will you be staying with us?"

"That's up in the air. Could you tell me if Joyce is here?"

"Yes, she is. How do you know Joyce?"

"It's a long story."

"Well, you finish with the card and I'll fetch her for ya."

The lady's behavior was alien to me. In my world, no one would be so careless. Here was a defenseless lady, who'd opened her door to me, a complete stranger. She didn't know me from Adam, and yet, she felt comfortable enough with me to turn her back to me. Maybe her behavior was common practice here in Shell Knob.

The elderly lady slowly made her way up the stairs while two small boys made their appearance in a flat out run from an anteroom, down the hallway in front of me, and toward a backdoor leading outside. They were out of breath, laughing and having a great time.

A few moments later, I could see the elderly woman descending the stairs, and behind her, the framework of a female dressed in tennis shoes and blue jeans.

It was refreshing to see Joyce. She looked relaxed, and I liked that look on her. I spoke first, "Joyce"

"Walter Eloy Goe"

"You remembered?"

"How could I forget such a funny name?" She beamed a broad smile and giggled. I suppose you're the one I have to thank for the ticket home."

"Not really, but, you can thank me if you like.

She reached out for my hand, "Come in."

"Thanks. I think I'd like that."